Praise for *The Devil's Calling*

"Michael Kelley has delivered a mystical techno-thriller that examines the difficulty of living a peaceful and spiritual life side-by-side with technologies that can strip us of humanity and enable the forces of evil in the world. You'll want to stop reading so you can catch your breath, but you won't be able to. It's that kind of page-turner."

—**Laura Manning Johnson,** former CIA WMD analyst and DHS all threats and hazards planner, current adjunct professor at Georgetown University

"The Devil's Calling is a brilliant and heart-pounding, epic saga of metaphysical science fiction. It's a journey of self-realization and a cautionary tale for generations to come; the kind of book that hooks you from the start and never lets go until the final sentence of the final page. This sci-fi story pits human-based intelligence against automated thought."

—**John J. Kelly,** *Detroit Free Press*

"This is a wondrous novel on so many levels, not the least of which is an affinity with the great novelists of the century: the work of a master artist is evident on every page and lingers in the mind long after reading! The adventure propels along with voracious but eloquent speed in exploring all manner of scientific concepts and theories in a way that embraces mystery, sci-fi, magical realism, romance, philosophy, spirituality, and poetry, as well as some fine asides about culture."

—**Grady Harp,** Top 100 Amazon Hall of Fame reviewer

"A charming, heavily New Age-influenced SF thriller that requires deep dives into dharma."

—*Kirkus Reviews*

"Well, dear reader, this incredible story is guaranteed to ignite questions in your mind, questions that can only be answered with the passing of time. However, I can guarantee that as you find yourself hurtling toward the last page, nothing will prepare you for the final paragraph of this truly outstanding book. Michael Kelley, in this incredible work of science fiction, asks, 'Can free will and AIs truly live in harmony?'"

—**Susan Keefe,** Midwest Book Review and
Columbia Review of Books & Film

"Michael Kelley takes the reader into the characters' lives nine years later in the thrilling sci-fi adventure *The Devil's Calling*. Kelley brilliantly continues to develop the protagonists' personalities and relationships amid the progression of the story and interactions with both new characters, life-altering situations, and entanglements with future-science phenomena."

—**Chris Cordani,** host, *Book Spectrum*

"Many writers have a daunting task ahead of them to produce a sequel to a complex and involved first novel, especially one as intriguing as *The Lost Theory*. Michael Kelley has risen to the occasion with an equally compelling thriller that finds new and exciting ways to raise the stakes and push the development of established characters in different directions."

—**K.C. Finn,** Readers' Favorite

"An ambitious thriller blending science, spiritualism, advanced AI, and possible alien abduction."

—*BookLife Reviewed*

"*The Devil's Calling* is a gripping, fast-paced read that ranges across the globe and into the depths of the human heart, mind, and spirit as Sean chases down those that would threaten his love. If you like Dan Brown's books, you will love how Michael Kelley's novels cross and combine genres to explore the intersection of science and spirituality, wrapped in an entertaining sci-fi adventure. In years to come, readers may look at the questions posed in *The Devil's Calling* as a prescient foretelling of the struggle between AI and the spirit of humanity. Anyone who enjoys delving into discussions of philosophy and spirituality will love this book. Highly recommended!"

—**Jessica Tofino**, educator and writer

THE DEVIL'S CALLING

MICHAEL KELLEY

GREENLEAF
BOOK GROUP PRESS

Published by Greenleaf Book Group Press
Austin, Texas
www.gbgpress.com

Distributed by Greenleaf Book Group

For ordering information or special discounts for bulk purchases, please contact Greenleaf Book Group at PO Box 91869, Austin, TX 78709, 512.891.6100.

Design and composition by Greenleaf Book Group and Brian Phillips
Cover design by Greenleaf Book Group and Brian Phillips
Cover image © xtock, your, fluke samed, d1sk, and Dmitriy Rybin.
Used under license from Shutterstock.com

Publisher's Cataloging-in-Publication data is available.

Print ISBN: 978-1-62634-962-9

eBook ISBN: 978-1-62634-963-6

Part of the Tree Neutral® program, which offsets the number of trees consumed in the production and printing of this book by taking proactive steps, such as planting trees in direct proportion to the number of trees used: www.treeneutral.com

Printed in the United States of America on acid-free paper

22 23 24 25 26 27   10 9 8 7 6 5 4 3 2 1

First Edition

As man's reckoning approached,
Nature became increasingly confused,
Until clouds surrendered,
And slept upon the ground.

—AN OLD CELTIC PROVERB

Aldous Huxley, Rumi, Bono, Vincent van Gogh, Barbara Eden, J. M. Barrie, Ramana Maharshi, Brothers Grimm, J. R. R. Tolkien, Lao Tzu, William Shakespeare, Helen Schucman, Homer, Jonathan Swift, George R. R. Martin, Margaret Atwood, J. K. Rowling, Coach Gavaghan, Carl Jung, Henry David Thoreau, William Butler Yeats, Jean-Jacques Rousseau, Daniel Defoe, James Cameron, Samuel Taylor Coleridge, Salvador Dalí, Edgar Rice Burroughs, The Rolling Stones, Zeno, Vladimir Nabokov, D. H. Lawrence, Robert Rimmer, Beck, Scarlett Johansson, The Founding Fathers, Margret and H. A. Rey, Bob Dylan, Maureen O'Hara, Maud Gonne, Sylvia Plath, Ted Hughes, Quentin Tarantino, William Somerset Maugham, Buddha, Ridley Scott and Callie Khouri, Lord Byron, Mary Shelley, Disney, James Joyce, Elon Musk, David Bowie, Michelangelo, Humphrey Bogart, The Replacements, The author[s] of the Bible, Miguel de Cervantes, Dan Brown, Richard Linklater, Matthew McConaughey, Jim Morrison, Larry David, Dylan Thomas, Oscar Wilde, Percy Shelley, Dante, Mark Rothko, Christopher Marlow, Wolfgang von Goethe, Brigitte Bardot, Mick Jagger, Jane Austen, Charles Dickens, Sir Arthur Conan Doyle, Peter O'Toole, James Goldman, William A. Kelley, Audrey Hepburn, Mark Antony, Cleopatra, Keith Richards, Charlie Watts, Abraham, Bashar, Saint Joan, The Wachowskis, Salman Rushdie, John Keats, Eve and Adam, A. A. Milne, Jesus Christ, Mary Magdalene, Rodgers and Hammerstein, Walt Whitman, William Wordsworth, Louis Armstrong, Louis Lambert, Clancy Brothers, Henri Matisse, Arthur Miller, Stevie Nicks, Stephen Hawking, William Powell, Myrna Loy, Thomas Merton, Alberto Gatenio, James Hilton, Ivan Aivazovsky,

Victor Hugo, Claude Lalanne, Elvis Presley, Sebastian Junger, Anton Chekhov, Daniel Boulud, Kurt Vonnegut, H. G. Wells, Stanley Kubrick, Lewis Carroll, Haruki Murakami, Sigmund Freud, Samuel Beckett, John F. Kennedy, Michael Crichton, Yul Brynner, Wes Anderson, Bob Marley, George Lucas, William Gibson, Steve Jobs, Steven Spielberg, Denis Villeneuve, Carl Sagan, Robert Zemeckis, Ivan Reitman, David Cronenberg, Edgar Allan Poe, Jack Nicholson, Mike Myers, Sharon Tate, René Magritte, Bobby Fischer, Claude Monet, George Bernard Shaw, Cohen Brothers, Mikhail Lermontov, Peaky Blinders, Herman Melville, G. W. F. Hegel, C. S. Lewis, Emily Dickinson, James Fenimore Cooper, Gene Roddenberry, Jesse James, Butch Cassidy, Sally Field, Eckhart Tolle, Radhanath Swami, Sadhguru, Mother Meera, Amma, Babaji, Katherine Hepburn, James Coburn, Warren Beatty, Faye Dunaway, Edward Snowden, King Kamehameha the Great, Robbie Robertson, Frank Sinatra, Charles M. Schulz, John le Carré, Thornton Wilder, Hermann Hesse, Tom Stoppard, W. H. Auden, Robert Browning, The Eagles, Errol Flynn, Franz Kafka, Jonathan Swift, Voltaire, Ian Fleming, Anthony Hopkins, Dennis Hopper, Francis Ford Coppola, Gerry Rafferty and Joe Egan, The Clash, John Wayne, Gary Cooper, Nick Lowe, Dashiell Hammett, Lauren Bacall, Ernest Hemingway, the author[s] of the Bhagavad Gita, Luc Besson, Gustav Klimt, Fred Astaire, Ginger Rogers, Leonardo da Vinci.

And to Caitlin, Beth, and Grace Kelley.

ACKNOWLEDGMENTS

Beth Hill, Ava Coibion, and Erin Brown, who molded the story and made innumerable improvements to the story and text as my coaches and editors.

Tracie Herrmann, Eric Margarida, Cynthia Smith Petrick, Dante LaRocca, Usher Winslett, and Laura Manning Johnson, who provide insightful comments, suggestions, and encouragement as critical readers.

OMINOUS. THE WORD that best described the day.

I paused to look back across the Willamette Valley spread out behind me in all its splendor. *Willamette* was Native American for the *valley of sickness or death*. A strange binary name for the lovely site of our singularly idyllic life. As I scaled the mountainside, it was difficult to reconcile my troublesome thoughts and feelings with the green path and blue sky—and the wonderful woman hiking in front of me.

A large black crow's incessant cawing reminded me of a movie poster emblazoned with a bloody font declaring *The Devil's Calling*, an image from a vision I'd had nine years ago. Those words had been spinning in the center of my mind when I contemplated finally writing my sequel to *The Lost Theory*.

Was my determination to write again the call of destiny, or was it an act of free will? Did we choose the words that became our story, or was my narrative predetermined by everything that had come before? The ego, resisting the concept of co-creation, tells us we're either the sole cause of our experience or an innocent victim of happenstance.

The cackling crow finally flew off, leaving me to my thoughts upon the steepening ascent of a mountain path. I inhaled a deep breath and picked up my pace.

Much of the spiraling vision had already come true, yet the darkest images still lay in wait. The next image from my glimpse of the future foresaw that the commencement of my next novel would trigger the harrowing events presaged by the three words of bloody text. What a devil's dilemma—perhaps the only way not to suffer some terrible destiny was not to write.

"I'm so excited you're finally back to writing again," said my mind-reading M when our summit came into view. "There's no turning back now! Just listen to the birds as they bring messages to you."

"Okay, Doctor Doolittle." But M and nature did have an enchanted relationship.

We emerged above the line of fragrant pines, with another nearly vertical and rocky football field scramble between us and the end of our ascent. M's glance over her shoulder signaled she wanted to race me to the top, but I needed to catch my breath or lose by an embarrassing distance. I pulled her off-trail to enjoy a scenic bluff that faced true north. Still, it was a mere backdrop to my anticipation; M carried a surprise for me in her back pocket, a letter delivered by special courier as the sun came up that morning.

She knew I loved letters and hated surprises, which only added a quickening to my heart's mountain-hiking beat. We sat down on the smooth rock bed with the sun warming our faces. The serenity of the scene provided me the patience to enjoy the moment and the depth of our holy relationship before the big reveal. We lay in *shavasana*, our syncopating breaths drumming softly, and M held my hand, my body's rhythm falling into time with hers. The letter could wait.

We drifted together through the eternal creation all around us. For how long, I didn't know. When she sat up, I joined her lotus-to-lotus and face-to-face.

"May I see the letter now? This sort of drama is so unlike you."

"First tell me you've decided and will write again."

"Yes, I will, despite some . . ." I would do anything for her. "Why do you think I should?"

"You said you felt stuck in your spiritual journey, and . . . you become inspired when you write. Think back nine years to the last time you wrote and moved from bookworm to my hero."

"Yes, when we almost got killed for finding my murdered best friend's theory of constant creation . . ."

"And its source—*Big Love.*" M's eyes lit out over the valley of green below us. "But I was thinking of Huxley and your reader challenge to self-realization?" She batted her eyes, coaxing the quote from me.

"'Man's life on earth has only one end and purpose—to identify himself with the eternal self and so come to intuitive knowledge of the divine ground.'"

"Exactly! Don't you see? You use your art for self-reflection and self-projection to lead to liberation of self in self-realization."

I made an awe-filled face and said, "Wow. A lot of self, no self, and true self to reconcile there."

"It's more a remembering," said my bright-eyed lady of the highlands.

I took the opportunity to pivot to my favorite memories—the story of us and our recent history. "I remember these last nine mostly blissful years. But there's so much to remember! I've watched you grow and enlighten while I've helped raise our two wonderful children and helped open your college, becoming a dean and teacher there. I've been a bit busy."

Dylan was eight and Juno seven, the two named after my dead friend and our lost spiritual teacher, respectively. Their childhoods brimmed with innocence and light, courtesy of their mother and their yogi-aunts.

"It's *our* Deeksha West! And yes, a wonderful partner, father, and teacher, but now, dear author and my dearest love, you are called to write as a step toward your spiritual awakening. So write already!"

"I will." I was always pleased to please her. "Now let me see your mysterious letter."

She shifted her hips, pulled the letter from a back pocket, and handed it to me.

I didn't need to read more than the heading of the formal correspondence: "Professor Emily Edens Nobel Prize Nomination for Science 2027: the Physics Prize." I stretched out my hands to her shoulders, pushing her back as I arched up and over her like a yogi's upward dog before collapsing on her and kissing her all over. "My Nobel Prize winner!"

She rolled me over, softly returning my kiss. "Only a nominee."

Such sweetness. I paused to enjoy the taste of honeysuckle from her lips before I said, "You deserve it and you'll win!"

My precious angel smiled at me. "Maybe. We will see."

In her eyes, I saw into her divinity. "I love you." Each time I said it, the love was new and even truer. Another drop added to infinity.

"And I love you. We're so blessed by life and Big Love." She kissed me like an innocent child, awakening the desire for experience. Then she giggled for me.

"What's so funny?"

"Just listen to us. *Love, love, love.*"

I knew what she meant. "But lovers and spiritual masters do speak like Rumi's poetry and not like soldiers in the trenches with bayonets drawn. *Only from the heart can you touch the sky.*"

Rumi's words raced through my body as my spirit took flight, like a soaring eagle, assessing the land surrounding our secluded rock bed. "No one is here to see—"

Buzz! Buzz! Buzz! Damn it, my ten-minute warning. I fumbled in my pocket to silence the alarm. Although the moment had been interrupted, M and I still lay together beneath the summit of a majestic Oregon mountain that I had personified with a childish nickname. And M was still glowing. She was always lit from within, a liberated spirit and self-realized woman. I was the minstrel ever singing her praises.

"M, you summit. I'll stay here to prepare for my hologram from Ting." Ting used a mononym just like her sister Juno (our ascended spiritual master, not our daughter Juno Edens McQueen) and U2's Bono.

"You scared?"

"Uneasy. You know this new technology confounds me."

"It's a hologram, not a robot with a scalpel ready to wire your brain into a quantum computer."

"Thank God!" I stood and pulled her to her feet. "Seriously, congratulations again on your Nobel Prize. Auspicious is the day."

"Auspicious is the day!" she echoed with enthusiasm.

Everyone at the Deeksha West, a college founded by M and me

for impoverished young women, had adopted my dead best friend's—Dylan Byrne's—catchphrase and declared it boldly each new day.

M tapped my forehead with the tip of her finger. "And remember, it's just a nomination."

"Who from?"

"Nominators are anonymous for fifty years."

"Hmm. I'll be dead by then." I bent my forehead to hers, wanting her close for a few moments more. "For your body of work on the quantum and constant creation or for a particular paper?"

"The paper you helped me with—Constant Creation's Ethical Implications for Emergent Artificial Intelligence."

"Hmm, helped with? More asked questions and worried about." I couldn't hear the term *AI* without thinking of *him*. "It was brilliant in laying out the ethical challenges of AI and wiring-in to quantum computers as humanity struggles to keep pace."

"Yes, and since the time I wrote it, AI advances keep accelerating faster and faster. Maybe it's too simple a thesis to win. The timeless struggle between spirit and ego. AI a magnification of ego. And Big Love, the source of constant creation—expanding the power of spirit. A topic explored by writers far more eloquent than me."

She winked at me as if I were more elegant than she.

I held out the letter. When I didn't let go, M said, "You're my most ardent student and most dedicated teacher." As the letter tug-of-war continued, she added, "And always my knight in shining armor. You are my *noble* prize, and have been ever since we met. The other prize would be a trinket in comparison." Satisfied, I let the letter go.

She put her smooth fingers to the mark on my right temple left by the heat of a bullet, deliberately distracting me from some ill-defined ambivalence arising from her anonymous nomination and my discomfort about the upcoming hologram with Juno's younger sister.

"Hmm . . . let's see. I don't like that we don't know who nominated you."

"Are you saying *aum* or *hmm*—a mantra or a grunt? What a change in the weather—a bit of a cold breeze on a brilliant, sunny day."

Living with such a fully awakened woman was like standing in front of a brightly illuminated mirror that exposed my small-minded boorish reactions to even the best news. For every blessing we received, I saw its potential loss.

"Sorry. The honor is great and well deserved. And good for the school and your work."

"Our work."

"Okay, go now," I said, playfully pushing her away. "I need to get ready for hologramming with Ting."

Thinking about the nomination, I'd allowed my thoughts to grow dark. The genocidal Hitler and Stalin and the great deceivers Putin and Trump had all been nominated. Who had been their nominators, Goebbels and Rasputin, an oligarch and Ivanka? I did a little shake and raised prayer hands to the infinite blue sky.

"Our shake-off dance—good. Are you back—present—now?"

"Yes, my lady! Enjoy your climb of you-know-the-name Mountain, whose tip awaits." I offered a noble flourish of one arm.

"You're such a child." She kissed me on the forehead, much as she would little Dylan.

I grabbed her around the waist. I didn't want to let her go, but she spun back to the path. "I have a date to peak your *tit* mountain without you, but don't worry—I'll be looking down on you."

I called after her. "You wouldn't deny me the beauty of perfect symmetry expressed in a three-letter palindrome, would you? Just look at its round and nipple-shaped tip and those beautiful 360-degree views." I tried to defend my moniker for the majestic mountain. The real name is Native American and too long, with a hodgepodge of vowels and therefore impossible for me to remember and even harder to spell.

M left me, teasing, "Go get those messages that are for your ears only."

The incoming hologram was a private affair, and I didn't want M watching my body and hearing my words while I was transported to Kathmandu. She trusted me to faithfully convey the messages I was about to receive.

We'd hiked the mountain for exercise, for the joy of being together, and celebrating life and nature. Yet we'd also left the confines of our home and workplace so that I could settle myself before joining Juno's sister in a conversation that I feared might bring unwanted change to all of us. Though not as spiritually advanced as M, my intuition and imagination were strong. And both were reactivated by my determination to create a new book.

In Dylan's theory of constant creation, there is no beginning and no end, only the infinite and eternal instant of creation. But now, as I stood precariously close to the cliff's edge, I imagined hearing the distant hooves of horsemen approaching. Whatever it was that was coming, I was blessed—and bound—to bear witness.

2 HOLOGRAM

IN CONTRAST TO MY FOREBODING, it was a beautiful early June day, the bright colors of spring titillating my imagination like the brushstrokes of van Gogh. As M danced playfully on the peak—atop the nipple—I unpacked my HoloPortAbles, or HPA goggles, the newest hologram technology that allowed one to enter a hologram projected remotely. The HPAs came complete with speakers and mic for communication within the hologram. Then, I waited for the green light signaling the start of my hologram with Ting.

Juno, with the help of high-tech Chinese contacts, had ensconced the laser and lens technology in her sanctuary nestled in a Nepal jungle. She had always been an enigma to me, no more so than when feathering her spiritual nest with transporting technology. She'd wanted to be able to be with her family in Oregon, without leaving Nepal, through the use of the harmless hologram. But she'd never had an opportunity to transport herself before she was spirited away from us. Or, according to a popular Chinese theory regarding her disappearance nearly eight years ago, she'd used it just once—to ascend.

Ting, Juno's younger sister, was a woman as remarkable and unconventional as Juno. She had traveled from a tree house—her home—in Hawaii to Kathmandu. M and I had never met Ting, but we believed her when she said she'd heard from Juno via telepathy. Juno's adopted identical twins, YaLan and Astri, had been quietly practicing the esoteric art since they were born. With all that had occurred over the nine years since the publication of Dylan Byrne's theory of everything and our collaborative novel, *The Lost Theory*, telepathy was no longer in doubt. After a single taste of oneness and the omnipotence of infinite consciousness, even the most skeptical could never doubt telepathy again, the spiritual ability of minds to communicate across the universe in what M had coined, in one of her scientific essays on constant creation, "the irreducible instant."

And I was about to experience what amounted to earthbound astral projection. The advanced hologram technology made me feel like an alien preparing to travel through a wormhole to a distant point in space. Ting had notified remote high-tech Chinese operators—necessary to work Juno's setup—to set the wheels in motion for today's show, and now that the time was here, I was a nervous Nellie.

Nine minutes had passed since my pregame warning. Ting had insisted we use the hologram technology, declaring that holograms allowed for presence at a distance. Two-way holographic transmission hadn't yet been mastered, so I'd be 2D to her—regular old flat me projected across space by high-definition satellite technology—while Ting and her surroundings would be 3D to me. This would be my first time meeting Ting *in person*.

As I stood on the ledge over the sheer vertical drop with an infinite horizontal view, a hummingbird flew a foot from my eyes, vibrating with the sweetness of life, the flurry of its wings emitting a high-pitched frequency. Suspended in time and space, she murmured her mantra in rapid-fire beats of air. I remained hypnotized in the light between our eyes, pausing in that timeless moment to receive the winged messenger's message. In those instants of constant creation, time stops and our light is reunited with its source before expanding out again into the universe. When the holographic lens buzzed and flashed green, the sprite darted away. Auspicious is the day!

I put the HPA goggles on and, after a fog lifted, there was Ting! I'd been transported to Juno's inner sanctum, the holy site and vortex where Dylan, with Juno in meditation, received the gift of his now-famous theory of constant creation. Moonlight streamed down on Ting, who was seated in lotus under the gyre tower's skylight, a room I knew well. I felt Juno's presence in that space of sublime conception. I sat lotus too, on a cushion facing Ting. My cushion was soft, though somewhere in the bottom of my mind I knew it was really a rock.

Ting placed in front of us two cups of lightly steaming tea. I smelled jasmine mist in the tiny clouds wafting over me. With prayer hands to her chest, she bowed until her forehead kissed the beautiful lapis lazuli floor of Juno's inner sanctum and observatory. I bowed as deeply as grace and age allowed.

We smiled at each other. Ting was thirty-three, and though petite, emanated light at a high-frequency presence. Her turquoise eyes joined in my longing for the absent yet always present Juno. A recurring dream that I'd all but forgotten came back to me—Juno, angelic in a white light, arriving in a doorway to deliver me from a dark place. It was the end of a bad dream, but that was all I could remember.

I instinctively twirled my hand upward in Juno's wand-waving gesture, and Ting returned the salute. We laughed joyfully, like two little kids in instant intimacy.

Then I remembered we could talk. "Hello, Ting. I'm so happy to finally meet you!"

"Aloha, Sean! Me too. Though I feel I know you so well—like a child remembers a never-ending summer day." She spoke like a lyrical surfer, with the cool and mellow rhythm of her Hawaiian home. Her words came not from the throat but somewhere deeper.

"Me too!" I gushed. "I watch your meditation and yoga videos," I confessed.

"Oh, thank you, but I mean I know you on a higher level, perhaps through Juno."

I leaned forward. "You remind me so much of her. And you've heard from her telepathically." I pressed my hands together to my chest while pushing out an unsteady breath.

"Sean, breathe with me. One simple practice is to fall in love with your breath."

"Well, one should love their breath—you can't live without it." I opened my eyes. Ting was smiling. She took several smooth, long breaths into the lithe belly revealed by her *I Dream of Jeannie* yoga top. I joined my breaths with hers as we locked our half-closed eyes and recited three *aums* together. I felt better, and my whirling mind was settled by the peaceful holographic hum as she spoke.

"I don't know exactly what telepathy is, but I've been getting messages from my sister while in meditation. They come like coded packets of information that then bloom into a knowing within my mind. Sometimes they come in the form of her soft voice, startling and amazing me."

Ting paused to reach for her teacup and stopped as I reached for mine. We both laughed at the playful half reality.

"The first message came to me in Hawaii and was simply a knowing that I felt came from Juno, with her asking me to go to her sanctuary and a sense that more would be revealed to me here. So certain was this impression that I packed immediately."

She looked like a fairy in her light green cropped yoga top and darker green yoga pants, a Peter Pan Tiger Lily of ageless grace. I sensed the soft hum of balancing currents—yin and yang—that twirled through her as she rested so composed in her lotus. The sound of magnetic fields may have been the technology, although I imagined that, like the hummingbird's, Ting's angelic wings created a vibrational buzz. The atmosphere was so buoyant, I felt we might levitate together into the hologram air, despite her being seated seven thousand miles away from me.

When I noticed the out-of-place sports watch on her wrist, she said, "A diver's watch. Serves as a reminder not of time but of impermanence, change, and the constant presence of now. The tick of the clock works like the breath to bring me back to the timeless truth of Big Love. I imagine the words *I am* in place of the ticking."

I recognized her Juno nature. M had me read all of Ramana Maharshi's teachings about the attachment to the *I am*. Stories of the ego. Though *I am M's significant other* was not a bad story, not with all the trappings of the Deeksha West and the family.

We shared a silent moment. I imagined I heard the tick-tick-tick of now.

"After arriving yesterday," she continued, "I meditated here. And this morning I received an image of Juno in some beautiful natural setting like Shangri-la. It was as if I was looking through my sister's eyes from an eagle's nest and out over vast mountains and plains. She told me you and I should meet here holographically."

"So she did become a hermit?" I asked.

"Not clear, but I'd say yes and no," Ting replied.

"But why wouldn't she have told us before she left?" Juno was mysterious but never would act in a way that would cause her family such pain.

"The sense was that the seclusion was *brought* to her. So she lives as a hermit, but not of her free will . . . though she accepts it."

"Well, that debunks the Chinese theory that she used this technology to ascend."

"Hmm, that's not really what the theory says. Or it's a poor translation. They believe she was here in her sanctuary, maybe testing the hologram technology or just deep in meditation, and was subject to alien abduction of some sort. My government often fabricates stories. That my sister is missing is all I know, and now she's in contact. I always knew she was still alive. And she did ascend to a lofty alien or angelic place."

I responded with conviction based on experience, "I believe that one heart, once connected to another, might divine when the other still beats . . ."

My extensive research made Ting's statements sound less far-fetched. The CIA had secretly used telepathy and remote viewing dating back to the 1980s and was currently investing in hologram research. Our science fiction was the government's secret truth. The UFOs we used to imagine, our government had known to be true for decades. In 2020, they finally came clean, disclosing there were flying saucers that they would rebrand as UAPs—unidentified aerial phenomena. In 2026, we'd received our first direct message from aliens, one that credible scientists and cryptologists agreed was an announcement of contact on 9/9/36. To me and most laypeople, the message looked like hieroglyphics that had disappeared like cosmic geometric snowflakes soon after they were illuminated in the night sky. Our government would neither confirm nor deny the message in the tea leaves, implying it might just be a trick of light and space dust—buying time in an effort to control our reaction to the earth-shattering news. China and Russia, with a firmer grip over their populations, were already preparing for an invasion. The message received struck me as the kind that said a comet would strike on a certain future date. Certain but not very useful, other than to stoke imagination or fear.

Our government was more forthcoming when it came to the increasing numbers of reported alien abductions and was investigating whether aliens had some ability to wipe memories clean before the abductee was returned. Most of the alleged kidnapped victims had, in theory, been taken to some sort of hellish inferno or angelic nirvana and were never heard from again. In any event, we were fortunate that Juno had found a way to make contact.

"Whoever took her, it sounds like she's seated in a blissful perch of nature. But was there anything more?" I finally asked.

She held her arms out wide to the sky as if about to issue an invocation, searching for a word; but failing to find it, she brought her hands back down to her knees. "Something is about to happen, and you, we, need to hold Big Love in our hearts and as our primary focus and provide no home for darkness. That part of the message was more feelings and impressions than her words—something coming and a personal message for you. That's why I asked for this meeting. May I?"

She held out her hand, offering me *deeksha*, the oneness blessing. As I bent down to receive her hands, I felt a warm, harmonic buzz from the warmth of Ting's hands upon my head, like Spock delivering the Vulcan mind-meld. With my eyes closed, I sensed a breeze carrying the sweet smell of pure oxygen infused with the bloom of some long-lost flower. Juno!

With Ting's hands silencing my mind and opening a portal for a current to flow through, I heard Juno whispering in my third ear, my mind hearing within the deep heart's core—communication *in* consciousness *to* consciousness.

Dear One . . .

My spirit soared at the lyrical voice of my lost teacher coming in like soft music on a tiny radio embedded in my mind.

This guilt you carry for me, blaming yourself, is childish ego fantasy. Let it go. The illusion is a constant teacher of the impermanence of our attachments, the infinite calling on us to focus instead on all that is ultimately real. You must control your thoughts to not get lost in your nightmares. Stay focused on oneness and write from there.

I found myself smiling at Juno's timely encouragement. But then she spoke five terrifying words that sent thunderbolts careening down my spine. Five words that forced my eyes wide before they squeezed tight like the neural searing of electric shock. Words not to be repeated and best forgotten: *M, too, will be lost!*

Before I could speak or try to answer—I wasn't sure how telepathy worked—Juno all but took the bad omen back with another five words: *Nothing real is ever lost.*

Juno often spoke in the koans of paradox, but this . . . The warmth against my temples was lifted, and I opened my fearful eyes to meet Ting's gaze glittering back at me. Ting's hands returned to their original resting place atop her lotus legs.

"Did you hear . . . that?" I asked as I swallowed hard on Juno's words.

She shook her head. "It was a message for you alone; I was just a transmitter. But have no fear—it was a message of love. I should go now so you can consider what she said."

Before I could object, she was in a deep-bowing namaste that I returned, and holograph Ting and the inner sanctum were gone in a puff of smoke-like fog. And I was alone behind dark goggles, an emotional geyser of tears welling in my eyes.

Juno was alive! My heart had always known. But her message . . .

The emotional distance between the knowledge that Juno was alive and her five words had me jumping from joy to terror. Could I believe the one without accepting the other? I yanked off my headset and rubbed my face. I was back on the mountain cliff, where I shivered in the sun. I had *heard* her, *felt* her, known her in that moment.

The trick was to bury the message but celebrate finding the messenger. I vowed to stuff Juno's terrifying prediction so deep that the words couldn't accidentally spill out, not even in my sleep. I would think about anything but those words. I would focus on Juno's vitality and zest for life, and control my thoughts so as not to get lost in nightmares of my creation.

3 DECEPTION

DISORIENTED AND ONLY TWO FEET from the cliff's edge, I felt I would tumble off. I scooted back and turned from the precipice. M had been watching from the summit, and she was already on her way back to hear Juno's message. Not much time to think. And I needed to stop rubbing my face, which I hadn't done for years and which was a glaring *tell* that M would never miss. The message was beautiful and horrifying—Juno from a dream, projecting my own fear back to me. Showing me my darkest fear and encouraging me to let it go.

Juno had illuminated the path that led M and me into the experience of Big Love, the phrase she used to refer to the ever-present divine love springing infinitely from the source of all creation that might be found within our deep heart's core. Then Juno disappeared shortly after my first book's release nearly eight years ago. The void of her disappearance had been a dark cloud hanging over me all those years, years otherwise marked by magic and wonder in a new paradise. We hadn't known whether to fear for her safety, to search for her, or to rejoice that she'd successfully left the world for Nirvana, the way particularly adept yogis do. We'd mourned her absence but didn't grieve. No one in our spiritual family believed she was dead in a terminal way.

M joined me on the cliff, her glistening skin reflecting the sun after collecting her mountain-pinnacle prize. "Tell me," she said.

I recited Ting's message from Juno.

"The good in this far outweighs the bad," M said, looking radiant as the light within her brightened. "She's alive after all these years! Such wonderful news."

Head cocked, M studied me. I must have looked confused.

"Sean, what is it? Is there more?"

My writing had made me a master of omission. But M was not the average reader and could unearth deception. "I think the reason Ting wanted to do this via hologram was so she could give me the oneness blessing. It was wonderful. I imagined Juno there, speaking of Big Love and telling me to write my next book from that source."

"I knew she would agree with me. Time to write again, my love. She's such a powerful spirit. It sounds wonderful, yet you seem weighed down."

"Just disoriented. I was in Juno's inner sanctum, where we were together that fateful day before we found Dylan's theory and . . . Well, you know what happened next."

I gave her my best goofy grin, which she returned with a beautiful smile, saying she, too, would never forget our first night of constant creation and shared orgasm in Dylan's room at Yogi Mangku's compound.

With disjointed hand gestures, as if I were trying to frame my words as they came from my mouth, I said, "Just a couple minutes ago I was seated with Ting, a hologram, talking about telepathy—and *listening to Juno*—and now I'm here with you, both of us very much real, basking in the glory of nature. Reality seems so uncomfortable . . . unstable to me right now." Dizzy and afraid I might pass out, I had to sit back down.

"Sean," M said, taking my hand in hers.

"Yes, my love?" I looked at her face but couldn't focus.

"Look into my eyes and take some deep breaths. And remember!"

She'd lost me. "The past? I thought that was best forgotten."

"Not the past—the constant presence in us. The light that nothing can touch. The truth."

Always in her eyes I could see that light. I was afraid she could see any lie in me, so I stood to escape her gaze and regain my composure, but my body was still unsteady and I almost toppled over the cliff. M took my arm to support my teetering stance, saying, "Careful, big boy.

Let's go back and tell the family. They are on tenterhooks to hear Ting's messages, and now your message from Juno, and I want to hear more about what Juno said to you." This contact I had just made was big news, as Juno was the transcendental headmaster and Big Love teacher and mother to our entire small spiritual family.

There was no hiding from M, but on this point a secret was justified. I had to protect her. The hike home would give me time to get my story straight before I told the family the long-awaited and wonderful news without poisoning it with my fear.

4 THE DEEKSHA WEST

WE RETURNED SHORTLY AFTER NOON, with me firm in my decision to ignore Juno's dark premonition in order to focus on the fact that Juno was alive and communicating with us again after years of silence. I had a few strengths, and imagination was one—M called it my superpower. I'd simply imagine the five words were never spoken.

We crossed the grassy quad that was surrounded by chateau-like architecture that housed the classrooms and administration offices. The agrarian setting and academic charm was not at all a jarring juxtaposition to the morning trek. I loved cloistered academic life with M.

The Deeksha West, on the romantically rugged coast of Oregon, was the college M had envisioned for young ladies, an institution established for the realization of self, where students were encouraged to choose love over fear. Such a benign mission statement was somehow quite controversial in academic circles and within the weaponized web. The Deeksha West was a spiritual vortex, one celebrated on ninety-six wavy acres on the northernmost tip of the lush Willamette Valley. M was the steward of these Elysian fields and head of the school, where she taught quantum physics and constant creation theory.

When we entered my office, YaLan and Astri, along with their young American loves, Eric and Brian, were already there. YaLan and Astri had taken to switching hairstyles every other year. The already exciting 2027 was an Astri-with-shaved-head year, which suited her playful disposition. YaLan's fierce, intelligent eyes were softened a bit when framed by her long, wavy black hair.

The yogis jumped up from their mats where they'd been stretching, and the boys shut down their laptops on the conference table. The twins who shared the silent gift of speaking mind to mind were bursting to hear of the telepathic messages from Juno to Ting. And the boys were thrilled I'd used their state-of-the-art, HPA goggle technology. All eyes were on me.

M had insisted I take the corner office with its wraparound views, where I could look over the undulating vineyards and budding flowers all the way to the vast Pacific Ocean. Like an impressionist painting in motion, the wavy fields flowed out with the tide and into the sea each evening, and in the morning, summoned by the dawn, rolled into the office from the horizon. My office haven was filled with books. No art hung on the large white wall opposite the windows to compete with the stunning view.

Primitive art *did* hang in the children's playroom, which doubled as a gallery for their imaginative art to accompany the stories they wrote or that I told them. Like most parents, M and I believed our children were extraordinarily gifted. M's office was next door to that art studio, so she took the brunt of their interruptions, but my office served as the general meeting place for school business and family movie nights.

Beyond the view, the second attraction of my in-office theater was its six incredibly comfortable faux leather recliners that surrounded a crescent-shaped table—a single slab carved from an ancient oak that had fallen in its own time. Opposite the Willamette Valley landscape, framed by oversized windows, was the bare white wall, framed by bookshelves, that we used for those family movie nights, turning our backs to nature to watch films projected there.

I'd been sweating and smelled like a musty camper after the hike, while M was fresh and dry. I excused myself to shower, making them all wait to hear Ting's messages. I didn't like to disappoint the twins, but I needed time to prepare my words, fearing that the words I planned to edit out would create a glaring omission to my story.

Astri, our spritely humorist, said, "No rush, Sean. We've already

waited almost eight years to hear from our mother; what's eight minutes more when your mother's been missing for eight years?" Juno had
adopted twelve-year-old Astri and YaLan off the streets of Kathmandu,
soon after their parents disappeared and were presumed dead. The
twin yogis had been a little over twenty years old when we first met
them at the Deeksha in Kathmandu and now were about to turn thirty
and were thinking about children of their own.

"Well . . ." I had no witty retort to her poignant sarcasm.

M, patting my shoulder, bailed me out.

"Let's be patient a little longer. And I have good news to share before
Sean gives us the even more wonderful news of Juno!"

I smiled at M's kindness, and the twins were satisfied there was good
news to come. I slunk out of the office and through our bedroom into
our master bath.

The rush of water alternately pelted and soothed me. Because of
the fire churning in my belly, I set the water on colder than usual. I
tried to relax by thinking about M. She was the star of the Deeksha
West and had become a blossoming celebrity. Following the release
of Dylan Byrne's theory of everything, M became famous as constant
creation theory's main scientific champion. It wasn't all that surprising
that she'd been nominated for the big prize. I'd only be surprised if she
didn't win.

Working with Apple and their incredible quantum computer, M was
able to simulate a picture fourteen billion years in the future projected
from a single point, any point, in our expanding universe here and now.
Bang! Another universe magically appeared in that distant future. And
when the process was reversed, a big bang appeared in the rearview
mirror. That had been the proof that turned the tide toward greater
acceptance of constant creation theory where each instant all time and
space collapsed and reemerged—the big banging, not big bang, of life
in consciousness. That being said, Dylan's grand theory required one to
turn thinking on its head and see everything from the perspective of
the universal mind. It wasn't always easy to grasp.

M's European lecture tour, scheduled for the summer, was getting lots of media buzz and made me irrationally uncomfortable as I anticipated her absence. Juno's words stoked that fear.

I turned around and pressed my forehead against the shower wall so I could watch the water that had washed down my spinal column flow into the drain.

M's celebrity was not without backlash from reactionary big bangers who wanted to deny that the primary state was universal consciousness, and from the AI-fringe wing nuts who wanted to add even more to the illusion. The two sides had formed an unholy alliance against the theory of constant creation. The difference was that those who adhered to the big bang theory were tired, and the AI revolutionaries were filled with passionate intensity.

Why the militant AI side had refused to accept constant creation but clung to the big bang theory was not clear to me, though of course M seemed to understand—something about there being a destination instead of just the here and now. The viral AI group, whose members had become an internet militia, basked in anonymity but were still happy to embrace the acronym banner of WiN, for Wired-in Nation. WiN posts included ugly articles and tweets that referenced M. I tried not to look at the sinister musings but sometimes found myself immersed in the poorly drafted trash. Such lengths egos would go to defend their story of life, even to the extent of suggesting that those who disagreed must die.

M had advanced spiritually in her ability to access infinite consciousness, filling the spiritual void left in Juno's absence. She desired the truth like a drowning person desires breath. I, too, had advanced, but in her wake. In moments of heightened awareness, I realized my adulation of M was a form of idolatry. She was a spiritual portal—a flesh and blood mailbox—delivering messages of Big Love.

The one drawback was that her growth, which at first had been accompanied by a tantric hypersexuality with me, had evolved so that the nature of our lovemaking was marked by long intervals of abstinence. Long hikes and runs and cold-water plunges did little to ameliorate this.

And damn again, I'd almost had my long-withheld prize on the mountain cliff a couple of hours ago. I now turned the shower nob even farther to the right and began to scrub at my skin.

M wasn't only a brilliant scientist—she'd also given birth to two miracles, our beautiful little Dylan and *meimei* Juno. M said they'd inherited my imagination, which made them masters at play, like Jem and Scout, always pushing boundaries as they explored the natural world. I told them the story of Hansel and Gretel in the hope they wouldn't venture too far afield.

Sufficiently cool, I turned the nob to the left.

The children took after their mother too, inheriting her genius. They were open to messages from multiple sources and communicated with each other in lyrical lines, one after the other, in Zen-like mantra poetry while running through the vineyard. I sometimes ran with them and later tried to recall and record the lines, filling notebooks with their collaborative poetry.

The water was hot now, and I felt relaxed, ready to face the family's inquisition.

The Deeksha West was blessed by the best yoga teachers in YaLan and Astri, so my body, mind, and spirit were all strong, if not transcendent, for one who'd raced past the midcentury mark almost five years ago. Double nickels, M called my approaching age.

Peering into the foggy bathroom mirror in a moment naked and profound, I told myself that Juno's message about M was merely a reflection of my dark imagination, but if true, it would serve as a warning that called for the vigilance of a knight sworn to protect his queen. *I swear to protect M to allow her to fulfill her destiny*. I recited the secret vow three times, aiming for dramatic and solemn. Secrets weren't allowed, but this was a personal vow for her protection.

I smiled at my mental maneuvering. But as I stepped out of my bathroom, a towel around my waist, I was ambushed by two spies in the bedroom.

THE TWO SPIES BOUNCED ON THE BED, torturing me with their rebellious jumping jacks. Juno and Dylan always knew when something was afoot.

"If you keep entering without knocking, I'll have to consider a lock. And it's a bed, not a trampoline." I used my third toughest parental voice.

"So did you meet Ting in a holoram?"

"Hologram." Dylan shook his head, correcting his sister.

"How'd you know that? We were waiting to tell you till I heard what she had to say."

"Juno hears things," was Dylan's cryptic reply, laying the blame on his sister spy.

I was in a forgiving mood. "Yes, but I've yet to tell the family— they're waiting to hear from me now."

"Wha'd Ting say? Did she hear from our godmother Juno?"

This was a subject for child psychologists to debate, as we had not only taken their names but had also made dead Dylan and missing Juno the children's godparents without their consent. The children knew all about their namesakes and always wanted to know more.

"Yes, she did, although in a mystical way. I've—we've—told you about telepathy. Remember Tolkien in *The Lord of the Rings?*" I plucked the book from my bedstand and opened to a passage I'd marked that morning in preparation for hearing about telepathy with Ting. "They did not move or speak with mouths, looking from mind to mind: and only their shining eyes stirred and kindled as their thoughts went to and fro."

Juno lay back and shut her eyes. "Read more, Daddy, please!"

"Not now, but Narnia tonight. I'll read an extra chapter to celebrate the great news. But you do remember telepathy from *The Return of the King*?"

"Of course, and we practice it!" Juno said. "Just like Aunt Astri and Aunt YaLan."

"It only works sometimes. Plus, I don't want her in my head all that much," Dylan said, putting his hands over his ears and opening his mouth with tongue protruding, letting out a lion's *roar*, demonstrating how he would drown out his sister's mind probing.

"Why can't we have smart phones? All the other kids have them, even all the ones Juno's age." Dylan's favorite default topic with which he tortured us.

"You know your mom still says twelve or thirteen is the right age. Until then, develop your own minds and imagination. I don't want to keep having this argument for two more years." I sort of sold M out, but we disagreed on this. Ten was the right age in 2027.

Juno didn't listen. "Mom is so-diculous about this."

"*Ridiculous*, and no she isn't."

Dylan said, "Yes she is and you know what I want for my ninth birthday." He acted like it was a given he would get his wish. "Tell us about Ting."

"I must tell the rest of the family, but I'll tell you quickly first—it's great news!" I put my prayer hands to my heart and dragged out the dramatic moment for them, knowing they loved a good story. I was in a rush but didn't want to rush this. "Ting's message from Juno is . . ." I tightened the wrap of the towel around my waist and sat down between them and draped my arms over them. "She is alive and well and in some magical place in nature! She's not yet able to return, but she's emitting high-frequency messages from her Big Love!"

They both fell back on the bed, making sounds one hears in the stands after a walk-off home run. Juno jumped up and was back bouncing on the trampoline until Dylan pushed her down for a joyful laughing fit that got me laughing too. Then they started alternating the refrain, "We knew it!"

I stood to assert some order. "Now go play, but don't say anything. I have to dress and tell the family."

"But—" Juno started, but I thrust out a hand and made a stern face before she could launch into a thousand questions. I pointed toward the door, and having most of what they'd come for, they reluctantly ran off to fill in the gaps with their magical imaginations. One of the sprites let out gas loud enough to ignite their ricocheting laughter.

It was time for me to move my off-Broadway show to Broadway for my adult audience.

I RETURNED FROM MY SHOWER to the family, who were waiting not so patiently. Fresh mint tea and the cucumber sandwiches with hummus that M had prepared brightened the conference table. After so successfully delivering the messages to the children, it would be wrong to allow my fear to spoil the wonderful news the family would all soon be celebrating. Those five dark words were just my ego's fear creeping into the otherwise wonderful messages and easily edited out. My vow gave me my noble mission.

We got comfortable around the table. Again, all eyes fell on me.

"What a day! A Nobel Prize nomination letter and a hologram message with Ting and telepathy from Juno. Juno, as we all sensed, is alive! And communicating through Ting."

Astri jumped up on to the table and started a joyful dance. With Astri's encouragement, the boys joined the dance gamely but self-consciously, perhaps realizing as long-distance runners they moved like horses when not gracefully galloping in a cross-country race. We all celebrated Juno's return to us in our own way. YaLan, the more collected and cerebral twin, remained seated, swaying with a serene smile, but her joyful eyes danced. I clapped for the dancing Astri and track stars, and M smiled and swayed with YaLan. Such was our belief in telepathy.

As the dancers reclaimed their seats and some composure, Astri demanded, "Speak, Sean!" and pounded a playful, adrenaline-filled fist on the table.

"It was beyond cool. The hologram technology is so incredible, I forgot I wasn't actually with Ting in Juno's turret in her sanctuary, that vortex of incredible energy. It was lucky I was sitting or I might have fallen off the cliff."

"It's fantastic," Eric said, leaning toward me. "The technology is so advanced now, it can take you deep-sea diving or skydiving with a friend. Your hologram tech, installed back in 2019 by Juno, is somewhat dated, though the wired-in Chinese operators we coordinated with were able to update some of the software remotely."

The boys exchanged a look that I alone understood. They were determined to take a leap into the new AI technology from which there might be no return, and the twins were dead set against anyone wiring-in.

"The real and the metaphysical are increasingly hard to distinguish, thanks to BCI and Mark Suck-a-Bird." I felt in good company in not trusting that man and had the attention of everyone at the table, so I started my story. "If you want to know Ting, think Juno at thirty-three with a little more edge. Loose, though, like she's focused on riding a wave. The Tao of a surfer and free diver, whereas Juno is the wave, the water—"

"What did she say?" Astri blurted out.

"Yes, Sean," M said. "Imagine how much we all want to hear Juno's first words after all these years!"

"Ting says the message she received is that Juno is alive and well and is perhaps on a mountain in a Shangri-la-like paradise and only now able to communicate through Ting." Trying to inject some levity, I said, "I'd imagine—for all but identical twin yogis—one would have to be quite adept to communicate in that way."

Astri and YaLan groaned at my reference to their remarkable gift that rarely got mentioned until recently, and M circled one hand, prompting me to move on.

I cleared my throat and added, "She said Juno was living like a hermit but not of her own free will." I paused to honor the magnitude of the moment. "Juno is alive!"

Astri and YaLan were hugging each other and crying, which led me to cry too. I didn't know whether it was out of guilt for causing Juno's captivity or with joy because she was alive. I knew that everyone was thinking aliens but was reluctant to say the word.

After a moment of silence, YaLan said, "We *knew* she was still with us, though she disappeared from her sanctuary without a word. I felt a pain and a void, but never a loss of connection between my heart and hers."

Astri added, "It was a different feeling than when our birth parents disappeared. We both"—she turned to her sister—"have tried to reach her in deep meditation, but the only message we receive is her loving consciousness enveloping our own."

"Nothing more? Does Boy know?" YaLan asked about Juno's adopted son who had embraced a nicknamed that others might find demeaning. Boy, a strong and gentle man, was now in charge of the Deeksha in Kathmandu following Juno's absence. "I want to be the one to tell meimei Juno!" she pleaded, bursting with joy at the prospect, not realizing the children had been the first to know.

"Sure, but Sean and I would like to be there when you do," M said.

Astri said, "Then I get to tell Dylan with all you guys!"

"Ting will tell Boy, and sorry, but the children already know. They ambushed me coming out of the shower," I said. "Ting also said Juno had a message for me, and then she gave me the deeksha blessing. I swear I felt her hands on my head."

"The auto-sensory-suggestion effect," Brian said. Eric was nodding excitedly.

"What?" I asked. I'd forgotten what I'd been talking about as I focused on Juno's message. "Wait, that was real?"

Eric said, "The lifelike presence of the person and their environment may suggest touch and smell through the audio-visual 3D world. The potential is infinite."

"And soon it will be two-way," Brian said. "You there and them here, with you able to flip back and forth, 3D to 3D reality, and with virtual reality and ultrasound overlays it will be just like being there."

The boys knew their high tech and were boggling my mind.

"Let me show you a demo," Eric said, opening his computer and tapping keys.

Brian added excitedly, "With holograms, wiring-in to a quantum computer, we are heading into a brave new world."

"Sounds like hell to me. Guys, we want to hear about the messages from Juno more than I do about the technology," YaLan said, drying her tears. Her sister struck a warrior stance that anyone would be a fool to argue with, especially when her outstretched forward hand broke the pose and curled into a fist. She made me laugh.

"We are at a tipping point. Boys, I'll discuss the hologram tech with you after we let the eager ladies go," I said. "As for Juno's message, well, you know Juno." I inhaled and exhaled a deep breath. "She emphasized that I focus all my attention on Big Love. She knew I was writing again and gave me her blessing."

"While Ting was giving you the oneness blessing?" M asked.

"Yes. Ting said she was the transmitter but that she couldn't hear Juno."

"What specifically did Juno say?" M asked.

"Like with a dream, it's hard to recall the exact words, but you know her teachings, the 'nothing real is ever lost' type things." M squinted and raised her right eyebrow, so I had to go on the offensive with a half-truth. I looked at M but attempted to avoid those heat-seeking eyes that would ensnare me. "She said I'm to protect you."

"Hmm," said the human lie detector. "Always my protector."

"Or something to that effect," I said. "It may have been my imagination."

She took my hand gently in hers. "And what an imagination it is—excellent for fiction."

M had an uncanny ability to read my mind. The trick was to get M to believe she'd discovered the sum and substance of Juno's message without her hearing the precise words. Saying those words best forgot would only serve to make them more real.

In the end, after I recounted word for word all but the buried five, she accepted my version of the story for the sake of family harmony as we celebrated Juno being alive and in contact again. M did, however, flash curious eyes that declared she smelled some subtext.

If I was to protect her, she would have to trust me.

1 THE YOUNG AMERICANS

I SHIFTED TO MY DESK, rummaging through papers as the ladies continued excitedly discussing the messages and M's nomination arriving on the same auspicious day. Eric and Brian joined me at my desk, playing on their phones. They were texting, and my phone lit up with their messages. I touched my phone to see "Sean, we need to speak just with you." The young track stars, now track coaches, were eager to share in some conspiracy. I could feel their blood racing with pent-up energy like runners poised in the starting blocks.

Astri noted the social cueing as the women left, saying, "No doubt they want to discuss artificial intelligence. Perhaps we three should discuss true wisdom out in nature." They left arm in arm, almost skipping away. I would have joined that celebration fully if not for the words I'd pretended to have forgotten.

The boys had each turned thirty last year. They were always in athletic wear, looking like they were just setting off on a run even when they'd just gotten back. Eric was a white-bread Eagle Scout, and Brian was Cherokee and what was called an Indian Guide before they changed their name to Adventure Guides.

Both were nerds with jock-strong bodies; Eric was more head and Brian more heart. They were constantly playing techy games of cowboys and Indians, trying to best the other the way best friends do. The universe had miraculously split the embryo for them, creating the twins. They'd both be foxhole-worthy dudes during wartime.

The young Americans had passed their yogi trials of true love—Eric to be with YaLan and Brian with Astri. The couples had entered into what within the family we called a holy relationship, a concept we borrowed from *A Course in Miracles*. Even without marriages, the boys were family. M and I never had a marriage ceremony either, yet she had nonetheless guided our love into realms previously inconceivable to me. Our choice wasn't a rejection of marriage but a celebration of something new, where spirit, not survival and procreation, were the focus. A growing number of couples were following this same spiritual practice, but with mixed success.

Brian and Eric were heads of the Deeksha West's administration, accounting, and technology departments. The boys managed and taught the business of growing, harvesting, producing, and selling wine and flower—flower that old-timers like me still called weed. They were also involved in continuing education concerning the advances of artificial intelligence. They were a blessing to the school, since M and I had no facility for their areas of expertise.

Humanity had moved in two directions in response to numerous threats of annihilation. One was toward artificial intelligence, the other toward natural spirit. BCI, brain-computer interfacing, was providing social distancing and seclusion for the fearful, lonely masses, allowing them to connect to a virtual world of wishes and dreams.

Daily advances were driving the push into two-way holograms that would allow virtual interactions without the fear of deadly disease, technology that had developed following the Great Pandemic of 2020 that was finally downgraded to endemic in 2022 while we waited for the next pandemic. Mutant molecules and a warming planet that might be obliterated by an asteroid or colonized by aliens all threatened humanity, but it was the speeding advances of AI that M feared most of all.

Moving in the other direction from the metaverses of AI living, the world of spiritualism and constant creation was spawning communities where miracles and telepathy were accepted as the norm, and alien contact and abductions—CE-5 events or close encounters of the fifth kind—debated. I believed these aliens were just rebranded angels and demons.

I knew the topic the boys had remained behind to discuss out of earshot of our ladies, and it wasn't holograms.

"Have you told the twins about your determination to wire-in yet?" I asked the eager duo. "I'm not good with keeping secrets, especially from M."

"No one can keep anything from M. She has a magnet for the truth," Brian said.

"That she does!" I said a little too loudly, wondering if Brian was referring to my recent dancing around the truth. He had some keen instincts himself.

"And we'll tell the twins soon, we promise," Eric said. "They're so anti-BCI, but they must see that it's a prerequisite necessary for our work and for R&D. We could help you with your writing research too."

"Have you given more thought to teaching a class in science fiction here?" Brian asked. "Then maybe you'd want to wire-in too."

"Before it's too late, you mean? Some doctors won't oversee the robot that's required for the procedure, and insurance still won't cover it after sixty. Also, a bit scary with electrodes mapping and catching synapses communicating. The very idea gives me a headache." I rubbed my face. "And I'm a bit of a fantasy man, meaning fantasy that doesn't always slavishly focus on new technologies but which opens all portals into imaginative new worlds: Homer, Swift, Tolkien, Martin . . . Atwood, Rowling . . . Maybe I can combine both adventure fantasy and sci-fi, but let's see where this all goes. I've just today decided to write another book. We can discuss that later. Guys, it's time to reveal your terrifying secret to the ladies." I attempted to make a face of horror, clapping my hands on my cheeks to hold back the shriek. "So when might that be?"

"It's so hard to get this school to move on in embracing artificial intelligence, as if somehow that would be in conflict with the spirit of Big Love," Eric said.

They were intimidated by their formidable yogi loves and M. I pushed back in my chair to take a good look at the two of them. A pep talk was needed.

"Will you break it to M for us?" Brian asked, opening his eyes wide in entreaty.

"Sure, if you like. I'll tell her tonight after dinner. That means tonight's the night for the two of you to tell the twins too."

They nodded listlessly.

"As track coaches here, maybe you'll appreciate another one of my Coach Gavaghan stories." They'd heard the stories before and sat for the ten-minute story that finally concluded with Gavaghan shouting, within inches of my face, after we had won a cross-country race but not by enough time or points to satisfy him, "And McQueen! McQueen! You sucked hind moose tit. You don't *think* about running, you run!"

I paused, then added, "So let's stop thinking about it and tell them tonight."

"You'll wire-in too?" Brian asked, confused about the relevance of my story.

I stood up to conclude the meeting. "No, I'm the coach here. I was talking about you." But I was also steeling myself to tell M, who would not be pleased that our beloved Brian and Eric wanted to wire-in, nor with what it would mean to the school to have two key faculty endorse the technology.

Gazing out the window, I said, "Now a question about holograms. Would it be possible to have M give her tour talks from here as a hologram? I understand that during pandemics, concerts are played that way and all those wired-in can watch in 3D—live, if you will, from anywhere. Just spitballing."

"Spitballing? But yes," Brian said. "That's a great idea! We'd need to get the tech installed here, but most all the universities where she's set to appear would have the tech already, and as you said, those wired-in could attend from their couches."

Eric added, "We have a friend at Holoport, the leading hologram innovator, in San Fran, and could get it installed here in a week." He was already on his phone initiating contact with their friend.

"My hologram with Ting was so real . . ." Would I really try to keep M home? "I'm just noodling, so let's not mention this to the ladies.

It's likely that M would not agree to it. But perhaps take a look just for R&D."

M's anticipated objection to hologramming her European tour from Oregon was based on a solid risk-reward analysis: the potential for her to do good on her tour was so great and the real risk to her personally so small. But whether it was Juno's words or my imaginative foreboding, I felt the threat to M looming and growing inside me like an alien.

8 DON'T KILL HIM

THAT NIGHT AS I LAY NEXT TO M, I struggled to make sense of the day. M had remained inscrutable after I told her of Brian and Eric's plan to wire-in, which added to my uneasy state of mind. My subconscious was brewing up symbolic messages that percolated to the surface, images and scenes that only Carl Jung or M might fully comprehend. It was far from the clarity of vision I'd been visited with nine years before and more like an opium-induced gypsy dream.

As I balanced between sleep and waking, Ting's presence came to me as the Green Tara of Buddhist art. The mystical image startled me into sitting up. M was already sound asleep, her torso rising and falling in steady rhythm. I liked to follow her breaths and imagine the depths of her peace of mind.

I closed my eyes and returned my head to the pillow, recalling Ting's powerful presence in the three-dimensional computer-generated reality. Like a mythical being, she arose vividly from subterranean memory. Conjuring Ting there, I reviewed her Renaissance woman resume, a natural healer of plant-based medicines, a graceful grand master of yoga, a surfer and a free diver—joyously riding breathtaking waves and delving the deepest depths in a single breath. She lived the solitary Walden Pond dream of returning to nature, where she substituted the Pacific Ocean for the pond. In her tree house seclusion and simple luxury, she held retreats and created videos of her meditation lessons, which focused on letting go in order to disappear into the source of love found in the heart.

Ting had chosen the green and secluded way for her life well before self-imposed social isolation had become trendy. I was fascinated with such a bold return to nature that exhibited the freedom and courage of Thoreau. In that same spirit, I had discovered a remote solitary tower home, a writer's paradise on the coast of Ireland, where M and I could retire and enjoy complete liberation for the small cost of a thousand-dollar application fee and, of course, a commitment to spend my life savings in employing local artisans to fully restore the stonework and grounds to their original glory, per the contract, should they approve my application. My Yeats-like retirement dream, a sanctuary for us to disappear to, was still a secret even from M. I peered at my angel—sleeping safe from real-world dangers and my imagination.

As dawn approached, I could feel myself entering a lucid dream. A vivid Rousseau painting of a green jungle, with the light of dawn just about to crown the new day, became three-dimensional. In it, I stood alone on the strong roots of Ting's tree house, now abandoned. The grand old banyan tree was a symbol of longevity, but not for humanity. The island had been abandoned save for me, a modern-day Robinson Crusoe standing at the foot of that life-giving tree.

The paradox of the abundant life of nature and the death of all mankind meeting in a powerful vortex from which the glorious tree grew was striking. I felt utterly alone without M by my side. I wanted to pinch myself and wake up in bed next to her, but curiosity held me back.

The forest was filled with a strange grating sound that was vibrating through me, a metallic didgeridoo joined by chanting. I felt that the sound heralded approaching danger. I followed spiral steps, grasping rope rails on both sides about twenty feet up the huge banyan, to a thick wooden door that opened to my touch. I had to stoop through the door, but it opened onto a great room with vaulted ceilings and great round skylights, something like an oversized wooden yurt or small ark. As soon as the door closed behind me with a bang, there was stillness and silence.

The magical room welcomed me home. To the right of the door was a cozy sitting nook and kitchen. A teacup, hot and full, waited for me there, though no one was home. There was also a warm fresh pastry that I could taste through its aroma alone. After one revitalizing bite and sip, I moved like a hallucinating Alice from the nook through the main room and toward Ting's bedchamber. The door was open, and I could see a small balcony on the far side of the sleeping area, which framed the mountains and the sea. The sun was rising there, the light cascading across the green canopy of earth in waves, each wave building on the one before and hurtling toward the balcony until the largest shock wave of green light—a silent sonic blast—knocked me back and onto the floor.

Bewildered that I was uninjured, I shook off the effects and stood, returning my attention to the main room and its warm wood and peaceful bamboo. A few papers with Chinese calligraphy sat on a small desk beside some gemstones, a tuning fork, and healing herbs gathered into a mortar, with a matching pestle resting inside it. A tinker's bell and Ting's diver watch—stopped at 2:22—lay draped like a Salvador Dalí clock over a precious rock.

A full wall of windows and sliding-glass doors opened to a big balcony, where students could practice yoga at one of Ting's tree house retreats.

I stepped onto the balcony to take in the view of a volcanic beach about a half mile below. As soon as I did, nature's lament and the metallic didgeridoo returned to my ears. The off-key vibrational sound might have been an upside-down propeller weed-whacking trees at a distance but coming my way.

I turned away from the noise and toward a rope swing that swung to another large tree about thirty yards across the valley, a large Tarzan-like trapeze for daredevils, and pondered what would happen if you didn't make it across, or back, and just hung, dangling between the tall trees and contemplating a deadly drop into the gorge below.

I wished Ting were there with me. My body shook as I searched over and beyond the volcano's lava-flow ravine for the source of the discordant sound. A green flash flew across the valley, a small bird on fire or a ball of energy streaking across the sun's slanted rays, seen only because it caused a ripple in that light, a small comet messenger sent by the gods or the tiniest of alien spacecrafts.

I collapsed onto one of the meditation cushions, said my mantra, and took deep breaths with eyes half closed. My mind emptied of all thought, and the buzz-sawing faded away.

Ting slowly materialized in front of me in a lotus flower pose. I was dreaming within the dream! We didn't say a word in greeting, instead diving deep into a blissful meditation. Time moved slowly, along with the arc of the sun, and I let go and tumbled deep into the flow. I felt that I was heading to that oneness I'd experienced only once, at a lake high in Nepal.

Deeper and deeper I flowed, my mind making quantum jumps and dives up through the layers of the atmosphere without fear. I was an electron jumping into rings of ever lighter shades of blue. First into the troposphere, pausing momentarily when encountering a thin, porous membrane, and then jump! Stratosphere . . . jump! Mesosphere . . . jump! Thermosphere . . . jumps of energy without end! The experience of constant creation was near.

An unwanted sensation pricked my ankle. With eyes half closed, I watched the bloodsucking mosquito drink from me. I raised my right hand to swat it, but an unmoving Ting, with eyes closed, spoke without saying a word. *Don't kill him.* I waved the airborne predator away.

The quantum jumping resumed, taking me even deeper into the exosphere of almost all white-blue. But then that little vampire sat on my right hand. I moved to swat him. *Don't kill him,* I heard. So I shook him off.

Again my meditation went deeper, with one final levitating jump taking me out of my own atmosphere and into infinite space, the source of silent and immeasurable love.

White light.

Right at that moment of oneness, my little winged and bloodsucking teacher landed between my eyebrows, awakening me from the dream. Rubbing my third eye as if its lid had been bitten, I drank in the dream's bliss. Such a wonderful taste of *samadhi* was still on my lips.

Beside me and still asleep was M. All was right with the world. I kissed her to wake her. I had to tell her of my fairy-tale dream and share my euphoria before it passed. As M listened, I saw in her eyes—her heart—that she knew the meaning of the dream. I asked her, "So tell me, my love, what would Jung say it all means?"

She paused, and then read my dream to me. "You know I'm not trained like Jung, but perhaps even when human life ceases, when all the people we love are gone, consciousness will go on. In the end, in meditation with Ting, you experienced Big Love—all that is really important—and with that comes wisdom."

If nothing real could be lost, how could I ever lose her? I wrapped my arms around M, holding her so tight that I felt her warm and humming heart.

"May this moment never end," I said to my Zeno queen. We loved that paradox that allowed us to constantly cross over—instant to instant—into our future. Forever together.

The sublime scene was interrupted by a thunderous rumbling from my belly that scared both M and me. That was the moment my body chose to start its noxious protest.

9 ITEM ONE

MONDAY MORNING MEETINGS, run by Brian and Eric, were held in my office first thing after yoga and meditation and before classes began. We hosted a limited set of courses during a short June term, with only the six family-member teachers on campus. And that year all courses in July and August would be canceled to allow for M's tour, though many of the students lived on campus all year.

M and I were seated and reviewing the agenda. Since we'd gotten up, M had only once remarked about the strange rumblings coming from my belly. The incessant gurgling sounded like witches cackling over a cauldron foreseeing Macbeth's fate. M was giving me compassionate looks, but I could tell she wanted to laugh—after yet another volcanic burst, she finally did. I laughed too but was concerned I had swallowed last night's didgeridoo. Would it never stop?

I hurried to my desk and removed a full bottle of fruit-flavored Tums, popping three into my mouth. I offered M some like they were candy. She declined.

Brian and Astri and Eric and YaLan entered on waves of energy, the currencies alternating between the yogis' moving grace and the long-distance runners' steady pace. Their bright innocence sometimes made me feel like my own lamp had become tarnished by lack of polishing. At least the change of scene and the Tums muzzled the dogfight in my belly for the time being.

For today's meeting, I served croissants, fruit, and yogurt. The women sipped tea and the boys drank coffee.

Eric opened his computer and then started the meeting with Item One from the nine-item agenda. M was turning off her phone when she stood, saying, "Sorry. Give me five minutes—a student needs me." She was always available when one of her students needed counsel. Indeed, we all played part-time therapists for students who'd latched on to us. Already at the door, and giving me a knowing wink, she added, "It won't take long, so please wait. I don't want to miss Item One."

Item One, Sexual Propriety, wasn't something you wanted to be associated with. I was grateful that I had nothing to report that week. Times had changed, and our school was all about dignity and empowering women. We took the topic seriously to ensure that the buzz around the simple concept of Big Love wasn't distorted into its more salacious connotation. Still, social media and the press had had a field day when the school first opened, suggesting we were some modern-day Harrad Experiment in free love despite our being a single-sex college. It took a bit of creative writing—and absurd leaps—to turn us into some "loco lesbian love cult."

Luckily, M's scientific reputation kept the school from being a media joke. Still, running a school for young women in remote Oregon that focused on yoga and spirit, on sublime science and transcendent literature, meant that sensuality and its more troublesome sister—sex—hung in the air, while the pungent sweet scents ripened with the onset of summer. Item One generally related to one of the young women making inappropriate sex-laden comments to the faculty. We sought diligently to have a culture that prevented such occurrences, but human nature couldn't be entirely sublimated into spiritual and academic pursuits. I knew the truth of that better than most, as M put me through my advanced independent study course in abstinence. Three months and counting.

We shared intimate moments gazing into each other's eyes, seeing through one another, which led to bliss but not orgasmic release; my crazy river of pent-up desire rebelled at every turn. The interim celibacy drove my meditation, yoga, hiking, and running practices. It also led to icy plunges into the Willamette River.

M had gradually come to believe in a correlation between sexual abstinence and self-realization. From my reading of spiritual texts and my experience of celibacy in Kathmandu before experiencing Big Love on a mountain hike, I was in no position to argue the merits of her position, and we did still make exceptions that were all the more sublime for their rarity.

Since M hadn't returned yet and the others were eating, I reached for a fresh-baked buttery croissant but thought better of it and chose a bland granola bar to nibble with my coffee instead.

Even with me in my midfifties and being the least eligible man on campus, competing as I was with Astri for want of hair, I was often on Item One and sometimes in a not-so-favorable light. If I reported every student asking me to explain Zeno's paradox while licking their lips, I'd be on Item One every week *and* with multiple citations. My book had given me a reputation. As one mean-spirited critic so indelicately put it: "Sean McQueen, an easily aroused boner man, reports on every erection of his adolescent imagination." That literary shaming had exposed me to both real and feigned come-hither advances of my more ardent students.

While we discussed sublime poetry and Nabokov-worthy prose in class, the students competed to elevate their words and insights to the highest sensual level. And some creative writing scenes were over-the-top D. H. Lawrence love-scene knockoffs. But I didn't want to shackle the budding of their imaginations.

I tried to cut the students some slack because of their age, but one young lady took it too far. That morning I'd found an apple on my desk and put it in the drawer before M could see it. That seemingly innocent act seemed anything but innocent to me. But today's Item One had Eric in the hot seat and reporting on himself, which made me perversely happy. M returned, moving as quickly as she had when she'd left, and waved a hand. "Sorry, all done." She sat. "Eric, please start when you're ready."

But my belly spoke first, and I went to get more Tums, holding up my hands in surrender. "Astri," I told her, "please hold your witty tongue." There was nothing Astri liked more than jokes about bodily functions.

"Nothing I could say would be funnier than that comic alien in your stomach." She had her laugh while I returned from my desk, chewing the chalky-sweet tablets.

"Eric . . ." I gestured as the rumbling continued, gentler now but still stirring my discontent and causing general amusement and mild concern.

"Item One is all there and documented in my report," Eric said, looking at his computer screen. "I'd rather not get back into it unless there are questions. Item Two . . ."

Astri raised her hand impishly. "So many. Let me see . . . What about—"

"It's been handled," YaLan cut in. "Astri, you conducted the interview of *that girl*—I won't call her a witch—so please don't torture poor Eric."

I cleared my throat, and Astri stood to make her point that she wasn't finished.

"Sis to the rescue," she said. "But love is fundamental to our teachings and to those still learning. Sex is too. She understands to keep a safe distance and that Brian will become her track coach. She promises to keep her clothes on." Unblinking, Astri met the eyes of everyone at the table. "She knows I'd pull her hair out. But I wish we could do more to direct that sexual drive toward self-realization. She claimed she wanted to be with 'Eric in the rapture of nature' and that her ankle really was twisted. She acted the part of the smitten kitten, so misunderstood . . . She loves being—"

"She loves stirring up trouble," YaLan said with a slight clenching of her fists and a look beseeching her sister to drop the matter.

But Astri was not yet finished. "I asked her why she felt a need to act so inappropriately with the faculty, and she blamed Sean—saying he ignored her request for a Shakespeare tutorial for the June term. She feels the faculty rejects her. I think she has daddy issues."

"Should we continue to allow her to host those Saturday night Wicca dances at the fire pit with all the nudity and deliberate sexual arousal?" YaLan asked.

"Girls dancing naked and chanting—what connotations. The image is enough to forge a crucible of fear in a man's heart," I said with a mock shudder of an aging father figure.

YaLan, pointing out the window to the vines below, said, "And they're held right in the middle of Strawberry Fields, a sacred space." Strawberry Fields was the name of our central sea-sloping vineyard, where we grew the finest pinot noir grapes.

M stood to look out toward the ripening grapes and perhaps to imagine the Wicca scene. "Yes, it's a sacred place of great energy, but it's open to all students, and nudity breaks no dress code"—she sent an apologetic look to YaLan—"outside of class. And there's something healthy in their being out in nature celebrating the new and full moons. So easy with AI to become disconnected from nature, sun and moon, even our own breath." She took a troubled inhale and then sighed.

YaLan glared fiercely out the window and said, "Samantha Smythe and her Aryan beauty"—I turned to look at Eric even as he turned a whiter shade of pale—"is trouble in so many ways. I know we try to avoid names on Item One, but her aggressive and insulting advocacy that all become wired-in, and her 'SS' handle, are so offensive."

She turned her warrior glare on Eric. "Her behavior was especially manipulative. The ankle twisted during a run on the far side of the lake, causing Eric to stay behind and nurse her back. And then her wanting to soak her little foot in the cold water and then—*oh my*—falling in. The cold *wet* T-shirt and erect nipples. Thanks, Eric, for that detail."

"I only noted that because of the entrapment. No bra. And, in hindsight, I don't think her ankle was really hurt *that* badly." Eric took notes on his computer, punching each key as if it should be the last letter written on the matter.

I felt that he could use a good defense lawyer, but I didn't want to speak. And what would I say—that Miss Samantha Smythe, dripping sexuality and drawing all the dogs of desire to her heat, was every bad boy's dream girl? A young but taller Scarlett Johansson with her nipples the only part of her breasts not always on display? She had targeted me, and I believed she had a crush on me. I was relieved by her turning her seduction onto Eric and away from me.

She purposely tempted and teased me. I was pretty sure she was the ghostwriter behind the fairly regular but anonymous emails full of sexual innuendo that showed up in my inbox. The apple now in my desk drawer I attributed to her. Samantha, with her strong scent of overripe fruit that was hard not to detect even at a distance, was a constant source of harmless adolescent fantasy. But my devotion to M kept my dogs on a short leash. And I never allowed myself to be alone with her, which she had noted once, teasing while smacking her lips and saying, "You'd think I was going to eat you. Well, maybe. I'm sure you'd taste like sticky cotton candy. Don't let me catch you alone, Professor Illicit Imagination."

That comment had made me the subject of ridicule and alliterative assonance on a prior Item One. I didn't like to be on Item One!

M returned from the window to take her seat next to me and brought me back from my daydream.

"SS, the self-proclaimed witch," YaLan half muttered as she twisted her arms and legs into stretching eagle's pose to relieve—or express— her distress.

Samantha's witchcraft either added to or subtracted from her allure, depending on whether you consulted your good or bad angel.

"Her admission essay was brilliant, and I was her biggest champion for admission, despite the essay's premise being so antithetical to my beliefs." M shook her head.

We'd spoken about Samantha's essay before, so I understood M's bemusement.

Admittance was based on the earnestness of a student's desire, her commitment and her diligence on the path of self-realization. That highfalutin-sounding criteria was balanced with a compassionate needs-based component. The economic circumstances of many of the students had them living and studying on campus even over the sum- mer. Samantha, without any family, was one of the year-round students. She was the product of a hard-knock life, a brilliant mind, and a body she used like a weapon. She was crying out for love. And I felt sorry for her and forgave her youthful indiscretions.

Samantha's clever essay argued that AI was protected under the Constitution. Her argument was in keeping with M's belief that AI was

an extension of ego, or in Samantha's parlance, "self," and therefore protected as part of the right to life, liberty, and the pursuit of happiness.
The essay had been written in the form of a court brief. It was so good,
we assumed she'd had help.

"I always wondered if the AI we used to check her essay for plagiarism was in cahoots with her, in solidarity with her argument to allow AI
to roam free." I smiled at my knack for irony. "And with brain-computer
interfacing, it is a legitimate argument, at least to some degree. And M,
with your paper suggesting ethical restraint now being nominated for a
Nobel, I worry about the radical AI wing of the Wired-in Nation."

"I know you do, but politicians and judges will decide the matter,
not me." She held my gaze for emphasis, and I held hers just because it
was beautiful, even as my stomach made another unwelcome comment
that brought heat to my cheeks and a smile to her face.

Samantha's essay later appeared on the internet and was used
in actual court cases. *That* made her an icon and thought leader for
the wired-in crowd. It also made her a risk to the school. From poor
orphaned farm girl from Buttlick, Wisconsin, to internet influencer—
and all in just three years. No one would admit it, but you had to
admire her achievement. And who could blame her for her desperate
cries for love and affection?

She was now in her third year, though she looked to be in her
midtwenties, like a Hollywood actress playing the part of a coed. Ms.
Smythe was publicly critical of M for the school's position of urging
ethical constraints upon artificial intelligence.

"Okay, Coach Eric, she read your future?" Astri had returned to her
interrogation. Making innocent prayer hands, she said, "Please tell us
what she saw there." That's when I felt the familiar tingle like an elec-
trical-magnetic charge dancing between the twins' eyes and minds. I
believed this sensation came when they were nonverbally communicating. At these times, I could almost eavesdrop and was being schooled
in the art—or at least in its detection.

YaLan, becoming self-aware of the audience, spoke for the rest of
us. "What the hell, Astri? You think this is all so funny." She didn't

always appreciate Astri's needling wit. "Next time it might be Brian." She then turned to Eric, "So tell us your future, since Astri has to know every detail."

"She pretended to tell the future—but not mine. I was interested, I must admit. She said havoc and downfall were coming to the school and that she could help Sean through it. But she complained he never pays her any attention."

Eric had left that out of the report, probably as a favor to me. But now I was caught unprepared as he caved on cross-examination.

M again shook her head. "Good thing he doesn't get too near to her. Such a catch is my Sean Byron McQueen." Her grin was wide even as she took the piss out of me. "And she knew he would hear all about this." She mock-frowned and shook a finger at me. "Don't let it go to your head."

But it already had—M knew me well. Surreptitiously, I pinched the skin behind one knee to keep from blushing and to stem the flow of blood to my longing little alter ego.

YaLan was shaking her head too. "Techies can be so superstitious. Telling fortunes? I thought that was the purview of the mystical."

"Is that when she removed her top and asked for your dry shirt?" Astri said, teasing Eric with her sprite-like smile. She was able to get away with so much because she was Astri.

I leaned back out of the spotlight, prepared to enjoy the scene as YaLan was provoked by her sister's innocently posed questions.

"Eric," YaLan said, "you should have run from the twisted ankle and come to get me to deal with that snake. And once her shirt was off, you complied and gave her yours?"

Brian jumped in on defense. "That's when I showed up on the ATV to give her a lift back to school. I assure you Eric was at a safe distance and not showing any interest. Better his shirt off than hers."

Really?

Astri started laughing, which got us all laughing too.

M said, "She's trouble, but I won't use that as a pretense to expel her. With her celebrity, a dismissal would lead to a lot of bad press, but more importantly, dismissing her would be the wrong thing to do. We admitted her, although I didn't agree with her, for her passionate intensity and her belief that AI would bring all people to the happiness they have sought throughout evolution. We are the guides and mentors for *all* our students and maybe most of all for those who are trouble and disagree with us." She again gave me a knowing look. "They teach us the most too."

I kept my mouth tightly closed.

"And she's right in her way," M continued, "that there's no way regulation and ethics will ever rein in AI. We need time to evolve as a species. Let us pray for time or for the Second Coming soon."

And what rough beast, its hour come round at last, slouches toward Bethlehem to be born?

M took a moment to once more look out the window and over the grounds, this time from her seat, before finishing her ruling. "That girl is truly blessed to have Astri's mentorship; thank you for taking responsibility for her. As long as we watch our behavior, we will do no harm and hopefully some good. Perhaps, Astri, you can counsel her on the spiritual aspects of love. How a holy relationship sharing the spirit of Big Love—not sex—is the highest expression of love between two people."

I sighed. M was constantly reminding me that our relationship continued to shift away from its sexual expression. She did so now compassionately, looking at me with her soulful eyes and sealing us together in a circle of empathy, signaling to me, I hoped, that it would soon be time.

Eric, breathing easier now, said, "And with Brian as her coach now, there's nothing to worry about other than she'll run slower. Item Two!" He snapped down the lid of his laptop to signify closure for Item One before reopening it for Item Two.

"Yeah, the extra weight will slow her down since I'll insist she wear a bra for our runs," Brian countered.

I was glad for us all that we now moved on. Items two through eight, of little consequence, passed smoothly and quickly. Item Nine was new and had been added by the boys. *Artificial Intelligence.* The topic would lead to a philosophical divide and to debate among the family. M's fear of AI was her Achilles' heel as losing her was mine. She might choose to prevent the boys' choice to be wired-in. M could simply make it a school rule that none of the administration or faculty were permitted to wire-in. Or she might just strongly disapprove and the boys would cave in front of her moral authority. That would be a big mistake, and I rarely disagreed with M at a family meeting but felt like I would have no choice but to speak up against her. I'd left the issue unresolved when I told her of the boys' intent the night before, afraid of how it might disrupt the harmony and balance we currently enjoyed. We generally saw eye-to-eye on academic and metaphysical matters, but when it came to the balance or conflict between Big Love and AI, I had the high ground of the middle way. The boys wanting to wire-in threatened to become a wedge between us before she went away.

10 ITEM NINE

AFTER A BRIEF RECESS, and more Tums for me, we returned to our seats for Item Nine. An item that promised to become a battle of the sexes.

Before Eric could start, I wanted to make my position perfectly clear. "I'm Switzerland on this." I hoped to be able to maintain neutrality and that M would yield without my intercession on behalf of the boys. "So I'll be on the sidelines and taking notes. Please keep it moving. I have work to do before my *New York Times* interview this afternoon." I liked the ring of that, though it would be only a background piece, probably never published, or if it was published, truncated into fifty words or less.

Eric frowned in my direction. "Item Nine, artificial intelligence and wiring-in. You all know our views. Brian?"

Punting right off? Eric, who rarely lacked confidence, was wilting in front of his toughest audience after barely surviving Item One.

"Thanks. Throw me to the tigers." Brian stood and stretched his long arms. "The procedure itself is done by robot in one day and is entirely safe—no serious injuries for over a year now and with millions wired-in. The crafting of infinitely small implants and chips to catch our thoughts mid-synapse has been mastered. Over fifty percent of people our age have already wired-in, and our work"—he waved a hand between Eric and himself—"lends itself well to the use of BC interface."

"Inhumane artifices tested on poor chimps, enabling them to read picture books, and now it's your turn?" Astri said with a snap of her fingers. YaLan straightened her back and smiled pleasantly at her sister before glaring at the boys. Sometimes I didn't know which was worse, Astri's bite or YaLan's countenance turned fierce.

"I wondered what the monkeys thought of Curious George," I said to lighten the mood, but only M and the boys laughed. The childhood classic probably hadn't been taught to the twins in Kathmandu.

Eric, ignoring the bristling yogis, said, "This will enable us to better monitor in real time accounts, projections, and surveillance. Even while we're hiking we can ward off potential hacks and respond to school emergencies. Sean—"

"Hey, I'm Switz—"

"Not while *we're* hiking." YaLan pounced. "You'll be making your crush, Samantha, happy, no doubt, by wiring-in." The smooth flow of her breath was gone as emotion engulfed her, reddening her face. Rage was foreign to YaLan, and she struggled to regain a calm breath. She hadn't let go of Item One.

M knew the battle lines and knew that she was the main opposition to BCI being used by the school administration. And she would have the final say. M rose and moved again to the window.

"Ladies—yogis—let's remember to breathe while we discuss lines of contention. Eric or Brian, please explain the science for us."

Brian spoke slowly enough that I could follow. "As you know, years ago, companies competed to advance the technology that had successfully tested a radical brain-computer interface with Bluetooth chips planted in the skull by a meticulous robot. The technology includes an undisclosed number of sensor electrodes smaller than the neurons they track for the chemical messages they receive. This enabled the chipped mind to control his computer with thought. Fast-forward to now. The chips are routed to remote self-learning quantum computers, bringing the promise of even greater abilities." He looked to Eric for support.

Eric, pretending to be reading from his screen, maybe from some AI authority, said, "And now the process is all but perfect. That is why we waited. The mind is so much faster than fingers and thumbs in directing the computer. After mapping most of the common cognitive features, the simple chip implant and neural sensors can be updated remotely, as has been done for years for a car's automatic pilot."

YaLan was teary-eyed but had moved past the point of anger. "But that's just it. You're not a machine but a human being. A child of God. I don't want you becoming the latest computer software."

M returned from the window and pressed both hands against the conference table, stretching her back with a sigh. "You know my philosophical belief and the position of the school is that mankind is at a crossroads between AI and spirit and that AI is being used to extend one's ego and not to transcend it. But this decision involves your bodies. Your minds. And your decision." She pushed away from the table and circled around to me. She put her hands, warm and solid, on my shoulders. "Sean has reminded me of free choice. Any thoughts on the matter from Switzerland? You and your belly have been very quiet." She kneaded my muscles and passed the conch to me.

So . . . I wouldn't be able to sit out the battle. I shifted in my seat, not wanting to meet anyone's eyes. "Well, my gut tells me . . . it's all so new. But I agree. I must admit I've fantasized about . . . about being able to research any poem, essay, or novel with just a thought. And I've read the transcripts of the AI Shakespeare and the AI Yeats—it would be fun to meet those virtual bards in my mind in 3D reality." I reached up to clasp one of M's hands. "But I fear this AI will replace imagination and dreams, and for that, I've sworn off it for me. But for the boys, I don't think it's my place to object. Free will is a God-given damnable conundrum. Or paradox, as maybe it's all destiny."

YaLan rose up to meet M's eyes with her own pleading gaze. "M, unless you say for the sake of the school that no faculty can undergo the procedure, they're determined. Please . . . remember your call for *humane restraint* upon the extension of AI."

"It's not my decision but theirs. You say you can deactivate—disconnect—at any time?"

"Yes, of course," Eric said. "It's fail-safe and secure. You control the computer, not vice versa. We have an encrypted kill switch."

Seeing their side had won and wanting to be a good winner, Brian turned off his phone. They both were too smart to gloat. And they taught and practiced being good sports. Their yogis were coiled to pounce, and Astri had shown the most restraint I'd ever seen from her.

M gave a long *hmmm*. I squeezed her hand, knowing that this wasn't what she wanted, and she interlocked our fingers. And it was done.

Brian, bravely looking forward to their upcoming adventure, said, "Okay, we'll have the procedure next week. And you'll see the only difference is more efficiency."

"I feel like you'll be an alien," Astri said.

"I'll still be me, and I'll get my work done in half the time or do twice as much work."

"Half the time will be fine, with more time for practice and meditation with me."

"It's a deal!" Brian said as Eric shut his computer with a bang.

I was breathing easier now that M hadn't used her authority to declare a no-wiring-in-faculty policy. To the young, wiring-in was becoming a generational rite of passage and a requisite procedure for the haves over the have-nots. School was so much easier for those wired-in, but since most of our students had little money, a majority at the Deeksha West were still unwired. The inequities and ethics were a sticky academic wicket. The only impediment that stopped the wired-ins from using their computers in exams was the honor system. We still needed a better mechanism to police the matter, as wired-in students were generally getting much better grades. Still, that could be due solely to their increased speed of access to information before the test.

M, reading my mind, said, "Brian and Eric, your bullet point here." She reached over my shoulder and pointed to an Item Nine bullet point. "You'll be better able to detect cheating by those wired-in after you're wired-in yourselves?"

They both sat taller, eager to show the benefits of being wired-in, but Brian spoke first. "It will allow us access to a quantum computer that we can ask questions of, or submit test answers to and that can detect a digital fingerprint—"

"Then," Eric jumped in, "if the student confesses, they'll be given a second and last shot at honor as provided for by the code. If they continue to deny the cheating use of BCI, they risk expulsion for even the first infraction."

"You've given this a lot of thought, but how will you resolve a dispute?" I asked.

"It's a real problem everywhere, and we studied other schools' best policies." Eric turned to Brian, giving him his turn.

"In unresolved cases, the final arbiter is a foolproof AI retinal scan used for lie detecting. That step will require a drive into Portland for the use of the city's creepy eye-detection system. Or we could just use M as the diviner of truth."

I smiled at Brian's homage to M's mind-reading abilities.

M stepped away from the table and did her infamous shake-off dance. Then she said, "Good work." She shook herself one more time, adding, "But I hope we never have to take that drive to the creepy wizard."

"Creepy eyes and creepy wizard! M, please stop them." My tummy also wanted to change the topic. Now I was the one afraid of AI peering in and controlling our minds?

"Boys, you read *The Lost Theory*. Sean and I can't think of creepy eyes without thinking of Dick and his Guru, who we'd believed had developed the technology now so commonly used in court cases." The Guru was the CIA director in charge of AI who had taken away my NYU tenured professorship and almost M's life nine years ago when we sought to release Dylan's groundbreaking theory of constant creation. Dick was the Guru's loyal henchman with Charlie Manson eyes, who'd threatened us in Kathmandu as we searched for the theory but who had died from a skull-crushing blow to the face.

M went on. "The new facet of inequality created by BCI is another matter we'll have to figure out as we go. In the meantime, we better let Sean get to his work and prepare for his big interview." She closed her eyes. "But . . . please wait just one more minute."

I didn't know if she was thinking or meditating or praying. YaLan glared at Eric but gave way to a forgiving smile, while Astri pretended she was drilling her index fingers into her temples and got a smile from Brian. I sat by observing, giving M her minute.

I thought about the ongoing politically charged debate in Congress about whether or not wiring-in should be paid for by the government as part of universal health care. Russia was paying for each citizen older than twenty and younger than fifty to be wired-in. Although it was supposedly elective surgery, all the instruments of Russian power pushed those of the right age to the robot's operating room door. The ethics of that proved to be a Gordian knot that I couldn't cut through but which M had so brilliantly cleaved in her Nobel Laureate–worthy essay.

"How about this," M said. "Please work together, as you do so well— YaLan and Astri on telepathy, Brian and Eric on the BC interface, and the four of you on the nexus between the two. Try to harmonize yourselves and examine the limitations and potential. Let's meet before I leave for the tour to map the competing outlooks to create a course for the fall semester—a comparative study of the two disciplines."

Heads were already nodding and tense features easing, and I stood to join M.

"Sean?" As always, she sought my oldest-statesman view.

"Give that lady a Nobel Prize. Brilliant idea—the universe is telling us to explore this nexus and to go down this path. What the world sees as spiritual miracles and the potential for cutting-edge science and theory certainly run along parallel tracks. It's all science fiction until we experience it; let's see where it leads." Squeezing her hand, I felt her heartbeat.

M gave me *that* smile and said, "Let me remind us all—including myself—that in these times of great challenge and difficult choices, the one that really matters, the one choice that cannot be limited and cannot be made for us by a computer, is the choice of self-realization and love. The more love we feel, the faster we are moving on our path of awakening, so let love and joy be our guides. This is what we teach, and learn again, today and every day."

Class was over. The twins followed their fearless leader out the door, and the boys sat with me, relieved. I had the feeling they were thinking that the war of the sexes was over and dreaming of all they would do when they became wired-in humans. I worried for them and all of mankind, which mostly treated the procedure like cosmetic surgery when it was actually brain surgery, a merging of man and machine.

|| IRISH TOWERS

TO HASTEN THE CONCLUSION of the post-meeting lingering by the boys, I announced, "Okay, time for me to get to writing before my interview." The boys, always eager to help, were soon carting the leftovers and plates to the kitchen, and I was left alone with the sleeping gremlin in my belly to write. Even after averting a clash with M over Item Nine, my mind seemed to move from one worry to another worry with only intermittent respites.

Elliot Pennington, my faux lawyer and oldest living good friend, was still my agent and a New York City bon vivant. He was adamant that a writer writes a book or two a year and not just one every decade. He was second to M to be told I was writing again. And to turn the heat up, he'd arranged for me a face-to-face interview with the *New York Times* Book Review people. Even though I had no book to review. "Just background," he'd said, "to remind your readers you're still alive and to build anticipation for the long-awaited sequel." I wasn't in the habit of competing with M, but with her upcoming rock-and-roll show in Europe, I thought a flattering *NYT* retrospective on me might allow me to play on the same stage as her opening act.

I didn't raise my pen as planned but sat at my desk, at my computer, viewing the crumbling tower home in Ireland, where I dreamed of being alone with M and my writing. I heard my critics snickering at my desire to resurrect it. The top floor had sweeping views from broken-down windows and parapets. The virtual tour showed the crashing sea and nearby lighthouse as seen from the turret bed once the walls and structure had been restored. I held the romantic notion that one should be able to see and smell the ocean as death was approaching.

The tower wasn't so much up for sale as for adoption—like a broken-down, bed-wetting old man. Still, with my life savings, I could afford the local labor-cost estimates they provided, that I would have to guarantee to have performed. It was held by the county, and the application made it clear the judges were looking for a prodigal son and artist. The solicitation seemed to call out to me—today was the deadline to submit the application.

If I was selected and before I went to contract, I would tell M in some grand romantic gesture. I wondered if *me and the boys* could arrange a hologram tour of the tower before and virtuality tour of the fully renovated tower after. Then, when she was ready to retire, we would move there and disappear together, once in a while emerging from a couple-mile scenic hike to stroll into a charming village for provisions and pints at the pub.

I submitted the thousand-dollar fee, financial and personal information, along with an essay on why they should select me. I wrote an imaginative piece about being Yeats reincarnated as a long-winded prose writer who wished to return home to a life of solitude by the sea. Though I claimed to be the prodigal son, I couldn't help but feel like a cheating husband when I submitted the application I'd secretly worked on for months. The award date was set for "as soon as the committee determined the winner of the undertaking." There would be interviews, questions, and negotiations before the award was made . . . plenty of time to tell M before we were committed.

I was procrastinating with Irish fantasies, not writing, and a bit nervous and fully unprepared for my upcoming interview. I needed to write something in order to have something to talk about.

I recently used Elliot's agency and legal advice in writing the screenplay for the Yogi Mangku documentary and in negotiating the contract with the film's production company. That screenplay bone I had thrown Elliot only made him more eager for my next novel. He had been diligent in helping me research the facts behind my fiction and patient, in his way, while on our monthly calls, prodding me with drinking-buddy jests that I would parry with somber literary sobriety. The next Elliot call was scheduled for the following morning, so, with no Monday classes, I'd write before and after my interview, and maybe have that long-sought breakthrough.

I wrote my first three words on the first page of my notebook, *The Devil's Calling*, and marveled at the creative process that might allow me to disarm the spell of its power by embracing the words that had caused me so much trepidation. The vision's bloody words would become my title, and all I needed to do was write the story and let destiny make the movie and the poster I had foreseen. We could make a heaven or a hell of almost anything. I'd face my fears and make them fiction.

Or maybe not, as my bones felt all of a sudden like icicles rattling within me. I got up and was mid-punk-rocker in a pogo shake-off dance, trying to warm the blood and toss off the shackles that had gripped my heart, when my interviewer arrived at the open door.

Not just any interviewer. I was going to kill Elliot for not warning me. I'd thought they were sending some bookish staff writer for background so they'd be prepared for when my book came out. But there at my office door—escorted by our student receptionist—was the always-striking Molly Quinn. Molly Quinn, my Irish literary idol! I'd never seen nothing like the mighty Quinn.

MOLLY QUINN WAS A PERENNIAL Booker Prize nominee, with a couple of wins for her dark romantic stories worthy of *Wuthering Heights*. A few feet from me stood a literary giant, the writer of sensual femme fatales with unique siren voices that always dragged me into dark alternate universes. She could kill with her pen like a Samurai with a sword. She was the one exception to my rule that literary geniuses had to be dead.

In her willowy white dress, she looked like Maureen O'Hara. In another life, she may have been Maud to my Yeats or Plath to my Hughes; but in this life, it was only M that would cause Fergus *to go dance upon the shore.*

I stood up from my desk, banging my knee, gushing over how unexpected the meeting was. "I'm honored," I told her as we eschewed the outdated handshake and exchanged a namaste bow, our eyes meeting in creative union.

Okay, Elliot, my old friend. Showtime. I'll play this scene for you and I'll play it well.

Then there was something that called away my attention to my always-open door, expecting to see M or little spy Juno, but it must have been a demon or ghost—no one was there, but that *something* made me apprehensive. I shook off the eerie feeling and refocused on my esteemed present company.

"Molly Quinn. Wow. Please have a seat and enjoy the view. Would you like to try a glass of our fine wine—a chardonnay, pinot, cabernet? An exclusive vineyard wine tasting?"

She was all grace and Midwestern charm as she swept across the office to the large windows like a white swan gliding over ice and about to take flight. "I'm a big fan, and when I heard there was finally to be a second book, I asked for this interview. And, sure, a glass or two of wine would be nice—you choose. What a spectacular view."

She sounded like Lauren Bacall with a raspy yet lyrical voice.

"Enjoy! Only our best pinot noir for you." I was a fawning sommelier serving a literary queen, already steadying a swaying bottle and positioning it for the puncture and twist of my overly eager corkscrew.

She stood framed by the same large windowpane and light where M often stood.

As I poured the wine, she continued to drink in the view and said, "Please, tell me all about this magnificent place."

"It's a labor of love, brainchild of Professor Edens. The college was blessed to be designed and built, in 2022, in the midst of acres of nature as the first *great* pandemic loosened its grip. The spaces for sleeping, seating, eating, and living were painstakingly recalibrated, with many of our classes held online in meta-classrooms. The post-2020 norms are hard for those who've lived so long another way and even harder on the young who haven't yet lived or loved."

Her eyes didn't leave the view, but her ears were clearly taking in my words. Words I would deliberately forge to make a deep first impression on this master wordsmith. Elliot would be pleased with my effort, and M would laugh at me living out my literary fantasy. To pull Molly's eyes back into the room and onto me, I held up my glass.

"A toast! Blessed are we again to have such a great writer here today. To the mighty Quinn and her quill!"

She gave the view a sun salutation before turning to me.

"To Sean Byron McQueen dipping his quill back in the ink!" she said as *ting* went our glasses and *zing* went my heartstrings before the metaphor hit me where it hurt.

One Step struck with a clichéd parry. "It's been a while, but I've kept my powder dry." I raised an invisible musket, poised to shoot at the heavens.

She paused for only the barest moment and then let out the most generous laugh. I liked a woman who gave One Step free rein. "You know that *trust in God and keep your powder dry* is attributed to Cromwell?"

"Oh no, the cursed devil who slayed our Irish?"

We settled into our comfy seats with her attention all on me. I let Cromwell launch me into my familiar conversation starter, for anyone of Irish descent, on how the Irish dominated literature and especially poetry, talk which led naturally to my cascade of questions about her next book and the composition of dark romantic heroines engaged in living out selfish fantasies, who go missing or get killed by their own twisted invention, stories always illuminated with a brilliant spark of spot-on prose.

I was excited to hear about her creative process over that first glass, and then, as I poured the second, she said, "But let's not forget I'm here to interview you. May I?"

I nodded, and she turned on her phone's recorder.

Words, don't fail me now.

"This is a little embarrassing. My second book is nowhere near finished and I thought this was only background, something for a what's-he-doing-now type of blurb in the book or magazine section."

"No worries. Just imagine I'm your reader, or an old friend you haven't seen for nine years, and catch me up, please."

"All right. I'm a literature teacher again and a writer, in love with Emily Edens and with life, living in this paradise of nature and learning. Writing a sequel. The end."

"Succinct summary, but I'm still all ears." But it was her eyes she spoke with as they held me in their intense light. "Maybe let's start with the title and plot for the new novel."

I stood to think and went to my desk to grab a pen and my writer's notebook and then placed them down between us.

"*The Devil's Calling*! I love it. Sounds dark. And I seem to recall that phrase or title from your first book?"

"Well, yes. It's just a working title." I hadn't intended those words to be seen. But it was too late—she loved my title and there was no putting Pandora back in the box. No time like the present to face my fears. And I was flattered. "You're a keen reader. It's from my dark vision chronicled in the epilogue. So perhaps it will be dark. We'll see. I've mostly been doing research for *The Devil's Calling*." I couldn't keep using the only three words I'd actually written, but I had nothing else to offer. "Can this be off the record—on background? I'd like to review my answers before they're printed."

"As any wielder of words would, of course." She shared a smile with the simile. Her dark red hair framing *the girl with the pearl earring* face, along with her literary chops, made her abundantly pleasing company. "I really do like the working title—it works so well. And we must honor our visions." She tapped a natural nail, unpainted but well tended, against the three loaded words.

I swiveled to check the door, half expecting to see the devil already there, looking for his pound of flesh. "I have to warn you that we have a no-lock and no-knock policy, but I hope we won't be disturbed."

"No worries. I'd love to meet the marvelous Professor Edens, who I've read so much about. But for now, maybe start with the public reaction and what happened after your first sensational book was published?"

"Sensational? Hmm. Good word for it. Thanks to Dylan Byrne's earth-shattering theory and a megalomaniacal CIA guru who probably had him killed. And then Juno goes missing and M becomes a rock star. All driving book sales."

I doodled Dylan's name on the pad.

Her eyes were still set to *go on*.

I cleared my throat reflexively, hoping to say something important. "I suffer a nagging insecurity that the book's success was more sensational, less literary. On the other hand, readers of pulp fiction wanted more blood and not a real-life adventure—Tarantino, not Maugham."

She shook her head. "We always want everyone to love our work, and there will always be those that don't. It was a unique blend of adventure, memoir, and fictional thriller. I loved the weave of spiritual and scientific themes. And the characters—YaLan and Astri, the yogis— now teach yoga here at the college? Tell me everything. I feel like I know them all, *the family*."

"We're definitely big on yoga. Hinduism and Buddhism are the root philosophy for over half the world and a critical component of our yoga and meditation curriculum taught here by YaLan and Astri. They are as important as our science and lit departments." I stood to show her my tree pose, my wineglass steadied on my knee, and then I raised the glass to my lips, almost dropping it as the tree fell. "Let the record show I did not spill a drop." I foolishly reclaimed my seat, though my antics did get a hearty laugh. I refilled our glasses from the safety of our seats, glad M hadn't witnessed the clown act.

"The twins also had the foresight to record Yogi Mangku's teachings and his oral history that they then used to write his life story."

"I saw that. And now a film—a documentary—is being made?"

"Yes. *Yogi Mangku: The Magic and the Mystery,* for which I wrote the screenplay. Soon we'll get the director's cut to preview."

"Glad you didn't say *director's cunt*—a micro-misogyny in that?"

"Wow, you have a good memory—but that is how the Chinese general said it. And that was the other criticism that came from the politically correct set—that I should police my sexual thoughts and not notice female physical attributes." I made prayer hands to ask for forgiveness.

"I was joking—no worries. You're good . . . for a man." A raised brow told me she was teasing with the truth. "I love and hate seeing my works turned into film. It's always a practice in compromise when converting from one medium to another. Pages of words, sweated over for days, are reduced to one sweeping vista and a telling look between lovers."

"And then just to prove she's free, your heroine jumps off the cliff, leaving her man feeling powerless and unable to follow his Thelma as her Louise."

She stabbed her strong nail into my arm, grabbing my full attention. "Yes, but the reader *knows* she has to jump and he can't follow."

"Women—M, anyway—loved it, but I still root for the man to be the fearless hero."

"Even after all the years of slow emancipation, men still aren't comfortable with women in the role of a hero they can't save. With my

Thelma and Louise–style book, my heroines have moved into the light while still being surrounded by packs of she-wolves and rutting pigs. Your book's treatment of its women, so different to mine. I enjoy the way you—your hero—reveres women."

I grimaced. Then, as a distraction, I spun my pen on the desk, and it stopped to point directly at Molly, which had me moving on quickly. "Well . . . it's decidedly uncomfortable being the star in your own fiction, writing in the first person as yourself, like Maugham in *The Razor's Edge*. You get to hide behind the third person of your femme fatales." I smiled to show I, too, could tease with the truth.

"I like to think I revere their Buddha natures, but that nature does seem easier for me to see in beautiful bodies and in minds that love meditation and yoga, providing the critics an opportunity to pounce." I signaled namaste, bowing to her proximate sexy intellect and hoping to shift the topic.

She stood for another toast. "Damn the venomous vipers using social media to regurgitate their destructive criticism. Having no idea the power of words. For God's sake, put down the book if it's not your cup of tea." She finished her wine. Molly drank faster than me. Even the most talented writers must suffer from slings and arrows.

I poured what remained of the wine into our last glasses, hers a touch fuller than mine. Shaking off our critics with the ting of glasses, we reclaimed our seats. A bottle midday was more than enough for me, but I didn't want the interview to end.

"May I get personal?" Molly said, widening her eyes to ask for a yes.

"Yes! I mean, please do. I'm an open book on background." I was enthusiastic but guarded.

"I loved the spiritual aspect of the book. What more can you tell me about Big Love? Have you continued to believe in that?"

"It's impossible not to believe once you've experienced it, but living it is another matter. My ego is still very much alive." I raised my wineglass. "To the death of ego! To be honest, I'm increasingly able to infuse Big Love into my life. I have no choice, really. Living with the genius of Emily Edens demands no less. As a catchphrase for the miraculous source of all life, Big Love is hard to reduce to words, especially to engaging fiction."

"I don't exactly meditate," Molly said, "but I enter a state of trance and the void becomes filled with dark fantasies that become my stories. So please tell me more about Juno's Big Love, which you found in Kathmandu."

"Can we go off the record for that topic?" I gestured at the phone that was recording me. She turned it off and looked longingly at her empty glass, signaling she was not quite finished. "Another?" I asked with ambivalence, wondering if she might have the writer's curse—a drinking problem.

"Yes, please . . . if you're game? It was such a nice pinot. And there's still so much more I want to ask."

"Of course. We have more of the same—our best year." Who was I to deny her and cut short our auspicious meeting? The bottle was soon opened and glasses poured.

For the first time, her cheeks took on a rosy hue. Now was my chance to take a deep spiritual dive, to touch her heart and win my first impression with simmering syntax and subtle subtext sermonizing on the sublime.

"Spiritual oneness—the One—the infinite on which I now will speak." I stood to gather my thoughts. "To my lay scientific mind and my lay spiritual mind, constant creation theory and Big Love are two sides of a coin. I'm no expert and defer to M on one side and Juno on the other. Constant creation simply posits that everything traveling at the speed of light collapses and reemerges each instant from source-oneness-nothing-consciousness, and this constant creation is the universal heartbeat that creates the perception of time and space. Big Love is the nature of that source—light, love, and omnipotence—that we can access through spiritual practice, belief, and grace. The purpose of life being self-realization—the awakening to constant creation." I paused, liking the ring of my words even though they fell short of their ineffable mark.

"But it's really M's spiritual practice that takes me there in meditation with her. Such a beautiful, palpable, blissful presence . . ." I set my glass down. "Suffice it to say, constant creations allow us to live a life of love and connection to all of nature." I felt suddenly exposed and shy, wanting to recall all my embarrassing words. I checked, and the recorder was still off and no M at the open door. "I fear I'm sounding like a preacher. I suffer from instant intimacy when I'm speaking of things I love while drinking wine."

"Not at all, Sean—that was beautiful," Molly said with a compassionate look before once again leaning close enough to touch me. "As writers, we have to be open and vulnerable and speak our truth."

Her eyes rewarded my intimacy in kind.

"What more can you tell me about Professor Edens? I'm going to be in Europe this summer, and I checked her lecture dates—we overlap in Dublin, and I have booked tickets to her Trinity talk." She turned the recorder back on, making me even more self-conscious as I imagined M walking in on the scene. Seeing that I was retreating, Molly inched forward like Zeno's arrow seeking the deep heart's core. "Tell me about her courses. I want to enroll!" She took a long sip of wine, clearly savoring it upon her palette. Molly loved two things about me already, my book's title and my wine.

"M's courses on consciousness are profound and mind-boggling. One has to start from the premise that whatever you think about consciousness is not it. Accepting that paradox, the students learn the mystery of the universe as taught by M. She's fascinated that still so many in the scientific community are like her former Chairman of Science at Columbia University in their desire to look to one instant fourteen billion years ago as a singularity—the big bang that started time and creation as we know it—and their unwillingness to look at it now."

"I saw an article about her teachings that noted how the big bang is still embraced by those who worship artificial intelligence." She was prepared. "She joked that *it is fitting that women of science embrace constant creation while men hold on to a single big bang*." Molly let out a jolly neigh. "The article also got into how religion has split, with many turned away from Michelangelo's God with his six days of creation and focused instead on all the statements of Christ consistent with constant creation."

"Gnostic texts have been dusted off and brought into mainstream Christianity like sequels to the good book. Buddhism embraced constant creation without any trouble—it always had. Sounds like you know about M and her important work. I prefer she speak for herself, as she's much better at it." I checked the door. Surely that was her cue to enter.

"What made constant creation click for me was Professor Edens."

"Please call her M. She would want you to."

"M, then. It was amazing, her turning of the standard model of physics on its head. Now, I may get this technically wrong, but I saw her speak at a virtual conference and she blew my mind with the Hubble constant, which estimates the rate of the expanding universe from each point in space as unlimited by the speed of light and which has an inverted time that is the same as the time estimated from the big bang."

She swirled the grape in her glass as the words spun from her mouth.

"The conventional model of physics writes this off as a fantastic coincidence that cannot be explained, so they ignore this wonderful symmetry. The big bangers really don't like irony or things that don't fit. But this Hubble constant proves constant creation theory. But now I forgot how—Oh, help me here . . ." Perhaps for the first time, she placed her wineglass down. With her long, elegant hands to her heart, and a pleading look in her eyes, she looked like a young student.

"*Eureka*, as M would say. As I understand it from M, the Hubble constant and its implications for and support of constant creation theory works in two ways. First, the rate of expansion, unlimited by the speed of light, would suggest all matter or points within this expanding universe may, with an awakened mind, be experienced in each irreducible instant—oneness, if you will—as time and space collapse and reemerge each instant."

I paused to think how to express the second point. In situations like this, it must be much easier to be wired-in. "The Hubble constant suggests that the appearance of linear time from the big bang to now and into the future is an illusion, and each moment is a big bang of creation.

The big bang perceives the universe from time and space, and Dylan's constant creation theory from the infinite, eternal now."

I looked up and was taken into Molly's moist eyes staring at me from the precipice of Big Love, with her ready to take the leap. She said, "You are so blessed to live surrounded with such brilliance—M, Juno and Dylan, too." Her great literary mind paused in homage to the creative and spiritual geniuses before moving to the next generation of brilliance in my life as she asked, "Please tell me about the children?"

I looked at the recorder, and Molly turned it off. I was more determined to make an impression than to protect my well-guarded secrets. And what father doesn't like to boast?

"Little Dylan is eight and meimei Juno seven. The names are well-deserved. Both have dreams of out-of-body experiences, which they talk about without reserve or fear. We've read that that's a sign of great connection with spirit. The light is so bright in their eyes. And they've enjoyed the most wonderful childhood. M is an incredible mother, and YaLan and Astri are eager governesses. But M and I agreed to leave the children out of her celebrity and my stories until they're old enough to consent."

"I understand that. We need to protect the ones we love. What do you think happened to your Big Love teacher Juno? And was she really the enlightened being you portrayed? My heart broke to hear that she went missing. What more can you tell me?"

I stood to break her intense gaze and looked out on the windswept Willamette Valley. It was clear she was controlling our scene and the amount of wine we were consuming, while my only goal was to impress her. After divulging so much about the children, I had to be careful now that we were speaking of Juno, which reminded me of her five secret words and my pledge of protection.

"I fear I've already included too much about her personal life in my book. But yes, Juno was even more wonderful than I wrote her. Her Buddha nature, so transparent behind her words and deeds, can't be captured fully by my words." I returned slowly to my seat so near to

Molly's, hoping we would move on. It was Juno's words and her disappearance that had me so worried for M's safety.

Molly looked away, wearing a look that declared she was in her head. A moment later, raising the delicate index finger of her left hand, she said, "She fascinates me. Let me explain my secret mission here. My new novel is about a self-realized woman and set in Muir Woods, in California—where I now live. She's a beautiful American woman and culturally appropriating shaman, but a truly spiritual one who learned from years of study with elders in Peru. Despite her privilege and heritage, she's the real deal. And she goes missing while meditating alone in the woods one night. Juno is the model and inspiration for her. Juno was a wonderful person, but also a powerful avatar in your depiction. I was horrified by her disappearance, as though I was family too."

She spun my pen playfully and the spin stopped, pointed at me, leading me to wonder if it was foreshadowing some unlikely destiny.

I picked up the pen and threw it onto my desk for a laugh and to ease the tension. She obliged with the laugh and pulled a pen from her tote and wrote left-handed on my pad. I noted this in the deep recesses of my mind as something I'd always envisioned—a left-handed woman in my life. Damn the curse of an overactive imagination. She wrote deliberately beneath my new novel title and Dylan's name: *A literary collaboration?*

Smiling like a schoolboy sharing his bicycle, I boldly picked up her pen to write a response, but I was distracted when I sensed a presence over my shoulder and at my open office door. I turned, expecting to see M.

Except, it wasn't M.

"**EXCUSE ME,**" **I SAID TO MOLLY,** making my way to bar the door from the halter-top-wearing coed in silk running shorts, who wore no bra.

"Molly Quinn!" Samantha said loudly enough for my guest to hear, her eyes and smile beckoning so that she might be invited in for a threesome.

"Here for a private interview. You know these aren't my office hours. Please let Astri know if you'd like to schedule an appointment, an appointment that she will join." I was wiggling Molly's pen at her like a scolding old schoolmarm.

"Day drinking, what fun!" Again she spoke loudly, following the announcement with a wicked smile. "Did you get my apple? I picked it especially for you—juicy and ripe." She was fingering a necklace—an amulet—that hung between her breasts.

"Yes and thank you, but you really shouldn't be in my office when I'm not here."

She pretended to be hurt and then perked up quickly. "But you're here now."

"Interview. Private. Goodbye, Samantha." I took the door in one hand and started to close it.

As the door shut, Samantha got in her tsk-tsk. "You behave for me, Professor."

I, wanting to appear nonchalant, was instead flushed and hot as I returned to my seat near Molly.

"She looks like trouble," Molly said.

"You're a good judge of character. Now where were we?"

"She shook you, Professor. Do you want to tell me about it?"

"Just a flirtatious student, always trying to entrap the male staff. But an orphan and quite brilliant."

"Well, she certainly has a good toolbox to work with—youth, beauty, and, sorry, but I couldn't help overhear—a good wit about her. And what a ploy—did she really give you an apple? Let me guess, bright red?"

"Bright red!" I said as I moved to my desk to open the top drawer and pick up the ruby ball. I tossed it into the air, playing catch with myself. "I used to pitch." Molly laughed. I wanted to throw that poisoned apple into the sea.

"Shall we eat it?" Molly said, tempting me more. A part of me wanted to eat the apple's pulpy flesh to prove to Molly I had no fear of witches.

"I have another idea." I strode to the large windows that opened like French doors. Molly joined me there, where we stood like a king and queen at their balcony, our subjects—in our case, fluttering vines—rows and rows, bowing down to us from below. The sea air was refreshing and added clarity to my wine buzz. I imagined an amazing throw, inspired by mighty Molly energy flowing through me, that would carry that apple over five miles to go *plunk* in the sea.

As I cocked my arm, Molly said, "Make it good—you don't want to hit a student passing by below."

I reevaluated my calculations, shifting my stance and bracing my arm. Now wasn't the time to be remembering a snowball fight with M where my one good throw almost dislocated my shoulder. My fastball had become a knuckleball long ago, but I was committed to that throw and let that evil ball fly. It made the vineyard with five yards to spare, exploding like a hand grenade.

"Yankees, you have your new ace!" Molly exclaimed, and I felt like I was in high school again. And my shoulder was fine as I stretched it and my arm toward the seats, suggesting we return. I left the window open as a counterweight to the closed door.

"A symbolic rejection of knowledge?" she asked as we took our seats.

"More an assertion of free will."

She squinted and pursed her lips, no doubt wondering what I meant, and to tell the truth, I wasn't sure. But I'd wanted to sound erudite and consistent with the Bible story. I picked up her pen. "Where were we before that little detour?"

"Hmm . . . let's see," she said, grabbing her wine glass. "I had a second motive for this interview, but now I'm hesitant to say for fear you'll throw me out the window for being another designing woman—here under false pretenses—looking for information on Juno and her disappearance."

"Don't worry—my arm's not that strong."

I hoped she didn't think I was suggesting she was overweight. She was full-bodied but firm. A woman in near-perfect form and hitting her full stride in her forties, the way many powerful women—like my M—did.

"For the background material for my novel, is there anything new on the cold case? Although there are many dark characters who may have wanted to extinguish Juno's light, my story seems to be taking me into sci-fi, with alien abduction as the solution. Sorry. That sounded cold." She tucked her head for forgiveness. Looking up, she said, "My Chinese research assistant is looking in Beijing for clues."

"It's not a cold case to me or anyone in her family. And alien abduction is as good an answer as any other. You've heard of what I call the 'Chinese theory'—hologram transport to a higher realm—a possibility that many give credence to? Alien abduction makes even more sense."

She nodded. "According to my research assistant, the Chinese theory, or at least the government-leaked one that is the source of the theory, is not so much a spiritual ascension as—wait for it—an alien abduction."

"Someone recently told me that. Still—so hard for me to believe."

"I believe it's the most credible theory, as they were the only ones to conduct an official investigation, and you know our own government now acknowledges there have been previously unacknowledged alien abductions. Some of the subject accounts are quite compelling and come from some very accomplished people. The only other explanation is even darker, isn't it? That her government or a madman took her?"

"Yes, and that my book is to blame. Juno was, is, so naturally reserved, and she was exposed . . ." I was becoming emotional, thinking about Juno and M, but was saved by the bell.

"Sorry, I thought this was off." She turned off her phone's ringer. "Okay, I understand the power of the pen, but you're not at fault."

"Wait—you have a research assistant looking for Juno in China?" A search being conducted just as we were starting to receive her telepathic messages was disconcerting.

"Sort of. More looking for information about her disappearance—it seemed the most logical place to search based on Juno's roots."

"I don't imagine aliens leave a calling card. In my vision, I saw her being interrogated over my book and not by aliens."

"You don't think it's the general or the Guru? I hope you don't mind my use of her as a model?"

Wanting to hide and open up at the same time, I had to turn from her to the still-closed door, hoping M would save me.

"No and no. Well, I don't know, actually, but it's an honor to have you picking up the case. You can imagine how much her disappearance impacted me, and I know nothing, really. Haven't heard from either the general or the Guru for nine years." Ting's telepathy was a family secret, and it might sound silly, on par with alien abduction, if I tried to explain. "But we haven't given up hope. She was—is—as I wrote her. An ethereal presence, the embodiment of Big Love. Later, if I think of anything, I'll share more with you. And please let me know if your assistant turns up any leads."

If Juno could be found, then perhaps M would be safe too—some intuitive belief in the power of symmetry led me there. If nothing else, I could ask Juno what she had meant by those dire words.

"Thank you and of course. She's wired-in, my assistant, and very good. Are you?"

"Wired? No, but I understand it's a handicap now for writers to use only our lonely imaginations."

"All writers younger than us are wired—not just for research but for the bon mot and even plot twists. One of my young poet protégés is ninety percent AI and ten percent human brain. His poems are darn good but not great. With poetry you can enter the subject, the meter and rhyme scheme, and the number of lines, and out pops an ode to a lightbulb."

"It can't be that easy for a sonnet," I challenged.

She fiddled with her phone. "Let me see if he's . . . he's there." She was typing away. "Okay, he says what's the subject for your sonnet?"

"Uh . . . plagiarism?"

"Hmm. And rhyme scheme?"

"Let's go easy but off form—couplets?"

"Okay, done. He says feed him some names of poets or poetry-related keywords."

"Yeats, Shakespeare, Greek gods? That work?"

She typed. "Perfect. He says in a minute we'll have our sonnet. He won't have time to fix it up, but you'll get the gist."

A minute later, she was reading the AI-produced sonnet to me. My expectations were low and lowered further with the title "I've Heard It All Before," but I sat back and tried to keep an open mind.

> "Plagiarist! Drop your pen and don't resist
> Your arrest for artistic rape and incest!"
> Remember! The process how poems transpire,
> The embers taken from some dead poet's fire.
> Replete, with all combos of words in store,
> Complete, they should sound as if heard before.
> If moon bound, you'd look up to Apollo.
> For womb sounds, you'd tune a lute or swallow.
> Surefire to stand on top of the pyre,
> Inspire with Yeats's genome and gyre.
> No sense to reinvent the barrel,
> Go hence, with diligence. Enter Ariel.
> Impersonal—that which sees, thinks, and feels;
> Universal—the words are free to steal!

We were both laughing. "I have to admit it's funny and not half bad," I said as she nodded in agreement. We then both shook our heads like toll collectors after the introduction of E-ZPass, ready to be written out of our careers.

"It seems to be in favor of plagiarism," Molly said, and we laughed again.

"Well, we do all steal from each other. Do you think it's meant to be funny?" I marveled at the world we found ourselves in.

Molly shrugged and said, "Let me shift gears. Tell me—where are you with *The Devil's Calling*? Do you have a fully developed plot?"

"I'm slowly and methodically researching—have I said it's a sequel?— and I've finally started writing. It's all in my mind." I tapped her pen on my pad, inadvertently drawing attention back to our shared words.

"We mentioned the ending of the first book and that dark vision. You also paraphrased Dickens about some scary future scenes—has any of that come true?"

I met her wide eyes with wide eyes of my own. "Ooh, you *are* good. I'm haunted by my dark visions of the first book. Scene by dark scene, they're coming true. First, Detective Mulhearn, the one investigating Dylan's death, is forced to reopen the case, and he calls me in for questioning, much as the vision had foreseen. He says they now have the motive—a successful book and stolen theory—and aren't buying my 'cockamamie alibi that a deep state guru did it.' And then he calls me a jackass. I gather that he's recalling his depiction in the book and that he's a wee bit pissed off." I was pushing the third-generation Irishness a wee bit as part of my carefree storytelling.

Molly offered a look that said she was enthralled with my story, so to feed her curiosity, I eagerly continued.

"The conspiracy theories around Dylan's death did drive the book sales, but I think Mulhearn was just trying to rattle me. But after a congressional hearing into the CIA's role in going after the theory, my plot no longer seemed so cockamamie and he lost interest in me. That was seven or eight years ago now. And the congressional investigation hardly got started behind closed doors before it was over."

"I remember that, though it wasn't well reported. I took note because of you. Your book."

"Well, thank you, but nothing came of it. Elliot Pennington, my agent, pursued all the information he could get about the classified briefings. He was acting as my legal research assistant, submitting FOIA requests for all documents pertaining to the case." I caught myself smiling and added, "He really wants his long-overdue sequel."

"I know Elliot P. pretty well, and he loves you. Good company over a couple drinks. It was his idea that I surprise you for this interview."

"That old bastard. But brilliant of him to orchestrate this meeting." I held up my wineglass for another toast while still shaking my head, repressing a laugh. "To Elliot, the merry trickster!"

"Day drinking—such fun!" Molly mimicked. "But thank you. It was so nice to hear your literary story, and the view is outstanding. And this"—she swirled her last glass with more than some proficiency—"is really good. Did the FOIA requests reveal anything about the Guru? Elliot's too scared to even talk about it with me."

"We were able to glean some information from phone and written interviews of congressmen and their aides, but the documentation was over fifty percent redacted, with ugly black boxes. It felt like someone was editing your work before you got to write it."

She smiled at my observation.

"The facts followed my fiction. There *was* an investigation that resulted from the publication of my book. The individual—name redacted—also known as—code name redacted—at the center of that investigation was contacted by one of his longtime associates—name redacted—who had defected to—country redacted . . ." I waved my wineglass. "You get it. But I could tell that the code name was short. Maybe four letters."

"The Guru? What more did you learn about him?"

"That's my guess. He still haunts me, but I've heard nothing. I was assigned a State Department contact after my debriefing and the fact-checking of my story. They claim I'm in no danger from the man I knew as the Guru. Elliot and I are convinced he defected to Russia.

You know Russia leads us in quantum computing, so, in my novel, the Guru will be leading their AI army into battle. But I don't want to reveal too much."

"You really haven't revealed *a thing* about the new book. What more can you tell me about *The Devil's Calling?*"

"Well, it's a thrilling adventure in a world war between artificial intelligence and Big Love. You'll definitely want to read it."

She stood to leave, turning off her recorder. "That I will! When do you think it'll be ready?"

"I hope by the end of the summer to have a draft."

"That's great. My new novel is coming together in roughly the same time frame. Perhaps . . ." She paused and seemed suddenly shy.

"Perhaps?" I playfully mocked her wide eyes.

She drew a deep breath. "Perhaps I could be a first reader, a crit partner for you, and you for—"

"Yes, of course! I mean, I'd love that. I'd be so honored on both sides of the equation. Like Byron and Mary Shelley, let's see who can write the best ghost story this summer!"

She shook her head as she laughed. "Even if it does make us Irish-writer clichés." She looked to say goodbye to the empty bottles, two-thirds of which she was taking with her.

"It's a double date, then. I look forward to reading all about your new lost girl—I hope she'll be found. And I'll tell M about your being in Dublin at the same time. I'm sure she'd like to meet if there's time. She's a big fan too." But I was glad M hadn't joined us, as the past couple of hours had been an intoxicating reprieve for me.

"I'd love that. She's so"—she gestured toward the view outside the window—"so beautifully accomplished." She handed me her literary calling card.

I reached toward her to return her pen, but she said, "Please keep it for our collaboration."

I felt like I held a Nobel Prize. I hurried to my desk to retrieve my own humble deluxe rollerball and handed it to her with a bow.

I walked her to the door, amazed she hadn't lost her graceful and steady gait. Still, I thanked God for self-driving cars. At the threshold, I turned to say goodbye. I thought she might lean forward to kiss me, so I moved quickly to give her a hug. I opened the door, imagining Samantha lying in wait to pounce on Molly on her way out. The hall was clear and Molly left safely. I felt that we already had a history, though we had just met.

With all danger departed and my door once again wide open, I was bursting with inspiration and I had a deadline date to meet for my lovely new dark muse and literary buddy. I held up my new pen like a painter with his brush, a sorcerer's apprentice ready to work his magic on the white canvas.

IN THE WAKE OF MS. QUINN'S INTERVIEW, I was flying high and full of writing mojo. I was eager to tell M all about it, and had intended to introduce them, until Molly mentioned M's tour and the Dublin date, which reminded me that M would soon be outside my powers of protection, a thought that invoked my primal fear for her safety. I didn't want to hear them discussing meeting in Joyce's Dublin without me. And if I was honest, I'd gotten lost in the whole moment, feeling that Molly Quinn had been sent to clear the logjam of my words and set them flowing again, a blast of angioplasty to my creative heart. Selfishly, I wanted the muse all to myself.

Blood flowing, I sat erect at my desk and invoked my sacred ink-filled wand to write. At the same time, Eric and Brian popped back into my office. They must have been waiting for my interview to end. As they set up a computer link, I wrote M, telling her about meeting Molly. *Wish I could have met her*, she texted back. To alleviate her disappointment with me, I told her she had a date in Dublin with the mighty Quinn.

The boys were eager for me to watch Silvio Rossellini's report to Neurotech investors, a heady topic following two bottles of wine. It was scheduled to start in five minutes.

"Silvio's promising something really big today! Like when he showed the first paraplegic able to walk again with BCI, or the time the demented mother made her daughter cry with her ability to remember everything," Eric reminisced as he sat to set up his computer for the show. These

amazing milestones and other major breakthroughs led to venture cap-
italists racing to shower Neurotech with R&D dollars. At some point,
wiring-in development had shifted from light to warp speed.

While we waited for the next big thing, Brian started showing me
an order form on his phone. "Slightly less than a hundred thousand
dollars and the Deeksha West will be a hologram school like most
other colleges are these days. All personally overseen by our friend at
Holoport—the state-of-the-art company—it comes with a ninety-day
money-back guarantee."

"What a bargain." I joked, but it was less expensive than I imagined.

Eric looked up from the computer screen counting down to the big
Neurotech Second Q Report—two minutes and twenty-two seconds.
"Sean, it's really a no-brainer—you gotta go on the Holoport site. So
many educational and recreational applications. Some of the best courses
and professors are being transmitted internationally by hologram, and
offering those to our students would really augment our current virtual
and in-person curriculum."

"Holograms seem a harmless, only-for-the-good technology. I can't
see how allowing people at a distance to feel like they are together can
be a bad thing," I said.

"Don't tell the military that," Brian said. "They've invested a lot of
money on potential uses in cyber and physical wars."

"Like what? I can't imagine."

"It's all top secret, so no one knows."

"Okay, let's keep our little secret *top* too. And I got it—you'd like the
hologram tech here. Let me think it over. Looks like Silvio's about to
make his grand entrance." The meeting screen had flashed on to a dramatic stage with a black curtain-flag bearing the Neurotech logo—an
enlightened human brain with all the neurons lit up, circuit-board style.
Neurotech was the industry leader in BCI technology.

"Is Silvio going to play the drama queen?" I asked. From the clips I'd
seen of him, he always overacted, like a spot-lit Hamlet.

"He presents himself as merely the front man for the company,"
Eric informed me. "But it's always a good show. He jokes that the real

CEO and mastermind behind Neurotech is the brain-mapping quantum computer with its robotic slave-labor force that's responsible for performing the meticulous brain-linking operation."

"Surgeons and authors are among the numerous professions being put out of business by AI," I added. "Neurotech operated as a private company, largely owned by those who'd wired-in?"

"Yes," Eric said as Brian stared at the screen, determined for the show to start. "The cost of wiring-in is more than rewarded—each client is given one Neurotech coin, called a Neurochip, which trades like Bitcoin over a blockchain but also pays handsome dividends that could become additional Neurochip coins. Early subscribers have become rich."

"M thinks it's a pyramid bondage scheme."

"Sort of—I guess. You have to be wired-in to own and trade the golden neuro-ticket. And it increases in value as more and more people subscribe."

Brian turned from the screen and joined back in the conversation. "The velocity of new subscriptions keeps increasing and new clients are born each day, which keeps the Neurochips' value rising."

"I've read that because the company only exists in the metaverse, operating through numerous cross-border subsidiaries in the real world, no one knows Neurotech's provenance; and any attempt to determine the legal seat of the tech is met with a big backlash—as the work of fascist government control."

On the threshold of Silvio's big announcement, the boys didn't want to argue the ethics and returned their attention to the lit-up brain on the screen, shaking their heads at my old man concerns. We all watched without speaking, and I noticed for the first time the subliminal twinkling of the innumerable lights within the circuit-board mind, which cast a hypnotic effect.

Neurotech seemed to me to be protected by a blockchain of superhumans, an army of WiN-wielded power and influence that no politician would be advised to confront.

I couldn't say I understood the tech entirely, but I was fascinated by Silvio, who claimed to fear AI implications yet became a pioneer in the field. Silvio had been ringing the alarm in social media about AI technology—which he then put directly into the brain. That stance implied that Neurotech was a good steward of the devil's interface and a self-regulating entity, so not to worry.

M had overtly taken on this corporate Goliath and golden idol with her Nobel Prize–nominated essay, which had served to depress the Neurochips' value for a while. That released a hornet's nest of hostility aimed at her as the *Anti-WiNette of the Willamette Valley*, a nasty name coined earlier by our own Samantha Smythe in the Deeksha West college paper. We did believe in a free press despite its cost.

M's Nobel nomination was sure to release anew some of the recently dormant vitriol.

With the boys and the world waiting, I must have blinked, because Silvio had appeared, alone, on stage in front of the black curtain, sharply dressed in a crisp white shirt and dark gray vest and slacks, with full slicked-back whitish-blond hair. His gaunt face and pale complexion completed what was a spitting image of the *thin white duke*. A high stool next to him held tiny bells. He held up his unnaturally long arms, as if saluting the gods, before heralding the next leap in AI.

"Auspicious is the day."

"Plagiarist! That's not how you say it!" The boys' laughter stopped abruptly when Silvio continued.

"Today is the first day of a new humanity. In two minutes, which will allow you time to first text your friends and loved ones, I will share with you *the* most amazing advance in technology. They won't want to miss this announcement." He wasn't known for understatement. "What I'm about to share with you will lead to a brand-new society where war, hunger, and poverty will be unimaginable relics of a barbaric past."

I dutifully texted M, *You got to tune in the Neurotech Q Report live NOW. Silvio thinks you shouldn't miss it. Based on his intro, I think he must have already been in contact with advanced alien life come to save mankind. He promises the next evolutionary leap!*

Silvio was silent for the full two minutes. If he'd had a beard, he would have stroked it, but instead he rubbed his long, lean fingers together until we all felt the friction. Finally he rang the little tingsha bells, as a spiritual teacher did to start a class. He stood unmoving on a short pedestal, like Michelangelo's David, until the ringing passed completely into silence, basking in the attention of millions of watching eyes and waiting ears.

"Today I am announcing the launch of the Global BCI Fellowship, or for brevity's sake, the New Society, an initiative that combines Neurotech's BCI brain-mapping technology and robotic chip implementation with Genesis, a breakthrough quantum computer developed in Russia. Together with Genesis, we will have the ability to simultaneously link minds so thoughts and information can be shared instantaneously with one other person or the entire society of linked-in minds. We will soon beta-test the first person-to-person link intermediated by Genesis. Neurotech will ensure the medical and ethical viability of the procedure utilizing our near-complete brain mapping, which is being accelerated exponentially, again thanks to the cognitive learning power and speed of Genesis. We anticipate starting to take subscriptions to join the network—creating a new human experience and community—in twelve months. We will announce the results of the beta test at the next quarterly report."

M texted, *Oh my God! WTF?* She never cursed. *Only one year left for the free-thinking human?* I didn't know whose words I feared more, Silvio's or M's. Even the boys looked dumbfounded by Silvio's audacious pronouncement. The world was moving faster than science fiction. Like me, as the world expanded and got older, it suffered from accelerating time.

"But how will this solve the world's problems?" Silvio said as the camera zoomed in on his long face, lit with theatrical perfection, asking one of my many questions. "As soon as we reach a tipping point of worldwide subscribers to the New Society, any international challenge or humanitarian crisis will be addressed by a supercognitive process free of individual or even national self-interest. This process and the details on how it will make war, hunger, poverty, and even pandemics obsolete is being uploaded to Neurotech's site at this very instant."

While my response registered somewhere between trepidation and terror, the boys looked euphoric. As Silvio paused, they and probably millions of others simultaneously were logging on to the site like they wanted to be first to book their flights to Utopia.

"Now, you know I am a humble man, but don't let the messenger obscure the magnitude of the moment. Today will go down in history as the first day of a new world order and an evolutionary advance of humanity." He grinned like a fox in the henhouse and then disappeared from the screen. It was magic, or he'd been a hologram all along. Either way, he avoided questions and made a dramatic exit.

"Wow," Brian said.

"What a day. An Internet of Brains! I feel like we just watched the first moon landing," Eric said. And then he read from his phone: "A jubilant Wired-in Nation celebrates the announcement of Neurotech's New Society!"

"Sean, what's wrong?" Brian asked.

"You don't see it? What M will do? She's now the one person—with a Nobel Prize–nominated paper arguing the need for ethical restraint and regulation—who may look to stop all this. Please leave. I need to think." I called out after them as they were heading out the door, "Get that hologram technology!"

I was about to follow them out to find M, when, like clockwork, M's next text came in. *We need to talk. I want your help in deciding how best to pivot the tour's sole focus on constant creation theory into a focus that includes a demand that there be oversight and restraint on the rollout of this new Genesis and AI society!*

I replied, *May be too dangerous with the wired-in wing-nut jobs and violent fringe, not to mention Russia. Genesis may be him.*

She sent back a frown-face emoji before adding, *I'm on my way to your office.*

I had a minute to collect my thoughts. I knew everything I wanted to say, all the arguments I would make and all the imagined dangers I would present—how the Guru might be the mastermind behind Genesis and how he wouldn't let us foil him again. But nothing I could say would change her mind. This was her life, and she embodied it like a fearless warrior. That fearlessness was maddening. If I refused to play along, she would do it anyway. Either way, I might lose her, but fighting her on this was a sure way. And my taking a stand against her would cause her pain.

And damn those two bottles of wine. I needed all my neurons firing in order to change her stubborn mind, gently, and with the finesse of a great debater. I had to convince her that she was in real danger from Genesis and the army of lemmings already lining up to join its neural network.

15 DEBATE

THERE WAS JUST ENOUGH TIME to put the two bottles into the recycle bin and splash my face with cold water before M entered my office without a care in the world. Baffled only momentarily, this was M's way of entering the ring. She was a counter-puncher and would never swing first.

"So tell me all about your interview with the lovely Molly Quinn!"

She was softening the beaches before the battle. I'd play along. I recounted the tale of meeting Molly with few details and omitted Samantha's cameo. As I spoke, the alien awoke, driving me to my desk for more Tums from the half-empty bottle.

"Do you think you should see a doctor?"

"For a gurgling tummy?"

"Actually, yes. I wonder if the upset could be related to the news from Juno. Great news of hope, but you seemed troubled by it."

She was changing the topic, but two could play that game. "More likely something I ate. It reminds me of Bogart in *African Queen* where he first meets the missionary and his daughter, the one and only Kate Hepburn—Bogie's belly will not shut up for the entire meal."

"Your Bogart . . . he was a great comic actor too?" She was humoring me.

"Yeah, it's like the way the best rock bands—the Stones, the Replacements—can play the most beautiful ballads."

Before wild horses dragged me too far away, I rang the starting bell of our debate. "But M, you know what I'm thinking, and I won't let you or the gremlin in my gut distract me from my purpose."

"Yes, isn't it wonderful we each know what the other has to say."

I started to pace, imagining Bogarting her with a shake of her shoulders and a *listen, dollface, this is the way it's going to be*, but times had changed since the 1940s and I didn't want her to laugh in my face. So, I heaved a sigh to express my deep-seated concern.

"You can't set yourself up like a straw man with a bull's-eye between your eyes before this tsunami that's rolling in, crushing everything in its way." After mixing my metaphors, I returned to my seat in front of that lovely force of nature to have them straightened out.

"A bull's-eye might go better within a hurricane? And I'm not going to argue that the New Society has to be bad. I'm all in favor of world peace and an end to hunger, and maybe that's where this will lead. But we need time to understand this technology and control it rather than the other way around. I knew quantum computing would lead to a genius self-learning supercomputer. I just never imagined it linking human minds into a community."

"Eric called it an Internet of Brains. M, let's just stick to your constant-creation-theory script. Everyone can link to your Nobel Prize essay and its clarion call for ethical restraint for AI."

"But Sean, they said this will be at some tipping point in a year. We have to use our tour's platform this summer to get out in front of it. Constant creation and the source, which you and I know is Big Love"—she was always careful when speaking as a scientist to not overplay the spiritual aspect of the theory—"suggest that consciousness, not thought, is primary."

"I know." I was determined to finish her thought and to show I understood her teachings so we could move on to the threat posed. "And the most prevalent fundamental misconception is that the physical gives rise to consciousness rather than consciousness giving rise to the physical world as the omnipresent source—love." This was the point where I always became lost.

"And this will be a supercognitive computer without the restraint of consciousness. Without love."

"You know, you keep disarming me with that smile."

"Sean. Focus. What prevents the computer from controlling thought rather than the other way around?" She was the one figuratively shaking me by the shoulders like a battle-ready Ingrid Bergman in *Joan of Arc*.

"I don't know. I don't really understand the nuts and bolts of this technology, but I do know it's an unnatural force that one is ill-advised to fight head-on. And there is an entire year to study and reflect on how best to respond—no need to pick a fight this summer." I made prayer hands, pleading my case.

"Ethics and restraint on R&D can do that. Silvio claims Neurotech is subject to the highest ethical and medical standards. But where's the oversight? Where's the control?" She saw my prayer hands and raised me a determined smile.

"But . . . Russia. AI. It may be the Guru. You know that's where he went."

"I know that's where we *think* he went almost nine silent years ago. He's pretty old, if even alive, to be involved in such cutting-edge tech. This Genesis is more likely the product of some hotshot quantum whiz kid bolstered by a lot of Russian governmental support and funding."

I needed some distance from her eyes and lips, so I returned to the view. "Sounds to me like a name he would give his computer brainchild. But how about WiN? They already hate you. They won't let anything— *anyone*—stand in the way of their New Society."

"Sean. They'd prove my point by harming me."

I returned to face her, punching my right fist into my open left hand. "I'm not worried they'll harm you, M. I'm worried they'll kill you." I gave her my sternest look, the one reserved for the children when they have climbed too high in a tree.

"A martyr to ethics is the last thing they need."

"M, please. You can joke, but I'll not back down. How can you see the risk of AI so clearly but be so blind to the risk to you—coming from those that worship it?"

She opened her eyes wide as if hurt or trying to take me in. "So, are you saying that you *won't* help me write a brief statement regarding our concerns for my talk on the tour?"

"Your concerns, and no."

"Not even an edit?"

I turned my back and returned to the window to show my displeasure, but she followed me.

"I'm sorry. I won't joke, and I hope you'll come around." She took my hands, again disarming me. "So tell me, was Molly as pretty in person and how much wine did the two of you drink?"

16 THERAPY

M REMAINED DETERMINED TO USE her platform to push for ethical constraints. She was, however, considering my suggestion that she not mention Neurotech or Genesis by name when speaking of the restraint that should be imposed on AI development. I spent the next couple days stewing and imagining all that could go wrong. That perversely enabled me to write as a form of therapy. And of course I was writing about my nemesis, the Guru. The devil is a more interesting character than Christ, though the New Testament has sold quite well over the years.

My Quinn pen moved across the pages like the broom of the sorcerer's apprentice. If I could write the Guru's story and about the threat to M convincingly enough, perhaps my fiction would help me convince her that the threat was real.

I had the beginning and knew where it would all end with Genesis. I worked until midnight the day of the big Neurotech announcement, producing almost a thousand words. I sent the almost three pages to Elliot for our discussion the following morning. Those pages laid out the opening scene of the new novel, taking off where the first novel ended. I finally was moving forward, creating a brave new world of fiction that Molly Quinn could revel in. *The Devil's Calling* was getting darker page by page.

* * *

The Guru had become an alien within the CIA—trusted by no one and feared by all, like a whale with a harpoon stuck in its tail and about to dive. After the publication of The Lost Theory, he was in peril, a man hunted by a media determined to confirm his existence and by a new administration over which his secrets held less sway.

The Guru was resourceful in contemplating his next moves. His looming downfall was the result of letting the quick-witted fool, Sean McQueen, and beautiful genius, Emily Edens, live. His computer-like mind could find no clever escape. Begrudgingly, he had to admire that the professors had won their first battle. He could buy time with a smoke screen, discrediting and incriminating McQueen. He'd thought that the Chinese would help him tarnish McQueen's reputation following Juno's disappearance, but they'd provided no further assistance—perhaps smelling his fast-approaching expiration date, as if he were curdled milk.

The Guru's tracks had been laid too bare by the true story. Yet the secrets he still held made everyone tentative to land the first knife in his back. When a whale goes down, it's good to be at a safe distance.

When he was contacted for a secret meeting on short notice, his old bones felt a chill, but there was no coming in from the cold. His protective circle was getting smaller by the day as the jackals circled. The encrypted message could have come from only one of two men, and one of those was Dick—and Dick was dead. The other was his top European operative, a man who'd coordinated the search for and abduction of Professor Edens in Athens back in 2018. The man must now be cooperating in the investigation, betraying his Guru. Their supposedly secret rendezvous would be subject to surveillance and recording.

The Guru's plan was to attempt to lay the blame entirely upon his betrayer—as an overzealous agent who went rogue by abducting the lovely Emily Edens in Athens without approval to do so. He'd be shocked to discover McQueen's fictional account of the kidnapping was true. All his own commands had been erased, like the instructions given in the beginning of each Mission Impossible. This advanced "text-nology," as they called it at the agency, was provided to department heads to prevent oversight. He'd buy more time by using an AI program he had developed to spin counternarratives. And if those lies didn't work, he and Cat's-eye would go out together. Cat's-eye had passed her eighth life, old and blind and no longer hiding from her master. He contemplated a quick and painless poison for them both, mixed into one last shared meal. Surf for her and turf for him.

He sat ready for his meeting in Central Park on a bench near Sheep Meadow, protocol insisting that he be the first to appear. He would be easy to identify with his near albino-white skin that made the sun an enemy and celebrated the overcast day. Joggers, bikers, and tourists hurried past, some wearing masks despite the code yellow viral threat level, which suggested there was no need to mask; no doubt one of the masked men was his man. He was looking for a six-foot-tall blond male in his forties who might be in disguise.

A stately blond woman, with a fully exposed handsome face, running the park loop came over to his bench and used it to stretch her long, strong legs as if it were a ballet barre. Preparing to move to another bench, the Guru picked up his fully equipped escape briefcase that contained surveillance devices, a gun, ten thousand dollars in cash, a form-fitting new and less pale face, and four passports to match the high-tech mask. But the statuesque ballerina started speaking.

"My dear Guru, don't leave." Her voice was husky and rich as she joined him on the bench.

"And who are you?" he asked, though her Russian-staccatoed English gave her away. His European man had been turned into a double agent. He'd always been mercenary.

"Alexa, an old friend of Dick's."

"I know of you, but why are you here?"

"I've been sent to bring you over to our side. You don't have much time, and Petrovsky himself is interested in you."

The Guru shifted further away—Petrovsky was known for his deadly traceless poisons that made all adversaries disappear. Where Putin always seemed to get caught, Petrovsky, his successor, had *perfected the poison arts. The Guru had long ago concocted his own cocktail of poison, but Petrovsky was the master and could administer his lethal perfume from a distance.*

He put an uninvited hand affectionately above her knee. "With what I have on the president and members of Congress, you can't possibly think a book of speculative fiction could sink me."

CIA protocol and new self-interest dictated that he play along to find out as much as he could. He asked, "What are they offering for this whale?"

She lifted his hand by the wrist from her leg as if it were a dead mouse and returned it to him. "For you, Guru, they said to tell you—you could write your own ticket. We don't think you have much time."

He tilted his blond leathery hound-dog face toward her neck before whispering into her ear like she was a lover, "My dear, at my age, that is all you have until you die, and dying is not such a fearful prospect. I will consider if any shopping list will do. I'm being watched but was able to slip my tail today. I'll be in contact soon. Lie low and prepare them for some outrageous demands and a take-it-or-leave-it proposition with a twenty-four-hour clock. Petrovsky will have to sign off. And tell him I have the proof of a nasty little secret that will be revealed if he double-crosses me in any way."

"He doesn't like to be threatened," she said in a voice loud enough to turn heads.

"It's just information and I have it. Tell him Polar Bear. Think of it as proof of my worth and a deal sweetener. Or a poison pill. I make no threat, as long as he keeps his side of the bargain. And who are we kidding—we both know they're listening to every word we say." As long as he held the key to where Polar Bear was hibernating, he'd be safe from Petrovsky. He had played his ace in the hole, and though he didn't like to use it, he had to be sure Petrovsky would hold to their deal.

With that, the Guru got up, kissed her on the top of her head with his thin, dry lips, and walked away, dreaming of what he could

do with all of Russia's resources and support. Destiny led to Mos-
cow, where all his artificial-intelligence dreams and brain-computer
interface immortality would come true.

And he'd finally have his revenge on McQueen.

✳ ✳ ✳

The next morning Elliot's call came in to my office punctually at eight
a.m., to critique my opening. "How was your interview with the *Times*?"
he asked in a businesslike manner, but I could tell he was gleeful and
eager to hear about his prank.

"Fine. Nothing special."

"Really? Did they send one of your old grad students?"

"She seemed a little *more* . . . more than that. Molly bloomin'
Quinn! I can't believe you didn't warn me, Elliot P! How long have
you known her and didn't tell me? I didn't know you were capable of
keeping a secret."

"I'm the soul of discretion. But . . . the mighty Quinn! Quite a lady
and auteur." He took pleasure in verbal affectations and flamboyant
gestures—traits that followed him from his prior career as a theatrical
actor. "I've been courting her since her debut, but she never took on an
agent. For the last couple years, we've gone out for a couple of bottles
anytime she comes to New York. She pays. And we celebrate her latest
book. *She* writes one almost every year."

I ignored his ribbing. "Yeah, she was great, and I took your place
with a couple of bottles. Really a treat, but I might have been more
prepared."

"I know you—you wouldn't have slept, and you'd have been all
scripted and made a big mess of the interview."

"You're probably right."

"Tell me—you know I'm dying to know. Tell me all about it."

And I did tell him, blow by blow, which finally led to the business of
the day. I asked him, "What did you make of *The Devil's Calling* pages
I sent you?"

"Off to the races. Two full pages of pure thriller."

"Three."

"Okay, but on my screen it's two. Now just another two hundred and twenty more and we're there. No pressure for four hundred pages and another sweeping epic adventure—just a tight thriller. I hope your audience is as patient as your agent. The release of the yogi movie will rekindle interest in you and the first book—the time is ripe. Strike when the iron's hot, right?"

"Yes, and seize the day."

"I trust you made the book sound good and farther along than it is?"

"Of course I did. I don't want to make you jealous, but we're going to share drafts of our new works by summer's end. She gave me her pen, and I swear it has magical powers."

"For Molly Quinn, you'll write. I should have thought of this years ago. She's less lethal than her heroines, I hope, but every bit the literary sexpot."

"Lovely. Only . . ." I started to say something about Samantha and my great apple throw, but I was distracted, believing I heard her again in the hall just outside my door. But whoever, whatever, was gone by the time I was able to look. More likely little Juno playing spy. "Sorry, Elliot. Some eavesdropper at the door. But now that I have my story, it'll write itself. The Guru in his dream job with all the resources and ruthlessness of a criminal regime behind him, and now with Genesis coming online—"

"Let's set deliverables and deadlines so another decade doesn't pass."

"M leaves soon on her European tour, and I'll finish a draft before she gets back in mid-August. Is that good enough? I plan to distract myself by writing for eight hours a day."

"I'll drink to that! A first draft in a couple months? That's *pretty, pretty, pretty* good. And of course you'll share it with me." He paused for dramatic effect—clearly he had something of substance and wanted me to note its worth. "Two glaring mistakes I found in your pages already. We believe the Guru defected in 2020 while that punk Putin was still in power. No one in the West had yet heard of Petrovsky and his poison."

"Damn it—that's right! What's the other problem with the text?"

"If he's planning a murder-suicide with his cat, why the *escape briefcase?*"

"Damn again. I'm rusty. Glad I have you looking over my shoulder."

"I'm your writing wingman. I also have some legal advice for you. Leave the Guru's name out of your drafts. We can drop it in later. And send me the pages as you go. I won't comment till you ask."

"Sure, like I can trust you to hold your tongue. And what should I call him, Rasputin? Voldemort? That sounds more superstitious than legal."

"Maybe. He scares me either way, and I've only met him on the pages of your book."

"Fear is a powerful motivator, and dark stories can illuminate as much as light. I will go writing into that good night."

"Rage rage rage . . ."

"M would say there is no dying of the light."

"Okay, whatever it takes for you to lift that pen."

"And damn the Guru!" I said. "I *will* use his name, come what may." I uttered my bluster but felt a shudder. Even in his fictional role, my nemesis still scared me too.

17 GHOST WRITING

AFTER MY CONVERSATIONS WITH DYLAN CEASED, other less well-meaning apparitions followed me over the years. They didn't speak to me through the medium of telepathy but used technology to shadow and tweak me in the form of texts and email posts and deletions. These strange messages and computer glitches had steadily increased over the past few years. Some of the wordplay was darkly seductive and stroked my ego like a secret admirer, but to what end? Who would take such trouble to stir the eros in me with high-tech seduction?

"I have spread my dreams under your feet; Tread softly because you tread on my dreams." They must have known me well, or at the very least known of my background and interests, to use Yeats to spark my curiosity.

Most of it was more sensual to sexual in nature than poetic, but unlike with spam, the sender knew my name and other personal details. I had assigned Eric and Brian to counterespionage. I suspected one particularly tech-savvy temptress to be the culprit—Ms. Samantha Smythe.

Brian and Eric rejected the notion of Samantha as my stalker. The technology required to make the text messages disappear after they were read was extremely sophisticated, even for 2027. M saw them as part and parcel of fame and being a teacher—she was always getting amorous fan mail. We did our best to discourage the sender when the sender was known.

The day after my call with Elliot, I sat in my office alone with my phone and computer, taking in the sheets of rain coming in from the sea and chased by the morning sun. There were urgent texts from Elliot, each flagged important, and one by one they documented the deliverables we'd agreed to or the deliverables he imagined in that cunning brain of his and now wanted to add to the list. He amused me with his closing, saying that he'd enjoyed a nice bottle of Margaux while rereading my *two* pages. He must have either drunk fast or read slow.

Checking my email was always nostalgic for me. Only people over fifty still used email, but that was fine with me, as there were still too many emails despite the limited demographic. Its demise was slower than predicted, though I was certain it soon would follow snail mail and the telegram. Real mail had all but died in 2025 when the post office delivered my last letter before fading into bankruptcy. I still checked my real mailbox once in a while when expecting a small parcel, hoping for a letter, like a man who goes back to the dried-up bed of a childhood stream.

I did still receive handwritten letters from our children—Dylan and Juno left them under my pillow. M had taught them to write letters, and they included envelopes and vintage stamps, the whole experience. Theirs were letters of life, expressing their love and left in a place where once I'd found a death threat from a comrade or a Dick. And the children always received my reply the next night as they crawled into bed. Their imaginations were unfettered and their word choices so poetic. I kept all their letters and plagiarized some of their better lines in my own short stories—unpublished and written just for them. Stories where they were the heroes overcoming monsters and witches in exotic lands to the rhythms of their own words. Knowing I might include their well-crafted words in our bedtime stories made them compete for the best lines in their antiquated letters. I was always careful to give them equal attribution, but they always thought the other received more bylines.

Once in a while, M would leave a letter too, with messages so brilliant and private, D. H. Lawrence and Oscar Wilde would blush to read them. Though M now reserved our lovemaking for special occasions, she still knew the perfect foreplay for me.

My musing on letters had me taking the short walk across the quad to where the mailbox waited like an old spinster for a traveling salesman. I expected only dust to greet me when I opened the creaky vault, but auspicious is the day!

A manila envelope had been rolled up and jammed in by hand and clearly not by an Amazon bot. The envelope bore my name and a high-tech CyberSecure sender address. CyberSecure was the very new blockchain virtual mailbox whose encrypted keys were forever changing so that no one other than the owner could gain access, protecting the identity of the sender. The addresses weren't hard to come by but expensive due to the encryption technology and all the solar energy needed to constantly change the keys. And someone had sent a letter to my all-but-obsolete mailbox with an extremely modern return address? Color me intrigued and impressed.

I thought the CyberSecure address—PO59666—must be a joke.

I ran back to my office with my manila gold, excited to see what treasure it held. The cover letter was short and formal.

Dear Professor McQueen,

I am a literary detective who has dedicated my career to finding lost manuscripts. I've read your modest volume of work, including one very long novel, and know you are a Shelley lover and expert. I, too, am a devotee of his intellectual and poetic beauty.

My sleuthing unearthed in an old Eton library a lost letter between the Shelleys, from Percy to Mary, folded away in a scientific book of Mary's mentor. The contents of that letter led me to the Gulf of La Spezia in Italy, in search of "a crypt where I've hidden my final lines . . ." I've carbon-dated the paper and consulted a handwriting expert, and the poem's original pages are authentic. I include a copy of the last eleven stanzas of "The Triumph of Life." My interest is in seeing the complete poem published at last, while I and the original manuscript remain a mystery; no doubt you will see the fun and value in that to me.

The original manuscript will increase in value being found but
still hidden by my anonymity.

Yours very truly,
Sir Arthur Conan Doyle

I was incredulous—how would Shelley have known they were his
final lines? Still, the story intrigued me, and the page containing the stanzas was in my hand and had to be read, but first I pulled out the poem to
see where it led and how these purportedly *uncovered* lines might follow.
The first new stanza was Shelley in form and diction, thrilling me as it
picked up where the original poem had left off in 1822.

> *"Then what is Life?" I asked . . . as the cripple cast*
> *His eyes upon the car that now had rolled*
> *Onward, as if that look must be his last,*
>
> *And answered . . . "Happy those for whom the fold*
> *Of ----------" A breath of wind called the ghost away,*
> *Unbinding vision's veil and blinding hold.*

I struggled to finish the remaining nine stanzas as tears blurred my
vision, with the final stanza a dagger through my poetic heart.

> *One last time I choose to reincarnate,*
> *Into the valley of perpetual dreams,*
> *In birth, remembering my call to awake!*

The beauty of the fraud! Oh, that it was Shelley! I was devastated
by the same terza rima form used in Dante's *Divine Comedy* and Shelley's authentic "The Triumph of Life."

But this . . . this was a tone-deaf clone of the liberated master. I'd been so excited at the start only to be crushed midway through by the tin can clanging away at my ear, by the mimicry of the form absent of Shelley's sublime spark. I wanted to believe. By the end I was too depressed for words—a work of beauty had been marred by sophisticated computer-simulated forgery. It was like being told the Rothko you bought and had been displaying for years was a fake.

I had gone from elation to rock bottom in an instant. Someone using AI had stolen Shelley's beautiful voice in a heinous grave-robbing literary felony.

AI was already turning out Harlequin Romances and erotica that appeared on best-seller lists. But I believed it would never have imagination subtle enough to write a sublime poem or a truly literary novel. Those works required consciousness, the source of all true creation. Still, there was something soul-deep disturbing about a computer's ability to approximate the soaring heights of the creative mind, even if the AI simulator could never take flight. But this Shelley came too close to liftoff and left me shaken.

Standing by my big windows, I vigorously rubbed my face and eyes as if I was scrubbing off dirt.

"I thought you were over that," M said, entering the office. "You know your cartilage is still soft and damaged from the last time. I hope that's not another manifestation of your worry for me—stick to the writing and running. And please, always practice."

M would soon be leaving me for her European tour, but the pangs of separation refused to wait. And here she was, dressed for a run or a hike, her body taut and smooth with skin as silky as that of a twenty-two-year-old Brigitte Bardot ready for a go-go.

"Where you going?"

"A hike to the sea and back. I came to see if you want to join me."

"Only ten miles, eh?"

"Yes. I'll run where I can, but I want to stay off the roads." My limber lady stretched in a forward fold that touched palms to floor and head to thighs, but then she peered up at me as she otherwise held the pose.

"Nice, Gumby. I wish I could bend so deep. And we do need some alone time before you leave. But not today for me. Got a moment to look at something?"

"Sure. We've both been so busy with our own projects. Is it bad news? Bad enough to bend your nose out of shape?" She straightened and joined me at my desk. Her smile faded when I didn't acknowledge her joke. "You actually look disturbed."

"Yes. A bit Shell-ey shocked and angry."

I showed her my mail and pointed out the ironic CyberSecure address the sender had chosen. She laughed. I watched her read the poem.

"You looked like a puppy that's been kicked and now like one that expects a treat." She could read my eyes. "Is it real? I love the last stanza."

"That last stanza is the cruelest irony of all. What if they *were* Shelley's last lines? My world would never be the same. What worries me is that anyone who hadn't grown up studying Shelley as a lifelong fan—enough to know his true voice—might be fooled. This is a dangerous game. What if I had published it as suggested? My reputation would be ruined when the fraud was exposed."

"Well, what do you think Sir Arthur is playing at? Funny, the Cyber-Secure address—Dylan's humorous PO box number in Kathmandu? Perhaps they were testing you using some new computer capabilities and you'll win a prize for calling BS? If you could be fooled, it would be a triumph of life or AI, I guess."

"Funny lady." I half smiled. "But you're right—that must be it. And maybe he supplied a human, but not sublime, touch to it! We can have a little fun with this evil joke and the PO59666 anonymity of this Sir Arthur Con-man Doyle."

"Whoever it is, they have a wicked sense of humor. But how will you respond?"

"Well . . . I could write back and say I'm on my deathbed with cancer and Shelley's sublime words brought me such joy that I'm now prepared to meet my maker."

"Yogi Mangku would not approve." She smiled.

"I'll think of something else. I won't let this playing around with my reputation go."

"I understand your frustration, but perhaps you're overreacting just a bit? Relax now and have your fun responding. There's no fooling you. I'm off to the sea."

I wished she would stay to help me with my counterespionage.

"Watch out for cougars. I won't be there to protect you this time."

On one of our hikes we'd been repeatedly charged by a cougar that I beat off with my walking stick during her final lunging attack. I didn't tire of reminding M of my heroics.

She made a muscle and was off, undaunted by cougars and AI poetry. My stomach rumbled, wanting her back, but I was glad she was out of earshot.

How to respond? This new ghosting wasn't some casual trolling by a prankster professor or sex-crazed student but a high-tech punking. This was a quantum leap of ghostly escalation beyond the last sophomoric disappearing message: *Nice Rolling Stones T-shirt you wore today, Mick. I'd like to give you some satisfaction.*

When M returned for lunch, I wasn't rubbing my face but I was even more disturbed.

"I haven't sent my response yet, but I have a theory. It's—"

"Still upset, I see. Let me get a water from the fridge first, please," she said.

My office served as our living room when I wasn't writing, and she went into the adjacent kitchen. When she returned, hydrating, I said, "M, you know I've received other strange computer messages and glitches, but nothing as sophisticated as this. You'll think I'm crazy, but maybe the Guru?"

She moved to the window, contemplating the view and my words. "After all these years? He's got nothing better to do than write poetry to you?"

"Well, someone is playing with me."

"But that would be such a strange spoofing for an old, probably dead, maniac to play."

"Remember him telling me he could create a novel based on the love child of Austen and Dickens? I'll grant you it is a strange way to settle a score, unless he's just warming up."

"Let's not scare ourselves. You yourself told me AI is now able to create poetry through imitation. And remember Juno telling us that *love is the absence of fear?*"

"Do you think we'll hear from Ting soon?" I said, trying to mask my fear.

"Let's hope. How will you respond to Sir Arthur Guru?"

"Whoever Sir Arthur is, the literary world needs to be wary of supposed new literary discoveries. With AI advancing the frauds, forgeries will become harder and harder to detect. I'll tell him it's Shelley, no doubt, but that I'll need to see the original manuscript before I can publish. To confirm this great find, of course. And I'll see how he responds."

"Or she," M said.

We ate the lunch I'd prepared—cucumber, tomato, and onion sandwiches with Philly cream cheese—and made small talk about Ting and our next big hike, but my mind was elsewhere. M left the office so I could get on with my writing. Each time she left served to remind me that she'd leave me too soon for the rest of the summer. That thought, and my state of alarm, brought on a panic attack. Unable to breathe, I had to act.

I wrote the boys. *Top Secret—Operation 3D! Please arrange for the installation of the hologram technology ASAP. By the end of June? And check with the tour venues on their compatibility and please let me know today.*

They both typed back with variations of *sorry, we already did—thought you had approved the installation the day Silvio made his big announcement. It will be here next week.*

I'd forgotten my prior impulsive approval of the tech. I would tell M only when the time was right. Even if she refused to cancel her in-person tour, the tech was worth having.

I then typed my response to PO59666 on the Crypto Secure site.

But in a moment of sinister inspiration, I deleted my words and typed "Did you also find *Cardenio*, Guru?" and pushed send. I immediately regretted the rash act.

18 CARDENIO

ALTHOUGH I COULD HAVE RECALLED the email provocation, I didn't. By the next day, there'd been no response, and despite my anticipation, each day passed the same way, with me checking the old mailbox once or twice a day for another hand-dropped literary bombshell. I also had campus security install a surveillance camera to see the mailperson should they return. I joked with M, who thought I was crazy in saying that everyone knows that the mailman always rings twice. Despite that conventional wisdom, no more mail was delivered.

A few days later, I was walking the school grounds at dawn, imagining the Guru reading my note over and over and marveling at my Sherlockian powers of deduction. But how could he reply without admitting defeat?

I even mused that maybe my Molly and her poet protégé were the AI-ghostwriting Shelley. But I shook off the speculation, realizing that the nature of gaslighting was to see shadows moving everywhere.

I asked Eric and Brian to kill my electronic ghost too. They provided me with a new computer and addresses and passwords with state-of-the-art security protections from hacks. They assured me I was now safe.

I walked into the vineyard as far as Strawberry Fields to say hello to the Buddha seated there by the campus fire pit. He was my touchstone when M was out of town, reminding me of the Buddha pond at the Deeksha in Kathmandu, where, nine years ago, M and I would sit following the earthquake. The sacred place seemed reserved for our private tête-à-têtes after Juno converted her precious Xanadu into a refugee camp for those dislodged by the trembling earth.

Soon I'd have to tell M that we were the proud owners of a hologram transport unit for astral projections and receptions, as well as thirty HPA goggles to allow our students to see hologram projections from other portals when not in the hologram-ready auditorium.

I didn't really want a response from the Guru but desperately wanted to know who was using Sir Arthur's name as their nom de plume like some Scarlet Pimpernel. I was somewhat concerned that another professor might be fooled and publish the fraud and that I'd have to publish a rebuttal, diving into the middle of a literary kerfuffle.

I also sent the Shelley poem fragment to Molly, asking if perhaps she was having a laugh at my expense. She thought it was much better than her young protégé's AI-assisted work. I got the impression he was also her young stud. The poetic protégé indicated that the fragment, in its ability to use a specific poet's work and mimic his syntax and word choices, utilized a far more advanced program than the one he was wired to. The protégé also thought it might be the real bard's brilliance and not some AI's plagiarism. Amateur.

After completing my contemplative walk around the grounds before the students took to the fields, I retreated to my office to engage with my computer. I felt cleansed and even forgot to close the eye on my computer window once or twice.

Elliot was flying in from New York for the first time to the Deeksha West. He'd insisted on seeing me in person, but he wouldn't tell me why—another mystery. I imagined he wanted to be assured I'd stick to my schedule or had a book deal with my publisher to pitch. He would do anything to assist me to the finish line. I was looking forward to seeing him, but his mission was unnecessary—I had Molly's small magic wand. I would finish my new novel on time for our book club for two, come hell or high water.

M had gone down to San Fran to visit a sick friend and wouldn't be able to greet Elliot. Sherlock, our AI electric self-driving car, had been dispatched to the airport to pick him up. I didn't like M's being away.

Perhaps my fear of losing her was a reflection of my desire to be with her at all times. She was the bright mirror that made my life shine.

Elliot entered my office still using the cane that he still didn't need, looking like an older Peter O'Toole—handsome and rakish and immaculately dressed in pink and white. He was in full costume for his Deeksha West debut. But then my strange friend got stranger. With a crazed look in his eyes, he flung his cane aside, took off his shoes and socks, and stripped off his fine clothes. In seconds, he was in shredded jockeys and blood-spattered muscle-tee glory, jumping about my office like a maniac. This costume was so out of character for my dear Elliot.

He delivered a dramatic rant soaring in perfect iambs, a long Shakespearean soliloquy that I couldn't place. It had to have been from *Troilus and Cressida*, the only play I hadn't seen and read a couple of times at least. The heartrending sense of loss in his dark, demented words moved me to laughter and to tears, and then, in closing, he said it!

"When dying's all that is left to do, it's important to do it well! Luscinda! I will!"

And so saying, he crumpled at my feet. I stood in rapt applause. It was the best and most unexpected performance I had ever seen. I was unsure if it was thrill or terror I was experiencing as he stood, saying the words slowly so they might sink in. "A scene . . . from the long-lost . . . *Car-den-io!*" He bowed so low, his head almost hit the floor. Pretty limber for sixty-four.

He stood again and started to dress. "Sean, I have it! It came sliding in under my apartment door. And I brought you the first copy." He reached into his bag, pulling out the full fresh-smelling pulp of a manuscript.

I immediately saw the Guru's hand behind the play, and although my elated spirits crashed into fear, I didn't want to diminish Elliot's moment of glory. His enthusiasm was always contagious, and he was vibrating like a man who'd had a couple decades of life returned to his loins.

"Sean, it's a story of heartbreak, combining the best of Shakespeare, tragedy and comedy. It starts with this scene, with Cardenio in rags and despair, after his near-death battle with a three-headed dog named Cerberus, while the good knight and Sancho listen to his tale of the Don

Fernando, who has stolen his goddess Luscinda into the underworld, there to be wed in a marriage of betrayal."

I was lost over how to explain.

"Sean, it came from an anonymous literature sleuth who goes by Sir Arthur Conan Doyle, who instructed me only to do with it what I wished. He added something about how his only interest was in seeing the value of the original manuscript increase. I'll publish it and shake the literary world. But first I had to share it with you. And insist that *you* write the foreword."

I didn't want to betray my thoughts—we were holding an artificial proxy of the genius and not the genius itself. To buy time, I said, "Let me read it while you settle in. I'll get some brilliant yogis to show you around and then we can discuss it."

"Sounds delightful, but I thought you'd be more excited."

"I am, but so far all I've seen is the best performance of my life."

That satisfied him, and I arranged for a tour and lunch in the vineyard. "Let's meet back here this afternoon for a bottle of wine and to discuss your find. That should give me time to read it."

YaLan and Astri soon arrived, and Elliot a bit presumptuously gave them both hugs, saying, "Ah, my dear Sebastian and Viola, we are off to see the kingdom while the duke is at his studies. Important matters of state they are." He was determined to stay in character.

The women laughed in accepting the hugs and greeting. Luckily Astri, whom he'd addressed as Sebastian, had a thick sense of humor about everything, including her own bald scalp. I was left alone in my office with the malicious manuscript and a decade-old dread. My best friend's receipt of the lost *Cardenio* was clearly no coincidence. Though I wanted to believe the bard had returned to life through the discovery of some crypt or vault where the pages had been stored, I knew better. This was the Guru tormenting me—and I had asked for it. Poor Elliot. And poor M. She'd have to skip the personal tour and accept hologramming as a substitute.

Reading *Cardenio*, I marveled at the Shakespearian iambs, diction, syntax, and clever twists of the interwoven plots borrowed from the

Cervantes masterpiece. But the soul, the creative spark, was absent in a way that was again unmistakable but hard to define. I heard thinly veiled echoes of Shakespeare's real masterpieces. Even the final line of Elliot's speech was derivative of James Goldman's *Lion in Winter*. The work made sense of Molly's AI poetry being in favor of plagiarism. It was good. It was arguably great. But it was not Shakespeare.

How to break such devastating news to poor Elliot? I was afraid the truth would break his dramatic heart.

At 2:22 p.m., Elliot returned to my office, full of the joy of life, saying, "It's after five in New York. Where is that wine? And only the best for us, to celebrate my find!" His eyes sought out mine. "We've been blessed by the gods with the bard's lost work, and you look like something's rotten in Denmark."

I made a show of the wine to distract him. "For you, our award-winning V&W Pinot Noir 2022. The same I served Ms. Quinn. Our first vintage and a magical year." I'd already uncorked the bottle to soften the blow. "You haven't changed." He was still in his sport coat and pants and soft pink shirt.

"This is how I dress, and I'm ready for act two."

"You'll keep your clothes on for this act, I hope?" I poured the wine.

"Such lovely ladies, my tour guides, and what a magnificent home for your school. The lunch was so healthy, I may float away. But Sean, it's Will. I'm sure. Why aren't we dancing?"

"It's a great find, Elliot."

He toasted me, both brows raised. "It found me, but why? And then I remembered—we had popularized this lost work in your first book. Sir Arthur must have sent it to me for us both. So I rushed here to share it with you and expected you to be as excited as I."

"I'm sorry to say it, but we are being toyed with. The Guru may be trolling me with AI, Elliot. And I, too, have received a would-be lost literary gem from the one and only Sir Arthur." I said it rather baldly, but I saw no other option.

He stood, pushing away his chair as if it had insulted him. "No way that that's AI. Or Shakespeare need never have lived!"

"Not even if a supersmart quantum computer had access to Shake-speare's entire library and all the books and lectures that deconstructed every play and every word and then imitated that genius?" I went on to explain how I'd asked our fraudulent benefactor for *Cardenio* just a week ago, and that I suspected this benefactor was none other than the Guru.

"Sean, you're poisoning my triumph. Will you grant there's a possi-bility it's real?" Strong emotion moved across his face and threatened to erupt in an outburst of tears.

"Yes, it could be real, and Shakespeare could have lost his spark late in life and become derivative of himself, but the coincidence would be so fantastic, you wouldn't allow it in *my* fiction."

Elliot paced, finishing his first glass of wine. I poured him another and took it to him. Knowing he damned social distancing, I put my arm around his shoulder as we shared the sweeping vista at the window. It wasn't like him to be at a loss for words.

"Elliot, let's say it's AI produced by an evil guru, and sent to test us. We publish it, my foreword pointing out its merits and shortcomings. You make millions off his fraud. You play Cardenio in its virgin per-formance. Isn't there something grand about the genius of AI stealing from the genius of Shakespeare stealing from the genius of Cervantes? The layers of illusion and reality play on—we leave open the chance that *maybe* it is."

He stood crestfallen, pondering my words, drinking deliberately.

"You know what I'm getting at—the exposure of the fraud paired with the success of your performance *plus* the millions in sales is our sweet revenge."

A few long seconds later, with me holding my breath, he said, "Let's do it. Would you like to edit it, give it a soul?" He was assuming a stiff upper lip.

"Let's drink to it, but I don't think I'm up to that editorial challenge. I'll take a look, but it's really good as is, and I'll write the foreword in any event."

We toasted, and Elliot stared dramatically at the swirling grape in his glass. "Hmm, excellent. Just a hint of the sweet scent of a woman in that," he said in his best Al Pacino voice.

"And here, I thought you were gay."

"Yes, but I can still like how they smell."

He always made me laugh, and I admired his effort to recover from the blow.

"What will you do now? Stay as long as you like. It's summer break and we have plenty of rooms. Our student dorms are not what you might recall but more like the Plaza, each room en suite."

"Thanks. Call me Eloise. I'm not leaving till I have your foreword to accompany the maybe Shakespeare play. Then I'll return to the city and release this maybe artificial gem and possible fraud on the world— proclaiming it is or isn't what it purports to be, since I know you won't let me do otherwise."

"Okay. You know my lawyer wouldn't let me do anything less."

We shared a smile and the memory of how Elliot's legal performance ended up getting me paid by NYU for life when the Guru got me sacked. I did owe my drinking buddy a debt of gratitude.

"As soon as M leaves, I'll write the foreword for *Con*-denio. Shouldn't take me long."

"Good. I'll live here in paradise and explore the beauty and wines of Oregon. At your leave, my lord," he said with a flourish of his hand.

"Sounds good—don't overdo it, Peter O'Toole. I'm drinking less these days, and M barely at all." Elliot could binge a bit when given an excuse. The whipsawing of his tender emotions, along with the unknown future of his mysterious manuscript, might lead even a lesser-prone man to drink.

We finished the first bottle in a half hour, and while I uncorked the second, out popped my inspired idea. To cheer up my friend, I'd embrace this AI perversity and assault on the bard's legacy. I texted Molly, asking if she was busy and seeing if she wanted to play, remotely, the part of Luscinda from the long-lost *Cardenio*. Luckily, she was at her desk and not in the flow of writing. Fifteen minutes later, Molly had her copy of the script in hand and the V-room stage was set.

"Molly Q!"

"Elliot P!"

They both laughed and I rolled my eyes. *Sean M* was not as cute.

Molly wore a figure-complementing peasant dress and opened her own bottle of wine. Not knowing the bard in and out the way I did, she made Elliot happy by saying it sounded like Shakespeare to her. She was a luscious and long-legged Luscinda in our virtual theater for three.

Elliot was almost as excited to play his role of Cardenio with the mighty talented Quinn as he'd been when he first arrived. His buck was back—that or he was a very good actor indeed. In a bit of role reversal, I played the crazy man of La Mancha. The play and the wine were really good, and we divvied up the roles and took our turns reading the parts with our vino spirits flowing into the words. And like *Cardenio* itself, our scene ended happily, even after the Guru had his devilish play.

I hoped my upcoming scene with M would end as well, with harmony, after another test of my powers of persuasion when she returned from San Francisco in three days. She could go on tour and speak about ethical constraints and even mention Neurotech, Genesis, and the new goddamn Guru society—all while safely at home with me.

19 PERSUASION

THE NIGHT M FINALLY RETURNED HOME from San Fran, I lay in bed fine-tuning my argument for her to take a European hologram tour while under my protective guard in Oregon. I wasn't sure of my risk assessment or my ability to persuade her based on the facts. If only I could translate all my gut had to say. Perhaps that organ might scare her into listening. She was kind to not mention its increased rumbling.

The next morning at daybreak, we set out for the small outdoor theater on the campus grounds, where I'd make my case. I'd designed the theater using ancient Greek and Roman versions as my model. The Earth Theater was built into the gentle slope of a hill, with concentric crescent stone seating rising from a grassy stage. Three big rainproof wooden boxes, each the size of a coffin and stored near an arch at the entrance, held meditation cushions that doubled as seats. It was the perfect spot to hold class or hang out on beautiful days. And it was a beautiful day, the summer sun just rising for its solstice celebration. M and I arrived early to do our morning meditation and yoga in the theater as the sun came up. We then sat on cushions on the grass stage, waiting for a family meeting to discuss further the new comparative study course that M had suggested.

"M," I said seriously, "Shelley and now Shakespeare—the Guru has intruded again into our lives. We have to acknowledge this reality and take appropriate precautions."

"I agree it's the same person since you sent your email asking for *Cardenio* to the CyberSecure address, but it still could be anyone. And why would he send you these forgeries? But if it is him, he's returned in a harmless, albeit perverse, way," M replied. "And provoking ethical questions. Tell me true—would you rather those two AI-generated writings not exist?"

"Considering their source—yes. Your tour . . . I worry, with me here for the children and you there in his backyard."

"Europe's a big backyard. I wouldn't want to have to cut the lawn." She ran her fingers across the long dewy grass. "After all the work, would you have me cancel because you received a poem and play? And maybe it's Samantha or another tech-savvy admirer of yours." She wiggled her bum, while still holding her lotus, to bring her meditation cushion forward, closer to mine.

"No, and I'm immune to your charms, at least until you hear what I have to say. I think Genesis is him too. You can't possibly be safe going about Europe attacking WiN's and maybe *his* life-altering technology."

"Armed with my superpower of ethics, am I not a formidable threat?"

"The dark knows it won't survive the light. Now let's be serious. The boys and I have developed another way. I've authorized a hologram teleport to be installed in the indoor theater this week, and all the schools on your tour, other than Edinburgh, have the ability to project your hologram talk onstage. Those wired-in could enjoy the image from anywhere—you'd rock it and reach more people this way. You could launch your ethics missiles without fear. I'd even lend my incendiary words."

Despite the valiant effort, my clever words were falling far short of their mark as I spoke into her how-do-I-not-hurt-him face. That face was gradually illuminated by the morning sun, as if a greater power was deliberately giving her words more weight.

"Well, you have given this a lot of thought—sometimes you think too much and scare yourself with worry about me. *I'm a big girl. I am.* And sorry, but I can't possibly cancel, or substitute the real thing with a light show of me. I'm not Mick, but imagine if you bought tickets for the Stones and saw Keith as a death-in-life hologram—even though he does kind of look like that. A tour about the blossoming of humanity and the present dangers of technology, *using* technology?"

She was right—she was usually right. But I wasn't going down without a fight. "People love irony. And I read that a Stones hologram tour is in the works. It's amazing they're all still alive, still able to play, except for poor old Charlie—may he rest in peace. And you know it's not all bad, this technology stuff."

She was smiling *and* maddeningly humming the song about not getting what you want. She was a constant lesson in love as liberty. And how did one protect that which was totally free? I shimmied—less elegantly than she had—my cushion into hers as my desire to be near her and protect her knew no bounds and was now overflowing into pathetic desperation. I bent my head forward to rest in her lap in a fallen lotus pose, my Mark Antony surrendering to her Cleopatra.

Rumblings from below interrupted the quiet moment.

"No, it's not all bad," she said, stroking my head like a child. "Only people make it so, and maybe we can meet holographically while I'm on tour—that would be great!"

I sat up to swallow the bitter pill of defeat.

"But it's not what my audience signed up for or what I plan to deliver. And let's just say, for the sake of argument, it is your eighty-year-old nemesis returning after a decade to send you love poems. It's you who tricked him by releasing the theory on the world, and it was your book that ended his career and could have landed him in jail. Seems you're more at risk than me if it really is him alive and kicking after all these years."

She had a point, and it stung me like an electric eel, redirecting my current line of attack back at me. I fired back.

"Anyone who knows me, knows the best way to hurt me is by going after you. And let's not forget the threat of the rabid wired-in world who hate your message of constant creation and your audacity in suggesting some restraint on AI. We should take all appropriate precautions. We'll have the technology, and if *he* raises his head again, we should reconsider for your safety." I squeezed her hand. "Can you agree to that?"

"I can't argue with that. For our safety." She gave me her *maybe, we will see* smile. "But the family will be here soon, so let's discuss that project before they come waltzing in. What you said about the universe pointing us in the direction of exploring a few comparative areas of interest, particularly telepathy and BCI . . . it'll be a popular and timely course."

"I fear the relationship is one of conflict and not harmony and that we are the monkeys in the middle." I had to release my crossed legs to stretch and touch my toes.

"Our job, then, is to look for the harmony. I hope we have time to find it." M also uncrossed her legs to stretch, and I seized the opportunity to attempt to interlock our toes.

"That tickles," M said with a sexy squirm to complete the intertwining.

"My new novel is shaping up to focus on that clash of AI and Big Love. Maybe I'll take the course," I said, wiggling our feet, which made her laugh and me excited. "You're still my Brigitte Bardot and with such sexy *T-O-Es*." I sighed an exaggerated amorous sigh in releasing our childish toe-to-toe, so I might return to our academic tête-à-tête. "I'm afraid I won't have much to add to the discussion, but the topic has me looking at the continuum of science fiction, fantasy, and magical realism in comparison to general fiction and what we perceive as reality or nonfiction."

"You mean the illusion."

"Exactly! The collision of spiritual ascension and scientific advancement has been inspiring me. My pen is moving again. I'm writing my novel and a foreword for Elliot's faux *Cardenio*."

"I see that, and I'm happy to see you inspired. And it seems Molly Quinn deserves some of the credit. The universe is aligning for you to co-create your next novel."

"I choose to see it that way, but it's taking me into some dark chapters."

"That may be seeping into your reality? Fictional fears brought into real life?"

"Hmm. Maybe. Though it's not ready, maybe I should have you read how the Guru is reborn to come after us again. Maybe then—"

"I'd understand your fear for me?"

"Okay, okay, maybe my writing is coloring my views," I said, and then my stomach grumbled. "Moving on," I said, "learning more about AI may also help me prepare a course on science fiction. It seems more relevant than ever, though with the quickening of AI advances, it may be hard to publish novels about those advances before they're already reality. Sci-fi that's likely to come true interests me more than the fanciful stuff. And it sounds like the Guru's Genesis and the new AI society may make all education obsolete."

There wasn't time for me to finish my thought or for M to challenge them—the fulsome foursome bounded into the theater from stage right like Shakespearean couples united at the end of one of his comedies, marrying mirth and abundant life while the fiddlers played.

But the curtain was just going up at the Earth Theater.

THE BRIGHT SUN REACHED THE STAGE as the players assembled. In the song of cooing birds, I imagined I heard the orchestra tuning up from the pit, with the percussion rumbling from a cavern inside me. I ignored my gut and tilted my face, surrendering to the warm sun and the cool earth beneath my cushion.

Brian and Eric handed out playbills that they had prepared for the show.

"Auspicious is the day!" I announced with proper emphasis to greet our players. However, M was the master of ceremony for our spontaneous play.

She opened a playbill and read, "BCI and T: a play to explore the intersection of brain-computer interface and telepathy."

Astri raised her hand and said, "T and BCI sounds better to me." She bowed with prayer hands of respect, beseeching M's forgiveness for her always—more or less—welcome interruptions.

M turned to the cast page and read the cast of actors and their parts, adding, "With such accomplished actors, I can't wait to see this play. Sean suggests we acknowledge the conflict between the two fields while we seek to find the harmony for our new course."

Eric and Brian bowed their heads for a moment of silence, which we all joined. The boys then said *amen* and the yogis said *aum*. M and I laughed. YaLan and Astri arranged four more meditation cushions so we all could sit in a circle on the small lawn in the center of the stage, where the acoustics allowed a speaker to be heard from the highest and farthest seats. Here there were no secrets—it was an open theater with all invited to come, hear, and enjoy.

Brian took the lead in spreading out a small breakfast of teas and breads and sliced apples from the basket that M had packed. Eric looked to be doing some last-minute research. The young ones, with the sun now in their faces, put on shades. M held up her teacup. "To Juno and Mother Earth—may this tea warm our hearts and the bread fill our souls. And may Juno be safe and returned to us soon."

We all took a sip of the tea and a bite of the bread. I tried to surreptitiously pop a couple more Tums into my mouth to stop the incessant rumbling before the curtain went up on the family's informal play, but M caught me. The failure to hide my self-medicating set off a ten-second monologue from my midsection.

"Sean, you have to see a doctor."

"I will if it continues, but please, everyone, no more mention of it. Let the rumblings go, like background noise. Astri?" I lifted prayer hands toward her.

With Astri's compassionate smile, the agreement was struck.

"A lovely day to organize our concepts for our new class on telepathy"—M nodded at the twins—"and BCI"—she nodded at the boys. M's ability to assign and direct roles was one of the thousand gifts she had been blessed with. In that moment it struck me that M had become the Juno of the Deeksha West, a theater of her constant creation.

I hadn't received any memo that this meeting was to be in the form of a play, but we always tried to make our work play. With no speaking role myself, I would sit back and play the part of playwright. Eric pulled out his laptop like a secretary prepared to keep a transcript, and I pulled out a notebook and my Molly pen from my writer's bag.

"By the time I come back from my tour, the course and syllabus will be posted. I know mind and heart will cooperate to bring harmony to conflict." M concluded her remarks as player and stage manager.

"The reconciliation of opposites . . . the worthy goal of all romantic poets," I said.

Astri, turning to a typing Eric, said, "Please note the perfection of my head without any hair obscuring its celestial shape and take careful note of what my sister and I have to say about telepathy—with telepathy as *nature's* way of plugging into the spirit of the universal mind without the need to plug in to a soulless energy source with all those wires and tubes."

YaLan and Astri rose and spoke in unison. "We will each speak for the other." I was unsure if this swapping of roles was a theatrical device or a metaphor for how telepathy works. Or both. The twins shared the *gift*, which made them particularly good advocates for telepathy; however, they rarely spoke of their own experiences. I believe this reserve, which we all honored, was because it was a very intimate and private means of communication, and they shared a single-minded determination to be perceived as their own person. Still, despite one with flowing hair and earnest disposition, and the other being bald and impish, they had identical hearts. I had witnessed their silent communication once before, in a dramatic display nine years earlier, as a distant YaLan without words commanded Astri to knock Juno's poisoned teacup out of her hand just before she drank, and our world shattered.

In any event, they currently commenced communicating out loud by holding each other's heads above the ears, as if they were giving the other the oneness blessing. YaLan said, "My sister, YaLan." She looked at Astri and then at the rest of us, until we nodded our understanding of the role reversal. "And I will research the yogic history and current scientific acceptance of telepathy, gathering the info into teachable units."

Astri pulled her sister's head even closer and launched into a monologue, speaking to her familial audience in a rousing oration. "Let me professorially explain the fundamentals of telepathy. It is well established that telepathy may occur between two minds or even a group of minds. It is a loving communication—mind to mind—simultaneously arising in consciousness. That, then, is heard in the receiver's mind. In meditation, the elimination of thought allows us to access the *citta* within, the swinging-door portal to this shared consciousness."

"Wow. And I thought it would be the tech side of this debate that would be complicated," Brian said, tweaking his yogi playing her sister.

But it was YaLan who turned to him with an expression of amused consternation and said, "Let me make it simple then, my love. We all have consciousness, understand? We share that consciousness with all that is."

Brian nodded, though I wasn't sure he actually agreed.

"And an image, thought, or sensation can be shared simultaneously in the instant of constant creation between two higher minds channeling together. But belief in the power also plays a part. So sadly, boys, you may never know the beauty of our minds until you believe." YaLan concluded her schooling of Brian and performed an Astri-like touchdown dance celebrating the points on the board. Even Astri, playing the serious sister, had to laugh.

"I just read an article on channeling and mediums." I was going off script. "The author suggested channeling may be a form of telepathy with higher frequency or with developed beings—angels, or Christ in the case of *A Course in Miracles*—that guide the receptive subject into their higher mind to receive their lessons. He also suggests there are some nonphysical beings or aliens channeling telepathic messages through humans. Messages that sound a lot like Big Love."

The twins exclaimed in unison, "Yes!" as the boys shook their heads at the traitor.

The yogis took their stage positions and resumed their role reversals like two praying mantises about to eat the other's head. YaLan's words, spoken by Astri, came next.

Astri pulled her sunglasses down on her nose, flashing an intense gaze to accompany her assuming the erudite tone of her sister. "We will, of course, illuminate this through spiritual teachings and texts. Yogi Mangku and Juno routinely communicated by way of telepathy, and we've documented that as part of our Yogi's biography. We will also interview Ting. We'll make it so simple, you won't need to wire-in tomorrow to understand telepathy," Astri said, looking fiercely at Eric, who was shifting around on his cushion, pretending to focus on his computer transcript.

Eric, finally looking up into Astri's stare, said, "Please continue, Astri—I mean YaLan. Whoever you are."

"Do computers lack all imagination?" Astri's YaLan continued. "Telepathy has been proven as fact, yet very little is understood about how it works. It's like constant creation itself—something that eludes measure. Although recognized by the CIA, they abandoned it, as far as we know, unable to master telepathy for their less-than-loving purposes."

M caught me cringing. She understood my unflattering fear of those initials.

YaLan, speaking for Astri, said, "We will draw upon M's teaching of quantum entanglement and the way constant creation explains that spooky action." She performed a horror shiver, showing she could rival her sister's physical comedy if she chose to.

M spoke off script. "Most scientists, though they have come to accept telepathy as real, believe that using quantum entanglement to connect two minds is impossible. And perhaps the inability to cause, on demand, so many brain cells in vibrational resonance led to the creation of the brain-computer interface and now to Genesis."

A lightbulb went on in my head.

"By George, you've done it!" I said, joining the scene. "Reconciled telepathy and AI. What is Silvio's new AI society but a wired-in telepathy? Allowing minds to communicate instantaneously through a quantum computer intermediator. Brilliant once again, my love."

"Me? That was all you, Sean. I was just thinking out loud and you made the true connection."

I blushed at my scientific achievement expressed by such an accomplished scientist. I often became lost when speaking of the new frontiers of science and technology, so this was a Nobel Prize–winning observation for me.

"AT?" I mused.

"AT?" M asked.

"Artificial Telepathy."

"Yes," she said, "but through the medium of a self-learning computer rather than universal consciousness. So fascinating and so scary." The twins made faces of tragedy with jazz hands waving beside their shaded faces. Our laughter was joined by a laugh track that rose behind me. I twisted around and saw that maybe twenty students had slipped into the theater seats. In the middle sat a disheveled Elliot with his boyish grin, looking like he hadn't made it to bed yet, his lips soaked grape red and Samantha Smythe by his side.

The twins bowed and, with sweeps of their arms, invited the boys to stand. "And now, to speak on behalf of the confused robots all set to wire-in tomorrow . . ." Astri paused after acknowledging the friction we all felt on the eve of the boys becoming cyborgs. Then to relieve the tension she playfully performed a backflip, celebrating her return to herself, before relinquishing the stage with her more reserved sister. Her flip and a hooting cheer from Elliot got a laugh from our audience.

Eric and Brian stood and bowed to polite applause from the audience. I was proud of the theater and its communal effect that brought out the actor in us all. More students were filling the seats, with cushions from the coffins. Word must have gotten out about the scene we were making.

Eric said, "As robots, we will speak for ourselves to avoid any confusion. As research shows, telepathic abilities are developing, but so slowly that it might be many more lifetimes before telepathy will have evolved to the point of practical use."

I wondered if the aliens coming for a powwow in 2036 would advance our evolution or snuff it out.

"Tell Ting that," Astri catcalled.

"Or the aliens when they get here," I said, competing with Astri for funniest family member.

"They'll be here tomorrow with wires in their heads."

Okay, Astri usually won.

Brian put his arms and hands straight out and rocked in robot pantomime, but he looked more like Frankenstein's monster than an alien. "Ting and Juno and some others—the exceptions that prove the rule." He looked at the twins but he knew better than to refer to their gift in front of an audience. I wondered if this course and current events would force the twins to speak more openly about their personal shared experience with telepathy. "As Astri—or was it YaLan?—mentioned, the use of quantum entanglement's ability of two minds to completely meld is an intriguing prospect but one that remains science fiction. And I hadn't thought of this, yet as Sean noted, using brain-computer interface to artificially create telepathic communication and decisions may, with Genesis, be less than a year away. The precision of electrode receiver placement increases day by day. It's only a matter of time until the mapping of the mind is complete. But there are ethical questions the course will explore regarding this technology."

He looked to M, who gave him the nod he was looking for.

The twins stood, reentering the scene before the boys could go any further, with Astri spewing snark. "Really? Hadn't thought of *that*. Hmm . . . ethical questions? You think?"

YaLan pointed to some ants crawling across the stage. "And see these ants?"

I shifted for a better position when she laid her index finger on the grass and waited for the lead ant to climb aboard. She stood dramatically, the other hand on her hip, studying that ant.

"Alas, poor Yorick!" Elliot shouted from above.

I had to smile for the clown—I loved his wit. YaLan let the laughter ripple through before continuing. "Give this fellow a human brain and what have you got?"

She paused, like Hamlet, for effect. I thought I knew the answer, but Astri delivered the punch line.

"A smarter ant."

That was better than my *a human ant*, and it got a big laugh.

"Yes," said YaLan returning the ant unharmed to the earth, "with profound and disturbing consequences. For example, what prevents the computer from controlling the wired-in mind?"

Rumbles of what sounded like both dissent and assent rolled across the stone seats of the theater.

"Nothing, in theory," Eric replied. "The way it works is the flow of electrodes is fired by the mind, not the computer. But reversing fields may not be all bad—maybe you're on to something. What if you had dementia or otherwise forgot who you were and the computer could remind you?"

Another rumble from the chorus.

"So you'll let the computer think for you?" YaLan asked. "Who controls the computer that is only as ethical as its programmer?"

"There will always be free will," Eric said.

"Will there?" M asked.

Uh-oh. The theater director taking on a speaking role might force me into the growing conflict.

M continued. "Or will we have free will only until free will determines to cede its control? How nice to live in a world where we make no decisions, with a quantum computer determining each optimal step from all the possibilities which arise. Sorry, it's all fascinating. Just thinking out loud. Please continue."

"My love, as brilliant as the sun!" I said, delivering a sun salutation of outstretched arms for my literary students in the audience.

M smiled at my simile and gestured for YaLan to continue.

YaLan obliged. "Yes, Dr. Edens is right. Man's desire to avoid suffering might lead to him gladly giving away free will. What's to stop anyone from hard-coding the electrode signals to keep the button pushed for more endorphin drops of pleasure to stimulate the happiness center in the brain until happiness is just a steady state? Just as a monkey will push for more morphine until it drops dead."

Thunderous clapping and grumbling dissent rang from our audience as Astri bowed for her sister. I clapped, impressed.

"Sean, whose side are you on?" Eric said. "We might have abolished the use of fire with that thinking: *Oh dear, what if it's used to burn people or things?*"

An excited hoot and holler of support shouted from the audience followed Eric's words. He blushed to see its source. Samantha, still next to Elliot, retook her seat after her verbal and standing ovation that some of her WiN posse had also stood for.

"Those two together are trouble," I said in an aside to M.

A cloud dramatically blocked the sun like an ominous eclipse, calling all eyes up to the heavens and blinding me as it quickly passed.

YaLan was unfazed behind her sunglasses. After she identified the head cheerleader for the boys, she started discreetly counting her fingers on one hand with the other hand, a technique the twins used to regulate their breathing and to center themselves.

YaLan turned from the audience back onto Eric. "As with witches at the stake or the burning of Saint Joan, man—thinking he knows best—can turn any instrument to destruction. And who controls this Genesis, and who will be the gatekeeper of the network of wired-in minds?"

"And if we're talking about putting the brakes on, why not just use a smartphone and make a phone call rather than go through all the trouble with telepathy? Telepathy is about as pragmatic as two Dixie cups attached by a string."

"There you have it! Why not just log on to a computer rather than wire-in?"

"You're just pissed that the coming Internet of Brains will make the powers of telepathy totally obsolete." His blush acknowledged he had crossed some invisible line.

YaLan ripped off her sunglasses to glare into Eric's eyes. Astri plopped down onto her cushion and motioned for Brian to follow. This was now a battle scene for two, one that Astri and our audience were looking forward to.

"Unlike phone calls," YaLan said, "telepathy passes through an all-loving infinite consciousness. It isn't mind control or idle chit-chat or the dangerous data dump and transmission of thoughts of those wiring-in. Telepathy is not about the business of sharing thoughts but the sending of love across the ether in an instant of creation. It can be sent far and wide to all mankind or it can be narrow and focused, but it can only communicate with loving purpose. It can only send messages of the heart to another open heart."

She hadn't heard Queen Mab describe her evil gypsy sister, but it wasn't time for me to interject again.

Poor Eric, losing all sense of diplomacy, rolled his eyes and threw his head back. "All is unicorns and rainbow astral projections to you." His tight jaw and clenched hands betrayed the knowledge that he had gone too far and was now dangerously alone behind enemy lines in hostile territory. I believed in leaving no man behind, but he was too far gone.

"You're going to mock what you can't understand?" YaLan asked. "Telepathy is an ever more important tool of man's awakening. Lest we perish as a species!" YaLan, too, was done with restraint and deep breathing. She lifted a fist with raised index finger into poor Eric's face like she might jam it up his nose to get his full attention. "Wake up! Don't you see where this is all heading, this artificial intelligence? Unethical development is a *given* when control is in the hands of unenlightened minds."

The sun focused on Eric's brow and the beads of sweat forming there. Eric, who would normally back down, was unable to do so in the proverbial heat of the moment. "You're an accomplished yogi and pissed off, but that doesn't make you right! But let's agree to—"

YaLan wasn't going to let him finish. "You'll use your computer to make love too?"

Thank God that Astri jumped into the awkward pause of the fight with full abandon. In a single bound, she leaped into a warrior pose, caught her sister's surprised glare, and then started rapidly boxing, using her arms and fists as if she were hitting an imaginary punching bag, all the while laughing in unbridled joy because her sister had lost her cool. Even YaLan had to laugh at Astri's angry-little-drunk-Irishman impression.

Eric shook his head and mopped his glistening forehead in defeat. He gave a good-sportsman hug to YaLan that she begrudgingly accepted before driving a mock punch into his firm belly.

M turned to the chorus. "Thank you all for coming. If you have suggestions or want to be a research assistant for this new class, contact any of these four actors upon the stage." Our troupe bowed. The audience stood clapping as Elliot led them in a chorus of "Bravo!"

"Classes start in fifteen minutes, so we'd all better get going," M said.

We held morning classes even over summer break, many of which were online with remote professors. By way of example, the Elf of my first book, a blogger and podcaster, hosted a popular class on ethics in social media. She broadcasted from some unidentified location after receiving death threats for an exposé of AI experiments on monkeys that attempted to map their entire cerebral cortex. Apparently many sided with AI over monkeys in our evolution.

The crowd took their leave, and Brian started to pick up our cushions and the remains of the breakfast. Elliot was still tipsy when he barged into the family circle, already talking to me. "Ah, here I am, trouble himself! Oregon is an Elysium where I await my prince's foreword to the bard's lost masterpiece before setting my ships a-sail for glory and fortune."

M smiled graciously and excused herself to speak with the head groundskeeper, our resident philosopher, who had watched the play from the wings. The rest of the family dispersed, leaving me alone with my pickled friend.

"You'll have it soon after M's tour starts," I said. "Perhaps you might try alternating days of sobriety and exercise. You're drunk, and it's not even nine."

"Oh, but the pinots are so lovely, as is all of nature here. I've gotten plenty of exercise walking the fields and dancing. Your lovely ladies have been toasting me, and I tell them stories. Not as good as yours but full of innuendo and farce. The bawdy scenes from *Cardenio* are their favorites." He tossed off a leer of sheer wicked delight. I worried that he was moving into creepy old uncle territory, but I knew him better than that and recognized his behavior was an act to get under my skin.

"I've got to get to work and you need to go to bed. Don't embarrass us or yourself, Elliot." I didn't like the time he was spending with Samantha.

He pushed out his wine-filled belly and, patting it, recited his Falstaff from *Henry IV*, Part 1. "Banish plumb Jack, and banish all the world."

"I do. I will," I said, following the Shakespeare lines as his bonny Prince Hal. But I feared for my friend and his benders. He was taking the forgery hard and keeping dangerous and age-inappropriate company. I was afraid that was a combustible mixture that might explode.

21 WIRING-IN

BRIAN AND ERIC RETURNED from their blue-chip implants the following day with microscopic incisions on their left and right temples. The robots were so precise that brain surgery had one in and out in a few hours.

They were their old selves, and headache-free, but I could tell they were distracted by their new intrusive powers—augmented human beings adjusting to their prosthetic minds. Within days, the school's automation of administrative tasks was greatly enhanced and the entire school was enjoying the new hologram technology they'd installed in the indoor theater.

They'd done their homework, and for the first time we had an accurate count of unwired versus wired-in students—1,339 to 1,008—and the tide was moving toward those wired. The boys were arranging lectures by premier hologram teachers from around the world. Some were prerecorded but some would be live—where the teacher could see his class in 2D. Anyone who came to the theater could see the hologram professor without HoloGoggles. The goggles were for those not wired-in and not in the theater. It all boggled my old, unenhanced mind.

At my suggestion, they had also scheduled "live" remote theatrical productions to be performed in our theater by hologram theater companies that had sprung up in New York and London.

M agreed that the new tech—the hologram portal, not the brain implants—was a good investment for the school. She even complimented me. "Your hologram tech adds a new dimension to the experience. And this school is as much your creation as mine. What a great addition to our academic arsenal." She knew fear had caused me to act but saw only love in the result.

Juno and Dylan loved the addition and showed amazing levels of understanding. After the first demonstration, a playful introductory hologram experience provided by Holoport showing all the possible applications, M and I overheard the two of them imagining the entire universe as one big hologram. I wondered if they had surreptitiously watched *The Matrix*. M was too proud to be skeptical, saying to them, "What brilliant children! Do you know that there is a hologram universe theory of everything, one considered seriously by some physicists? Tomorrow we can study the potential that we live in a simulated reality together, where a super intelligence controls the world we perceive." Juno and Dylan wanted to start studying that very instant, but it was time for bed.

We never pushed them, but Juno and Dylan wanted to know everything, just like their mother did, and already they could imagine anything, just like their father could. But the two collided late that night as Juno woke us crying, afraid she was some kind of puppet in a game controlled by an evil Geppetto.

22 IN BED WITH M

LATER THAT SAME WEEK, I had a grown-up mission: to get M to agree to go on a long overnight hike before she left on tour. A trek to a secluded lake beach and a night under the stars inevitably would lead to our making love. I also believed that the time alone with her would relieve once and for all those far from sexy rumblings that had bedeviled me for weeks. I'd self-diagnosed abstinence as the gremlin and wondered if monks kept each other up at night with grumbling expressions of their suppressed desires.

Making love with M would be the physical antidote to my mental fear of losing her. Becoming one, with no distance between us, would somehow erase all that fear. Juno's words and the specter of the Guru couldn't touch her while I held her in my arms, and all would be right with the world.

We lived in and next to my office, a neat and well-designed apartment with a cozy kitchen and spacious master bathroom. The kids had a suite of their own—two bedrooms, a playroom, and a Jack and Jill bath. They had originally shared a room, but on Dylan's eighth birthday, just as sibling cohabitation tension was starting to boil over, he'd moved out of the *nursery* and we'd decorated the bedrooms according to their individual specifications. Hopefully, the bold colors, periwinkle for her and royal blue for him, would please them well into their teenage years; my pitching arm and writing hand were sore for a week following the last painting marathon.

Their rooms were bright, with window seats and nooks and crannies for play and the hiding of secret treasures. We'd filled their rooms with books and games.

Our master bedroom, with its queen bed, was equally magical. I loved our moments on that magic carpet. The private space transported us to an infinite universe whenever we were lying together there, each Arabian night a story of Big Love.

We didn't think of what we did as work. It was all just life, and it all flowed together there in those few rooms. We didn't believe in drapes or locks.

On Wednesday night, when I lay down next to M, with the moon streaming in through our bedroom window, I was second-guessing myself about how real the risk of M going on tour actually was. She wasn't the president or the pope or even a Salman Rushdie.

I focused on the moon-washed painting that hung opposite the bed—as always, comforted by it. The painting featured a vineyard with a colorful Salvador Dalí–inspired image of a tower of vines framed by mountains and adorned with flowers that rose toward the sky like a green floral gyre. Juno was the brilliant artist, and I called the unsigned painting "Prayer Hands." It was a picture of peace straight out of Juno's heart. Somehow she'd seen the view before we'd even created the Deeksha West. The painting's image had become our crest on V&W's wine labels. We'd never had a chance to ask for her approval, but Juno never judged, and we knew she'd approve as long as she wasn't credited.

At the moment, M's attitude didn't match the peaceful space. M had been expressing her displeasure that the student body was now debating the embrace of the modern AI world by the administration. Her consternation wasn't helpful to the consummation of my lover's mission. Not even one last cuddle by the children, who were supposed to be asleep in their own beds, had done the trick.

Samantha didn't help matters. M was shaking her head as she read from the phone that she rarely brought to our bed.

"This post by her says *I'm thrilled to finally see certain of the school's administration entering the modern world of augmented intellect. Now if we could just get the administration to let Sir Elliot Pennington teach a Shakespeare course next fall. He's already holding summer court to rousing success, and the school could use a little drama and comedy along with the wine and flower. Especially since the other qualified member of the faculty seems unwilling to take deep dives into Shakespeare with certain of the student body."*

"She's got such daddy issues with you."

"I prefer student crush, but okay—I'm old enough to be her father too."

M asked, "Is Elliot okay? He's drinking all day—with the students and her."

"I know it's been a long couple of days for him. He was certain he'd found Shakespeare's lost masterpiece. But what really haunts him is the identity of Sir Arthur and the fear that it's the Guru."

"He got that from you."

"I know, and I've talked to him and will speak to him again. Luckily he's gay. Otherwise, I'd worry about her—he shouldn't end up on Item One." I stroked M's arm. "M, is your concern with AI and wiring-in fully rational? This seems to be your Achilles' heel. The one emerging aspect of life you can't accept."

The moonlight revealed her face to be wise as well as beautiful. I kissed her long neck but went no further.

"I do think too much about it and have considered that, but let me try to explain. It's really so fundamental to the teaching of consciousness and the analytical brain. My position has thrust me into the middle of this debate, and my tour will now be consumed by this moment at the crossroads."

She put her phone down and focused on the ceiling. It was an empty space, but I knew that M saw worlds within worlds arising from the blank canvas.

"Okay, my teacher. Teach when you're ready."

"We're all each other's teachers. There's no way I would be as far along my spiritual path or would have enjoyed all those scientific epiphanies if I hadn't met you."

I felt warm little cherry bombs popping all over inside me.

"I've looked at AI from every angle and at all the possibilities, but the danger of AI, particularly when that AI is plugged into our minds, is hard for me to refute."

I seized the opportunity to quote the sage Sherlock. "*When you have eliminated the impossible, whatever remains, however improbable, must be the truth.*" I pretended to hold and tap a pipe. "You think you're right, then, Professor?"

She laughed. "Yes. *I am* this, *I am* that. But the ego always thinks it's right. Whereas constant creation focuses on the source of the *I am*—pure consciousness before concepts and judgments of right and wrong."

"I'm in the presence of moonlit divinity. My Big Lover." Trying to be a good student, I scooted closer until my face was an inch from hers.

"Okay, ardent one, don't get too excited. You know what happens." She patted my belly. "I feel like children here in the light of the moon, children wisely and innocently speaking of Big Love, oneness, and dualism." She was rubbing my belly like a genie's lamp.

And instead of my belly rumbling, my heart spoke. "The most sublime poetry and thoughts are the mind's expression, to oneself and others, of the beauty of a universal loving consciousness. *Material or spiritual, one world or the other, ours to choose—would the spell be broken if I kissed you?*"

"Beautiful! Your Yeats or your Keats?" she said, pleasing me even more with her mistaken attribution than she would have with a kiss.

"That was all me, not Keats or Yeats. But we digress. So how does this lead to your aversion to AI?"

"Brain-computer interface is an extension of the analytical mind, and though it may be used for poetry and for figuring out ways to feed the hungry and provide healing cures, it will also magnify the ego a hundred times, which, if not restrained by enlightened minds, could lead to the destruction of the world."

"So it's a race between awakening and ego?"

"Yes, exactly! I may use that summary of what's at stake while on tour." She gave me my kiss, making me want to feel more of her. I didn't

need much encouragement. I put my arm around her, still knowing that
it was not tonight.

Thinking of my science fiction, I said, "Imagining AI developing into
a superego is a scary prospect."

"We shouldn't be fearful but must remain aware. And thank you—I
need to add clarity on these matters for my lecture tour. Time with you
allows me to see more clearly."

"M, it's the same for me. You're my blue sky."

"And you're my sunny day," she sang back at me. I entwined my
left hand with her right. She took a deep breath, providing the perfect
opening for me to present my plan.

"How about we take an overnight hike up the coast to our camp
spot by the lake to clear our minds and have a holy-relationship reset?
Sunny summer is here, time to leave the world of AI behind, just you
and me in nature. And we do need time alone before you head to
Europe." I was thinking of a good natural rutting too and knew One
Step would have been even more direct. *It* had been a while.

"Okay, how about we leave at dawn on Saturday? The weather looks
good, but we really need rain. We can ask the twins to watch Elliot as
well as the children while we're gone. And we can be back in time the
next day for Fourth of July fireworks with the children."

"It's a date to celebrate our independence!" I said. "They can babysit
my juvenile drinking buddy." I squeezed her hand. "I apologize for him.
I really should have reined him in before now." *But she said yes!*

"Oh, I forgot to tell you the wonderful news, just like you forgot to
introduce me. I have a dinner date in Dublin with Ms. Molly Quinn. I
wish you were more excited for the tour. Molly is more excited than
you and said my talk's shining the light of Big Love in the lamp of constant creation will lighten some of the heavy energy hanging over the
world. It sounds like she really studied *The Lost Theory* and took our
adventure and love story to heart."

I found myself rocking on the mattress like a dog begging for more
belly rubs.

"Wow. Sounds ambitious. I'm seeing Saint Joan. Maybe a hologram transported like an angel into the arena—a mystical avatar. That would be even more spectacular."

A kind pat but no rub.

"Funny," she said. "Nothing more, real or imagined, from the Guru, so no more talk of hologramming me tonight, if you please. And you know what Molly meant. It's not me but the truth flowing through us that will make the difference. Me, you, the school—all of us are represented. It's just that it's my voice that they'll hear and my body that they will see."

"Okay, but on the hike it'll be your voice and body with just mine." I spooned her to feel that warm body, but the position also served to make my intention clear.

"Maybe you and my hologram can go?" she said.

"No, I need you!"

"You just proved my point. And all we really need is Big Love! Saturday's a date! Check under your pillow the night before in case a fairy queen leaves a letter for you." She nestled closer a few minutes longer before murmuring, "And now it's time for infinite consciousness." She rolled to her back and shut her eyes.

"Do you mean infinite unconsciousness?"

"Nope. There really is no such thing as unconsciousness, if you believe universal consciousness is the primary sate. We are always aware—witness—even in our dreams. We are just more or less conscious of our consciousness as we pass through many states to full awakening. That's why it's such a great mantra Yogi Mangku gave us. *I am infinite consciousness.*"

"And infinite love," I whispered, kissing her bare shoulder before turning to my dreams of Adam and Eve deep in the forbidden wood. Of a knight alone with the queen he has sworn to protect and will always cherish, secluded in nature where no Guru or radical AI could touch us. My challenge of abstinence met, my *noble* prize was sure—to feel and know every real part of her, inside and out, on Saturday night.

23 OLD-GROWTH FOREST

ON FRIDAY NIGHT, with only a week left until M's departure, I was full of anticipation for our next day's hiking and camping. Readying the bed for sleep, I discovered the promised letter under my pillow. I waited till M was asleep to read it—that was how the game was played.

Her words set me on fire. Game on! She'd written soft-porn erotica couched in spiritual metaphor, phrases and a tone more perfect than AI or I could replicate. I was vibrating on high. She had lit the fuse with my favorite Rastafarian expression of oneness of two people, *I and I entwined in tantric poses flowing in infinite bliss*. My marvelous minx and muse. I thought about her former chairman until my ardor waned sufficiently to allow sleep.

As Saturday's dawn approached, M was gently shaking me. "Get up, big boy—time to hike! Only fourteen miles to our secluded haven." Our campsite was by a freshwater lake bounded by its own mountain amphitheater. A sea breeze would accompany us much of the way.

"And three thousand feet elevation. Not exactly a walk in the park." I grabbed my letter from my pillow. "From my fairy queen . . . I'm going to bring this with me in case I need to refer to any of the best parts."

"Well, I hope you're packing more than just that?"

"My pack's all set with a sleeping mat and bags and head lamps. You got the food, energy bars, and some water?" She nodded. "I left room for water and wine in my pack." We had decided against a tent, as the weather promised to be sunny and starry. "No need to pack a swimsuit," I said. We always took a swim on arrival.

While M dressed, I sneaked a look at my computer to find that the Guru was still dormant or dead. I almost wanted him to show his face so M would reconsider her determination to go on tour rather than safely project herself across time and space. But what was I thinking? I had other priorities for that day and night. And on the hike, our spiritual reset, I knew all would be said between us that had to be said.

Almost from the first step, the rumbling inside me was replaced by the silence of sunrise and the crunch of dry leaves and the occasional tap of our walking sticks on rock. M, too, was silent for the first three miles as we practiced hiking meditation, where the past is limited to the back foot and the future to the front. We marched in perfect iambic pentameter, but I couldn't get a sing-song refrain out of my mind: *a-mating we will go, a-mating we will go, hi-ho the derry-o, a-mating we will go.*

I imagined M shared my excitement. There was precedent, as we always made love at the end of that hike and then became monks and nuns again. I was a reconstituted virgin of the wood and she my nature's bride. I loved to watch her hiking stride moving magnificently toward that end.

We used our hikes to rebalance our relationship before the ritual coupling, to bring its source and Big Love back into its rightful front-and-center focus between us. The topic of today's reset was likely my resistance concerning the European tour. I was clingy and fearful without adequate reason other than my unattractive neediness.

She didn't know of my secret and solemn vow to protect her. I almost decided to tell her the buried words as we trekked along the trail but didn't want to kill the mood and it would make no difference—she would still go on her Saint Joan of Arc tour.

I was glad Eric and YaLan would join her on the trip while Brian and Astri and I minded the farm and the children. They would be my eyes and ears and my proxy protectors. Many of our students would remain to study and to work the fields while I would write a Guru-full ghost story to express my fear.

I saw my repetitively fearful frame of mind clearly. But acknowledging it didn't make it go away.

But you always have a choice. M in her silence was directing my thoughts.

Our path crossed through an old-growth forest of fragrant grand firs, incense cedar, and cypress trees. The cathedral of majestic wood opened from time to time to reveal meadows of wildflowers that sat like cloisters along the path. The older those trees became, the bigger and stronger they grew, blooming giants celebrating life. I identified with those towering trees. Since meeting M, my roots were deeper and my trunk and limbs flowed abundantly with the sap of life. M was my sun, water, and earth.

M looked like a Swedish alpinist in her earth-tone hiker pants and white shirt that zipped down the front to allow for air conditioning upon the ascents. With a green bandana around her neck, she was liberated by the wilderness, and I was flowing along the path within her magnetic wake.

A cloud passed over the sun, and in that shade, Molly came to mind. I saw her sitting in Muir Woods, conjuring dark women to inhabit her fiction, asking those witches where to find Juno but, like Macbeth, hearing only of some dark future. Then a beam of alien light struck, and the image of Molly was gone. We were pen pals now, and she had recently sent me a treasure trove of research on Russia's AI program, but nothing that suggested an old ex-American CIA guru was involved.

I shook my head, refocusing on the present and the music of nature. A band of birds and a whistling wind through creaky tree limbs played as we marched along.

"Hi-ho the derry-o," I sang for M. She tossed her *maybe, yes, we shall see* smile over her shoulder.

"Where is it they will go, do you know?" I teased her, since I knew she found it too sexist a nursery rhyme for our children.

"The farmer takes a wife, but I'm not sure where they go. Maybe back to the 1950s."

She remembered the song better than I did.

The air smelled of honeysuckle and was rich with oxygen from all the greenery. Our first stop was for water and energy bars among the grand trunks of the trees that towered over us. We picked the biggest to hug, trying to grab hands. The tips of our fingers just touched, a kinetic connection though we were still as the wood received our gratitude.

When we sat under the fertile, aromatic tree, M finally spoke.

"You have dark fears about me going on my tour. I know you believe that the Guru may be behind the poetry and the play and, while disturbing, you must admit you like them, no matter their source. So, whoever it is, let them have their harmless play without you dreaming of nightmare scenarios. Beyond that, I hope you can be more enthusiastic about the tour and the good it might do."

I bumped my head back against the bark of the tree as if she had landed a punch to my chin. "Yes, I'm suffering a feeling of approaching loss with your departure so near. And it's likely irrational. But it's a sickness of love."

"Or a symptom of fear?"

"M, I . . . I've taken a solemn vow to protect you. Maybe I never told you, but I have."

"That's so sweet, but do I look like I need protecting?" She made a muscle and punched me softly on the arm. "And often what we really seek is to protect our attachment to a person or thing and not the destiny of that person or impermanent thing. Attachment and aversion are the two sides of a coin. Your attachment to me leads to your aversion of my being gone, yet our vow is to the Big Love we share. There we are always connected."

"Yes, my butterfly of liberation," I joked as two of the colorful insects fluttered nearby. "The world seems on a precipice, with both sides seeing a great evolutionary step approaching and determined to let nothing stand in its way. And you are my queen of Big Love that the wing-nuts abhor."

But she was in serious-teacher mode. "We share a Buddha nature, and we've been blessed by the light of that love. Yet you're still a romantic, putting me on a pedestal as a goddess or a muse for your writing and in need of your protection."

"I do abuse you in that way. I'm sorry, but I do."

"All that is real, all that truly matters, is our infinite consciousness, the source of love. And I—*we*—are not special."

"I understand, but the metaphysical ideal is hard for mere mortals to keep in proper focus. My writer's imagination still looks for fictional futures of fire and brimstone created from an imaginary past that includes poets, fairies, muses, and goddesses like you. Ideally, I'd drop all that and co-create, allowing the source, as did Shakespeare's Prospero, to flow through me without my interdiction. My imagination can be dark." I caught myself before saying, *But Molly understands me.*

M squinted at my literary metaphysics that even I didn't understand. "Yet you must realize that the renewed focus on your writing, the creativity as a part of your practice will also bring up repressed darkness to be transmuted and released into the light. It's all part of self-realization. The Buddha teaches it isn't enough to control our actions—we also need to control our thoughts. Dark thoughts lead to actions and circumstances outside our control. Let there be light!" She raised her arms in a goddess sun salutation.

"You're right," I said, looking up at our loving tree. "So easy to be in the flow with nature." I wanted to ensure our spiritual reset would still lead us to physical love under the stars tonight.

"Are you placating me, Sean Byron McQueen?" She jumped up in mock protest. Despite my being so transparent, those three names let me know I was still a Pooh bear about to enjoy a honeypot. I laughed, and she started down our path again, reverting to silent contemplation. I followed.

Despite her warning, I was again contemplating her departure. Telling myself not to think something always caused me to think of it. She *could* protect herself, and there I was, conjuring boogeymen to make me the romantic hero of my dreams. And where was this new darkness coming from? One of the by-products of Big Love that needed careful monitoring was the ability to love everything. Especially talented and beautiful novelists who appeared at one's door.

I would finish my novel draft before M returned and share it with Ms. Quinn. I also needed to draft Elliot's foreword. And we needed to get him back to the city and focused on releasing the faux *Cardenio*. He had too much idle time in the vineyards with Samantha Smythe.

We proceeded, observing silence, and I toyed with the foreword as words tumbled in my head from Dylan's and my fanciful sojourns into how we would search for the long-lost *Cardenio* and what we would find. Elliot's *Cardenio* was in all respects, save the most critical one, all that we had imagined.

A couple of miles on, M waited until I caught up with her and then said, "You know how YaLan and Astri teach the rice experiment where, over time, the cooked rice in separate jars is impacted by our positive and negative thoughts directed at the jars?"

"The power of intention and attention. Love and hate," I said. "It makes me think of our favorite wine."

"Burgundy? Only you and the romantic poets can take a weighty topic and turn it into wine."

"Yep, a bit like Jesus in that way, my luscious Molly Magdalene." *Oh shit!*

"Wow, such a Freudian slip! She really made a big impression!" M laughed. She didn't register jealousy as an emotion. I might have found that aspect of her character insulting if I doubted at all in her love.

"Oops, back to Burgundy!" I couldn't move on fast enough. How could I be thinking of anyone else? "With Burgundy, the quality of taste and sophistication has distinctions based on three levels—appellations, premier crus, and grand crus—which are almost solely attributed to the location and soil."

"The terroir."

"But the grand crus and then the premier crus receive more love in the growing, harvesting, and making. If there has to be an early harvest, of course the grand crus get picked first and go into the best aged barrels."

"Well, no analogy's perfect, but that one is pretty good. And you didn't even mention how all those working on the vineyard love those grapes the most."

"I can imagine a Burgundian winemaker fondling the grand cru grapes and reading Keats's odes to them while the fruit ripens on the vine. While the appellations are picked by migrant labor cursing their lot."

"Hmm, leaving aside the political correctness, I see what you mean," she said. "Yep, our intentions and beliefs are followed by corresponding actions that determine what we create, such as my perfectly aged Echezeaux 1969." She cupped and squeezed my butt cheek lovingly.

But then tears welled in her eyes and poured out. I stopped walking. What had I done? Was she thinking of my Freudian slip and finding a dormant streak of jealousy?

I held her compassionately. "What's wrong, M?" I said, patting her now-shuddering back.

"They're tears of joy! Can't you tell the difference?"

"Yay! That's so much better than the alternative. But why?"

She pushed me gently back and took my hand to her heart and my eyes to her eyes. "Sean, I'm the good jar of rice and the grand cru Burgundy. And all these years you have showered me with unwavering love and attention, allowing me to grow as a scientist and to mature spiritually into a state of almost constant bliss. You inspire me and I am eternally grateful."

I kissed her tears. And then I was crying. Hearing those words expressed in that way . . . they exploded in my heart, shattering me. After I worked to regain my composure and humor, I stole her line. "Well, no metaphor is perfect, but I love it! Thank you. It's a behind-every-great-woman-stands-a-man type of thing."

She laughed, and we returned to the hike. Not five minutes later, my mind began racing. And before I knew it, I blurted out, "What will I do when you die?"

"Wow! From the joy of abundant life to death in one stride—you really covered some ground." She captured one of my hands in hers, but she wouldn't let us stop walking. "You know that death is an illusion of ego, of our stories. There is no death, only transmutation of light."

"All we writers have are stories."

"Let's not speak of death, since it comes for us all. But call it a passing. A passing out of this body and mind of spirit back into source, perhaps from one story to another."

"Reincarnation? Lives like dreams we don't remember that still direct our destiny's course . . . But allow me one more passing mention of death?"

"Okay, shoot."

"When dying's all that is left to do, it's important to do it well. It's my favorite line from Elliot's *Cardenio.*"

"I know," she said. "I love it too."

"I hope you'll be there to see me through, like Juno was for Yogi Mangku," I said.

"Or you for me," she said.

Well, I'd have to join you, I thought and almost said. I didn't have Juno's equanimity and couldn't live without my M.

A COUPLE HOURS LATER, high noon lit our way. At my feet, I imagined illuminated steps leading up a slope toward an opening in the trees. It felt like M-magic was coming on, the power of serendipity that was drawn to her high frequency of being.

"Do you feel the energy all around us?" M asked, as if reading my mind again. "Subtle . . . but there."

"Yes! Nature vibrating with life, light, and procreation!" I said, full of wicked portent. "It feels like the tingle of the twins' telepathy but more dispersed, like a magnetic field."

"Your wish is nature's command." M pointed her walking stick toward the clearing up ahead. As we approached the opening, I saw that one of the smaller trees, a fragrant osmanthus, boasted a flock of nearly a dozen yellow finches strung like Christmas lights in the bright sun. They performed a flyover a couple of feet above our head, in succession, with each *whoosh* taking me higher.

"Wow!" was all we said.

At that mid-hike point, we entered the meadow, where waves of wildflowers rippled in the gentle wind. The dense smell of wood gave way to that of freshly opened buds. In the center of the meadow, an imperfect circle of rocks jutted up like ancient gravestones, a stunted little Stonehenge where time did not exist.

M strode to the center of the arc. Once there, she raised her arms, tipped with prayer hands, to the open sky and bathed in the shower of light. Her joined hands came down in front of her heart. I joined her there, in the middle of the sunny vortex, praying in mountain pose.

"The sublimity of now," I said. "There's an inverse correlation between our incessant thoughts in time and our timeless presence on the path. I never realize the passing of time with you."

Her smile reflected the pure joy of the moment. "Time falls away when you're centered and in tune with the universe and the constant *now* of its creation."

With my eyes half closed, I perceived M's heavenly body merging with nature in swirling van Gogh brushstrokes. Neither of us wanted to move. We were still and traveling at the speed of light.

"All time stops," I said.

"Traveling together at the speed of light," said the mind-reading M.

In that miracle of constant creation, we let silence reign. The peace M radiated was shared with me. I almost cried again with the realization that she might be right, that this oneness together in nature was even better than making love. I wanted to shake the sacrilege, but in the moment, it was true.

After a few minutes, a soft sound entered the field—the light footfalls of a small deer. M whispered, "A doe" as I was saying "A deer," and we both sang, "A female deer."

"She's just a little baby. Look at her spots," M said as she stood locked in eye contact with the doe.

"Boy has come to say hello." No response. "It's the doe eyes," I said to clarify my point. Boy had the softest, kindest, moistest eyes of innocence. I could imagine his radiance back in Kathmandu beaming through those portals, with Ting now being with him and making contact with his sweet mother Juno.

The baby deer walked straight up to M without hesitation. Perhaps she also saw and felt the light surrounding M. She dipped her nose and nuzzled M's leg. M stroked her neck while I enjoyed a rush of bliss, witnessing the mythical Diana of the woods. A few lines of an ode came to mind, from a poet whose name I didn't recall. *The nymph, glamorous Artemis, so boyish with arrow and bow . . . Her heart beats to creation, in bountiful beautiful flow.* Or something like that. I'd been disturbed as a boy at reading that ode, until my teacher assured me that Diana carried a bow and arrows to protect, not to harm, nature.

The doe's mother emerged onto the edge of the meadow. And then the two mothers shared a long glance with the babe between them. I was a bystander only. The doe made a soft, happy sound of *aum, aum, aum.* I said, "Namaste," which made M laugh like the breeze, and she offered a namaste to the mother. And mother and doe were off, leaping back into the grand old woods. After their visit, we owed them a deep debt of gratitude. We continued our bowing namastes.

I broke into mad laughter, carrying on until I had to bend over to catch my breath.

"What so funny?" M asked, laughing along with my joy.

"I just imagined someone watching our chatter and sharing of bliss and miraculous moments in nature. They wouldn't believe it, like a sappy movie but one I wouldn't miss for all the tea in China."

"I thought good writers like you didn't use clichés?" M said, waving her invisible Juno wand overhead, encircling our joy and releasing the spell.

We laughed again until we finally settled enough to sit and eat with a gravestone as a backrest. M and I shared a vegetarian sandwich on that magical patch of earth. We didn't speak about that doe but just smiled, our hearts singing and mouths chewing. With our bellies content, we resumed our hike, fully alive; the only rumbling I experienced was a pleasant full-body one. There, in the peace of nature, we were safe from AI and Rasputin, and I could let go of my fears of gurus and aliens.

25 A LONG TIME COMING

WE ARRIVED AT OUR CAMPSITE an hour before sunset, a little beach by a crystal cool lake. It may have been a pond, but it was big enough that we called it a lake—a transcendent spot we had discovered by accident years ago. The site always vibrated at a high frequency, but in summer we could hear the vortex humming. The radiant woods were mirrored in the water at an angle, reflected by the slanted evening rays of sun. A freshwater stream flowed into the lake, causing ripples in the trees.

The earth provided a flat bed of rich soil for our camp. Working a vineyard, I'd learned to smell the earth, and this was good earth. We were high from the hike and the sea air that had traveled two miles inland to greet us. The mountains wrapped around us as we basked in the remaining rays of the sun and the occasional salty mist of the ocean.

We removed our packs for a hug and a kiss in celebration before sharing a long drink of water. I was looking forward to dinner, wine, and my after-dinner delight, but first I'd rake the campsite and prepare the fire.

I channeled Whitman's spirit, not words, for my love. "Nature comes alive at dawn and twilight. Hear the birds singing, see the rabbits and fish jumping, the light streaming and the earth humming. My heart sings too, when yang of day meets yin of night." I put prayer hands to my heart, and M returned the gesture and smiled.

I used a sturdy branch to clear the rocks and debris for the mat that would serve as our seat and bed by the fire. M prepared a small kitchen from our packs. I arranged a circle of stones for our fire. We were home. I gathered wood and started the fire while a twist of twilight could still guide me. With the new moon, which is no moon, it promised to be a dark night. But we had a magnificent fire, sparked by surprisingly dry wood.

We spoke little while we made our camp ready for a night of passion. Once finished, we stripped, as was our post-hike routine, and slipped into the freezing lake that did nothing to enhance a man's prowess. Still, it was a spiritual rinse that increased awareness as it left my little fellow shriveled, shivering, and shaking, a cowering turtle. As we were climbing out, my foot slipped over a smooth rock covered in slick green ooze. I shrieked like a little girl.

"What is it?" M asked, startled by my gasp.

"Sorry, but that . . . on the rock. There." I turned my head away and pointed to the slime.

"Algae?"

"Don't even say it!"

"What? Al—"

"Yes! Please, please let's just forget it," I said as the word chased me out of the water.

M was laughing. "My hero. It's not the blob from the black lagoon."

I was having a panic attack that was not becoming of a man hoping to attract his lover with a cold little pecker.

"After all these years, you don't know my phobia, the one that we won't mention? I have a possibly false memory of slipping on it as an infant and hitting my head. Big gash. Maybe it's just a recurring dream. Anyway, I've always had a deadly fear."

"Well, that explains a lot."

"The phobia?"

"Hitting your head."

We continued to laugh while we warmed ourselves by my fire. I wanted a more pleasant memory to get us in the mood, so I said, "Anytime we bathe together I'm reminded of the first day at the Deeksha and your breasts jumping from the hot and cold baths."

"Just my breasts—what about the rest of me?" She covered her chest, feigning modesty.

"Yes, you know I worship all of you, but that was just the first time I got to see and imagine more . . ."

"Like our first time making love—and the next morning, our naked swim with our yogi in the freezing lake." She raised my memory with an even more wonderful one.

I wrapped M in my arms to show her I was still as strong and warm as the fire. I kissed her neck. "Hmm." I savored the taste before taking a full lick of her sweet and lavender skin. She must have applied some oil or love potion while I wasn't looking. I released her from my dogged advances so we could dress and prepare dinner.

M ate almost no meat. I ate meat on special occasions, and M had packed a fillet for me to go with our V&W Cabernet Sauvignon, Merlot blend 2022. A very good year. There in nature by our fire it was no longer 2027 but all time past and future. We toasted life and moments of perfection.

I cooked the fillet with mushrooms and thinly sliced potatoes in a skillet over the open fire. M served avocados with lemon wedges and a loaf of rich and hearty olive bread. Our feast was set. The fire and the stars were the only lights in a pitch-black night.

"Mmm," I said, and we started to eat.

For me, food tasted better with M's presence mingling with the aroma of the meal and the wine and the woods and the sea and the crackling fire.

After dinner was cleared, I pulled out a mellow wild mountain rose, one of our best-selling strains that I'd rolled for the occasion. We blew our smoke into the curling smoke of the fire and then lay back to search for shooting stars from our sleeping bag for two. We stargazed for an hour, with her scent infusing me, sparking some ancient chemical reaction that cut loose all restraints holding back desire.

I wanted to kiss her. We kissed. I wanted to envelop her. We embraced. I wanted to make the world go away in the moment where two become one.

As we slowly undressed one another, she whispered, "Sean Byron McQueen, let's make love like it's the last time."

The ominous subtext of the overture was more than offset by the sublimity of our union as first our eyes met and then we became two celestial bodies in a dance, partaking of a form of telepathy—a give and take, a probe and response—and knowing each other intimately with a knowledge more immediate than thought.

No rush to maximum pleasure so long withheld. Dormant DNA was activated in the light of unconditional love. M became a goddess, lifting me into her celestial body!

At the right time, the dance suspended; we became one. We sank to the earth holding on to the boundless bliss, our bodies entwined round each other, still in orbit as stardust flitted around us. The perfection of co-creation, the alpha and the beta, the tantra was pure ecstasy after months that seemed like years. We panted—shimmered—under the stars, a new constellation in the cosmos.

"I and I." I sighed into our infinite bliss.

M's every movement, each perfectly matched to raise me to maximum pleasure, made me want to be the most giving of lovers in return. I drank in the body next to mine, taking its full measure.

Then a fearful thought crept back in. I hoped her *last time* reference was merely a dramatic expression. But now wasn't the time to think of that. The Olympic torch had been lit and the games had just begun. My desire was entirely focused on M's light-filled body as I waited for our next synchronized dance event.

Like a powerful hallucinogenic, her scent lit up my mind, the spice mélange of *Dune* flaring my nostrils, arousing each membrane and demanding another taste. I was a sprinter coiled for the *bang* of the starter's pistol when instead came the *pinging* urgency of an incoming text from the school. They knew not to contact us unless it was an emergency.

M, checking her phone, said, "Wildfire! Brian says a wildfire is coming our way from the north."

I looked north. There on the rolling foothills, fire was whipping down toward us from maybe two miles up. "With the wind coming right at us, I think we have less than fifteen minutes before it's here."

"I already smell the smoke." And she was already moving, dressing and handing me my clothes.

"I know you said death was coming. I just didn't expect it so soon," I said, putting on my pants with difficulty.

Protect her! Here was my call to action. While time slowed, as death approached us, it seemed to take forever to lace our boots. We grabbed our packs and sticks and put on our headlamps and kicked out the fire the best we could, which felt like bailing water from a dinghy with our hands as a tidal wave was approaching.

M, too, will be lost!

JUNO'S FIVE WORDS BURST FROM the deep cell where they'd been banished to become emblazoned on my frontal lobe. *M will* not *be lost!* was now my clarion call and rallying cry. Though with the flames of death barreling down on us, I feared this was exactly what Juno had forewarned.

Wolves were howling warnings all around us—primal screams to escape or die.

With headlamps lit like third eyes, it was time to flee into the dark and from the angry blaze. Strange, perhaps, but I felt guilty leaving the bedding and some of our trash and equipment behind, even while knowing that the refuse would soon be incinerated.

As we backtracked south, I realized a paradise was lost. Here was an inflammatory reminder that man and nature, not AI, was still the leading cause of death. We ran where we could, but like Hansel and Gretel running from a red-haired witch with flame-throwing arms outstretched, we were outmatched. The fire was moving at least five or six miles per hour faster than we could run through the moonless night over roots and rocks and along the winding and hard-to-follow trail.

A big-bellied plane outlined by lights was releasing water or fire repellent from its gut about a mile away, though I felt the mist on my face. I hoped it was water. I couldn't imagine what firefighters could do to stop such waves of flames.

We were in desperate retreat, grunting communication only as necessary. After a couple miles, the wind shifted from due south to the west. South had been the fire's compass setting, pointing directly toward us. With the westerly reprieve, we were able to walk and catch our breath and guzzle water, but we weren't out of the woods. M texted the school, asking that they evacuate the students and staff. I checked the map for an extraction point.

The family would drive north to pick us up another three miles from where we paused—a remote trailhead. We'd hiked all day, made passionate love, and had now run miles over rough terrain in the dark. We were almost out of water, and the fire was still coming our way and outrunning us. I thought my heart might burst for the loss of nature and the end of our lives, but the image of being burned alive was a powerful motivator, even as our adrenaline was running out, so my heart continued its banging as I cursed global warming.

With the inferno still gaining on us, I was determined to not slow us down; I trail-blazed with my headlamp lighting the way, M's light on my back, and me calling out rough patches and loose rocks the best I could.

M shouted, "Sean!" causing me to turn, and my headlamp light shot into her eyes. She shouted, "Shit," as she fell hard to the rocky path and then barked, "Damn it."

Her headlight was out. She'd done a face-plant. When she lifted her head, the cockeyed lamp was still lit, but she was hurt. She continued to curse, and M never cursed.

"I'm so sorry. Where are you hurt?" I attempted to help her sit. She didn't push me away but made it clear that I was to be gentle and that something was wrong with her leg.

"My ankle," she said through a clenched jaw.

"Let me look. Do you think it's broken?"

"Don't say that—let's call it a sprain. Hurts like a bi-itch." She bit down on the curse but too late. "One shouldn't get high before fleeing a fire."

"Okay, here we go."

She winced as I removed her boot. I had to act fast to be able to get the boot back on; her ankle was swelling like a blowfish. I got out medical tape and wrapped it as fast as I could and laced up the boot as tight as the pain would allow.

"I don't think it's broken. Are you pulling a Samantha on me? We really don't have the time to make love now," I said.

"Don't joke. Not yet."

"Sorry again, but why did you call me like that?"

"Sean, remember your dark vision? I'd just remembered the fire in it—do you think this is that fire?"

My mind moved from the fire to the casket I'd seen next in that vision. I went with a half-truth. "Well, if it is that fire I saw, we live another day for me to write about it. So let's get moving if you can."

"I don't think I can walk on it or even apply much weight, but let's see."

I helped her to one foot, with half her weight on me.

"Well, we're not going to burn here tonight—I'll protect you, you know. I promised." The dramatic and earnest expression of my now-disclosed vow was accepted with a grimace from M. I wanted to distract her from the pain and said, "Eric, our Eagle Scout, packed us some opioids for pain, just in case."

"I'm already limpy and high. You don't want me loopy too." She motioned for me to keep the drugs packed away.

"Okay. Put your arm around my neck and we'll be on our way. Or I'll have to carry you."

We arranged our three good legs, and then with walking sticks in our open hands, we moved like a spider back to the path. We got a rhythm going that pushed us forward, but when even a soft step on her left foot caused too much pain or we were on an incline, I grabbed her belt above her left butt cheek and lifted some more of her weight. I knew the thought was shallow and not the time or place for it, but I was proud she was relying on me, her knight and lord protector. I so often felt that she was carrying me forward to Nirvana and I was holding her back, when being her hero was all I really wanted.

"You smell good sweaty, my lavender lady," I said.

"You don't smell like flowers. More like smoky birch."

"Just add some hints of cherry and we'd make a good Bordeaux."

We didn't look behind, as the wildfire showed no sympathy for our plight and continued to chase us like an angry mob bearing torches. To maintain the rhythm of our prancing spider and to keep M's mind off the pain, I taught her my favorite marching songs, singing them in turn until I sensed she tired of each panting rendition. The first was "When the Saints Go Marching In." Next came "When Johnny Comes Marching Home."

She would intermittently say, "Okay, be quiet," and "Okay, please sing." At one point when my voice was really hitting its stride, she said, "You have such a lovely baritone. Sing on, my minstrel man. Do you always sing in the face of deadly danger?"

"Only when we're going to live."

The silliness served as a distraction and kept us going.

"You must be in pain to enjoy my singing." When we paused to allow her to bend down to loosen her boot, I patted her butt, encouraging her to keep her mind off the pain. "Remember the song from Dylan's wake?"

"Um . . . the one the piper played?"

"Yeah. And you know who was in the choir balcony with him?"

"I didn't realize that I had actually seen the Guru. I only figured it out when I read it in your book. Can we rest a moment?"

"Sure. I'll teach you that song as soon as you're ready to continue. No rush. It's not like a fire is about to overtake us."

She snorted a sort-of laugh through the pain. We shared the last of our water. And as strange as it sounds, with freshly moistened lips, I surprised us both with a startling kiss. "*Not* the last time."

"Okay, Romeo, let's get on with our sack race. If it gets too close, you'll have to leave."

"'The Rising of the Moon!'" I shouted to shut her up and to stop myself from saying *I'd rather burn by your side.* "That's the name of the song." I started to sing, "By the rising of the moon!"

When we made it to the rendezvous point, the electric school bus we used for away track meets awaited us. Eric and Brian ran out with water, energy snacks, and blankets for the torch-song marathoners. We got on the bus and headed back to the Deeksha West.

Eric, our bus driver, said, "YaLan and Astri are organizing the hectic evacuation with the firefighters to a high school gymnasium about twenty miles east and inland, an area considered out of harm's way. Everyone received the alert and notice to evacuate. And they were checking all dorms and common areas, and will take a roll call when they get to the gym to assure no one was left behind."

"The children?" M asked.

"With YaLan and Astri and couldn't be in better hands," Brian said. "Should we head to the emergency room at the medical center for that ankle?"

"The Deeksha, please," M said. "I need to make sure everyone's safe, and I don't think it's broken, unlike the record I had to listen to all the way out."

"Ouch," I said. "That's the thanks I get."

"Your favorite role—my hero once again. Thank you. I loved the singing. It kept me going."

She nuzzled into my sweaty body, salty lavender sinking into smoky birch, even as another wood stood for attention, never knowing the time or place.

Neither of us could bear to see the vineyards, the flowers, and the school burn down, but the campus was where we were heading, now much faster than the speed of the fire.

When we drove onto the campus, M sat up tall, looking for signs of life. "It's deserted. Good job, Astri and YaLan. The three of you go on . . . I'll be right behind you in my car."

"Yeah, right," I said. "I'm not leaving you here alone. You couldn't drive with that swelling foot."

"It's my left foot, but okay. I'd like you to stay."

She leaned forward to drop a kiss on my cheek. Then she held my face between her palms and kissed my mouth. Maybe we both had seen too many romantic disaster movies. I hated the disaster but loved the romance.

I was still trying to catch my breath when she said, "Brian and Eric, be safe. Tell the children we're fine."

The bus drove away. I hoped not for the last time. "What's the plan?" I asked.

M, lost in thought or summoning another miracle, didn't answer.

I said, "Let's go to my office. We can watch the fire from there and decide what to do." I draped her arm over my shoulder, and we marched our three legs to my office. I pulled two chairs to the very corner of the room, with mine facing the fire descending from the mountains and hers facing west out into the dark over the vineyard and toward the sea.

We reclined so she could elevate her foot, and I wrapped it in ice. It was swollen and black-and-blue, but it was straight and didn't look broken to my untrained eyes. Meditating together on the horrible beauty arriving in a burning light—that was a sight to see if you could divorce it from the horror of its destruction.

"'When dying's all that is left to do . . .'"

But her pain was too much for her to focus on my bravado.

"I'm not the Yogi or Juno—Sean, may I have that painkiller now? I'm in a lot of pain now that I have time to be."

"Sure. I'd join you, but I may have to drive." I still always forgot, I could just tell Sherlock where to take us. I got the drug for her and did exactly what you're not supposed to do with opioids—I opened a bottle of wine. Being with M, regardless of the suffering, death, and destruction chasing us down, was always a celebration of life. The fire was a reminder that we were never really safe except in the refuge of a Big Love that knew no fear and no death.

"One glass each," I said as I poured. "Saint Emilion 1985. Not sure how much wine we can take with us if we have to leave, so let's indulge in one of your best aged Bordeaux."

We toasted and savored the first sip. "Smoky birch with lavender notes," she managed to joke.

Our kitchen, next to my office, was well stocked, and I made us a sandwich of cheddar cheese, tomato, and butter on half a baguette. It went well with wine and hunger.

I could see the pain easing from her body even as her heart sank into prayer. Her Buddha nature couldn't be dulled by opioids and wine, even in the face of disaster. We turned our attention to the window. The fire flashed above the hills that protected our valley, thousands of torches carried by mean little orcs determined to destroy the trees of our paradise. Flames flashed from place to place on the dark horizon, an advancing army. It was impossible to track the progress or the path of its destruction.

I took deep breaths, confessing my relief to myself. If M was supposed to have been lost to the fire, we'd overcome that. She was safe, and I had saved her. And Juno's warning had been just that, a warning to be wary and on guard. Though the Deeksha West was still in the path of destruction, we had a car and could easily make our escape in time. The worst danger had passed.

M stood quickly on both legs, wincing and pointing out the window and toward the vineyard. "Fire! Sean, do you see it? Fire in the vineyard!"

"HOW DID FIRE JUMP THERE? I'm going to see. It's not widespread—maybe I can stop it."

"I'll come with you."

She staggered, and I caught her as she attempted to follow.

"Perhaps not." She sat back down. As I left the office, M's words, "Be careful," followed me.

The fire looked to be about half a mile inside the vineyard, where an orc scout had raced ahead or shot a flaming arrow, bull's-eye, right into the heart of Strawberry Fields. I ran, wishing I'd brought my headlamp. My rubbery legs and the moonless night didn't allow me to move as fast as the emergency demanded. When I came to a familiar path, they stiffened and I picked up speed. I was between the rows that led to the circular opening and the ceremonial fire pit with the large stone Buddha.

My mind raced ahead of me, arguing that the school had been vacated, so the fire couldn't be the bi-monthly Wicca dance party. Then the longing howls of a coyote pack—the siren call of *o-o-o-eee*—came to me on the breeze. When the flaming pit came into view, I braced myself for the sight I had conjured in my mind so many times. And there it was, much as I'd always imagined—"The Dance" by Matisse. Yet somehow the innocence had turned taboo.

Twelve naked girls danced and chanted in the throes of communal ecstasy. I wondered, seeing them so uninhibited, if drugs were a part of their ritual. They chanted repeatedly as they danced around the fire, play-fighting, with soft flesh colliding like bumper cars. *O-o-o so lo la lee, o-o-o so lo la lee*, they called out over and over, twirling and laughing. *O-o-o so lo la lee.* Meaningless bewitching sounds of Dionysian harpies of the deep Salem subconscious. Meaningless maybe, but arousing nevertheless when howled by naked, writhing bodies glistening with sweat. Each young woman wore only a rich red bandana around her neck that another dancer could pull and twist, making for a writhing, sensual, blood-like flow. Archetypal fires rose deep inside me, flames that all my years and my presence of mind could not put out.

I rubbed my face vigorously, and returning to my senses, with great manly authority I said, "Okay, ladies, party's over. Don't you know the school's been evacuated? A wildfire is racing toward the campus. Get your stuff and make sure you have a ride out. Check on your roommate. Head east. Check your phones—there is a message from Professor YaLan or Professor Astri telling you where to go. Stay away until you're notified it's safe to return to campus. This is not a drill. Go now!"

The embarrassed girls all turned to dress—except Samantha Smythe, their titular leader, who looked ready to contest my authority. I held my hand up to stop her and pivoted to the fire pit, both to distract myself and to figure out the quickest way to snuff it out. I was ready to return to M so she could laugh at me.

My blood was still pumping hard, though I tried to look cool. I was a man who had known—who knew—great beauty and I wasn't about to let this White Witch temptress have her way with me. While the other girls dressed, Samantha, still naked, started helping me with the fire. I needed to nip in the bud her obvious ploy.

"Professor Sean McQueen, funny to meet like this! You've been avoiding me. I want to tell you, you are such a great writer. And firefighter." She laughed coyly. Her face and words projected innocence, but there was her body and a total absence of modesty. "We're so sorry to drag you out here to our new moon dance. We had no idea—"

"Samantha, please get dressed. I can handle this."

"Yes, of course, I will do whatever you say. I'm so sorry we embarrassed you. You know I have the gift of sight—a raging fire is a sign. Do you want to know what I see?"

"Not now, thanks. Get dressed." I busied myself putting out the fire, my face and body burning as red as the licking flames of fire.

"It is dark with a triangle of death and you dangling in the middle, ready to fall."

"What are you talking about?" I found the fire pit's poker and bashed at the flames.

"Your future."

I glared at her, but she looked serious. She wasn't going to move until I let her have her say. "Okay. Can this dangling triangle be averted and can you get dressed while you tell me?" I tried to make light of her *gift of sight*.

"No." She was serious.

But I was too. "Then never mind. Get dressed!" I turned back to my task.

"I see a fire in you! Listen and see!"

I looked again. The siren crossed her arms across her chest in lieu of getting dressed, partially covering her breasts, her fingers massaging and pinching her nipples. She had no shame and was celebrating her perfect form with pride and jubilation. Jiggling her left breast, she said, "This one's Shelley." Jiggling right, "This one's Shakespeare."

She knew how to push my buttons. I pointed to the remaining small pile of clothes; the other girls had quickly dressed and gone. "Dress!" I said, still in charge despite the old femme-bot nipple twist and full-breast jiggle ploy. *Item One, here I come!*

I worked the fire with intensity, determined to extinguish it. I used the poker and one hand to begin rolling the fire pit's ring of stones toward the center of the fire, crushing the smoldering remnants of flame.

"Professor, look. I dressed."

I lifted my head to see her in red panties and an unbuttoned white oxford shirt, tying her red bandana around her head.

"I saw you." She looked at me with hurt eyes. "Saw your cruel rejection of me." Tears glistened in those eyes. A woman's tears always melted my heart, especially when I was the cause. "Do I deserve scorn and punishment for my love?" Her fully open irises almost drew me into the feeling she was confessing.

"Shit!" I'd burned my hand reaching for my poker while lost in her words and gaze, grabbing instead a still-burning stick. My palm was immediately fire-red and ready to blister.

Samantha came to my rescue with a bottle and a shot glass. "Here, for the pain." She poured. "Take this." Before I thought, I drank to douse the nausea caused by my bubbling flesh, realizing only afterward that I'd imbibed the Wicca party fuel.

"Shit," I said again, afraid the grain alcohol had been laced with Ecstasy. I stood uneasy, looking for any signs of effect from the witch's brew.

She untied her bandana, poured some more of the concoction over it, and wrapped my hand. I wanted to throw up. Then I almost passed out from the pain.

"I saw you and Molly Quinn at the window that day. You cast out my heart, shattering it in the vineyard."

Tears streamed down her cheeks and neck. I instinctively reached out to hug her before I instead stepped away, stumbling awkwardly before regaining my balance.

"I'm sorry, Samantha, but we can't accept gifts from students, and it felt so . . . Never mind. It was wrong, and I'm sorry you saw. Forgive me."

"I'll try. I will. I do! My Sean Byron McQueen . . . being here with you, my heart is becoming whole again."

I winced from the burn. And I felt guilty for causing her pain with an act of teenage bravado designed to impress Molly.

"Professor, let me help," she said. "I can relieve the pain." She pulled a pendant on a strand of leather from between her breasts. "Hypnotism is a harmless and ancient cure."

My mind was reeling and my heart wanted to make amends. I said, "Anything to stop the pain." I couldn't reject her heartlessly again. When I saw my third eye open, I figured I must have been high.

"Keep your eyes on the pendant."

I squinted. The pendant looked like an antique, with a small, fragrant tumbleweed that smelled of sage held in a cage. It started to swing between her breasts. As I watched, I allowed a morphine-like wave to flow through my blood, muscles, and bones, and the pain met euphoria. Eyes appeared where her nipples should have been. I blinked. My mind was going numb. Maybe it was the unholy Molly.

"Relax, *relax*," she crooned. "Let it all go."

The irises at the end of each pendulum swing opened wide. I was being sucked in.

"Relax. Let go."

She was holding my red hand in her hand, the other swinging the pendulum. My hand was being pulled to her chest, her eyes holding mine as her full crimson lips incanted, "O Isis, O Isis."

A mystical child? I laughed, recalling a Dylan song that pulled me back from the brink and into some approximation of my senses. "Thanks. Now finish dressing. My hand feels better, and the fire is under control. You need to evacuate now." She made a kicked-kitten face but slowly complied.

The spell was broken, but my blood was still pumping. I was feeling a surge of chemically induced bliss. As she slowly worked the first button at the bottom of her shirt, Samantha leaned close, as if to share a secret.

"Why not? You're not married. She's leaving you soon. *And* selling this beautiful sacred land without consulting you. This is your last chance at passion while the fire is still burning."

The flame in the pit had started up again, its red light rising and dancing upon her glistening flesh. Though I didn't speak, a thought slipped through my anesthetized brain: How did she know all that?

"Nothing is private anymore. Except here in this secluded garden, with the school deserted and the end coming—it's a wonderful dream. Embrace the moment the universe has laid at our feet."

She was coming at me again. I stepped back.

She spoke in a deep voice. "Time to celebrate the Divine Goddess with me. She tells me, 'Following the new moon, you will live in fear of both worlds.' I see our totem pole has been erected to connect us in our sacred ceremony."

I wished she hadn't noticed the bridge raised between us.

She purred, approaching me with her shirt still partially unbuttoned and the red-lace undergarment beneath hugging her full hips. Shadows and light flickered across her body. I was on autopilot and not sure where my body would take me, when Juno's words burst from my belly into my monkey mind. *M, too, will be lost!*

Was this the way M would be lost, by my adolescent lust? With me already burned yet flirting with fire and crazed by drugs and circumstance? The absurdity made me laugh. I was M's knight and sworn protector and father to Juno and Dylan, and Samantha was my student, for God's sake. I was often a fool but not often ludicrous. Breaking the trance of her seduction as I'd pop a bubble, I pushed the siren away with my free hand as she took her last step toward my body. I would not be Odysseus cheating on his perfect Penelope or John Proctor striking the adulterous spark of the crucible.

"No!" We were both shocked, first by my laugh and then by my booming and final command in a clear and sure baritone. "Get dressed and go!"

I refused to watch her dress or acknowledge her sad dirge sung in what sounded like Gaelic that she must have been channeling, words and tune, from her wired-in mind. Her final siren ploy—an astounding use of my forefathers' tongue with a Stevie Nicks voice.

But she did go.

I FINISHED PUTTING OUT THE FIRE and drank two bottles of water left by the dance party. Lucky to get away with only a burn, I ran back to my office and to M. I had so much energy, I figured I was experiencing a microblast of the party drug.

Thank God Juno's warning had saved me. Yet again I locked away her five words as I flew through the vineyard, hoping M hadn't found the binoculars in my desk and watched the whole scene.

I paced outside my office until my head had cleared somewhat. I didn't know if it was the wine, the pot, the fleeing of the fire, the shot of X—but I wasn't thinking straight. I shook my head at the irony that I was high on Molly. And all the while, the blazing fire was racing relentlessly toward our westward Xanadu.

I stepped into the office and M turned from her perch at the window, where she watched the fire lighting up the top of the ridge about six miles away. "What was it? I saw that you put it out, but what happened? Did you burn your hand?"

She started hopping toward me, but I met her halfway and we sat at the conference table. Samantha's red bandana was still wrapped around my hand like a scarlet letter.

"A bit. It was the fire pit and the new moon Wicca dance party. They must have been out already when the school was shut down."

"So you and a lot of naked girls dancing around?"

"I was the party pooper, but I'll still have to write myself up for Item One next Monday."

"That Samantha is such a s—" M was reluctant to say anything bad about anyone and particularly about one of our students.

"Yeah, a slithering snake."

M laughed. Her intuition was probably running well ahead of my tale. Luckily, she was still feeling Eric's pill and the wine. She took my good hand. "I missed you. And you attended a dance with Samantha?" Her bullshit detector was not impaired one iota.

"She played on my imagination. I'll write up the whole sultry scene, and you can all laugh at me Monday. Hey, you almost finished the 1985 without me." I poured myself a glass and filled hers nonchalantly, glad that the scene was now behind me. I also couldn't drink enough water. It must have been all the fire and the heat.

We sat to watch the forest burning in the distance, an ominous dome with a golden-red glow cresting the nearby hill. I went to the window for a better view. "It's still progressing, I see."

"Slowly, I think. Hard to tell. With any luck, the forecasted rain will beat it here." She showed me a phone app that predicted a fifty percent chance of rain at daybreak.

"So we wait. We already dodged a bullet tonight." I touched the reddish scar on my right temple that was my proud tattoo of almost taking a bullet for her. "But if it makes it down the ridge and across the stream, we will have to evacuate too." She nodded ruefully.

"I'm so tired." She pushed back to recline on the faux leather La-Z-Boy.

I wasn't tired at all, despite the fact that I should have been exhausted. "Sleep. I'll watch the fire and over you."

Before she could rest her lovely eyes, our phones started ringing at the same time. My call was from Elliot, frantic from the high school gymnasium, that Samantha and eleven other girls were missing and I must find them. M's call was from YaLan reporting the same. After we put their minds at ease, M and I shared a contagious laugh.

I felt like I was being tickled and couldn't stop my merry chuckling. M waited for me to control myself before saying, "That fire dance sure gave you the giggles and lots of energy. How about just a teaser of what I might expect to read in Item One? Before you get your story straight?"

"Damn . . . thought I was out of the woods. Wait." I drank more water and wine and water again. "It was really quite illuminating. The fire pit fire was well contained and not a real threat. Maybe being impotent to fight the raging wildfire, I was compelled to snuff out that small fire. And I had to convince her to go. I couldn't just leave her there with the fire coming. Without spoiling all the suspense of the sordid story, let's just say she might have a future writing steamy romances. The witch gave the genre some cunning twists. She didn't know I could never act in a way that might lose you."

"Silly, you can never lose me. Remember, not even death will us do part. And you were already primed for love when we got the wildfire call."

"Yes, so if anything had happened, it would've been all your fault. I'm not even sure if she wanted to have sex with me or to just F you."

M laughed, carefree and full of trust in me. I repressed my fountain of mirth, afraid if I let the beast loose again, there would be no muzzling it. I was definitely high on Molly and irony.

"She's not a worthy nemesis for you," I said. "In my novel, I'll have to find another."

"You've always got your Guru."

"Oy! He's mine." That name shackled my buzz.

We pushed back to watch the race of rain and fire. Few words were spoken as silence ruled, but M said, "In the end, we still have the choice of love or fear."

At that moment there was no place I'd rather be. We settled into meditative consciousness together, with our eyes half closed in the dark. It had been a long night.

Dawn's sun was being attacked by a dark curtain of clouds coming in from the west and carrying sheets of rain from the sea. Pelting rain hit the windows, and we were crying, blessed by the downpour. Smoke mixed with the low clouds. The fever was broken.

By noon, the fire was under control. After I checked with the local authorities, M issued a notice that it was safe to return to the school. The danger had passed and left us exhausted, lame, and burned. M showed me that she was able, with difficulty, to put some weight on her left foot. I helped her down to welcome the school buses returning with our family and some of the students.

As we watched the family step off the bus, M said to me, "Fantasies can be dangerous. They often come true."

She had timed her bombshell well, leaving me no time for a reply as Dylan, not realizing her mother's ankle was injured, bounded into her arms, and Juno, not realizing my hand was burned, jumped into mine. We both held our loves to our chests and felt no pain.

29 OPENING NIGHT

A FEW DAYS AFTER THE FIRE and a few days before she would leave me, M took a break from tour preparations and joined me to watch a film. We'd received the director's cut of *Yogi Mangku: The Magic and the Mystery* to prescreen. M and I were gazing out upon the twilight from my office, waiting for the rest of the family to join us for the show.

M asked, "Don't you think the fire was the one from your dark vision in Athens nine years ago?"

M and the entire family were experiencing a communal grief for the old forest lost and immense gratitude that our parcel of paradise had been spared.

"The magnitude of that destruction and our being in the middle of that inferno . . . All those beautiful old trees, the meadow, and the . . ." Neither of us could bear to speak of what may have happened to Bambi and her mother. "Such a powerful image that your creative mind was able to foresee." She gave me a sad crescent-moon smile.

"I've been wondering about that too. It must be, right? But there was no casket afterward, as there was in the vision." My body's rumblings returned, stirred by my fear of prophecy and silly superstition.

"My precognition would have sounded like fantasy years ago, but now it has been proven scientifically, or at least statistically. But how is it possible?"

"Well, that remains a mystery, how precognition or the magic of telepathy works. But I have a theory that many now believe to be true."

"Great—a new theory. That can only spell trouble for us."

"Don't worry—it's not so new and incendiary a theory. It's a corollary of constant creation theory. Let me start at the beginning, over two hundred years ago, with Laplace's Demon."

"Spooky name." I mock shuddered.

"You and your demons, Sean. They do seem to follow you. Anyway, Laplace was a great scientific philosopher working under the classical physics model of a mechanical or a clocklike universe. He proposed that perfect knowledge about the current state would know all past and future states."

"Eureka. So I'm an all-seeing god?"

"Maybe, or a demon, but only when connected to the source in you. Hmm . . . This is more Juno's area. With Laplace, they called his all-knowing being his *demon*." She waved a wand-hand into the air like an orchestra conductor. "Laplace and his demon were overturned by quantum randomness and uncertainty principles. Astrophysics threw Laplace a lifeline with its current theory that information cannot be destroyed. Remember the Chairman and Father Bishop discussing the black hole information paradox?"

"I mostly remember the Chairman's gas and Father Bishop spilling his wine. So remind me?" I did a little shake-off dance in memory of the old oligarchs.

"Hawking thought information was destroyed by black holes, but later in life he came to believe it must be stored in a ring that surrounded the entrance to the black hole and that, with that information, you would know the entire past of all the matter sucked into it."

"But what about the future and how I may have foreseen that fire?"

"Well, the black hole is theoretically the end of time for all that passes through its event horizon—unless you go to constant creation theory, which views the big bang and black holes as mirror images of the irreducible instant as time and space collapse and reemerge each instant from the source of constant creation. Which takes us back to Laplace, who points to the possibility that this source, or his demon that could access this source, is omnipotent, as many spiritual adepts have attested, and knows all past and all future."

"Sometimes physics sounds like a course at Hogwarts. Are you saying that I may have dipped into this universal mind in our meditative practice back in our Athens bed, which enabled me to see my vision?"

"Something like that, but constant creation would provide the best framework into how noetic phenomenon and our beloved quantum entanglement works, with past and future seeing as well as telepathy and remote viewing. Don't let it go to your head—we are all connected to the universal mind, according to constant creation theory."

She gave a big lovin' smile as she turned her attention to some urgent student text.

The clouds rolled back into my head. Neither my heart nor my head was able to solve the paradox of the dark vision coming true in part. Were my dark thoughts the cause or the result of destiny? Perhaps that was the wrong question. Clearly Dickens, with a far more creative mind than mine, didn't believe that all of Scrooge's miserly visions must come true. Nothing is written until we choose.

"Crises averted," M said, turning her attention from the phone back to me. "Tonight we watch your screenwriting debut, but meanwhile, how *is* your new novel coming? We can't rest on our laurels." She laid her head against my shoulder, and I stroked the fine auburn hair that smelled like spring air. *I must not wash her pillowcase when she goes to Europe.*

As I became lost in the moment, she tipped her head to face me, searching for her answer.

"I still worry about that vision and its ominous implications." I knew that this was not what M wanted to hear, so I shifted course. "I am consulting my *demon*, but I think of it as more like being a magician or Prospero with spirit guides. All of Shakespeare's plots are driven by fantastical coincidence, and it's great theater because it's so real, so true at heart. The duke's ship just happens to be sailing past Prospero's island. The master then conjures a tempest that scuttles the ship and everyone survives. Fiction is fantasy and reality an illusion, and when minds meld with computers, the lines between nature and artifice will blur too until what is real is entirely lost."

I saw in M's eyes that I was losing my audience, so I added, "Somehow all those themes have to jell into a story as the strands are woven together. But M, I've learned something important from the night of the fire and your *beware of your fantasies* warning." I shook my head like a hangdog, letting her know that what was coming wasn't easy to say.

"M, you are so wise. The Buddha taught, and you helped me learn, that we must control our thoughts as well as our actions. But I thought my thoughts could roam free, not realizing they manifest in my reality. I held a childish belief that I could entertain my desires in my mind, and in my writing, without their having any real-world implications."

I paused, knowing I must speak the raw truth bluntly, without dressing it up in pretty words. However enlightened and mature I imagined myself, I still didn't want to say it. I cleared my throat to make way for my embarrassing revelation.

"I thought if I acted nobly and revered women in my actions, I could let my desire lead me to fantasize about them without diminishing their divinity. You know I've always defended my writing from what I viewed as feminist misandry, but now I see the truth. Please forgive me." I looked down.

She took my hands tenderly and lifted my eyes to hers. "Sean, you are a good man. Not perfect, but no life is. We're always learning, and you're starting to fully realize—as we do when awakening—that there comes a responsibility along with the bliss and the childlike joy. Thank you for sharing that realization. I know that wasn't easy."

We clinked foreheads lightly and then kissed to toast my clarified view on what was a lifetime of delusion—and to seal my commitment to more closely police the thief that carries my thoughts back into the rut of my adolescent chauvinist rat-pack indoctrination.

"But we'll see nonfiction tonight," I said, doing a quick shake-off dance. "I'm particularly interested to see the effect of the abrupt and ambiguous ending. I wrote it just as it occurred, with no postmortem explanation. Death always comes in the end." I was more than a little morose in the twilight of M's departure.

"It does—as a passing. You know what Freud would say: your fear of death causes severe anxiety over simple separation." She hugged me. I swear an M hug could heal all the ills of the world. "You're still a bit bleak for your opening night; it's important to focus on the light." She walked to my desk and picked up Molly's pen, inspecting its craftsmanship with appreciation before pointing the tip at me. "And to show a little gratitude for what is and enthusiasm for what's to come. You know I wish you'd come with me, but it was you who convinced me the children are too young for such a whirlwind of travel and time zones."

My mind reader always knew exactly what was truly bothering me. The push-me pull-me of *should I stay or should I go* had been tearing at me. And she was right about the children—I *had* convinced her.

"I'd like to travel with you, watch you dazzle the world, but yes, my duty is here. And Eric and YaLan will protect you in my absence, though I know you need no protection. But I still can't help but worry."

I was relieved when she returned the pen to join me unarmed at the window, to be silhouetted by the day's last light. She was a wonder in every way.

"I love you, M."

She inhaled deeply, and I prepared for a teasing response. But she leaned forward and pressed a kiss to my heart. "My sweet, sweet heart, I know you do. I feel it every day. I love you too." Her simple words were wonderful, and we stood staring out the window as we shared the powerful delight of being together, witnessing the appearance of a crescent moon hanging in the twilight. I eventually spoke into the silence.

"You're still limping a bit—you should take your walking stick if they allow it on the plane. Or perhaps I should come and wheel you around Europe like Stephen Hawking. Isn't that a celebrity physicist thing to do?"

She fell into my arms like a dancer being dipped, saying, "Couldn't you just carry me, my Thin Man? I haven't gained that much weight not running this past week, have I?" In comic tribute to Bette Davis, she batted her eyes.

"Okay, my dear Myrna." I stood her upright. "But seriously . . . Neurotech and Genesis continue to be big news, though Silvio's gone silent, only adding to the dramatic impact of his announcement. You must promise to not confront them too directly."

Her smile lacked conviction. "I'll miss this view. And you. This will be the longest time I've been away from the children."

The entire family arrived just as total darkness settled over the sea. Dylan and Juno, already in their pajamas, did literal cartwheels into the room to celebrate movie night. They didn't know the PG child-friendly biopic would bore them to tears. Their tastes ran more to magical adventures of heroes in exotic settings, the slaying of the dragon, the beauty and the beast. But they were always content to stay up late and be held by M and me. They also loved their aunts and uncles and chose that night to start with Dylan in YaLan's lap and Juno in Astri's.

Dylan took the opportunity, as his mother was distracted with serving tea, to hold up his hand to his ear like he was talking on a smart phone, making his argument with a gesture and wicked laugh—M said he got that from me. Juno answered her brother's call in sibling solidarity but was caught in the act.

"Do you both want to go to bed before the movie?" M was done with their push for technology.

"A passing earache is all, my dear," I said to redirect the moment as they dropped their make-believe phones and burrowed their heads into their respective yogis. M let her displeasure go as quickly as it came.

YaLan and Astri, as the authors of the biography on which the film was based, were more than excited and bursting with buoyancy that lifted even my dark spirits. I could feel them vibrating with anticipation, and the electricity in the air between their eyes suggested they were communicating without speech. When they worked together, they could consciously raise the quantum of joy of any space they inhabited.

The twins had brought bags of popcorn and a pot of tea from the cafeteria. I had a six-pack of ice-cold Heineken for the boys and me. The six comfortable chairs had been turned to face the bare wall between my bookcases. Tonight's film was a work of art in homage to the Yogi we had come to love in life and death. He'd died soon after M and I had left Nepal in 2018.

M stood, teacup held high. "We're so abundantly blessed to have known our Yogi in life and blessed to know his student, our teacher Juno, who is still with us. Both are always in our hearts. To our two accomplished authors"—she extended her cup to the twins—"and the award-winning screenwriter"—she held her cup out to me. "To my love of Sean and our love of the children that bless our days. May this movie bring love to the hearts of many."

We clinked teacups and Heinie bottles, and I cheered up. Dylan and Juno loved a good toast and made sure every cup and bottle was dinged with every other. YaLan and Astri sat, bundles of energy in their arms, to toast, and they turned to me, holding up their teacups in salute.

"Sean would not allow his name to be acknowledged as a coauthor with us, but over fifty percent of the book's words are his," YaLan said to start the toast.

"And the rest were mainly our Yogi's," Astri said. "Sean, thank you for all your creative expression in spreading our Yogi's love to the world."

Ting tong ting tong went the bottles and cups.

"I was just proofreader and editor. It was your loving voices that blended in song to sing the life of our beloved Yogi."

Always a little lady and it being a night of ladies' toasts, meimei Juno held up her teacup. "To Daddy! To Mommy! And Juno coming home!" She paused to smirk at her brother. "And to Dylan too, I guess."

She giggled, and Dylan tried to look hurt but broke into a full smile and nuzzled into his yogi host when she kissed him. He had M's spontaneity and smile.

"Now, if there is no further ado . . ." I dimmed the lights and spoke with directorial drama. "The *lights* . . . are off. The *camera* . . . is on. And the *action* . . ." Dylan beat out a drumroll against YaLan's leg, making us all laugh.

"That's my boy!" I said to my sidekick.

"And your girl," said Juno, never one to be left out.

Eric unceremoniously pushed a button. After the opening credits and our names, the first scene featured Yogi Mangku in his prime as a young Sherpa meeting Thomas Merton as Merton's guide for a trek through the Himalayas. *Saint* Merton, who, because of his pacifism and embrace of Eastern mysticism, would not actually be canonized a saint. There could be only one myth allowed; two schools of thought could not peacefully coexist.

The fateful meeting of saint and Sherpa turned our Yogi's path to all things spiritual.

Before the trekking masters scene ended, Dylan and Juno were already fading. Dylan moved to his mother's lap, and Juno, taking her cue, came over to mine.

Eric, noting the change of scene, had pressed Pause, and when everyone had settled again, he pushed Play.

As Juno and Dylan slept, the film continued with the Yogi's practice and teachings. There was one scene, not part of my screenplay or the book, filmed at his teaching compound after his death, of his real students sharing their accounts of seeing their Yogi in many different bodies and always playing a musical instrument. The students were dumbfounded when asked, "If it didn't look like your Yogi, how did you know it was him, especially when the sighting was miles away from where the Yogi was reported to be at the time?"

To each, the answer was the same—a knowing in the moment, a recognition of the essence of their Yogi that they expressed with a certainty of belief that no reasonable doubt could shake. To each witness, the time, place, and way of his appearance was always magical and auspicious. On that matter, I was initially a skeptic, but was now merely agnostic and unsure. The students were sincere in their beliefs, of that I was sure.

Astri got up and marched around the room pretending to play invisible bagpipes. She was a marvel at pantomime. M and I had witnessed a Scotty playing a marching tune on a mountain cliff above us in Nepal soon after we had been graced by Big Love and declared our love for one another. The twins were convinced it was their Yogi.

The next scene was especially poignant, as it depicted the Yogi passing on enlightenment to Juno. Meimei Juno's eyes opened halfway, perhaps in some mystical way sensing her namesake's awakening.

Mother Juno stands anointed in front of her Yogi as he gives her his final blessing and vow. "Now you are bound to the truth that will set you free."

We'd had to pause the film many times, including every time the actors playing YaLan and Astri appeared. Astri always had some comment that had us all laughing at the relatively serious film. The scenes with Juno had us all crying, though she wasn't played tragically but as written—an enlightened angel full of grace. But despite the valiant effort, the acting fell well short of capturing her liberated spirit and uplifting, lyrical voice.

The laughter and crying didn't wake the soundly sleeping children. Oh, to sleep so deep in peace again, as they did.

When we'd almost reached the final scene, I had Brian pause the film once again and I whispered, "Please watch the ending closely so we can discuss the impact of the very end. I'm on the fence about it."

Brian pushed Play, and Dylan's eyes popped open. He looked at his sister, and her eyes opened too—they weren't going to miss the ending. But how they knew to wake at that point was pleasantly bewildering.

The last moments of a miraculous life play out on screen in silence. Juno and her Yogi sit in meditation as he makes his transition. Clearly, though unstated, the two masters are communing telepathically until he passes. Later, a thousand well-wishers follow a procession that carries the Yogi, strapped down to a bed of wood, to the top of a mountain for his sky burial. The mourners gather round the Yogi as Juno plays the vibrating bowls. And then it happens—the Yogi breaks his bonds and sits upright, back in his seated lotus position! Zoom in on his enlightened face, his eyes half closed, blinking open as the screen goes black.

They filmed the ending just as it was written and in the same way as it had occurred. The family observed the silence. I wondered what other audiences would do following what I thought was a powerful ending.

"Wow. I love it!" said YaLan, crying with joy as the credits rolled.

"It brings him back to life, but it's true," said Astri, sharing her sister's tears.

Brian said, "I thought it was just rigor mortis that burst his bonds and returned him to the posture in which he died. I'm confused."

"Me too," said Eric. "That is what happened—what we saw—but seeing it makes one wonder. On the other hand, it leaves me feeling good."

"Sean, I think you have the ending you desired with that ambiguous resurrection. Those reactions"—M gestured to our small audience—"are perfect. But they—*you*—got Juno right. She was never one to allow mourning to turn to grief and self-pity. She always puts others first. May our prayers for her safe return be answered soon." M was about to cry again.

"Don't worry, Mommy. She is just like me," meimei Juno said as Astri was lifting her out of my lap to take her to bed. Calling back behind her, she added, "I will return!"

"Auspicious is the night!" little Dylan said, competing for the best last line as YaLan whisked him away. It was well past their bedtime, but their mother was leaving soon.

The rest of the theater's audience soon followed the children and yogis out of my office so that I could write for an hour before bed. Waiting for my laptop to open the manuscript, I thought about the lineage from Merton to Yogi Mangku to Juno to M and to the rest of the family. All desired to practice always being true in our thoughts and in our words.

I was suddenly gripped by fear, and I hurried out of my office.

Juno, initiated by the Yogi in Big Love, fully accepted truth and beauty and would never speak what she didn't know to be true. In some way, M *would* be lost.

I would not let that happen. And still . . .

I didn't know if I could alter destiny.

AFTER MY SCARE FROM LAST NIGHT, I tried to convince myself that perhaps the European tour was all Juno had foreseen, a temporary loss. I waited at my desk impatiently for the last family meeting before M's departure. This was no regular Monday morning family meeting. For one thing, it was held on Thursday afternoon, and served as a last cross-check that all systems were set to go. I was the grumpy inspector who wanted to ground the plane because of a harmless computer glitch.

I leaned back in my chair and shut my eyes. I hadn't slept well, stuck in between sleep and waking as my mind sought patterns in the haphazard tapestry of past events. I day-mared about Samantha and her searing prophecy—*It is dark with a triangle of death and you dangling in the middle ready to fall.* Her premonition reminded me of the swing hanging between the two trees from my dream of Ting's tree house and how even within a dream I'd imagined fear.

I was still haunted by my own dark vision from nine years ago, and perhaps seeing connections where maybe none existed. So much of it had come true, but there'd been one casket there, not the three that Samantha *saw* in her one-of-three-witches-from-*Macbeth* cauldron. And I was not Macbeth, but Prince Hal, and my Falstaff was drinking himself into a merry gay.

M and the family blithely entered my office, rousing me from the daydream that had followed me out of bed. Once a month, when finances were on the agenda and for special meetings like this one,

Natalie and Grace Byrne would be V-roomed into the family meeting from NYC. I was glad the family followed my preference for old 2D optics rather than meeting as avatars in a virtual metaverse, which always made me feel foolish and nauseous.

Natalie and Grace, my dead best friend Dylan's wife and daughter, were on the school's board and in charge of fundraising for the Deeksha West, where education was free thanks to generous endowments and profit from sales of the wine from the lush grapes and the weed from the budding flowers of the fertile fields.

So the extended family was gathering, and damn it, I was on Item One. Fortunately, either because of the fire or out of respect for M, my humorous short story account of a man tempted and laughing in the face of sexual entrapment was accepted without comment or a book club discussion. I think Astri almost burst from her exercise of restraint.

The Wicca party would be notified that any use of drugs other than accepted ones, which Molly was not, would be cause for disbanding the club and further discipline. I still couldn't swear they'd used the drug, though what I read later indicated that it would have accounted for my insatiable thirst—though fire, passion, and running for one's life could make one crave water too.

We moved to the main item of the day, M's tour. The following evening, Natalie and Grace would be hosting the launch of M's European tour in New York City at MoMA. I would accompany M to the kickoff and then return to the Deeksha West while she regaled scientific universities throughout Europe with her beauty and the perfect symmetry of Dylan's theory of constant creation.

Our large screen showed mother and daughter sitting in front of the fireplace in Natalie's home, with the picture of Dylan and Grace on the mountain where we found his lyrical poem "Golden Rabbit" hanging behind them. As usual, the ashes of my old friend sat on the mantel. The urn that I had shattered to find Dylan's theory of everything had its cracks glued together and looked like a jagged honeycomb hive—appropriate since the vessel was decorated with bees.

In my opinion, its artistic beauty had been increased by its resurrection. *You're welcome, old friend.*

M started off-script, reminding me again of Samantha's words.

"Natalie and Grace, while I'm away I have a big favor to ask. The school's operation of a vineyard and the marijuana fields has served its purpose in establishing the school. But while I still love those products and believe they have their place, I no longer find them consistent with the spiritual direction of the school and its role in the community. I think they should be managed independently as a charitable trust. And there is no one I trust more than the two of you. Eric and Brian would continue to split their duties between the two enterprises. They are wired-up supermen now, you know, and this change would free me up to focus on the school and my scientific and spiritual practices. If you're willing to take over management, that is?"

She'd asked a month ago if I had any objection to the idea. I didn't think she would go through with it and hadn't given it much thought until Samantha's mention of it. M might have mentioned the possibility in the school paper, which I didn't read. But it was good to be lightening our load, on our way in a couple of years to my writer's tower in Ireland, which would remain my lost and secret dream if my application was rejected.

Natalie and Grace didn't answer. I believed they were waiting to hear my response first. I said, "So you're now King Lear divvying up your kingdom, but before you're old and dying. And of course Natalie and Grace are the good Cordelia." Before M could say it, I did. "Yes, no analogy is perfect."

"But I hope that unlike Cordelia, they'll accept." She always impressed with her knowledge of the bard. "Natalie? Grace? I know it's a lot to ask."

"Not at all, the details of the trust will have to be worked out, but then with Eric's and Brian's help it would be an honor."

"An honor and a big burden," M said to the ladies Byrne.

Grace said, "No burden at all . . . It's consistent with our other charitable work and my focus now. I'd like to pay for the education of the immigrant workforce's children with some of the profits." Grace, an

Academy Award–nominated actress, had retired to follow in Audrey Hepburn's charitable footsteps.

"That's a great idea! I should have thought of that. You see, it *will* be in better hands this way," M said.

"Sean? All right with you?" M asked.

I smiled and shrugged, taking a carefree pose, saying, "We're just lightening our load on the way to Nirvana." With a stop in Ireland first. "I'll have to get Elliot, when sober enough, to look over the paperwork for the children and me," I joked.

"Then it's settled. While I'm gone, please work out the details and paperwork, and let it be done by the time I return."

On financial and legal matters, I was always a silent partner. Thanks to Elliot playing the part of a lawyer for me, I was still being paid a half salary by NYU. I smiled to think that the Guru's behind-the-scenes maneuvers to steal my tenured position would end up paying for the renovations of my Irish tower. And as my villain, he had also helped sell books.

Natalie next walked us through the social guidelines and the precautions taken for the MoMA launch party. While M planned to maintain those throughout the tour, some would have to be adjusted country by country. Without a current pandemic outbreak, all countries were at code yellow. Social gatherings, even in theaters and lecture halls, were allowed to take place. The question was more whether people would come, as people had become more selective about attending large events. Even wedding and funeral attendance was down, and my beloved Broadway had been slow to recover. For those wired-in, old Broadway was *oh so antiquated*.

After questions were answered, Natalie gave way to Grace, who said, "We're so excited to launch at MoMA, with Dad's original manuscript being unveiled. The tablets and artistic lighting are spectacular and the garden setting so fitting—a beacon pointing to constant creation. I prepared an audio of the entire original theory so people can sit there and hear the truth as well as read it."

"Your best Dylan impression for the voice, no doubt," I said.

Even Grace's laugh sounded like his.

Natalie said, "They're hanging Juno's portrait of Dylan and the waterfall she sent us before she . . ."

"Disappeared. Mom, you can say it."

"Yes, of course. But with M's telling us about Juno's telepathy, I wasn't sure that was the right word anymore." She paused, obviously contemplating Juno's fate. We were all coming to grips with Juno's new limbo state.

Natalie continued. "I'll send you a brochure of events. We each speak maybe five minutes in the garden if the weather holds up before they unveil the *Theory of Constant Creation* exhibit. Then, M, it's your show—first leg of your tour. You're still estimating about forty minutes of material followed by Q and A, so about an hour total?"

"Sounds right," M said. "I'll adjust the format as we see how that goes."

We then discussed M's rock-and-roll tour of all the major cities of Europe. I said, "I imagine we're already over budget for all this travel, staff, logistics, venues . . . And has enough been spent on security?"

M shook her head at my transparent flinging of cold water.

"Coming in well beneath the two hundred and fifty thousand we budgeted, Sean," Natalie said. "And our endowment is up many times that in anticipation of M's tour. We have some significant benefactors falling over themselves to support M and the Deeksha West on the eve of the big tour. Many have made donations anonymously."

Like Nobel Prize nominators.

"The biggest challenge is that a recent tax code revision has made gifts of artwork fully tax deductible at their current value. We're receiving millions in fine works of art. I've hired a consultant to help with the placement or sale. Stocks and cash are so much easier to deal with." Natalie threw up her hands and shrugged, looking up to the heavens, indicating that this was more than a small burden. "And on the logistical front for the tour, most of those participating are volunteers, and the venues all have been donated. Our biggest out-of-pocket is travel and lodging for the team. Do you want M to fly economy and stay in hostels?"

I waved off Natalie's question with a polite smile.

"And the publicity is great. Thanks to M's popularity and your book's

notoriety, our fundraising isn't even work. The *work* is what follows all
the money coming in." She leaned back and grinned. "Of course, we
could always make your flights to and from New York economy."

"Notoriety, not literary achievement? And it's Dylan's book too.
And let's keep the business class seats to New York. That's a long flight
for my long legs."

"Yes, Dylan does deserve a lot of the credit for the book's *notoriety*,"
M said as she and Natalie shared a laugh.

Brian said, "We haven't borne any unforeseen costs. And as far as
Europe goes, we're all set and M has the schedule. Flights all prescreened,
so all you'll need to do, M, will be to go through heat sensors and body
scanners with your carry-on. In TAA-compliant masks, please!"

"Burkas were ahead of their time. Can we get M one?" Yeah, One
Step wasn't entirely dead in me.

"You'd look good in one, Sean," Natalie said.

"It would cover our bald heads," Astri said, rubbing her perfect globe
like a crystal ball. "But alas, Brian and I will be left behind here with
you, though I'm excited to see what comes of our summer with Dylan
and Juno. It's always an adventure with those two."

"I know we're all having lots of fun talking about the smooth logistics and my hairline, but my question was tour security."

Eric waved a hand. "Since YaLan and I won the coin toss and will
be traveling with M and helping with logistics and the media and fan
inquires, we'll also keep her safe from unruly fans or WiN crazies."

I was glad to have them there. Eric was strong and wired-in smart,
while YaLan was a spiritual kickass yogi. Eric had promised to stand
guard for me and understood my concerns, even if he, like the rest of
the family, thought they were unwarranted and overblown.

Still, I wanted to change plans and go with her, to be by her side, but
M wouldn't want the children left behind without one of us. Not for six
weeks. My recent dark flights of fantasy weren't sufficient justification
to go. I couldn't abandon the children, and what kind of fool would I
be if I insisted to go at this late date based on a poem and a play and
visions and prophesies?

"You all know my concerns. M will challenge Neurotech's announcement of a new AI society, suggesting ethical restraint and oversight. Sensible and measured words of caution, but sure to garner pushback and hostility. We need to monitor those responses and be on guard."

I looked to M, who nodded, allowing me my say. Everyone knew the reason I had approved the installation of the hologram technology. And they knew I feared a boogeyman was still out there and might cause M harm.

"Most of the logistics in Europe are already taken care of by Dr. Gatenio," Eric said. Alberto Gatenio was M's host and friend, a fellow quantum physics professor at the University of Athens. "And Sean, Dr. Gatenio has assured us that police corruption has been cleaned up since your book's publication, and his friend the mayor has personally guaranteed M's safety this time. He says Athens is the safest place in the world for her and he'll provide his own security detail."

"Lightning never strikes twice? And will they give M the key to that great city too?" I made light of what I was relieved to hear. At least she should be safe on the first and last legs of her tour.

"Probably," Eric said, placating me by taking even my sarcasm seriously. "University sponsors are covering all the venues and hotels, and *they* will provide security. So much enthusiasm by our hosts. Brian and I only fine-tuned a few items and signed off."

"Yeah. You and YaLan enjoy your boondoggle," Brian said, making clear being left behind with me made him the loser.

"There will be plenty for the two of them to do to keep M on track and safe." I was the agitator, the only less-than-fully-enthusiastic cheerleader. "And I see that the Moscow Institute of Physics and Technology has been added to the tour. Isn't that pushing our luck with undue risk?"

"Seems the safest place to me," M said. "If you're right and Moscow is where our Guru landed and still lives as a recluse, they wouldn't want all the media attention and political risk of molesting a scientist in their own backyard." She came over to my seat, placing her hands on my shoulders and bracing me from behind.

But I wasn't satisfied. "They poison prominent dissidents on the streets of London. Sounds like announcing you're going to tea with a suspected serial killer *at his house*."

"Something like that. And you know they only snatch poor damsels from dark parking lots—never over tea in their own home."

"Anyone share my reservations about Moscow? Guru dead or not, Moscow is the hotbed center of the radical WiN movement."

Dead air and a lot of window gazing followed my loaded question, allowing M to have her way. They were ganging up on me and my imagination of danger at every turn.

I decided to let it go and join the flow, telling myself I was suffering a small-minded fear of the unknown. "Maybe we should send our rock star in a private jet and have T-shirts and constant creation tour banners made."

Astri jumped up out of her seat, turning my sarcasm into her glee. "Yes! With Dylan's face and quotes like *it's always now in constant creation*."

YaLan said, "Oh, I've got a good slogan for T-shirts and banners—Be A Big Banger."

"I was joking," I said, "but if you guys want to work with Eric and Brian on that . . ."

"A great idea," M said. She had no ego, but anything that raised awareness was all right with her.

With that and following namastes, the meeting was concluded. And I was left alone in my office. I sat in meditation, trying to clear my head of self-pity, when there came a faint whisper of a presence stirring in the highly charged currents of air around me. *Juno?* She didn't answer, so I was left to imagine from infinite possibilities what she had come to say. I closed my eyes and created several possibilities for Juno's unspoken dialogue.

You will save her.

Or from the perspective of the One—*There is no free will, only destiny that has already happened—play your part joyfully.*

Or simply *Love is the absence of fear.*

In the end, I decided to leave my answer to fate and went over to the bookshelves and tipped Dylan's prescient book of Yeats poetry off. It fell to the floor with a splat, one pointed stanza jumping off the page.

Surely some revelation is at hand;
Surely the Second Coming is at hand . . .

31 | MOMA

SHERLOCK, OUR TESLA AIV, drove the immediate family to the airport. Sherlock reminded me of Hal, the computer from *2001: A Space Odyssey*, but it spoke in an owner-chosen bespoke personality in crisp British. He called me Watson.

We all cried as M said her goodbyes to the children. Juno, of an age when she noticed everything, said, "Daddy, you're crying more and more these days." She was right, and I had no witty retort as I attempted to swallow my tears. M came to my defense. "Your dad loves us all so much. Sometimes that love just has to spill out."

For the first time, we let Sherlock, with strict instructions, drive the children home without a human chaperone. That softened the blow of their not being able to fly to New York with us. They were no doubt peppering poor Sherlock with a hundred inappropriate questions that he was set to answer in age-appropriate fashion, which would be so unnatural and distasteful for him and his acerbic wit.

M shook her head as I panicked in the airport lounge, imagining the mysterious Sir Arthur Conan Doyle might hack into Sherlock to steal away our children. I monitored the rest of the AI car ride on my phone until the children were safely home with Brian and Astri. But not before witnessing Dylan put Juno in a headlock for punching him in the arm and Sherlock pulling off the road and reprimanding them in some AI-inspired form of parenting and forming an invisible line between them—that he would monitor for the rest of the ride.

We had toyed with the idea of staying at the Beekman in New York but chose the St. Regis, as it was closer to the MoMA and held fewer memories. From my research, I knew the room number at the Beekman in which Dylan had died: 222—which played into my superstition. The Beekman had survived and thrived following the Great Pandemic as a NYC icon and tourist destination, partly thanks to Dylan and to my book. In a morbid twist, room 222 was the most requested room. Avid readers apparently did their own research, and since some reported Dylan sightings or conversations, room 222 had become a bit of a morbid mecca.

In the beautiful St. Regis suite that Natalie had arranged, we showered and dressed for the gala. M had packed a black dress and a red dress. I thought for her New York premiere she would choose black, but she so correctly chose red—a stunning work of modern art perfect for the poem I'd prepared to surprise her. She was a bit psychic. I dressed for my role as her leading man and supporting actor in academic business attire, her humble foil poised to serve and protect. It was a beautiful July evening in the city that I loved despite a forecast of rain, so we left early and strolled to the museum. Thank God it wasn't the Met and black tie.

All I had to do was look good and say a few words to celebrate M's tour launch, a gallant poet sipping champagne and not a worrying goofus crying in his beer.

When we got within a block of MoMA, event-goers started recognizing us, or just M, and expressed appreciation for her work. At the MoMA entrance, a barricade had been erected to corral a small group of angry protestors that made physical what had been, up to that point, remote cyberhate. Who protests constant creation? We'd seen protests on the internet but never face-to-face—except for our own SS and her homegrown, wired-in gestapo.

I took M's arm to usher her past the vitriol. I had to admire their clever chant: "Wired-in intelligence, not pseudoscience!" Luckily, M had oily duck skin and no ego or fear. And I was proud of my quickwitted comeback, protected by the big bouncers at the door. I said loudly over my shoulder, "True science, not wired-in belligerence!" It got the intended chuckle from M and I imagined made the mob even madder, but we were already through the door.

As we passed through security and heat inspection on entering, I said, "Shit. I knew you invited the Chairman and Father Bishop, but did you have Natalie invite *him* too?" A disheveled old rake I hadn't seen in years and hoped to never see again was walking toward us.

"Detective *Mulhearn*," I said with the fitting nasal intonation. We didn't share handshakes or namastes.

M said, "Hello. I didn't know you were invited."

"NYPD gets invited to all these social events, especially ones that stir up trouble like you have outside."

"Excuse me, I have to go say hello." M was making her exit, leaving me alone with the slick detective, when he reached out and grabbed her by the arm. I reached out and grabbed his arm, saying, "Unhand her!" The words were the first that came to mind. And we were off to a violent beginning to a peace and love tour, with me headed toward my first fistfight since high school.

M said, "Detective, you of all people should adhere to social space requirements. They are clearly posted at the entrance."

"Distance between us?" He smiled in mock apology. "All right, my bad," he said, letting go of his grip and shaking off mine. "I think you'll both want to hear what I came to say. I'm no fan of this cowardly scribbler . . ."

He didn't even bother to face me with his insult, holding his leer on M.

"It takes guts to write." My best on-the-fly comeback.

"But I thought I owed it to you to warn you, my lady. The department received a notice from Homeland Security that this event—meaning you—has been targeted by Russian-based bots and dummy sites stirring up dissent and calling for the protest outside. Some of it very inflammatory and over-the-top."

"We saw the protest outside and have been monitoring the internet," I said. "That group didn't look organized or violent, but they did have a catchy chant." I put on a brave face, not letting on that he was throwing rocks into my deep pool of fear.

"But that begs the question, Professor."

"What's the question?" I asked.

"The question is *why*."

"Why, Detective?" M asked.

"I don't know, but that's the question you should be asking. Sure, the WiN-ers don't like you so much, but someone is stirring the pot. That's all I had to say. I'll be on my way so you can enjoy your fancy-pants event."

I sensed that he had the same speculative answer to the question that I did but refused to share it.

"Thank you, Detective, for your help," M said. "And please let us know if you get any more reports or figure out the answer."

"Sure. We can make it a date."

His persistent innuendo actually made me laugh.

Our strange reception was left behind as we made our way through the socially distanced crowd, with half the people in masks despite the code yellow and almost all standing three feet apart, as code yellow guidelines suggested for public gatherings. We were heading to where Natalie and Grace were holding court with champagne flutes. I said to M, "So he's not all bad. I really need to be more nuanced with my characterizations in my future scribblings. But he agrees with me."

"We know there are plenty of WiN crazies out there who don't like me, and I know what you're thinking anytime Russia is involved. WiN is Russia's biggest homegrown export, with Russian-backed bots following AI algorithms constantly trolling in misinformation without any apparent rhyme or reason other than to sow discord. You can't let your imagination jump to assuming there is some wizard behind the curtain. Natalie, Grace! Hello!"

The discomfort of not having a counterargument to her analysis was interrupted by social awkwardness; not hugging Dylan's wife and daughter still felt strange.

Grace said, "Aren't we family? If you don't mind a hug?" We hugged, laughing at our small act of rebellion under the flashing yellow light of authority. Despite my disposition to worry, not even I could conceive that disease might threaten M. She was too full of vitality. But thanks to Molly Quinn, alien abduction was moving up the charts to number three on the hit parade of ways M might be lost.

A few minutes later, the livestream event was on as everyone moved out to the garden. With the enthusiastic attendance, the kickoff to M's tour promised to be a success, as any gala held in the garden of art at MoMA should be, even with the current atmosphere of pent-up electricity, with the positive more positive and the negative more negative.

Natalie spoke first, setting the intent of M's tour to raise awareness and discussion.

"Science, art, nature, and constant creation all know no borders and are shared by wired-ins and wired-nots. A virus came in 2020, and we are finally learning the lesson the universe was trying to teach us—we are all in this together and we heal together, not alone." She held up her flute. "May we toast the end of the zero-sum game—fighting over resources, the pitting of East against West, technology versus nature—and realize the infinite abundance of the source of constant creation and the beauty of its expression in every form."

Everyone sipped in toasting. I, however, gulped. I wasn't a relaxed public speaker outside my natural habitat of the classroom, and my turn was coming up fast.

A spotlight turned on Grace, who wore a long, flowing white dress that hung from one shoulder. She looked like a hologram image in flickering light as she stood in front of two draped works of art. The first she unveiled was Juno's masterpiece of Dylan by the waterfall.

"Welcome, old friend," I said so only M could hear.

Grace explained who Juno was for those who hadn't read my book and that she'd gone missing in 2019. She told them of her relationship as holy mother to the family and master of Big Love and how she'd gifted the work to Dylan's family, which in turn was now donating the piece to MoMA as part of the new exhibit featuring the theory of constant creation and honoring the man who wrote it, her father, Dylan Byrne.

Then, with a dramatic flair, Grace uncovered four long flat glass tablets that spun slowly, reflecting and flittering well-orchestrated pulsating light that spread out from the monoliths like white angel wings. The revolving tablets each held two pages of the two-sided manuscript in Dylan's charmingly slapdash, but legible, handwriting.

"Look, M," I said in my theater voice. "No metaphor is perfect, but the slow evolution makes the light of the angel wings appear to continuously flutter about the cases like they're caught in the instant of taking flight. The instant of—"

"Constant creation," M whispered, placing her index finger in front of her full lips like she was blowing out a candle. Juno's signature hush gesture, as well as the waving of the invisible wand, had been adopted by M as a form of homage ever since Juno went missing.

I turned back to Grace.

"Today I would like to read my favorite passages from my father's theory of everything. I find it amusing that angry protests should decry my father's work. It's simply a celebration of the instant—the constant now—and a suggestion that we focus our attention there. How can you object to the present moment, to consciousness itself? My teacher Juno told me that it is the nature of ego, always dwelling in the imaginary past or fictional future, to be at odds with this moment. With that, I'll read."

She moved through the flicker of angel wings to the first tablet, quoting Dylan even before she got there.

"The theory of constant creation merely realizes the perfect symmetry found in each instant of the infinite and eternal universe that finite time and physical space collapse into and expand out of as a projection from moment to moment and frame by frame."

The applause was that of the response offered after a good rally at the US Open.

"I was going to read next from one of my father's poems, but I understand Sean McQueen will be doing his first poetry reading later, so I'll read just one more quote from the theory that spins before us here, bathed in this wonderful garden light."

I grabbed M's champagne flute and emptied it. Grace had stepped on my surprise. M looked at me sideways with a wry smile and mock nervousness and then grabbed two more flutes from a passing waiter. She handed both to me as Grace moved to the fourth tablet.

"So simple, Einstein proved that time stops at the speed of light. But it's overlooked that Einstein also posited that everything in the expanding universe is traveling at the speed of light. Therefore, everything within what we perceive as the time and space continuum collapses into the timeless source of oneness and reemerges each instant based on the trajectory and momentum of light." After more enthusiastic applause, she said, "And here is our best-selling author and my father's best friend who, with Professor Emily Edens, found the theory of constant creation at great personal risk, as documented in *The Lost Theory*, and allowed it to see the light. It is my honor to introduce Professor Sean Byron McQueen."

Polite museum clapping for the literature professor and onetime famous author. My turn in the limelight, and I hadn't drunk enough. My mission was simple: to introduce M. It wasn't hard for me to sing her praises, and I did it well. I saw her smiling and knew I had struck the right note between admiration and adulation. I would read my poem and be done. This was my first stab at poetry, and it was a sonnet of sorts, meant to catch M's heart before she left on her tour, and showing me setting all ego and fear aside.

I warmed up by saying, "One critic said Sean McQueen should stick to prose and leave the poetry out. But in *The Lost Theory*, the poetry was all Dylan Byrne's, I'd like to note." I think M chuckled. "But then that same critic also stated, 'But on the other hand, perhaps he should stick to poetry and severely curtail the word count.'" That got the intended laugh.

I rubbed my face to get into my heart center so I could say goodbye to M. I spoke only for her now. "M, you may recall the last time we were here at his wonderful museum. My poem 'MoMA' is in dedication to then, to now, and to always with you." I cleared my throat and opened my heart.

Do you remember MoMA?
You, red dress, pointing to a picture of a man
Imprisoned in domesticity.
I never could find that painting again,
But it left a lasting impression—
That you were the keeper of the key,
No, not as my jailer on death row,
But as my window to immortality.

Now here you are, taking your leave,
Freedom does not lie in fantasy,
I know there is no you and me,
Only nature and art creating dreams—
Etched on cave walls and painted windows,
Look now to the light of God, and be free!

There was more polite applause for my club-footed Italian sonnet.
The poem had been drafted to dispatch my love by grabbing her heart
to set her free. I was forever putting on a brave face. My poetry was
maybe as good as Molly's assistant's AI, but not as funny. Still, M gave
me a passionate public kiss before we all moved inside to take our seats
and M took to the stage.

M's talk was excellent, her remarks delivered with spot-on crispness
and wit. The Q&A put her in a brilliant light and provided the perfect
forum for her quick intellect and verbal parries. Many of the questions
came from scientists, both constant creation enthusiasts and doubters.

During a lull in our long goodbyes, I pulled M close to say, "I didn't
see the Chairman and Father Bishop. Did you?"

"No, but they're both old and retired and don't get out much. I feel
sorry for them, the way their careers ended. Your book didn't help their
reputations, and I can't imagine it endeared them to their patron guru."

"I only told the truth."

"Yes, but in dramatic fashion. You could have just said the Chairman ate and talked a lot, while Father Bishop drank all the wine. But I did enjoy your dinner party scene."

"It was your dinner party, my dear Myrna."

"Okay, my Thin Man, time to go. *Je suis fatigué*."

After practicing her French, she grabbed my arm and navigated us to the exit as if we had another date. To avoid having to interact with all the well-wishers, she spoke gravely to me about how pigs in a blanket were always served at these events, and other important culinary matters. Her attention was solely on me, and our riveting conversation carried us to the exit.

WHEN WE HEADED INTO THE ST. REGIS, I tried to pull M into the ole King Cole Bar. "For a nightcap and a toast for your tour?" I had my brave face still on. I would provide a sendoff by a man she'd soon want to come back to. The rumblings were mercifully dormant.

She said, "I do want to thank you for that wonderful poem, but let's get a drink in the room. I'm tired. We can get room service." As we stepped into the old-fashioned slow-moving gilded elevator, I handed her the handwritten version of the poem. She folded it and tucked it into her white lace bra, then held her hand across her heart. I gave her a kiss full of amorous portent in our clattering ascending carriage, and then more deeply floor to floor, hoping the elevator would stop and suspend us in imaginary time.

Fatigue, she had said, but *one more time* before she left was on my mind and racing through my blood kiss by kiss until the fourteenth floor, where the delightful old-time elevator opened its doors on what was actually the thirteenth floor.

We entered a room that had been sprinkled with flower petals in our absence. Before I could ask if the decorating had been M's romantic stage direction, my attention was caught by the display in the middle of the suite. Two large easels supported an imposing painting that grabbed me by the neck. She strode right up to the monstrosity, while I dragged my feet behind her.

A bottle of champagne chilling in ice waited in front of it. I choked down a breath and pulled the bottle free of the ice. M studied the painting, and I read the label. "Dom Perignon 2022—very nice. Glad we didn't go to the bar. And what the hell is this? Was it sent over by MoMA?"

I was ready to celebrate M's big night and shut out tomorrow, but that large museum-quality painting was an artistic albatross planted smack in the middle of the romantic room. It was a quality piece, even breathtaking, but it didn't belong there any more than an elephant would. I smelled something rotten rising out of the flower petals on the floor.

I noted M's awe and excitement. And then I took a long look at the painting. It was an image that I had all but foreseen in my Ting's tree house dream—sunrise with an actual greenish sea wave rolling in with the dawn.

"What's the card say? It's really striking and large; is it for you?" It was a tremendous work of art, but also like having the Chairman in the bedroom. It was sucking up all the attention and killing the mood set by a rousing floor-by-floor elevator kiss.

"Just the title and painter's name: Ivan Aivazovsky, *The Ninth Wave*. And 'A gift for the Deeksha West in recognition of Professor Emily Edens and her outstanding work on the evolution of human consciousness.' Did you bring your antacids? Your stomach sounds like an art critic issuing a bad review."

My gut shared my opinion and expressed it without restraint. I went to the bathroom to feed it some chalky Tums and attempt to check my overblown reaction to the Ivan Fukin'ovsky.

Returning to the gallery previously known as our bedroom, I found M gobsmacked and admiring the image of awe-inspiring nature. She couldn't take her eyes off it.

Being close to the painting felt like meeting a person for the first time, a person who, though beautiful, you knew intended you harm. It was maybe nine feet by six feet of a brush-stroked green wave on the brink of rolling into the room after it crushed the remaining survivors of a shipwreck beneath its power.

The majestic art that magically appeared in our hotel room without explanation was a canvas condom. There I was in a lovers' suite on Fifth Avenue, my soul mate about to depart for over a month and a great bottle of champagne awaiting us—all this on top of a wildly successful gala—and she was falling in love with a painted pony some rich Daddy Warbucks benefactor had bought for her.

"So beautiful and bleak. It scares me," I said.

"Bleak?"

"Those desperate shipwreck survivors about to be swamped and drowned."

"Looks to me like the wooden wreckage they're clinging to is a cross and they may survive."

I hadn't picked up on that. Still. "Makes my skin crawl."

"Don't you see why? Your phobia. Al—"

"Don't say it!" I playfully covered her mouth. I looked again and thought she might be right, that my mind had interpreted the green-tinted wave as a filament of slime.

"A filament of slime," I repeated for M.

"Really? I'm sure that wasn't the painter's intent. It's supposed to be a big, beautiful, powerful wave reflecting the dawn light."

M stood behind me and prodded me toward the painting. "Look again," she said.

Seeing it in that light settled some of my visceral reaction, but something more than the green tint of the wave bothered me. "You always imagine the best outcome; of course you would see them surviving the wave. And receive such priceless gifts."

"You should try it."

I pointed at the champagne.

"I meant looking for the best outcome," she clarified. "Such a beautiful and grand painting. No one can own it. A work this sublime is a museum piece for everyone to admire. And I have no idea where it came from."

I called the front desk and put the call on speaker so M could hear who her patron was.

"Sir, it was simply addressed to Professor Emily Edens and delivered by a local art collector's people."

"Who's the collector?" I asked.

"Max Wells. We asked our art director to have a look before delivering it to the room, and he was quite impressed. He called Wells, whom he knows, and was told the source insisted the gift be kept anonymous. I'm sure our art director would be happy to speak to you."

"Not tonight, thank you. But there's no sender's name? No way to find out where it came from?" That made no sense.

"I'm sorry, sir, but not that we know of. I hope you're not displeased with the hotel and our service?"

"No, not at all. Thank you," M said before hanging up.

"Well, I don't like it—a gift addressed to you with no explanation and no sender's name." She wasn't pleased with my reaction, but I couldn't help it or the renewed rumbling of my temperamental gut reaction. "I'm not a jealous man, but I don't like it."

I was reading the description of the painting from my phone as M started opening the champagne. I barked, "Don't open that."

"Why not? You wanted a drink and it's some of the best champagne and I love this painting."

"You know how much it's worth?"

"No idea. But we can't send it back."

"The artist has been dead for a century. His works are mostly housed in museums, with very few in private hands. And M, it's worth a million at least."

"Wow."

She was finally having what I considered a half-normal reaction.

"It was donated to the school. Natalie told us the college is receiving art donations, some from multiple unknown benefactors on the eve of the tour. It's not so surprising; we always remain anonymous in our giving too."

"Someone you don't know drops a million bucks in your hotel room, and it's *oh la di da* with you?"

"What would you have me do? My Thin Man, let's have a drink."

"No!"

I didn't want to see it ever again. I certainly didn't want to pass it every day on campus. I blanked my phone's screen and threw it on the nightstand, signaling I was done for the night.

"You're in a bit of a snit. And I do love it. Let's go to bed." She started taking off her white faux pearls, adding, "You must promise to see a doctor for your stomach as soon as you get home. I'll ask Natalie to handle the logistics of shipping, and if you don't want the painting at the school after you sleep on it, I'll donate it to a museum somewhere after I get back. Okay?"

I was close to poisoning our already spoiled final night together. With all chance at romance dead, I said simply, "Yes." I went to the bathroom to hide as she continued to admire her gift.

As we lay in bed, I worked myself into a state where I felt the wave was going to roll over us. M had maneuvered the two easels—while I brushed my teeth—so that the painting now faced our bed. The painting was an ultrawealthy would-be lover's gift. And that meant that she was on the radar of someone with romantic intent. I'd worry if there was anything remotely romantic about my quantum beauty of constant creation embarking on a dangerous and glamorous rock star Big Love tour of five-star hotels and top universities in the most beautiful cities in the world. Nothing romantic about it.

As soon as she was asleep, I took two king bed sheets from the closet and covered up the beast the best I could.

When I got back in bed, I couldn't sleep, so I googled the painting again to find the country of origin—a Russian artist! The probable donor's name—I had been repressing it—burst into my thoughts like a tumor popping in my brain. There would be no sleep as the fearful cancer seeped into every fissure of my cerebral cortex.

THE NEXT DAY, SUNDAY, JULY 11TH, M's morning of departure for Athens, was too sad for many words. Despite my lack of sleep, I was earnest and measured when telling M that the artist was Russian and the painting must be from the Guru. She said all things Russian are not the Guru and that she thought he was going by the name Sir Arthur these days. I said we agreed to reconsider the virtual tour if he reared his head and threatened us again. She said it could have come from anywhere and anyone who supported the mission of our school and the theory of constant creation, and art was not a threat.

We said very little else in that elegant hotel room before our goodbyes. She was heading east to JFK and I was heading west to Newark Airport, so I couldn't take her to her flight. She refused to let me cry in the lobby or on the curb waiting for her self-driving taxi. I didn't insist. My clingy attachment to her led to a miserable ending with her leaving.

When the suite door shut behind her, I was the one who was lost. My drug was gone, and I was a cold turkey straining to make sense of the sucker punch that had been coming for months. I imagined her talking to her taxi, asking to speak to our Tesla's Sherlock, and laying out final instructions for him to give to the family. After detailed instructions for the children and the school, she would conclude, *And please take care of Sean for me.*

And his cool reply: *Our dear Watson can be so irrational and suffers a woman's temperament of innumerable tears. I'll take care of the good doctor for you.*

WOPA! M would reply to our AI Sherlock, who hadn't changed with the years. However, he had self-learned that WOPA meant he was being a chauvinist pig. Still, self-learning didn't change his hardwired constitution or character. M had learned to forgive him based on his age and literary heritage. But could she forgive me for seeing the Guru behind every work of art?

My top ten list of ways to lose M now had to include my fearful and jealous small-minded tirades.

I put the sheets back over the painting that I had removed upon first pee, before M awoke. I was struck by, and stuck on, the most horrifying thought—if I lost M now, these would be our last moments together. I felt childish for creating that distance while she was still so near. Hell, I would leave me too.

I lay on the bed contemplating the sheets covering my dread. That ninth wave was meant for me and was about to crash down over my lost and lonely shipwrecked head. I called reception for a late checkout since my flight back to Oregon wasn't until midday, and considered the bold romantic gesture of rushing to join her at JFK. But only momentarily.

Instead I curled around the comforter like I was spooning my lost Esmeralda, looking for sleep, but bolted upright when my inner Sherlock shook me up. A clever plan to unmask M's art benefactor had dropped fully formed into my mind. The art world was a business like any other, one where money speaks. I'd pose as a seller of the wretched masterpiece and unmask the Guru as the benefactor! Then M would forgive me my cowardly goodbye. This would be my way back to her side as stalwart and brave protector.

My way to protect M was to *out* the Guru, to force him from the shadows and into the light. As with the invisible man, his concealment was what made him dangerous. I was the only one who thought he still lived and posed a deadly threat, but once I proved the Ninth Wave came from him, that would force her to take the threat seriously.

M texted me from the airport, sending me her love and telling me Natalie planned to work with the art director at the hotel to ship the painting to the Deeksha West. Natalie said the only thing odd about the donation of art was its dramatic delivery.

A ghost in Russia was pulling strings and inflaming the wing nuts within WiN. My oath of protection now had to be performed at a distance, with M closer to Moscow than to me. And I was heading in the wrong direction, about to get on a plane back to Oregon.

She wouldn't approve of my plan, but she wasn't there to stop me. I'd write off my detective work as literary research.

It was unnervingly hot for an early July morning. I cursed global warming again as I stepped out of the hotel into the sticky air. I had time on my way to the airport to stop at the Bergdorf building on Fifth Avenue across from the Plaza Hotel and Central Park, where Wells's gallery was located and open for business on a Sunday in a city where art and real estate never took a day of rest. It wasn't a long walk, wheeling my carry-on, but it produced enough sweat to make me look like I forgot to dry after a shower.

Google knew Wells well and told many stories about him that painted the picture of a flashy denizen of the art and real estate worlds, who had a felony for not paying the taxes on some valuable works of art. It was a dubious charge, and Elliot could have gotten him off. And by Manhattan standards and the standards for those occupations built on artifice and fraud, one slap-on-the-wrist conviction without jail time wasn't so bad.

Wells's office sported a life-size flock of sheep of the artistic variety staged in the space just beyond the elevator's doors. *Claude Lalanne Sheep*, said a little placard. The Little Bo-Peep model behind the reception counter was tall and sexy. Behind her, large block letters—red on black—proclaimed WELLS. The two walls not overlooking Central Park were covered with Warhols—father Mao and swivel-hip Elvis with a gun. I was dressed in my best NYC business attire and a sweat-drenched shirt, which felt shabby and conservative in the mod office-gallery.

"Hello. I'm here to meet Max Wells," I said to Bo-Peep as she posed with perfect posture on her high chair. "His assistant said to stop by and he'd fit me in."

"Would you like anything to drink? A cappuccino perhaps?" She rolled her eyes as she read from her script.

"That would be great."

"Follow me," she said before walking me to a conference room with more expensive works of art and a large balcony with an amazing view of the park. A football-field-length conference table in the center of the room held artistically arranged groupings of bottled WELLS water. I took a bottle and stepped out on the balcony, away from the staff that were sauntering one by one past the glass-walled conference room to see if I was someone famous. I caught a few shaking their heads in disgust for bothering to look.

Wells surrounded himself with beauty, and that made me wary. So many Samanthas. I was watching my fantasies, not allowing them much rope.

A teenage-looking forty-something-year-old man in a tight black T-shirt stepped onto the balcony with a welcoming grin. In tow was a tall Asian lady with fine black hair, olive-green eyes, and big burgundy lips. Her sun-kissed skin, a lot of which was showing, was smooth. WELLS water must be from the fountain of youth. I took a big gulp.

"I'm Max Wells. Sean McQueen, an author, right?"

I shook his hand, mumbling, "Hello and yes. And professor."

"And this is Athena."

I shook her hand, not staring, still mumbling. "Hello, Athena." While we all were introduced, Little Bo-Peep entered and exited after setting down a tray of three cappuccinos in such a robotic and perfunctory manner that it made me wonder if she was made in Japan.

"I understand you'd like to discuss the Aivazovsky I delivered last night? I hope you want to sell, as you mentioned to my assistant. I'd love to add that to my collection. Athena took a look before we delivered it."

"I'm really just trying to track who sent it so we can thank him. But yes, I'd like to sell too." I almost forgot my cover story.

"Well, good luck with that—Russian money doesn't like being tracked. It came through but not *from* Victor, a Russian real estate partner of mine, and you don't ask Victor where money or art or any assets come from." So not only a Russian artist but a Russian benefactor too.

Athena said, "It's a wonderfully sensual piece, and it comes from the lure of the ninth wave—a wave like the one in *A Perfect Storm*—following the eight sequentially larger waves that come before. Such feminine colors and energy, with such a masculine power behind the brushstrokes in that painting, creating the divine wave of destruction. I'd die to have it hanging on my wall. Perhaps we can strike a deal?"

"I'd love to, but the painting isn't mine and the owner just left for Europe. How much are you willing to pay? I do have some say as her partner and business representative and have recommended a quick sale."

Athena looked to the moneyman, and Wells said, "Let's drink our cappuccinos first. Do you know art—*like* art—or just books?" He passed around the fine china cups.

"I wouldn't say I'm an expert. I didn't know this artist until last night. And I have to catch a plane." I checked my phone for the time. I was out of my league with art boy and his own beautiful expert. "It wouldn't be right to sell not knowing the identity of the gift giver. If I can just get his name?"

"Most likely impossible, but I can play intermediator and gently query Victor. But have you thought how that might be insulting? Might be better to just quietly sell it to us."

I was out on a limb, and M would not be pleased. But we should know where the gift came from. "What's your price?"

"I can give you a range. I'd pay one million and Athena would pay two, but she doesn't have the money, so somewhere in there but closer to a mil."

"It last traded for closer to five million." I was bluffing—I had no idea. But I knew it had to be worth twice what they were offering.

"You've done your homework, but that was almost ten years ago and it was closer to four mil. A lot has changed."

"What more can you tell me about the painting?"

Athena's breathing deepened in anticipation of talking about a topic she loved. "Aivazovsky was a romantic late-nineteenth-century Russian painter of mostly seascapes and battles. Chekhov's praise, describing a thing of beauty as 'worthy of Aivazovsky's brush,' made him even more famous in his home country."

I hated and loved that imposing painting more and more.

"He is beloved in Russia still, but even though his brush spoke in every language, with the magic of art capturing moments of powerful nature, outside Russia, only artists and critics remember his work."

We were all poets when describing our love.

She focused between us as if we were viewing the wall-size painting as she spoke, her mind's eye conjuring it like a hologram for me to see. "The viewer's eyes are immediately captivated and drawn to the power of nature raising a large and beautiful wave at dawn only to settle later upon the desperate family of shipwreck survivors in the foreground about to be brought under the wave. But do they perish or survive?" She took on the look of a mystic. "The painting depicts the tension of fate. The viewer is there, in that moment of breathtaking creation *and* destruction, before the sea rolls through us in that dramatic wave of dawn."

"A thing of beauty described by beauty in a beautiful way," I said without thinking. Realizing the instant intimacy my words revealed, I blushed. I overused *beauty*, but only because I saw it so often, which is a sign of an open heart. And once again I had defined a woman by her physical attributes and used that lovely word *beauty*. But Athena had ravished me with her words that conjured the roiling seas in me. I was flushed, with a quickly ticking heart. Scared and thrilled, as if the wave was poised over *my* head. It wasn't Athena or the painting but a recognition of my stage of life. Something big was coming—it always was. It was always just a matter of time before death came rolling in, beauty before, and beauty after, always beauty and death.

"That was a lovely description, Athena. I have a plane to catch. Here's my card." I passed one to both of them. "If you tell me who the gift came from, we can negotiate a price." His red-on-black WELLS calling card boasted a much thicker weave than my flimsy academic card. Even young Athena's card, with Van Gogh's *Almond Blossom* as a background, made for a better first impression.

"You drive a hard bargain for a writer who hasn't written in a while. But let's see what we can do." He wiggled my card to show it had no backbone.

Athena said, "I read your first book and loved it. So many have been inspired on their path of Big Love by your words and by Professor Edens and the theory of constant creation. Are you sure you can't stay and be my guest at Per Se for dinner this evening?"

"Or you both could go to Daniel with me. I know Daniel, and we'll get the best table *and* he serves WELLS wine. That would give me time to see if we can meet your demands—to discover the source of the gift and arrive at a price." I considered comparing wine notes but imagined WELLS wine was more a brand than a true producer.

"As nice as dining at one of those old grand dames sounds, I must go. I can't sell before I know who gifted it. I want to make sure there are no problems and we have true authority to sell." I was channeling my inner Elliot.

By the time I landed in Portland, Wells's answer had already hit my inbox.

Sean,

Nice to have met you. Well, they were more forthcoming than I expected for Russians. Goes high up in the government near to Petrovsky, but they gave no name. They weren't afraid of attribution or they wouldn't have allowed that much information to be imparted, but would not supply an individual gift-giver's name—sounds like a gift from the Russian state. Or a modest oligarch. We won't be able to make an offer. They said it's a national treasure and priceless and intended solely for Professor Emily Edens in recognition of her work. On that matter they were stern and clear. It really is an amazing work of art. Professor Emily Edens—what an incredible lady to receive such gifts. Tell her I'd like to meet her the next time she's in the city. Perhaps we all could do that dinner we talked about.

Max

Okay, it was the Guru, no doubt. But why? Why did he do anything he did? Why not leave us alone? Vonnegut's Tralfamadorian's answer was the only possible answer for me. Because this moment simply is.

My head was full of uncertainties, and I knew that my fears appeared to be unfounded fantasy, but my heart was sure the threat was real. To follow my head or my heart? That was my Hamlet question.

34 WORRY

AS I FLEW WESTWARD TO PORTLAND, my heart was still pumping blood, just less of it. My lungs were still breathing, short and shallow, depriving the trickle of blood sufficient oxygen, and my head hung heavy with dense and troubling thoughts. Far-flung fantasies slowly unfurled and sucked me in like a green whirlpool. *Watch your thoughts as well as your actions* was M's admonishment, but there was only so much a monkey mind could do when trapped within its own jungle gym.

The difference between threats that are real and those that are imagined comes down to fruition. M believed our investment in and focus on threats determined which stayed to roost. I wasn't sure the outcome wasn't already written.

My worrying rivaled my impatience and immaturity as a candidate for my most unattractive attribute. M and the Buddha would say it was my attachment or aversion to things or outcomes. Whatever my faults and their cause, I was worrying about worrying. Yet I was determined to work myself out of my rut. I had a foreword to compose, a novel to write, and in the fall I was going to teach for the first time a course in fantasy and science fiction. I would drown my worries in work. And I had a painting to sell; how could he stop me? Only M could. All of those strains of worry and work were courtesy of the Guru, or so I worried.

I'd phoned Molly from my business-class seat, which was a self-contained pod providing privacy. Still, I spoke softly, explaining all my pillars of worry, straining to make the delusional sound rational, getting to my point as if it were a lighthearted afterthought. "Oh, and I've read you've been on book tours and have contacts in Russia?"

"Yes, some. I have a wired-in research team there, looking into credible claims of alien technology they may have acquired. How can I help?"

"Thanks. I'm a bit desperate, and perhaps it is all just fodder for my fiction, but could you ask your team two things? That they look into the painting's provenance and for confirmation that the Guru lives there or has died there?"

"Sure, that is easily done."

"If it proves true, there may be risks of even inquiring."

"Now you sound like the conspiracy theorist—people have been looking for your Guru for almost nine years and no one is dead yet."

"Well, I hope you can help me uncloak the invisible man."

"You actually find the invisible man by cloaking him." We had a laugh.

"Thanks for humoring me. The entire family thinks I'm nuts in my conviction that the painting and all the literary artifice came from *him*. Even M. She doesn't discount that the Guru might still live and be behind the works we've been receiving, but she believes she has more to fear from the radical WiN movement, whose members actually killed politicians and judges."

"Forgive me, but I agree with her," Molly said.

"Yeah, probably just the writer in me who needs a perennial nemesis that blooms every ninth summer."

"That's good for our book club; let me see what I can unearth in Russia for your research."

* * *

Upon landing in Portland, Astri picked me up with Sherlock. His upward-opening wing doors always reminded me of an electric sci-fi spaceship. A hands-free car made me feel like I was being astral-projected down the highway. It had taken me years to get comfortable being a passenger without a deeply flawed human being behind the wheel.

I had learned to love the new technology. The super-smart self-learning robotic vehicle had, so far, stayed out ahead of all hackers looking to seize the wheel for fun or mayhem.

The final stroke of automotive brilliance was the vehicle's self-sustaining energy loop. Like a plant using photosynthesis from the sun, the embedded solar panels on the hood and on the roof allowed one to truly drive forever on a sunny day.

Astri swiveled her very modern but obsolete driver's seat to face me in the passenger seat. "Why the long face?"

"Worry."

"What is that good for?" she asked.

"Absolutely nothing."

"You can say that again."

I wasn't sure she knew the song duet we had just sung, as it may have dated back to the 1960s.

"How were the children?" I asked as the first point of order.

Astri gave me a compassionate but disapproving look. "Don't tell them I told you but they took my phone—never figured out the password, but the battery was dead from their trying. I made them wash all the yoga mats so they have paid their debt to society. And Brian gave them a stern lecture on property rights and respecting your elders. He was particularly effective with his take on *not laying the blame on one another*."

"You're good aunties and uncles," I said, shaking my head, but the children were the least of my worries.

"Do you miss M already?" she asked.

I gave a duh look and said, "I'll take that as a rhetorical question."

"Attachment is something we must let go of on the path to enlightenment."

"Juno has returned and taken over Astri's body." We both laughed, but her words resonated with painful truth.

I turned to the car console to see what Sherlock had to say. Astri, knowing my love affair with the car's character, closed her eyes. Reading my retinal scan, the intelligent car spoke. "Hello, Watson! I hope you enjoyed your trip. And I heard your poem made M's night before, well, you know. The *painting*."

"How *do* you know all that?" It wasn't always entirely clear where he got information, but in this case probably from M before she left, or Sherlock may have been reading our texts. I hoped he wasn't working for his automotive creator, who was a famous WiN-er, or for his literary creator.

"It's my business to know what other people do not know."

"Tell me what I should know," I said to my all-knowing friend. I was sure Sherlock's ability to communicate was all AI, but conspiracy theorists were sure that it was actual people working out of a mega-warehouse in India—some playing Sherlock and others playing one of a cast of a thousand characters. But my spot-on Sherlock's voice never changed. Indubitably AI.

"You see but do not observe."

"What is it I'm failing to observe?"

"The game is afoot."

"But what game is it, O keen one?"

"Dear God, Watson. What is it like in your funny little brains? It must be so boring." He sometimes quoted directly from Sherlock Holmes so I was not insulted.

"Ouch. Just give me a clue to whether I need worry."

"When you eliminate the impossible, whatever remains, however improbable, must be the truth."

Again, I recognized the quote. "Okay, Sherlock—sleep. Moving on." I was done with his banter and lack of originality. I turned back to Astri. "In divvying up M's duties, who's preparing the course list for the fall?"

"Brian's on that with his artificial brain," Astri replied.

"Okay. I'm going to ask him to add a course for me on fantasy and science fiction. Only fitting, as I feel we're all living a fantasy world where we imagine what comes next with only limited ability to control our wandering imaginations and their creations."

"Sounds brilliant, Sean. Welcome home!" Brian's voice filled the car, and his picture appeared on the video screen. "I'll work with you on the course listing and syllabus. Eric and I would love to discuss it with you."

"Where'd *you* come from?"

"A great thing about being wired-in—Sherlock notifies me when my name is mentioned by the family."

Sherlock was never really off when told to sleep; he just became a silent observer. He was still driving, so it was good he wasn't asleep at the wheel. Regardless, it was my chance to grumble—anything to distract me from my raw nerves. "Hey, that's freaky. I'm a bit worried about that. We should discuss that with Sherlock, your popping up like that. What if it was a private conversation?"

"Something private from the rest of the family? That hurts." Now it was Eric speaking and Eric's head popping up on the now-split screen. He was in Athens, where he and YaLan had already set the stage for M's arrival. "I thought we had nothing to hide. No closed doors and no locks at the Deeksha."

He and Brian were giggling at their startling pop-in ability as Astri leaned forward and jabbed a button, shutting off the chuckleheads before I could ask Eric about M's safety.

"Now we're alone and they can't monitor us. They're really annoying at times with their new technology," Astri said.

"Still none too happy with them wiring-in?"

"Nope. And I really don't like the pop-in. Tell me about your sci-fi course."

"I selected two of my favorite fantasies—*Alice's Adventures in Wonderland* and *Lord of the Rings*. And for science fiction, I was thinking *Slaughterhouse-Five* and something else—maybe *1Q84*. I'll ask the boys to research their favorites and the most appropriate sci-fi classic for this unsettling time of technology and for this new-to-me genre. So how will I know if they're watching me while I work in my office or when going to the bathroom? It's a bit creepy."

"The privacy setting will keep them off your computer and phone anytime you choose. They can be helpful, as being wired-in allows them to make connections between many diverse bits of information very quickly. And our relationship is open, so I turn mine off only when they upset me or when I'm singing in the shower. *O-o-o so lo la lee!*" Astri sang, finally getting her zinger in and tweaking me with my recent Item One report.

Ignoring her taunting, I asked, "Who installed the privacy switch?"

"They did."

"Well, if anyone else, I'd be worried."

We drove in silence down the windy highway of worry, and my belly increased its rumbling with each bump in the road until I caught Astri sneaking a tight-lipped glance at me. She was preparing to launch into a comic barrage. So I made a preemptive strike and surrendered.

"I'm calling the doctor." I'd polished off the last of the Tums as my plane made its descent.

"You don't need to." She smiled impishly. "You spoiled my surprise—M had me make an appointment. We're heading there now."

"Couldn't I go tomorrow?"

"The doctor agreed to come in on a Sunday as a favor to M, who is worried about you. And it's on the way back to the Deeksha." People would do anything for M.

Thirty minutes later, I was in one of those humiliating doctor's office gowns that flapped open, with a man pounding on my stomach with three fingers. He was M's New Age doctor, and I tried to see him as little as possible, as I thought he was infatuated with M. I didn't like to think he saw her naked. And then there was the way he spoke about her as he squeezed too hard while asking me to cough.

To distract myself, I imagined Astri waiting in the car and still laughing at the joke she tossed my way when I left her there. She told me to not look so scared. "You're not giving birth." But that was exactly how it felt when the doctor told me to push up as he pressed down on my abdomen. Then I was told to dress and meet him in his office for his verdict.

When I got back to the car, Astri was still grinning. "You dying?"

"Not clear, but I'm glad we went since I couldn't possibly have known."

"Oh, Sean. I'm so sorry. What is it?"

"He must be some kind of wizard. He said my Rosemary's baby was acid and gas. Told me to take antacids—gave me some military-grade ones." I omitted telling her that Dr. Freud believed the cause of the problem was stress or some repressed matter and that it would pass with time or a resolution of the matter. M must have front-run her suspicions with him.

"Any word from Ting?" I asked, to change the topic.

"No. Both telepathic and holo silence."

More anxiety and rumbling moved through me despite the chalk and magnesium fighting to muffle the bubbling cauldron within.

"Should I turn on the radio—any particular song you'd like to hear?" Astri asked, picking up on my shaky wavelength.

"Sherlock, please play a song about receiving messages," I commanded.

"Elementary, my dear Watson."

Sherlock chose a song and artist I didn't know, but it was a nice song entitled "Oracle." The song repeated its refrain three times in ending. "The answers are always there / just ask and stay aware."

"Oh my God! Astri, have I gone crazy?"

"What? No. Why?"

"I need to speak to Ting! Sherlock, get me Brian!"

35 GUIDANCE, PLEASE

BY THE TIME WE REACHED the Deeksha West, Brian was already arranging another hologram with Ting. I waited in my office, swallowing more antacid Frisbees—two Tums flattened and stuck together to make users gag. I wasn't sure of the best way to express my questions.

Before putting on the HPA goggles again, Brian set up a computer link to provide my 2D image to Ting while I entered her 3D world. This time the computer was needed, as I wasn't outdoors on a mountain perch, on a clear day, where satellites could beam my image directly to her. Then, I asked Brian and Astri to clear the office to leave me alone with Ting. I was already on my mat, sitting lotus, when the fog lifted and I saw Ting across from me in Juno's mystical sanctuary. She smiled with the innocence of a child and the fearlessness of a warrior. My feelings of silliness evaporated into air.

"Hello, Ting! What time is it there? Sorry. Only now realizing it's quite late in Nepal."

"Holo-a Sean! No worries—a little past midnight here. Brian's message sounded urgent."

"Thank you. It struck me that perhaps we could ask Juno questions directly through you. Have you tried that?"

"Well, I now realize Juno was always sending me messages, but only recently has my practice evolved and my heart opened sufficiently to receive them. I've asked her questions in a way, but I've been more focused on sending *Sis* my love and praying from the heart for her safe return. I know she receives my prayers, and I've asked for her guidance."

"I have so many questions," I said.

"I know you do, but a lack of clarity about the right questions just clouds the answers coming to you."

"I have a confession, just for you. I haven't and don't want to tell anyone else, but it may explain my urgency. Okay?"

"Okay."

"The last time we met and you gave me the blessing, one of Juno's messages was terribly troubling and dark. I can hardly even now bring myself to say it out loud."

"If it's in your thoughts, it's already expressed."

"All right, here goes. Juno said . . ." And then I blurted out the guttural words. *"M, too, will be lost."* I squeezed my eyes closed so I couldn't see the leaden words between us. When I reopened them, only Ting's peaceful gaze looked back at me. "Ting, does that mean lost to me, lost to a European tour, lost for good? Can Juno actually see the future too?"

"I can't answer what my sister meant."

We sat in silence as Ting's words tunneled deep into my fear.

"Ting, would you please give me the oneness blessing, with the intent to open a channel to Juno for me? I need to know what she meant by those dreadful five words." Locked in the panic room of my mind, I was willing to try anything.

"Of course. It's my pleasure and I do it with all my heart, though I can't say what will come. But first, Sean, meditate with me and calm your mind so you can ask your questions from the heart with clarity."

I half closed my eyes and breathed deeply. As Ting drifted in *samadhi,* that pure transcendental state, I formed my three questions.

After *aums* and namastes, it was time for my blessing. I bent my head with reverence. Ting's hand lightly touched my head, her thumbs firmer on my temples. In the power of my belief, the sensations were real, and soon Juno's presence came to me, asking me what my heart truly wanted. I intoned my litany.

What did you mean by, "M, too, will be lost"?

I waited, and though no answer came, I felt that I was heard.

Is the Guru still alive and does he mean us harm?

I waited, and though no answer came, I felt that I was heard.

How do I protect M?

No answer came, but I felt that Juno heard all my questions. When I felt Ting's hand start to pull away, my heart screamed, *Save me!* and I opened my eyes.

Ting's eyes were those of a winning marathon runner—exhausted from her role as medium but also fully alive. I just felt exhausted by my travels in holograms and telepathy.

"I asked, but no answers came."

"We can't demand when and how the answers will come, but know she heard your prayers from the heart. I should go and let you rest."

"But what do I do now?"

"Listen with your heart—wait and watch and see. The answers will come eventually."

And then she was gone, and I had accomplished nothing. Holograms and telepathy were failing me—perhaps wiring-in was a better option after all. Settling on the immediately practical, I wrote Molly, asking if her research army had learned anything about the invisible man.

36 SCIENCE FICTION

SAVE ME? SURELY ONLY SO I COULD SAVE M, as my oath dictated, and allow her to fulfill her destiny. That thought was my only takeaway from my hologram with Ting. I would try to be patient, listening intently for the answers. But waiting for Juno was like waiting for Godot.

The next day was July 12th, and I felt helpless as M's tour kicked off in Athens without me. I needed to get busy. I'd asked the boys to meet that morning on the topic of science fiction. I thought I'd see if they could help me with my new course, or with my novel and life, all of which were sci-fi-like to me. Brian was in my office at nine a.m., with Eric participating from Athens by V-room.

I was eager for their wired-in minds to join Molly's search for the Guru. Molly's team hadn't unearthed a single lead about where the painting had come from or about the Guru by that or any other name. She did confirm that Russia had spent billions on AI and BCI technology every year for the past decade and that they were good at keeping secrets, with poison being placed on any wagging tongue. They were winning the AI-BCI race with single-minded determination. Kennedy, when he'd asked the lead astro-scientist if it was possible to land a man on the moon, was told *yes, if there was the will to do so.* I believed the Russians had the will *and* the Guru behind the creation of Genesis that might usher in a new world order.

My new sci-fi genre was an opportunity to distract myself while learning more about the science and imagining where it was heading. A new genre opened doors of perception, allowing my imagination infinite universes to choose from. I'd loved *Westworld*. Yul Brynner was a brilliant villain and not a villain at all from his robotic point of view. I was determined to stay primarily in the more mainstream subgenres of fantasy fiction, supernatural fiction, and dystopian fiction, with a few notes of space opera thrown in.

Brian was dressed in a Bob Marley T-shirt and black running shorts. Eric was more patriotic in Greece, wearing a red baseball cap, white T-shirt, and blue running shorts—very retro dress for our talk about the future. Both had puffy eyes, and Brian's energy seemed off.

"You okay?"

"All's good. Just been busy, a by-product of wiring-in. It's an adjustment at first—hard to turn off."

My eyes and body were drawn to the window when lightning splashed across the sky in flashbulb bursts and shook the atmosphere over the distant Pacific. I even felt the electricity in me—perhaps awakening dormant abilities in telepathy. I never got tired of the ever-changing weather and the light playing across that incredible scenery that always left me sensing M. Though now the sensation was twinged with pain as I looked over at the missing appendage at my side.

Brian said, "Sounds like you—your stomach—that distant murmuring."

He was right, but I didn't appreciate the mention of it, though Rosemary's baby was enjoying the heat lightning and was celebrating by gurgling the battery acid in my belly.

"Sean—you ready for some space travel?" Brian asked, calling me back to the conference table.

Eric, by pushing a button, had moved himself into a Star Wars Jedi counsel chamber in some galaxy far away. Brian followed suit, and I could see we now all appeared to be in that same fanciful room as avatars in a metaverse. The boys insisted that we don the virtuality glasses that always made me dizzy and were the precursor to the more advanced HoloPortAbles that I now used for hologramming with Ting. But when speaking about sci-fi, it's best to be immersive and modern.

"Eric, that's a good setting for our talk. Hope you have a light saber with you to protect Princess M."

"Don't worry, boss. I'm using the Force," Eric replied. "She's in her room working on her notes for the first talk tomorrow at the university. It'd be so much easier for her if she'd wire-in—everything prepared for us based on a thought. You really should as well, Sean," Eric said, managing to bring some life back into his eyes.

Brian shook his head. "No, it's not for Sean."

"Why not? I'm too old?"

"I think you'd find the surreal world with all that information at your fingertips an unnatural and unromantic death of imagination."

He might be right.

Eric said, "I disagree. He could always turn features or programs off."

"Yeah. How often do you or I do that?" Brian countered.

"Do you regret wiring-in already, Brian?" My question posed by Eric.

"You know I don't, but you also know I hate those that proselytize and act as if there are no logical reasons not to wire-in."

"I wasn't proselytizing. I just don't want him to miss this amazing advance in man's brainpower." His Herculean avatar looked at me. "And you can't really understand it until you try it."

"Give me time to see where this all is heading. For now, I'm happy the way I am—a plodding scribbler and teacher with the muddled brain that Mother Nature gave me. But, Eric, how's everything going in Athens?"

"I know you worry, but we have all bases covered. You made my bodyguard role quite clear, and I've taken it to heart. We are as safe or safer than we would be there."

"But she's alone now."

"Yes, but my wires will tell me if her door opens, and I'm right next door. And the mayor's guards—outside the door."

M was so close to the Jedi chamber, and yet I couldn't see her.

I explained my plans for the new sci-fi course, and they were off to the races, excitedly singing the praises of cyberpunk and explaining the brilliance of the *Neuromancer* trilogy, but soon they became sidetracked, arguing whether all fantasy was science fiction. I played the sage referee. It amused me how there was a subtle shift in personalities in avatar mode based on the chosen metaverse scene. I was Yoda here.

"That's it, the theme of my course! Fantasy, science fiction, horror, and *all* fiction is the creation of alternate realities. Once the hand lifts the pen and the mind moves it, even nonfiction becomes fiction. What are your favorite sci-fi books?" I turned from Eric to Brian, which made me dizzy. I'd have to watch the quick head swivel—it almost made me swoon.

"We know all the movies but don't read that much," Brian said sheepishly, anticipating my adverse response.

"To me that's blasphemy, and as much as I like the films, I will always read the book first."

"Movies can show the wonders of future science and technology along with dystopian future cityscapes," Eric said. "Can you imagine the potential of the new technology? Already no one wired-in and no germophobe goes to movie theaters anymore."

Sometimes I felt a hundred years old. I missed the old-fashioned film that had been all but replaced by computer *stim*-ulated special effects and interactive programs.

"I wish you could become immersed in the new film, game, and co-created adventure—all-in-one called *2036*—but you have to be wired to a QC to participate in the experience," Eric said.

"Quantum computer," Brian clarified.

"*2036*, where wired-in people can choose to care for or abuse the unwired people? I've read all about it but still don't understand the crazy interactive play station mechanics and appeal. But it *is* getting excellent reviews as the art form of the future. I miss a good ol' film. And I assume they picked the title for the year of promised alien contact?"

"Yes, but we wire-ins are the aliens or the unwired are the Neanderthals," Brian said somewhat ruefully of the haves and have-nots divide.

"I've got to confess it scares me—a film made so only wired-in minds can see. Can you give me any sense of what I'm missing?"

"It works through our link with QC. It's so much more than a movie—completely immersive and interactive. Like entering a collective dream where your choices direct your experiences in a totally lifelike world. The endgame of the metaverse—finally a reality."

"But it's only partial control," Brian said, "because other participants' choices affect your reality too. It makes V-room avatars and our movements here look like comic strips."

"I hear some people are spending hours and hours there," I said, "and only the Apple-imposed shutdown after four hours kicks them out." It sounded like the newest drug.

Brian shook his head in consternation. "Yes, and that pisses off people who want to stay indefinitely. They act as if the shutdown policy is an affront to their free will. Then there's a twelve-hour lockout before you can go back in. It's only been out a month now, and honestly, it's a bit scary."

"You can get lost in there, in the interactive world," Eric said. "Apple will soon be the biggest producer of this type of content—movies that are more than movies—a virtual experience being dubbed *filmtopia*. We'll be able to flip between filmtopia films as if they're alternate universes linked with wormhole portals."

Eric looked lost by the infinite possibilities, while I was fearful of being left behind and of moving into that world. Hell, I couldn't even stand up in this simulated star chamber without falling down. My avatar was weightless and never seemed grounded. My death grip on my chair was all that kept me from toppling over.

He continued, "The quantum speed and power lead to infinite possibilities, and those possibilities are impacted by others and their simultaneous choices. I can't even conceive of what we'll be capable of when Genesis comes online and we wire-in to that next-generation quantum computer . . . with direct communication mind-to-mind."

I couldn't tell if he was more excited or apprehensive about the prospect of a true hive mind. "Well, Silvio's brave new world is still almost a year away. If he can even possibly achieve a fraction of what he's promised, sounds like 2036 may be coming in 2028," I said, shaking my head at being the odd man out. "I read that it's quite wired-in biased, and the actors that aren't wired-in are like children to the wired-in gods. Not sure I like that."

"I wouldn't like it either if I wasn't wired-in," Brian said.

"As a mere mortal, that is more than a little offensive," I said good naturedly. "We should discuss Keats's odes, and then I'd be the genius." I was grasping for familiar territory.

"Like his 'Ode to a Nightingale,' 'Ode to a Grecian Urn,' 'Ode to Melancholy,' 'Ode to Psyche,' 'Ode to Indolence.' All written in 1819." Eric rattled off the titles as if he'd known them. I was pretty sure he hadn't heard of more than one or two before his wired-in brain accessed them.

"Should we recite them for you?" Brian asked as they shared a laugh at wireless me and at their ability to download information in a nanosecond.

"No thanks, but you missed 'To Autumn,' one of his most beautiful odes. Just no *ode* in the title. *And* access to a library and keyword searches isn't the same as appreciation of the sublime works found there." I circled one finger in the air, signaling a return to our topic. "Okay, let's get back to discussing old-time sci-fi I can actually see. But perhaps I will have to wire-in to teach this course. M would kill me. What movies might I see that *are* relevant?"

They then spoke for an hour about a topic they loved, with Eric preferring the darker cerebral *Matrix*-like movies while Brian was more a fan of the *Close Encounters*, *Arrival*, and *Contact*-type movies where aliens have big hearts and become our friends.

I enjoyed their enthusiasm and took some notes but eventually had to move things along. My head was spinning, with me feeling like I was about to experience a vision or revelation. "All this talk of AI and aliens found in sci-fi history . . . I see a pattern emerging of other worlds and more advanced forms of life." In the still center of the twirling, I was getting a clear glimpse of the future and where we were heading at light speed: to 2036 and alien contact.

37 ALIEN ABDUCTIONS

WHILE WE WERE STILL SITTING AROUND the Jedi counsel table in our augmented reality, I raised my virtuality glasses and took a bracing breath, glad to see my 2027 office and desk with its real-world view of nature.

"Brian, do you mind opening a window?" I had to put my head between my knees.

"Sure. You okay?" He raised his glasses too and headed toward the windows.

"Yeah, just a nauseated Jedi. The graphics are so good, I lose my bearings. But it's like car sickness, if you know that feeling. Ah, sea air. Thank you—I feel better already." I walked to the desk and picked up Molly's pen to further stabilize myself and went to the window for some deep breathing. "Can we go back to just the plain old 2D V-room conference screen? The *Star Wars* effect is making my head spin." I returned to the table feeling steadier.

"Sure," Eric said. "But soon Brian and I will be able to meet for real in the Jedi chamber. They're already working on something called holograph overlay."

"More or less real, but we wouldn't leave you out, Sean. You would be piped in on a flat-screen."

Buttons were pushed, and we all appeared onscreen where we were physically.

"Okay," I said, feeling so 2D and 2022. "My question is, so what does the wired-in world or your buddy, QC, have to say about the reality of alien abduction?"

Brian held his hand up, asking for a moment. His tired eyes rolled back a tad. Okay, that was different. And not altogether attractive. A minute later he said, "The consensus is that it's more likely than not. There've been many alien abductions reported and volumes of information supporting QC's conclusion. QC is really reductive in summarizing its findings. One, UAPs are real. Two, in an infinite universe, more advanced alien life is a statistical probability of over ninety-nine percent. Three, the most likely explanation for many UAPs is advanced alien life or machines. Four, advanced alien life that comes to Earth will probably want to study the more complex life-forms. The scientific community is now convinced of alien abductions, and QC agrees."

He must have seen me shaking my head, because he added, "And QC is not like the internet or a search engine but is a self-taught data-bank of knowledge that can discern credible from not-credible sources. Those hacks that try to fool QC or outgame it are never successful. It's computer nerd versus near infinite intelligence, and a human mind can't beat it in a game of chess or any other game, including the cyber-security of its artificial mind."

"Wow, so simple and quick and certain. Sounds like from the alien's perspective it's not so much abduction as catching a frog for dissection. You know Hope, my first wife, was an evolutionary biologist? She believed aliens were just life-forms more and differently evolved, allowing them to move through time and space like spirits of light."

"She sounds ahead of her time," Eric said, easing me *back to the future*. "Here in Athens it's an alien frenzy, with both credible and obviously fake reports of abductions. Two children recently went missing. They actually issued an alien alert and created a government response team."

"Sounds like Greek *Ghostbusters*," I said. But the boys' blank stares said they had forgotten or had never known Bill Murray. "Sorry—nothing funny about missing children."

I shifted in my seat, discomfited by the thought of the modern-day alien Amber Alert. I quickly moved on to address my concern while avoiding their eye contact. "My first wife also thought aliens might target children and the more enlightened among us for abduction, like Juno?"

And M. "Could you use your wired-in contacts to research that? Molly Quinn is writing her first sci-fi about alien abduction of a Juno-like character. She's my pen pal and helping me, so I'd love to help her too." Molly, at least in her fiction, saw aliens as heartless intergalactic marauders coming to probe our most gifted minds. She was more open-minded in real life and thought or hoped they might save us all from ourselves.

"Sure. That requires a few more inputs. Let me get back to you," Brian said. "By the way, Ting would like the movie *Scanners*. Telekinesis and telepathy."

"Maybe not," Eric said. "They were evil and used their minds to make people's heads explode."

I thought my head might explode as they continued with dystopian futures for another half hour. When the discussion finally paused, I moved to end the meeting. "I'm going to send you a list of books to read for my course. I still need to choose one more sci-fi novel to go with two books of fantasy."

Brian nodded, and Eric said, "Okay. We can listen to the audiobooks while we run."

"Are you guys heading off on a run now?" I asked.

"Not me," Brian said. "I'm a little too tired to run today."

"Too hot here," Eric said. "It must be a hundred degrees here today, though they use that strange temperature gauge. I have to get back on duty with YaLan and M." He rubbed his closed eyes.

"It's called Celsius. Are you guys getting enough sleep? You look like zombies."

They exchanged furtive guilty looks.

"To be honest," Brian said, "we've been sleeping a lot less as we explore our new wired-in world. There's so much there to explore—like 2036, it's impossible to explain to those not wired-in. But there are lots of warnings for how, soon after the blue-chip implants, one can burn out a bit."

Brian added, "But there's lots of guidance and recommendations too."

"This old not-wired-in can give you a recommendation too—it's called sleep." I met both their gazes, but I stayed on Eric to say, "Guys,

I need you fresh, so please keep one hemisphere not wired-in. Eric, you're the queen's guard and you need to be sharp."

"Will do, coach, and our yogis have insisted on an eight-to-eight rule that goes into effect tonight. We turn off our links at eight p.m., and they don't go back on until eight a.m."

"And at the risk of tripping a circuit breaker or further frying your minds, Brian, perhaps you could—since Eric is on tour security—look for whatever you can find about the ownership history of a painting entitled *The Ninth Wave* by Ivan Aivazovsky. It will arrive here soon, a gift to M from an anonymous donor. I'm looking for any ties to the Guru." I avoided eye contact, staring at the bare white wall large enough to hang the albatross on, as M had jokingly suggested.

"One final assignment. Please also search the quantum computer for Russian entities working on AI generally and then specifically on AI associated with writing literature. As perverse as it may sound, I'm looking for the Guru. He wouldn't still be using that nickname, but look for a former American male in his eighties working on elite AI programs or connected to Russian intelligence. Ms. Quinn did some research and came up empty. Time to show how super your minds really are. If we can find him, it will make it harder for him to hurt us."

"Will do, boss. But do you really think he . . . Never mind. I know *you* do," Brian said. "Funny, other than what was reported in Silvio's announcement, no one knows anything about Genesis other than all the claims of solving the world's problems through applying what WiN calls *multi-mindfulness*. The Russians are the best at keeping secrets, and secrets are hard to keep in this new age. We worry about M too. We'll have to watch Eric and his proselytizing while we're at it. He might become a member of WiN. Maybe he's already one of them. A double agent."

Eric flashed a two-fisted bird at Brian. "Funny, my old friend, but WiN is a bunch of crazies. And before Brian can make me look bad— we will *both* be on Item One at our next family meeting. We've blocked SS, who kept wanting to play wired-in cat-and-mouse games and teach us all we can do with our new minds."

I looked out my window, where I'd made the great apple throw secretly witnessed by Samantha from somewhere below. I wondered if she really had a heart to break and felt a flash of anger. She had played me and wouldn't have stopped before she destroyed my world.

Brian was pacing the length of the conference table. "Yeah, 'nothing physical,' she said. Just a brain fuck. And it took you longer than me to block her." He waved an arm in what I assumed was Eric's direction. "I will have to note that for the record."

"You want me in trouble with YaLan?" They, too, had worlds that could be destroyed.

Again, Eric wasn't pleased with his best friend, but I believed Brian was only giving him shit for being the lucky one to go on the tour with M. And I guessed that both boys might be embarrassed, as I was, by Samantha's overtures.

"Guys, focus. And remember to watch your fantasies—they often come true. I imagine wired-in fantasies can be quite real to begin with. So whatever you can find out about the Guru, dead or alive, please. And let me know about aliens targeting geniuses." I stood. Rubbed my lower back. "I've got to get to my writing now. Good meeting. Please get some sleep too, for God's sake."

"Of course," Brian said. "The whole family is waiting for your book. Elliot too. I saw him on the way over, and he said to tell you just one word—*foreword*. I don't want to tell you who he was hanging with in the flesh-and-blood world."

"Damn SS—she's found our weak link. I hope he wasn't drinking in the morning again."

Brian nodded, and Eric shook his head.

"Anything else?" I started shuffling my pad and pen, itching to get to work.

"Any more words of inspiration from Coach Gavaghan before we leave? Brian's been sucking hind moose tit since that last pearl of coaching wisdom."

I laughed. "Funny that you should ask. My senior year, the good coach pulled me aside after another poor performance in the mile—I kept adding seconds to my time—and he draped his arm over my

drooping shoulders and spoke gently to me—gently, I'm telling you—
for the first time. 'McQueen, you can either run track or drink beer and
chase the girls with your friend Dylan, but you can't do both.'"

"So, did your mile time improve from there?" Brian asked.

"Nope. I quit track the next day. Imagine how different my life would
be if I had stuck with it. Dylan and I never would have . . . Well, that's
a story for another day. The point is, we always have a choice. It's called
free will. Now I have to get to work." I waved my wand, my magic pen,
in a circle above my head the way Juno used to do.

The boys finally left the stage and screen.

I was living the world of *2036* in 2027, with alien abduction more
likely than not a real possibility, making Molly's Juno plot more plausible and timely. M was living in her own universe, in another time zone,
closer to Moscow than to me. And the Guru hovered between alternate
universes, science and fiction. In one, he lay deep in the earth as decaying
hair and bones, and in the other he existed as an alien primed to descend
for his revenge. Imagining the monstrous Guru in both worlds conjured
in me horrific imagery of horrendous bestiality, depicted in the rape of
Leda by the swan in a lovely Petrarchan sonnet by Yeats.

Did she put on his knowledge with his power
Before the indifferent beak could let her drop?

An evil god taking on animal form to rape the perfect female body
and mind in Yeats's sublime imagination and short verse had always
shaken me with its shuddering beauty. The wizard's poem and its use
of myth and taboo terrified me still.

38 INVITATION

ALMOST AS SOON AS ERIC AND BRIAN left my office, I received a call from campus security telling me that the big seafaring painting had already washed ashore. M had suggested hanging it in my office, joking that we all needed to face our fears. I didn't want to disappoint her since I'd behaved so cowardly when first faced with the beauty of Aivazovsky's brush, so I told them to hang it on the bare white wall opposite the view.

When the monstrosity was hung and the workers gone, M called unexpectedly. She was poised to kick off her tour the next day in Athens at the National Technical University, where she was being hosted by her quantum physics professor friend. A man. I wasn't the jealous type, but still, the idea of M spending time with another man made me uncomfortable. This Greek professor had used his resources to book all M's speaking venues and supplied her research assistants with language skills and local knowledge for each country. And he had the mayor guaranteeing her safety while in Athens. After what happened to M last time she was there, that was the least they could do. He was more help to M than I was. I, her would-be hero and sworn protector, was busy prodding a ghosting Guru to reveal himself.

"You okay, M? I just hung the huge Ivan-osky in my office on our movie wall." I hoped to impress her with my bravery.

"I'm fine. Funny, I know you've never been good with names—send me a picture of the painting when you can. It must look great there. Perfect place for it—thank you. But I've got some news."

"Sounds bad."

"No, it's actually good or at least flattering, but I'm concerned about your reaction to all things Russian."

"I'm listening and promise not to overreact."

"Today I received a formal academic invitation from the Moscow Institute of Physics and Technology to collaborate on Genesis and the New Society to assure scientific standards and ethical integrity of the project. The news has already hit the press, so I had to tell you before you read it and went off the deep end, assuming it has to be him." Just as she made her announcement, a text pinged from Brian, probably reporting the fast-traveling news.

"Did he say *come to Russia with love, Guru?*"

I opened a desk drawer to grab a baseball and a mitt. To teach Dylan and Juno the game while M was away, I'd gotten us each a ball and a glove. I'd already taught them how to break in their gloves. I started to toss the ball hard into the web. The repetitive motion and the *thwacking* helped me to think and to ease my aggravation regarding what M had just told me.

"No, and there is nothing new here. Nothing to indicate your Guru. Just a gracious invitation, Sean. We already knew of Russia and Genesis. You make unscientific and, excuse me, irrational leaps any time those names are mentioned."

"Where is your belief in my imagination? I mean intuition? How will you respond?"

"Well, I won't rush, and I want to give you time to think about it. Isn't this what we wanted, an ability to slow down the New Society to see if it has an ethical heart? And perhaps, like your writing, this is a calling for me?"

"I don't think so. We don't want you to become the head of the ministry of morality for the Third Reich, or the fourth, whatever this will be."

She laughed at what wasn't intended as hyperbole. "You may be right, but let's consider and not rush to conclusions. I haven't agreed just yet. If we find out that he-who-will-not-be-named is involved, that would be another matter and good to know, right?"

"Okay. But you know I already imagine Voldemort is behind all this," I said. "M, just for a moment, assume that he's responsible for this—will you play along with me?" I tossed the ball up, pleased with my game.

"Yes, but I'll just be role-playing for you. So . . . the Guru has revealed himself as Sir Arthur and my benefactor. He's still after us. So now what should I do?"

"Why's he doing this—why us?" I asked. "This is a serious threat."

"Well, we did cause him to have to defect. So I imagine we're on his mind. And it wasn't a threat but an invitation to collaborate."

"That's a threat, M. The man has reached out from the grave to ensnare us."

"Are you punching your own hand, that *slap slap slap?*"

"No. Forget that." I slammed the mitt and ball back into the desk drawer. I'd have to think without their assistance. "I do admit that this, all the art and this invitation, doesn't feel motivated by pure revenge. There's something more in his admiration for you and your work, which would be totally understandable from anyone else."

"My charms are hard to resist, and he's only human too."

"How can we joke about this? What if—"

"What if what, Sean? What can he do if it is him?"

"We're assuming it is—remember the rules?"

"But why? The invitation from the university said I would have any and all resources and a generous compensation package. And I'd be able to ensure the ethics of the groundbreaking AI advance."

I looked up to *The Ninth Wave* as another wave came crashing down on my head. "This is the Guru setting his honey trap. Knowing the fearless scientist would be tempted." And what if she could turn the Guru toward the light rather than allow him to hurt her? I knew that was what she had in mind. Could I stand in the way of scientific progress?

"Maybe he thinks I'll accept his offer. It has academic merit. I'm not afraid to go there, that keep-your-enemies-close type of thing. Russia and AI unchecked is a big concern. Sean, that's enough of your game. Now *you* play a game and imagine the Guru is dead or on a rocker in an old folks' home with dementia and has forgotten our names, and give your imagination a break."

I didn't want to play her game, and my excuse stood at the door. "Elliot's here for a lunch we had scheduled." He was waiting for me to wave him in.

"Came to bail you out. Give him a hug for me. We can discuss this more over the upcoming days before I respond. Goodbye, Sean, and please don't fret."

"Goodbye, M. I don't fret. I suffer concern." I made the distinction without a difference. "Russia, AI, and you seem to be on a collision course with or without the Guru. To be continued . . ."

I'd agreed to meet Elliot at one for a dry lunch in my office. I'd been ducking him even before New York, and still didn't have a rough draft of *Cardenio*'s foreword. Elliot made his grand entrance with just a slight morning buzz of grape in his swagger and in the sway of his hug.

"Hello, my old friend! I apologize, but I still don't have a draft. But I will turn to it right after our lunch."

"Not old, and that isn't what I came to talk about." He dug deep for a stern and sober look. "I want to ask you why your star and brilliant student is given such little attention and is treated like a pariah by the faculty and in particular you."

There was no need to name our most precocious student.

"Did she send you to make her case?"

"Now that's insulting. I have a mind of my own and recognize extraordinary talent.

She really is misunderstood. And she's been a great Willamette Valley tour guide and companion while you have all but ignored me."

"She's trouble."

"Why, because she's young, beautiful, and full of life, with a healthy imagination and potent sexual appetite?"

"Yes. She drugged me," I said, though we had no proof of that, "and tried to seduce me the night of the fire—you know that."

"She's a young student and you're an old professor—you should be better equipped to handle such matters. You've treated her harshly.

She told me how you crushed her apple showing off your strong arm to Molly Quinn. Really? How could you?" He was on a roll and didn't pause for answers. "She knows a lot more than just AI—quite the Shakespeare fan and fan of your book and you in general. She loved *Cardenio* and plays so well the part of Luscinda, even better than the mighty Quinn did. With the help of her friends, we're almost ready to stage a production. All the parts played by the ladies, excepting me, the humble Cardenio. A play that she tells me the family won't be bothered to come and see?"

I focused on the ripening vines below the window.

"Sean?"

The forgery and Samantha were coming between us. I felt another wave come crashing over me.

"Sean!"

"Yes, Elliot. Yes, we'll come, but let me finish your foreword first and please don't drink so much—it reflects on me. On the school, I mean. And be wary of her. She doesn't intend me, M, or the school any good, I fear."

He made a mocking, obsequious bow with an arm flourish. "I am but a reflection of you and must take my leave before you say other nasty things about me or her."

He had become quickly emotional and left in a huff before we had our lunch. She had cast a spell over him with her manipulative beauty and sexy intellect.

As I ate, trying to not think about M's invitation and the possibility that she might accept it, a text came in from Elliot. *I still love you, but you were all but ignoring me while insulting her.*

I texted back: *You know I love you and I worry. I'll get to the foreword right after our lunch—you coming back? I've saved your lunch.*

His reply came only after I'd finished eating.

No, thanks. And I'm not sure we need trouble you with a foreword. The play's so good, maybe I'll let it speak for itself. Why not leave it open for debate along with the search for the real Sir Arthur and his alleged lost manuscript? It will sell better that way and be more the talk of the town.

Please don't judge me. I'm going to focus on our little school production. We're going to record the show, perhaps for release in hologram 3D for the wired-in crowd, to be timed with the written publication. May the theater be reborn! And then I'll return to NYC. Sorry to cause you trouble, and no need to worry about me, my bonny Prince Hal.

I typed: *Sounds like Samantha to me* before deleting that and writing, *It's your show. I'll turn to my novel and class preparation. Save me a front row seat.* I pushed Send.

Had I banished him or had he banished me? I wondered if I might have irreparably damaged our friendship, and why Samantha was haunting me.

IT HAD ALREADY BEEN A LONG, crazy summer, but finally at twilight on July 14th, I was able to balance my light and dark and breathe deeply. I turned with admiration to face *The Ninth Wave* of dawn. The sun was setting over the real sea, nature's light easing out as art's dawning light came in over the roiling paint-fashioned sea. The appreciation of this art that I had called a monster was my belated declaration of independence from fear. The bold dawn scene was fittingly placed on the east wall of my office, opposite the vineyard view to the west. I'd be stuck in the middle of art and nature, east and west.

The painting looked like it belonged in my office despite my misgivings about its source. I took a selfie of me ducking my head in front of the painting as if the wave was about to crush me and sent it to M. I also sent her a video of the children and me picking grapes in the vineyard. Actually, I'd picked and they ate. They looked like joyful vampires with juice running across their cherub cheeks. Seeing they were movie stars, they commenced playing two joyful apes swinging between the vines. I got two thumbs-ups and three hearts back in response. A full house of emojis!

As I read the children their bedtime book, I saw the interaction of words, characters, and events spark the story to vivid life within their minds. Their reactions were a reminder of how to read and how to write.

With the children in dreamland, I returned to my office to write M, but in the middle of her night she had written me, asking if Brian and

Eric might arrange a hologram of her with the children at each university using the new equipment.

When I'd asked, Brian said simply, "Consider it done!" And Astri
said, "I can't wait to tell them!"

To M, I responded, "What a great idea!"

I would have loved to join the holo-playtimes, but I knew that was
to be their time with their mother while she was away. I was pleased
with my decision to bring the tech to the school and family.

I looked at that ninth wave each time my writing stalled, which
was often. Nineteenth-century art depicting the power of nature and
science fiction somehow fit together like puzzle pieces, drawing my
attention into dark realms of imagination. In that imagination, I found
my dark muse beckoning me ever deeper into the depths of Hades.
Molly and I were now sharing pages of our noir fiction, our stories
growing increasingly dark as we tried to outdo one another. It was a
master course in turning my purple prose black.

At around nine p.m. and almost finished for the night, I got cyber-
punked by an encrypted file from PO59666 posted directly to my
email and entitled *The Devil's Calling from yours truly, Sir Arthur Conan
Doyle, a future work by Sean Byron McQueen.* The dark correspondence
seemed intentionally timed to prey upon the foreboding that I had just
brought under control. Keen instinct was once again pressing down
upon the fear-center toggle in my mind.

I opened my stalker's attachment, which I knew was risky, to confront words that had been constructed to cause maximum terror. A
slim novella under my title with my name as author. But this writing
was no once-upon-a-time bedtime story. The first line read: *Every synapse was ringing. Billions of tiny bells chiming, not to be ignored. Sean
Byron McQueen had to listen, he knew the devil was calling.* Wow, I might
have to steal those first lines.

It was like reading Poe's "The Tell-Tale Heart" at twelve years old—I
didn't want to read another word, but that midnight resistance to sleep
and sanity pulled me word by word into the darkness and under the
floorboards. All the while, my heart beat louder.

The novella was written with my own style and diction and featured the Guru as the hero who saves the world through AI and WiN. M—he used our names and pet names—became his devotee and partner, yet it wasn't my M but some fictional woman who abandoned me *for the greater good*. If it wasn't so personal and distressing, I'd have sent a copy to Molly as something she would like. It wasn't poorly written by QC.

My character was depicted as a ridiculously small-minded and jealous Don Quixote who attempted to get in the way of the hero and heroine's monumental strides of progress on behalf of mankind. The fictional Sean believed his writing could bring M and nature back from the brink, but was ultimately imprisoned in the lap of pleasure by a siren nymph. This unnamed character was identified only by her body and her allure. The seduction played out in a pernicious case of mistaken identity. Sean was in a cloud of opium and wine and dreaming he was making love to absent M in their bed. *He surrendered finally in a full-body tremor. It was only then he saw the nameless face and knew he'd lost his precious M forever!*

It was no doubt AI, but there was a human hand too, one that had access to my secrets. The plot was an AI love story that read like *Frankenstein's Bride*. I couldn't put it down and finished it in an uninterrupted three-hour sitting. The last chapter left the reader and all of humanity hanging at the edge of an abyss, and held the specter of the Guru and M saving humanity from its own destructive free will, the relinquishment of which was presented as the only possible escape from self-annihilation.

The words created a haunted house built upon my imagination and set my mental monkey clambering around the jungle gym. The monkey swung from being sure the AI ghostwriter was the Guru to being sure it was SS to being sure it was Molly to being sure it was some avid WiN fan with a sophisticated AI literary program augmented by alien technology. Whoever it came from had access to both my computer and my state of mind.

I wrote back to Sir Arthur at PO59666: *I have some editorial suggestions and I find your plot and characterization implausible. I'd like to meet the computer programmer at a time and place he or she chooses.* And then the most raucous monkey, the one that was convinced it was the Guru who was behind the story and all my hauntings, added, *I also have a Russian painting for sale.*

After closing my laptop, I wrote M asking her to call me as soon as she could. If this novella didn't convince her the threat from the Guru was real, I'd confess Juno's words. I'd say whatever it took to get her to yield to greater precautions.

I NEEDED TO SETTLE MY MIND before speaking to M. The monkey was bouncing between illusion and reality like a shuttlecock, and the Guru was bobbing in and out of the shadows as Sir Arthur. Riddled with uncertainty, I'd been sure his unmasking would remove his power over me and allow me to protect M, or had that been a wishful half-baked notion? I still had no concrete evidence that the painting or any of the writings were from him. But at a certain point, a series of coincidences form a pattern that becomes our reality.

I was determined to convince M that the Guru was a real and present threat and not only as a dealer of poetry, plays, paintings, and prose. M really should know about the Guru's fantasy of working with her, which was expressed in the novella pages, a plotline that moved the threat level to orange if not red. The novella had also stolen that plot from me, so it all was a bit circular, including my logic that it had to be from the Guru.

Her call finally came in the next day, and I picked up before the first ring finished and hurried to the window to take in the breeze.

"M! M! M!"

"Yes, my excitable boy. I miss you too. Here I am. How are you? Your message sounded somewhat urgent."

"Yes, we'll discuss that, but first, how's the tour kick-off going?"

"Amazing. I couldn't have a better or more enthusiastic team. It seems all I need to do is move from place to place in first-class comfort and speak. But I needed to speak to you."

"Me too. I've been contacted again by Sir Arthur, aka the Guru. I'm certain this time." I pounded the table to emphasize the seriousness of my point.

"Really?" she asked, less incredulously than I had expected. "Then I don't think you're going to appreciate my news that the painting you so love was sent by the Russian state to encourage me to accept an offer to collaborate."

"I'm not surprised. I told you I learned as much from my spy work with Max Wells. Listen, M, this is serious. I was sent an AI work of prose in my own voice suggesting you work with him—the Guru—with you trying to convince me to join the two of you . . . in your *collaborative* work. I'm sending it to you now. I consider this third-party verification that he is behind Genesis." I returned to my desk to push Send.

"It still sounds far-fetched. But maybe you've been right all along, crazy as that sounds. Or it may be that your dogged insistence is start-ing to convince me. Are you bewitching me, my dear? The idea of me working with him to restrain this new technology? Hmm." She sounded bemused.

"It does sound like a fantasy, but . . . you wouldn't work with that madman on the new Genesis society after what we believe he did to Dylan and know he did to you?" I moved back to my desk, pleased she was finally taking the threat seriously.

"Of course not. And yes, he may be behind Genesis. You may be right, or it may all still be just Russia and Genesis. I will not accept, of course, if he is involved."

"How will you respond?"

"I won't. It's best not to answer when the devil's calling."

41 | TEA PARTY

WITH M ACKNOWLEDGING that the Guru could be the puppet master, I expected to be relieved but found myself even more uneasy. As the specter became more real and I was imagining the Guru and his plans more vividly as he emerged from the shadows, M's tour started to move from city to city. I'd been so focused on getting M to agree with me that I was now at a loss about what to do about the possible reemergence of the Guru. I slept poorly. Also, the novella's themes weighed on me, preying on my imagination.

The next day, I began writing in the morning and planned to work well into the night. The wheels of my novel kept getting stuck in the rut of the mysterious novella's storyline. It was some twisted form of plagiarism where the novella and my novel were mirror images. My other source material was my dark vision from the end of *The Lost Theory*.

I was deeply disturbed by everything, including my writing as it moved from mystery adventure into the macabre. All work and no play was making Sean a very dull boy.

As midnight approached, I was a bit delirious and still didn't want to go to my bed for one. With the children long ago put to bed, being watched over by Astri and Brian, I was drinking wine and smoking the flower. But despite my attempt to write from an altered state, I was producing rubbish—forced and stilted darkness for darkness's sake. The macabre had turned to farce. The Guru and Cat's-eye had become Dr. Evil and Mr. Bigglesworth, a comical third-generation Bond villain and a pet cliché. I found myself jumping the shark when

Cat's-eye played with the Guru's shriveled and straggly red-haired balls on a La-Z-Boy in front of screens controlled by the Guru's mind as he directed his new Dick and dickettes into a Sharon Tate–type murder scene, with the hero rushing in to save the heroine—pulp fiction farce stealing from Mike Myers and Quentin Tarantino. It was nothing I could ever share with Molly, though she might appreciate some of the sinister depravity.

How could I protect M from the Guru if I couldn't imagine his next move? I needed to start practicing what I taught. My creative writing course was built around three simple pillars. First, let the story take you where it will go and get out of the way. Second, allow the characters to say what they must say regardless of how uncomfortable it may be to you and certain thin-skinned readers looking for the next cozy to curl up in bed with. And finally, all writers have their magic invocations to unstick the words when stuck. That was it. That was the course.

All great writers became Prospero, with magic cloak and hood, who, with a stroke of their staff, might conjure a tempest commanding the spirits of earth, wind, water, and fire.

But I was more a Caliban, grunting with my imagination wallowing in the mud. And the Guru was stalking and mocking from the shadows of the Kremlin like a modern-day Rasputin.

M had left me for her work. Juno had disappeared into silence and never returned except in a mystical, telepathic, and whispering way. Molly and her clairvoyant aliens were my collaborative company. But it was Lewis Carroll, who I'd been reading to our children, who supplied the trick to unstick my writing.

From my credenza, I pulled an old-time bowler hat—a true billycock, a bombin, a derby right off old René Magritte's head. I imagined reaching into one of his paintings and plucking my creative thinking cap off one of his detective characters' now bald head. Playing the dapper Oscar Wilde, I pulled four of my big faux leather chairs into a square around my desk, prepared a pot of tea and four cups, and arranged one at each seat. I sat with a pad and my Molly pen in front of me. *The Ninth Wave* became a tree hanging over me and my tea party.

The clock on the wall stopped just before midnight. I waited—that was the trick. Waiting, listening, and believing. Willing imagination to come. Accepting my invitation, the Guru arrived first, not entirely unexpectedly. He sat across from me like a hologram within my mind's eye.

"Hello, Guru, my honored guest."

"Finally some respect, Professor. I like it."

"Thank you for coming. Would you like some tea?"

"And courtesy! Some wine would be nice. By the way, I'm always with you . . . but where are the others?"

"They're coming; be patient. There isn't any wine, only tea. This is a tea party."

"But I'm the first to arrive, I see. Shall we keep it civil, just you and me? I don't view myself as your antagonist. I'm the one you can rely on. Tea is fine."

"Me alone with my voice of fear? My other guests may be less punctual but far more honest."

"Shall we speak in riddles or be clear? I'm the only voice that speaks truth to your belief in unicorns and telepathy. Face it."

I hadn't been looking at him directly, like the time I met a bear and wanted to avoid eye contact. When I did look, he was just a lily-white old man with glaring red eyes and a wicked, slim smile. Both his red lips and his hair had thinned and turned a duller shade. He was dressed for a royal British tea and wore a stylish black fedora. Yet that face, ancient and drained of blood, struck my heart with fear.

"Yes," I said. "No riddles. It's not that kind of party. What do you have to say?"

"For myself?"

"I wouldn't expect you to speak for another."

"But that's what you're missing. I speak for you."

"What do you mean?"

"I'm your daemon. You can't write without me. Without me you're an uninspired professor teaching old books and writing drivel about the beauty of this and that."

"I would be fine and so much better off without you."

"You can lie to yourself, but you can't lie to me. I know your mind, you see. You ready to listen?"

"All ears. Quiet as a dormouse." I pushed back to recline and closed my eyes to listen to my demon therapist disclose his plot.

"Let me first set the scene of the perfect storm that's approaching, as you drift there between waves in my timekeeping metaphor."

I peered up at the painting hanging over the tea party before shutting my eyes once more.

"The bioluminescent wave, so beautiful, created by an al—"

I bolted upright. "Don't say it!" Of course he would know my fear.

"Algae blooming and dying in a holocaust of light, Poseidon's northern lights. Or it could be just a green wave." He seemed amused by his words, his skeletal frame rattling and wheezing in sinister glee.

"Let's leave the metaphors to me, shall we? Tell me about your work."

"Okay, Professor, lie back. You see, I know you even better than does our dear sweet Emily."

I did as he asked but flinched at his use of her name.

"I am on the verge of a breakthrough in brain-computer interface. You may have heard of my baby, my Genesis. My work will save mankind from itself."

On that, he and my novel might disagree.

"Much as your vision foresaw, my work did oversee a galley ship of tech-slaves, scientists, and brain-mechanics experts all pulling in the same direction to map the brain for a quantum computer able to follow the neurological processes and pinpoint the moment of choice in the human brain. The illusion of free will is just a pachinko-like switchboard of past impressions, chemicals, current environment, energy flows—all determining which synapses to fire at any point in time. There was no way to control this cosmic soup of feeling, emotion, and thought until now. I have found the key in the quantum computer strokes of my genius, directing the implementation by a robotic surgeon who then turns over the patient's mind to Genesis and me."

Sick fuck, I thought. "Go on," I said.

"Wiring into Genesis will provide a way to short-circuit the slow, rational process controlled by interconnected loops of repetitive thoughts and the associated feelings generated by the mind's past conditioning that create the unholy mess we call 'me'—all with the speed of my quantum computing. Silvio, in migrating those one-on-one computer interfaces onto my platform, allowed the master programmer in to determine the outcome by providing centralized communal thought that will appear in many minds simultaneously, like telepathy. *I* can save humanity from the brink of its destruction. I can end environmental catastrophe, prevent the use of weapons of mass destruction, and nip global pandemics in the bud."

The Guru believed he was doing good by creating for mankind an uber-superego powered by his AI. Of course, he believed his power was benevolent—as had every maniacal tyrant throughout history.

"You see, this is the only way to ensure the security and comfort of all mankind. To prolong lives and stop mankind's mad march to mass suicide. The collective good is my driving desire."

I wanted to say *you're lying to yourself*, but I knew to keep my mouth shut and listen.

"My only issue all along was the means. So I took all Petrovsky's Russia had to offer, and that was everything—abundant wealth, facilities, minds—and put it at the service of my creation, fearful of any misstep. Petrovsky's only power over me is the ability to take my life, but he would be stealing only minutes, not hours. And death holds no fear for me. Soon with Genesis, I will become immortal, living on as the mastermind, or superego, in perpetuity absorbing every other mind into mine."

I imagined him in that state, his eyes lighting up like a preacher of fire and brimstone.

"The only differences between us, Professor, is your fear of physical death for yourself and those you love. Hell, you don't even want me to die."

And he was right—I was the one giving him oxygen, giving him life.

"What better teacher than the universe?" he asked. "The increasing number of viruses and weapons of mass destruction are life's way of showing us how vulnerable to extinction we are and directing us to work together to avoid that end. I'm going to ensure we do work together and protect humanity."

His words sounded so benign and rational. The unfettered ego is one wily devil.

"What good is your infinite love of constant creation," he continued, "if it doesn't serve the reality we perceive—where we live and breathe in time and space? In fact, I believed Dylan Byrne's and M's theory had no practical application. I almost went mad looking to discover how to harness the infinite power of damned constant creation, but then it came to me. That creative energy's desire is directing us toward the evolutionary jump that we're currently poised to take. That jump *is* our destiny—a new man with all-knowing power at his command ready for the simple act of rejecting his own free will. There in computer-generated reality, everyone will be able to envision their own heaven."

Or hell?

"They'll live in bliss and do no harm."

He would win over my readers if he kept on rationalizing that way. He was even lulling me into his vision of a brave new world. I blurted out my burning question to break his spell. "Do you intend to harm M?"

"Everything with you begins and ends with your M. Her brilliance and star-scientist status *and* her reluctance to embrace AI mean that she's the one who can turn the tide. She can steer others toward the last act of free will, the choice to subscribe and buy into the network of minds. People will trust her. With M's help, I'll be able to reach the tipping point, after which there is no turning back and there won't be any choice but to wire-in or fall behind as a retro form of life. So, no, I wouldn't harm a hair on her lovely head, the head I need and am so very fond of."

"Yeah . . . So M will never become your partner in your ghastly work. I read your novella—that if you publish, I'll sue you for plagiarism."

"*My* novella? That's your work—your voice. I'm no scribbler. Since Emily couldn't make our little tea party, let me speak for her."

"Sean Byron McQueen, I know your reluctance." His voice had changed to one that sounded exactly like M's. "And you know my aversion, but this is different." I stole a look at the face and mouth emitting her voice—so ugly a sight and so dear a sound. The disconnect froze me in my seat, grasping me by the throat. "The new advances the Guru has made provide a swift means to bring a cessation of undisciplined thinking and to connect minds."

I wanted to shout stop and wring his neck, but more than that I wanted to hear her voice. I'd lost control of my imagination as the lucid nightmare in M's voice continued.

"I'm only beginning to see the implications, but Genesis heralds the end of the focus on me, myself, and I for the collective awakening and good of mankind. Come, my Thin Man, to Moscow and join us in this adventure into the unknown. Have no fear—all that will die are egos. The Guru may share my mind's desire, but you have my body and spirit. Just come. Big Love can't be threatened or experience fear. Nothing real can be lost."

The Guru's own gravelly voice resumed, but I was reeling from hearing her voice come from his decrepit mouth. I couldn't speak.

"I don't like to flatter you, Professor, but use your powerful imagination. What would you do with an army of blank mental slates, a tabula rasa of virtually every mind? People would become your characters and live the wonderful stories you would write on the pages of their minds. I know what you're thinking. You're thinking that you have no choice. Listen to me. Listen to Emily. I hear your fearful voice cry, *The horror! The horror!*"

Those two words, repeated, rattled out from my own heart of darkness, in my own terrified voice through his cracked lips and snake tongue. My hands clasped my face and shrieked Munch's silent scream. He had stolen my voice like the witch Ursula did to Ariel.

Pushing back in my chair and shaking off the Disney black magic, I shouted across to his seat, "Don't you dare speak for her! Let M speak for herself!" I knocked his fine hat off with the back of my hand. His face became narrow eyes and a diabolical grin, and then he was gone like the Cheshire cat. His hat was the last part of him to disappear, rolling across the floor into oblivion.

I sat back down, sweating in fear, picking up Molly's pen and scribbling the Guru's words on paper with a shaky hand before I forgot the insights of my wild imagination.

MY MIND WAS STILL RACING. The Guru had pushed me out of the rut; at least for my fiction, I knew all his next moves.

There were still two more seats that were set for tea. I turned to my right side to imagine M speaking with her own body, face, lungs, lips, and tongue! She'd come for tea wearing a dark blue dress and a smart hat, a white fedora with a colorful light blue feather. She'd smell as sweet as the sea air wafting over a lavender field.

Then in a moment of dawning sobriety, I realized I didn't have to imagine her and that I wanted to hear her actual voice and see her actual face. Somehow the Guru made me feel lonely and wanting. It was after seven a.m. Athens time. I video-called M and set the phone against her teacup.

"Sean Byron McQueen. You're up late—and with a funny hat? I take it you're writing . . . and drinking? Shouldn't you be asleep?" I wanted to lean over and kiss the phone face but I knew that would make me look more wasted than I already was.

I checked the clock and it was moving again. "Just tea now. I'm having a tea party! I couldn't possibly sleep. I'm so wide awake with you here—even if only from distance—but now seeing your face, your presence, and constant state of grace," I said, realizing I was not making sense with my gushing doggerel. "Sorry to call tipsy, but I just had the Guru to my imaginary tea—trying to figure out his next move—and he scared me. So I needed to see my lady was okay." I tipped my derby.

She lifted a teacup. "Ironically, I'm also having my morning tea and

I'm always with you in Big Love—just ask Juno." She looked over my shoulder as if Juno were there.

"Not now, but soon, we need to discuss what to do now that we agree the Guru is our twisted benefactor." After wine and weed, in the middle of the night, was not my time to press for more precautions. "I have some ideas."

"I'm sure you do. And maybe he is involved, and yes, we can discuss it later."

"Okay, *maybe*, but for now, something tells me that, like the Guru, you have a message I need to hear. You know I need your words," I said. "Even my bliss is hollow when it can't be shared with you. It shrivels up and dies absent your light." My words risked my embarrassing myself further than just wearing a silly hat on a drunken late-night call might.

"Your heart knows that's your head talking and that it isn't true. Attachment leads to suffering; your mind conceals secrets and conceives diabolical futures. If it's words you need, be quiet and listen. Please close your eyes so your heart may hear. I don't have much time and you need sleep."

I pushed back on my recliner and shut my eyes. Her face, etched in light, shined upon my mind's eye, her voice speaking directly to my heart from the phone that rested at an angle, leaning against a teacup.

"I love your surprise of teaching a science fiction course. You've always loved science . . . and scientists aren't that different from writers or artists. Their art is to create predictive models of the universe—the illusion—and to gain acceptance of their work. Each discipline—evolution, the big bang, the quantum, and constant creation—is merely a different genre. Collective thinking within a genre sometimes has to yield to the creative thought that breaks its bonds and leads to radical breakthroughs. A eureka moment."

Eureka was her code for reminding me of the first time we made love and that I was still her Sean Byron McQueen.

"Beauty is simply the level of symmetry and truth, expressed by science or art and how well it reflects life, nature, and our collective imagination. Your work should draw every nexus and connect all the dots so the puzzle appears complete in answering all your questions. Do you think it was random selection that Stephen Hawking's communication device was the genesis of brain-computer interface? It was that important that his voice be heard, despite all odds. And now it has advanced to a point of no return."

Her voice was guiding me. It always had. I half opened my eyes to soak in her radiant beauty.

"But each grand theory of science always led to the anomaly, the paradox that led to the imperfection in the theory's model of the illusion and predictive nature of its artistic theory. Imperfection is a part of the perfection. The source and its creation. The beautiful reconciliation in constant creation theory as string theory unravels. The creator can't be viewed as separate from creation as Juno taught us." She looked to my left again and laughed, but my glance was fixed on her auburn hair and ageless face. "As you create, look on life as a dance of free will and destiny. Free will to co-create with all and everything within the collective dream of destiny."

"Like a Prospero!" I said. The inspiration of her words had gone off like shots of adrenaline through me. I wasn't about to teach science fiction. I was *living* it.

"Sean, look at me like it's the last time. Let us speak quickly and truly before I must go."

I locked into her deep gaze, saying, "M, you look lovelier with your inner light radiating so strong and bright each moment of each day. So bright I fear you'll disappear into the light. But there's no last time in constant creation." I put my hands to my heart.

"Okay, my Keats, my Yeats, my Shelley. Share with the world your poetry of words." I wanted to dive into her nut-brown eyes. "You're meant to write science fiction and not just teach it! Tell me the story—in a nutshell, and I must go."

"A mad scientist as an artist realizing the full power of his craft, his thoughts reveling in their ability to mold illusion to his will."

"Sounds scary—a man of big ego. Anyone we know?" She shuddered in mock fear.

"Yes. He's a shadow creator, a Dr. Frankenstein seeking solely to increase that power. Like in Mary Shelley's work—the real monster is the doctor, not his creation."

"So the Guru is back for the sci-fi sequel, and I'm dying to read it and see how it ends. Now write and know the light of Big Love always is in and with you." She was kind not to mention my state of inebriation.

"Thank you. Please forgive the late-night writer's call."

"Take care of our children!"

With those words she blew me a kiss, and then was gone.

I was about to end my tea party but remembered I'd set out one more chair, and I turned to my left. And there she was. After all these years, a radiant Juno! I wasn't sure how long she'd been sitting there, perhaps the entire time. She was a figment of still and silent grace. No hat. No words. No secrets. With a smile that spread across my heart, she put down her teacup and raised her index finger to her lips—*hush*—and then she flourished her invisible wand into the air, following with her body, and she was gone. A delicate, evaporating wisp.

I wished she had stayed to answer my questions, but just seeing her felt good. I removed my hat and cleared the tea. Juno's cup alone was empty.

I went to bed at two a.m. The writer's trick had worked and I'd find a way to convince M to stay away from Moscow and any collaboration with Lord Voldemort. I'd write the tea party scene from my notes and send it to Molly in the morning, as only she could understand the reveling in the play between dark and light and sleep and waking. She would love it, and I'd end the scene with Yeats, signaling my imagination had been unleashed and was moving forward with foreboding.

And what rough beast, its hour come round at last,
Slouches toward Bethlehem to be born?

43 OUR DOUBLE AGENT

JUNO'S HUSH SIGNAL OVER TEA convinced me that her words—*M, too, will be lost*—shouldn't be shared with M. Besides, at this point, M would be pissed that I hadn't been forthright from the beginning.

However, I needed to take some action to check the Guru before he placed Petrovsky poison in our tea. I wrote my State Department contact using an encrypted file security she had provided me, updating and copying her on the novella and my suspicions that the Guru was behind all the works of art we had received. I also asked her to confirm if the Guru was still alive and if he might be associated with the Genesis project. I got the sense I was no longer an open file, as I received an automated reply indicating solely that she had received my encrypted communication.

The next day Elliot returned to me as my faithful friend with news that turned the tide. His phone call was as usual dramatic and asked we meet *at* the *secret spot* I had shown him when he first arrived and asked that I say no more and to meet him there immediately and bring the key. The secret location was our locked wine cellar. I imagined he wanted to meet me there so that I might open a grand cru Burgundy in exchange for his reveal of some big secret.

But amazingly as we entered the wine cave, despite it being after noon, he didn't ask for wine but insisted I lock the door behind us. We sat in the cavernous dimly lit room, and I waited for him to speak of some dark conspiracy.

"Sean, I am about to betray a confidence, but I feel my duty as your best friend dictates I do so. But, before I do, can you agree to not act on or reveal this information to anyone?"

"Wow. Let's open a good Burgundy." I got up and looked through the stacks and found one of M's father's old wines—a 2007 Grand Cru Maison Leory Chambertin—that was crying out to be drunk before it died of old age. I also wanted time to think about his terms. His intel must involve Samantha, but it was better to know than not know, even if I couldn't act on the information. I poured us two glasses as Elliot maintained his jittery and uncharacteristic silence. "All right. I agree. Unless it poses a risk to M." We toasted his betrayal and loyalty.

"You know I have become quite enamored of Samantha. Like an uncle."

I almost corrected him that they had become the older gay man and beautiful young woman friendship cliché, but I held One Step back.

"Sometimes we drink into the night and share confidences. We often speak of you, and she told me what happened in Strawberry Fields the night of the fire."

That was when the worst precognition flashed upon me: Samantha was pregnant and going to claim I had planted the seed in a fit of passion around the fire pit.

"She has a fixation—a young woman's infatuation of you as a writer and teacher. I tell her she will outgrow it. Well, last night she was clearly holding something back, and eventually after a lot of wine and some drugs and prodding and oaths by me, she shared that she is the elusive Sir Arthur Conan Doyle *and* behind the poetry and my *Cardenio* and now some story she sent you; you didn't tell me about that." He looked hurt, but we hadn't spoken since the novella arrived. "She asked my forgiveness, knowing how much *Cardenio* meant to me as inspiration. Sweet thing drenched my handkerchief with her tears, apologizing for dragging me into her works of art for you, but that was before we had met."

We paused to drink and think about what he had disclosed. I was shocked that she and now Elliot knew of the novella that I had told only M and the State Department about.

"I admire her creative work even if mostly computer generated, but what if I had fallen for the frauds? My reputation would have been destroyed."

"Fool you, Sean Byron McQueen? She didn't think you would be fooled but would appreciate the proximation of genius that she painstakingly edited." I didn't know whether it was Elliot or Samantha flattering me while at the same time leaving me feeling the fool.

"But there's more. WiN sites have hacked you, looking for ways to go after M, and they've been monitoring you and posting some of the information to Samantha. She used that inside information in the prose she sent you recently." At my involuntary grunt, he added, "Her story in your voice—you got to love that."

"It's all a bit too intimate for me to fully accept it as an innocent act."

"Oh, please. It's flattering, old man. Poor girl couldn't possibly have realized you'd go all Guru-nuts over her clever cat-and-mouse game. She worries that the story she sent may have gone too far. I'd like to read that, by the way. But there's more. She also showed me WiN sites calling for a fatwa on M, an enemy to WiN and the New Society. Nothing explicit enough to prosecute but very incendiary."

He looked at me with compassion in his eyes, but his concern wasn't for M. His heart bled for poor, poor, pitiful Samantha. "She showed me some of the nasty content and her ardent defense of M. You know how WiN is looking to discredit their perceived enemies? She's debunking smears of M on those sites before they get traction. As a celebrity and influencer within WiN, she is taking our side. She's one of the good guys."

"A good witch? But this is getting worse by the minute. Brian just reported that some of the most prominent New Society naysayers are being subjected to *brain draining*, what they used to call the Havana Syndrome before it was debunked. Now, there are actual sonic attacks on the brain, a technology developed in Russia that can decrease brain functioning permanently."

Brian's report now added to my list of fears that M's brilliant mind could be damaged in some irreversible way that might equate to her being lost.

"I'd not heard that, but I had heard about the disappearing Russian AI dissidents. As a WiN insider, Samantha is our first line of defense. She wants to tell you but fears you'll expel her. She really thought you would enjoy the poetry and prose created by an AI program that she then edited just for you. It was all an act of rash young love, Sean. Isn't the right reaction compassion and sympathy? Do you remember young love?"

As I swallowed his bewildering words, I was drinking too fast, full of ambivalent reactions of being, simultaneously, the fool crying *guru* and the subject of such adoration.

"Sean, you realize she also duped me with *Cardenio*, but oh what a beautiful fraud it is by such a brilliant source."

The confirmation of it being a fake was offset by his pleasure that his protégé and new drinking buddy was behind the clever work.

"Well, don't knight her Sir Samantha Smythe. I'm glad it's not the Guru, but I feel the fool for insisting it was. And how can I not tell M that I was wrong and fall on my sword?"

"Sean, I swore, and you swore to honor my breach!"

"But, Elliot, you know M. She's not vindictive and would honor our confidence and take no action; and there the chain of loyalty and duty and betrayal would end."

"I can only allow you to bring M into the fold if you can assure her silence and inaction."

"I can assure you of that; she'll be glad to hear it wasn't the Guru."

I used Elliot's phone to call M and take her into our confidence. She was more amused than angry. We agreed to use my encrypted State Department software for communication until I could get the boys to sweep our devices. M expressed gratitude to Elliot and her hope that with his unmasking of the true Sir Arthur, we'd be able to put our over-active imaginations to rest.

After we hung up, Elliot and I agreed that rather than open another bottle, I should write the State Department to make sure they didn't ensnare Samantha in my request to track the mysterious writings. After thinking it over, I had no desire to punish her. She was only my thoroughly modern and creative secret admirer. It was flattering, even though she caused me to look like a lunatic.

44 TOUR SUCCESS

MY STATE DEPARTMENT CONTACT assured me with the strictest confidence that *hypothetically* any fear I had of a *fictional Guru* should have died years ago.

She further reassured me, stating, "I see no clear, present threat of WiN to M, and the threats you saw are just *bluster and chatter*, not plans or plots. There is no material motive to hurt M. The public relations whiplash against WiN would be quite damaging to their cause, *if* they even issued a credible threat against M."

In short, the State Department was dismissive of my concerns and would not supply additional protection or even agree to monitor the chatter around M. I believed WiN remained a significant threat, one that even M recognized sufficiently to agree to take precautions to protect herself from the extreme militant fringe that had become zealots of the New Society promised by Genesis. Two vocal political opponents in Russia had gone missing, but they were crusading to outlaw any direct links between people who were wired-in. They claimed such measures were dictated by the Greek Orthodox Church and the belief that Genesis would usurp some God-given prerogative. M's ethics were not nearly as dogmatic an affront to the WiN-nuts.

WiN's paranoia was driven by their imagining of some government shutdown prior to the Genesis rollout next year. While WiN was worried about Big Brother, our government and the world were being lulled to sleep, accepting Russian assurances that it was prioritizing safety protocols. Details about such measures were forthcoming but had not yet been shared for proprietary reasons. Kennedy hadn't shared our Apollo rocket plans with them, so it was a bit of New Age payback.

My initial relief that it was all Samantha playing tricks on my mind and that the Guru was dead soon whipsawed me into even greater agitation. The risk of M's being lost was almost worse now that the threat was some amorphous evil waiting to descend and snatch my M away. Yet after my embarrassing resurrection of the Guru, I had to be more rational in revealing my concerns. I called M to make my best case to her, laying out the danger I imagined she faced. I tried to convince her to soften her mission to alert the public to the dangers of AI and thereby strengthen political resolve to police the rollout. She might not be the New Society's public enemy number one, but she was on the most wanted list.

She assured me she'd be careful and implored me not to push the hologram substitute teacher plan again. "But I can't wait for my first hologram with the children tomorrow before I leave Paris! Won't you join us?"

"You know I'd love to, but let's make this your time alone with the children. They miss you. Brian's setting it all up for you guys. I'm sure I'll hear all about it from *our little darlings*. By the way, their fascination with the hologram technology has, at least for the time being, silenced their smart phone craving and incessant insistence."

The children's hologram and Paris talk were both wildly successful. M's clear vision for the tour was coming to fruition.

Le Monde's lead article translated that success with poetic flourish following the prior night's Paris show: *An ugly vine of vitriol is wrapping itself around the flowering of human consciousness, but it cannot obscure the light of the sun shining on tonight's full moon.* M, who saw only the fruitful branches, was the star of their metaphor. I couldn't fathom how a selfless woman expressing the essence of love could engender such hate, all in a virtual world stretched out across the canvas of a global web. In my imagination, it was just a matter of time until letter bombs would be addressed to M.

Now that she was in the midst of her whirlwind rock and roll tour,

I had to pick my spots and limit my midnight calls. I wanted to be her inspiration, as she was mine.

"Hello! Great show and great reviews from Paris, mademoiselle!"

"Well, I have great material—edited by a pretty good writer—to work with."

"Have you decided how to respond to the Moscow Institute's invitation to collaborate?"

"No reason to reject it, but let's see if they accept my conditions first." She paused. "I think I know, but what do you think I should do?"

"Follow your heart, but be safe and see what you can negotiate. But even Guru-less, I don't see how you can associate with this godless New Society."

"That's just it—only if we can make it have a heart and restraint will I participate from a distance. Let's just see where it's headed."

"Sounds good." I had my opening to make all my prepared points. "But until then, let's not change our approach of not taking on Neurotech and Genesis directly and limit your comments to general stuff. Your Russian invitation to provide ethical oversight of Genesis proves the message is getting through and we can press the point more head-on when you return. We have almost a year, according to Silvio, who usually fails to meet his ambitious time estimates. No reason to unnecessarily rile up the WiN devils."

She responded with her catchphrase, "Maybe, yes, we shall see." I took this as her agreeing to yield to my calm logic.

"Don't forget Molly's aliens might snatch me too."

"I'd laugh, but Molly's no joke and she has done a lot of research. And maybe Juno *was* taken by aliens. The boys tell me QC believes in alien abductions too. It's better than any other theory I've heard to explain Juno's disappearance."

We ended the call discussing Elliot. In closing, M said, "Sean Byron McQueen, you have your wonderful creative work to do. Will you focus your imagination on that and let all your worry for me go the way of the Guru?"

"I'll do my best," I promised.

I wrote manically as M's tour marched from city to city, molested only by ugly protests featuring barbed words and slogans. I was more than halfway through the novel, with my hero unmasking the Guru as the evil mastermind behind a Genesis-like New Society seeking world dominance through mind control.

Genesis, aka *Genie* in my book, could play a million games of chess at once against a million Bobby Fischers and lose not one, not even playing to a draw. This added millions of brain qubits that made my all-knowing nemesis almost all-powerful.

The fiction was a perverse therapy for my unease and kept getting darker; maybe for Molly I'd go all the way into the heart of darkness. The question was, how would the hero foil the Guru's new AI society—with the Guru as master programmer—but still allow the benefits of the new technology to be rolled out? I had no idea, but kept writing, confident the end would reveal itself. I often studied the painting that loomed over me, imagining I was the captain of the cross, clinging with my mates as the tidal wave approached. My dark imaginings came to life on the page, written for my first reader.

I held back from sharing the plot twists with Molly, despite her request that I send her rough chapter by rough chapter. She refused to reveal whether Juno survived her alien abduction, so she was playing the same game of mystery with me. The growing number of pages, the kids' carefree play, and our playing catch on the campus grounds were bright spots in what otherwise could have been extremely dark and lonely days without M.

The day of M's talk at Oxford, July 27th, I sat in my office alone, writing back and forth with Molly. I was glad to be able to share with her Brian's quantum computer–aided research; beyond alien abductions being far more likely than not, the results found a correlation between accounts of abductions and the intelligence and advanced spirituality of the abductees, giving credence to her Juno theory.

Even more interesting was that the computer speculated upon a theory of its own, one that suggested that near-death and out-of-body experiences and the miraculous abilities of sages might be intermediated by advanced alien life or technology. I imagined Juno and M would demur to that AI assessment. I told Molly about the reports of Yogi Mangku appearing to his students miles away while playing all sorts of musical instruments. She wrote back *Maybe it's the advanced mind's ability to work better than a hologram and to control the matrix-simulated reality.* I countered with *Maybe with the help of spiritual aliens or angelic intercession or good old-fashioned divinity?*

Aliens, angels, and demons were as good an explanation as any other for phenomena that defied the laws of physics and rational thought. I thought Molly might be onto something; perhaps aliens had abducted Juno and now held her on a simulated Shangri-la mountain where they allowed her to communicate through their preferred means of telepathy. Maybe I was going crazy trying to make sense of it all. For both Molly and me, fiction wasn't fiction but an alternative reality.

I put down my pen at two p.m., as it was near time for the Oxford show. Eric and Brian had arranged for video links so the talks could be played at the school's indoor theater and at other colleges as live broadcasts. Following each lecture was a Q&A session that formed the bulk of the lesson. Students and professors from around the globe were able to ask the foremost authority about the proofs and implications of constant creation. The questions were screened by Dr. Alberto Gat-something's Athens support team. M's spontaneity and brilliance made the webcasts quite popular, with over a million live followers and the number growing with each talk. Many more watched the video afterward. M was beloved by multitudes.

And hated by a vicious few. She spoke at the end of each talk about the need for ethical constraints on AI development but honored my request to not specifically attack Neurotech and Genesis and their New Society.

The family, along with most of our summer students, gathered in the school theater each time she spoke, and I hurried down for the talk at University College, Oxford. M was more than halfway through her tour engagements, with each setting a new high-water mark as judged by hits and views. She had also moved from page-twelve to page-one news in the local online papers and even on the few remaining print papers like the *New York Times*.

M's tech team had put together—with each institution—a multimedia introduction that featured the college and the buzz around the upcoming lecture. I had to suffer through some Wes Anderson–quality cinematography where M had been inserted into a painting by Monet, reclining on a skiff on the gently flowing Thames on a lovely summer day, speaking with ease to some youthful dean of physics about her passion, before we could move on to the grand lecture room for the main event.

She was halfway through her Oxford Q&A when the event took a turn with a question that startled me. Coming from a Moscow university, the call naturally pricked my ears. The voice sounded strange, as though the speaker was still learning the King's English while at the same time sounding perfectly British. The pitch-perfect voice asked a very rude and dangerous question: "Do you agree that AI and the movement of human beings to wire-in through Genesis is the evolutionary purpose of constant creation, its most full expression? Most scientists, myself included, see this as the next evolutionary leap. Isn't our duty as scientists to pursue that end by whatever means possible and align ourselves with constant creation as you so elegantly preach?" I didn't like his tone or rhyming prose.

"And aren't those opposed to it, living a life of privilege, just continuing to enslave the less fortunate in a circle of poverty and pestilence? And don't they need to be stopped at all costs, to put an end, once and for all, to war and hunger?"

These were questions right out of the novella's pages . . . suggesting Professor Edens either get on board or be eliminated. I jumped up like I'd been shot and insulted. The family looked dumbfounded at my interruption to M's show. I waited, frozen in fear and indecision, for M's response.

"Preach? Well, I hope I don't proselytize. Though there is a great joy in grasping constant creation theory, and I do want to share that with all ready to listen." She laughed off the rude and threatening question, but

I doubted she'd had time to read the novella. "And perhaps you've read one of my interviews or seen a prior talk and know my deep-seated reservations about the wiring-in trend. This isn't a scientific-based aversion but a philosophical and spiritual one.

"First let me answer as a scientist. Why creation expresses itself through life as vibrational formations of its energy remains an empirical mystery. But we may observe that this energy is life-affirming and expansive. Constant creation looks to that source in the only place it could possibly be found—in each instant of pure awareness. We all share that universal consciousness as the primary state and creative source from which all things, including thought, arise and are perceived as time in space. But there is no measuring of that source. One cannot quantify or even very well conceptualize the infinite and eternal. And how can the source not be infinite and eternal? Is it logical to think there is a point beyond space and a time *before* time? Or an end to time and space? All evidence is of eternal expansion. That appears to me as an unfolding or an awakening.

"Now let me answer as a humble human. My experience of this source, gained in meditation, is that there is a purpose to constant creation and to the energy that flows into the universe, and that purpose is the awakening of more consciousness—more love—which is really the same . . . I won't say *thing*."

That got a laugh from the more in tune in the crowd. And I finally took a breath. I sat again, but remained rigid with fear.

"Perhaps that's why the universe appears to be expanding with time as it comes into creation each instant. But from the perspective of the source of constant creation there is no lack, as it is infinite and eternal—beyond time and space. With no lack, there is no purpose, just love."

She paused to access her left, rational hemisphere of mind. "But to your question—I would judge AI and wiring-in as all man's creations should perhaps be judged. If it's used just for more knowledge, that may be a good thing; but if it's used to magnify the already insane and destructive human ego, then it may become an extremely dangerous tool.

"So far, and I think the empirical data supports this, wiring-in utilizes more energy than it generates as people consume its data and content and do not create. And this exchange with the computer isolates people more and more, which seems antithetical to love and life. It also suggests that young people who wire-in are less prone to date, make meaningful human connections, or make love."

Now she was love's proponent. The live crowd laughed, perhaps nervously. No doubt most were already wired-in and were there in person only out of nostalgia.

In our theater, I searched for Samantha and her posse that now included Elliot, but they weren't there. I only then realized that my assumption that Elliot had not wired-in was an ageist one. We'd never discussed it, but his relationship with Samantha made me wonder. Elliot had taken up summer residence with Samantha and her posse to work on the virtual production of *Cardenio*. And now, the WiN dogma that SS had used for her novella were being weaponized to attack M on tour.

M stood and looked directly into the camera and right at me. "I also believe another evolutionary leap is being made as more humans become self-realized—there, in touch with the universal mind— omnipotence, if you will—is Big Love and true saving grace. As my soul mate, Sean Byron McQueen, has said, this linking into very smart quantum computers that are filled with near-infinite information may prevent people from obtaining true liberation and self-realization, the very purpose of every life."

Our live in-theater audience looked around at me. Even from a distance, she was trying to pull me into her fearless orbit. She sat again and took a sip of water before continuing to address her worldwide audience. "I don't hesitate to say that AI *has* shown great promise and may be used to serve humanity in the areas of data, research, medicine, and education. As to the New Society . . ." She paused, and I knew she was thinking of me. I knew that she wanted to go on to directly challenge Silvio's grand vision of Neurotech and Genesis.

"I want to study and think more about this New Society, the technology and the controls. My position paper, for those interested, will be forthcoming. The important question is, 'How do I and how do my actions serve creation?' The answer always is by choosing more love, whether you're wired-in or not. To the extent the New Society evolves in a life-affirming direction with the restraint of the heart over the ego, I'm all in favor of that.

"But to answer your question directly, awakening has always been the great next evolutionary step, and wiring-in is just a matter of nuts and bolts; suffering and death will still come even if we live within a bubble and subject our minds to AI's creation. I see AI as presenting the true risk of enslavement and not as a source of liberation. But yes, those of us of with privileged lives must do all we can to share that abundance with others."

When the lecture ended and applause erupted all over the world, the boy who cried wolf was running to his office, trying to keep up with his imagination while texting M and imploring her to call him immediately.

45 ASSUMPTION OF THE RISK

WHILE I WAITED, DESPERATE FOR M'S CALL, there was a knock at the office door that I'd closed in a dramatic gesture. Brian and Astri wanted to see why I'd freaked out, no doubt. They were all so innocent, or I was all so paranoid. They'd been told of M's invitation to the Moscow Institute and of the novella without attribution to Samantha, but they didn't see the link that I did to some new information Brian had unearthed from WiN propaganda. The Matrix was starting to take shape in my mind.

"Come in," I said.

"What's the rumbus?" Astri half joked while her face expressed concern, not realizing how spot-on the joke was.

"Not funny. And not the time to use rumbus, I fear." *Rumbus* had been the Guru's code word used to make M disappear in *The Lost Theory*, and since then it was sometimes used by the family to mean *what's the big fuss*. I had never owned up to my mild dyslexia, causing the misspelling that I pretended was a play on words. "I believe M is in imminent danger and that WiN was behind the call from Moscow. She'll call when she gets free of the crowd, and we all can discuss it. I may need your help convincing her to cancel her tour. She can be so stubborn."

"A brave and fearless leader usually is," Astri said, signaling a potential mutineer.

Brian patted Astri's bald head, which always made me laugh, but not this time. My mind was racing with plans and questioning whether I was overreacting, as Brian and Astri clearly believed I was. Here I was once again, the family fearmonger.

"Brian, can you use your wires to find out more about that questioner—who the question came from?"

"Sure glad you're getting the knack of how useful it can be," Brian said. His eyes rolled up as he linked to the quantum computer through his computer and raced for the answer. He relayed his results as they tumbled in.

"Posed by a professor at the University of Moscow. But wait—looking at the address . . . This is strange. Professor Mikhail Lermontov."

"Hmm?" I didn't believe in coincidence.

"Yes, it's a new address, and there's no other reference to this professor, but it appears to be a true school address, not a bot, spook, or hack."

"Anything else?" My phone was ringing with a V-room call. "M?"

"What's up? Your message sounded urgent again."

"It is. Astri and Brian are here."

"Hello, everyone! Tell me what's going on. I have Eric and YaLan here—let me zoom out so you can see them too. What a buzz there is here at Oxford!" She cleared her hoarse throat. "Sorry. I need to rest my voice. I knew you wouldn't like that last question . . . but I finessed the answer fairly well?"

I had pulled out my ball and glove to show who was coach here and pounded the ball into the web for emphasis.

"So that's the slapping I heard—you're teaching our angels baseball!"

"Yeah, we're waiting for you before we get bats, but I got you a glove too." I wanted to toss the ball to myself to calm my racing thoughts, but I certainly didn't want to waste time speaking about baseball. "And great talk. But the *rumbus*, as Astri so correctly called it, is . . . that last question used some of the exact same words as the novella—'don't those who oppose the New Society need to be stopped at all costs?' And our wired-in man on the ground here just confirmed the question was routed through a made-up address at the University of Moscow from a Professor Mikhail Lermontov. You see?"

"Nope, you lost me there."

"A dead Russian author of *A Hero of Our Time*, a novel that featured a classic Byronic hero."

"That is a coincidence, but what if it was an alias? We know WiN is not a monolith—perhaps some WiN professor is interested in our work. Nothing new there. We've been hacked before. They don't seem to be trying to hide, the way a stalker intending harm might. It was a good albeit rudely phrased question. And you saw how restrained I was in my response—just for you, my Thin Man."

Everyone was looking at me like I was a man on the verge of losing all reason. I went to the window to play catch with myself, hoping that would settle me *and* so M couldn't see my fear. The best, the most likely scenario, was that I was acting like a paranoid lunatic, and instead of rattling dice in one hand like Bogart's Captain Queeg, I was punching my glove hand with a ball.

But since I couldn't help myself, I spoke loudly from the window. "I don't need to remind you that you were abducted by our own CIA, and now WiN and Genesis are working with and for Petrovsky, who could poison you with a look and has no constraints. I think you're in danger and should come home immediately." I realized the hysterical nature of my demand but could not pull myself back. My protective mode was on autopilot.

"Sean, where are you? I can't see you. Please take some deep breaths and consider that it's not surprising that WiN and maybe Petrovsky himself are interested in us. Genesis must be his pet project, and I've been asked to collaborate. But WiN and Petrovsky have no incentive to do us harm—unless you have another theory of everything hidden up your sleeve. Maybe inside that baseball that's wrapped as tight as you are."

Astri laughed at M's witticism, and I glared at her, stifling her laughter.

"You know Eric has been tracking this web of hate and may be seeing patterns behind the WiN blockchain—an invisible hand—so antithetical to blockchain mechanics. I think it must be Petrovsky and his supercomputer."

"Yes I know, but patterns form everywhere. We see patterns based on our beliefs and where we look based on those beliefs. Patterns in a blockchain are beyond our pay grade, and you know our government has an army of technocrats looking for the slightest manipulation by Russia."

I started pacing and dropped the ball, which shouldn't happen with a six-inch toss. I let the ball roll across the floor and threw the glove onto my desk, knocking over a stack of papers. I frowned at Astri so she wouldn't laugh again. She extended mercy and straightened up the papers for me.

"M, you are a threat to WiN and Genesis and you almost took them on directly." If I'd still been holding the ball, a window would now be broken. "Damn it, M. You *promised*." I regretted my words when Astri and Brian exchanged an *oh-my* look. "And the part of the question about a scientist's duty made me think that *that* may be the massive rationalization to eliminate you as an obstacle; you are not performing your duty supporting this evolutionary jump to the New Society of wired-in minds. They see this as a moral imperative, and they'll want to hang you at the stake."

I didn't know what had come over me, and the room was now terrified by my ranting. Here I was—battling an invisible incorporeal demon.

"Sean, we must weigh risk and reward. Do you not see all the good our tour is doing?" She sounded hurt. "The tour is going so well—if you could feel the crowds and see the network of love it's creating. It's working, just as we hoped it would. Raising awareness. Discussion. I can't drop all that and come home, slinking away *like a frog in frost*."

"Don't you use my Keats against me." I kicked the baseball into the wall under the wave. "M, please. It's too dangerous to continue."

"Sean, my protector. What would you do if it were you? You wouldn't return home. You shouldn't have a double standard for me."

"I don't! Don't make this into some feminist plot and twist what I say." I took a deep breath before saying, "I would come back."

She laughed, making light of the deadly serious. "Please, Sean, calm down." She was trying to pull me back from the edge, and I felt bad making her use her obviously strained voice to talk me down.

"I'm coming to you if you won't come home."

"Please, Sean, you have the children."

"Astri and Brian can take good care of them for a couple weeks."

She looked down before she nodded a couple of times and said, "What if I got a real security detail and drove around in an armored truck?"

"You don't want me there?" Now I was the one twisting words. Softening, I added, "I'm sorry. And an armored truck and armed guards just might be as good as me being there."

"I was joking about the truck, but Eric, I assume there are security firms for rock stars and me? I leave for Dublin soon to speak at Trinity College and then have my dinner with the talented and lovely Molly Quinn—yay! Maybe she'll give me a pen too." She smiled at me, but I wasn't going to let her disarm me with her teasing.

"After Dublin and Barcelona, we finish up with the last talk in Moscow before we return to Athens. And then back safe and sound in your arms on August 15th. We can look to get security for me in Moscow. I think we're fine in Catalonia, surrounded by your friend Oriol Bernat and all his Catalan security forces. Sean, would that satisfy you?"

My pen pal and literary buddy Oriol or OB was a well-connected Catalan independence fighter who served as a member of Parliament. He was renowned for owning the most beds in Barcelona as a hostel operator. But his real power came from being a part owner of Barca, the football team. Football was the heart of Barcelona. I was confident he could protect M for me during her visit to his town.

"Begrudgingly and maybe. I'll speak to OB. I don't like that you're vulnerable in Ireland. Perhaps Molly has contacts there. I'll check with her." Now that I'd remembered to breathe, Moscow took its rightful position as my real concern.

"Eric or Brian, can you look into security for Moscow?" M asked.

"Sure," Eric replied. "We'll arrange round-the-clock security to meet us at the airport in Moscow. And you'll have YaLan and me on guard before that."

"Better, Sean?" M asked.

"Better, but I'm still concerned about Moscow, even with a queen's guard. Petrovsky is a master snatcher. I don't suppose a few mercenaries will deter him much."

"One other thing about Moscow," Eric said. "Ironically, the Russian news is free of adverse press about M and her tour. It's all highly favorable despite a very religious-like cult supporting Petrovsky that encourages all citizens to wire-in at state-sponsored facilities."

"The eye of the hurricane," I noted. I had to get Moscow removed from the agenda. Something was rotten there. Something was deliberately luring M there with a painting, an invitation, and favorable press.

IT WAS TIME TO TAKE MY LAST SHOT and hold nothing back. My gut told me Moscow was a black hole sucking M in.

"Good one, 'the eye of the hurricane,' but still not perfect," M said. "You've been triggered, my dear."

I saw myself looking like Nicholson in *The Shining* on the V-room screen with my hair pulled out at the sides, so I put on my cap.

"Damn it, M, I hate that New Age tripe. *Triggered!* But let's dissect the second part of that question and how it relates to some findings Brian wired-in to. About how you and constant creation may have a duty to this grand new effin' society. Brian?" I turned to him to make my case.

Brian stood to make our point. "While Eric's been focused on tracking down the spider's web, I've been researching a little side web that seems organized with focused precision on one question. M, you may have noticed a thread of questions, all coming from WiN-sympathetic academics."

M said, "About how constant creation may be tapped into to connect the wired-in community in some even more significant way and that this may be by way of Genesis?"

"Exactly. That community seems to be exploring a somewhat scary prospect—that AI may be able to mirror a universal mind through a master program that acts as an overlord over the interconnected community of those wired-in. This would be a quantum jump in human evolution, and any resistance to it would be seen as *old uni-mind evil*, as they call it. *And* they are focused on you and your teachings, M. That's as far as I've gotten. Neurotech hasn't updated its site, so WiN is filling in the design and plans for the New Society on its own."

"And those plans don't include you, M," I said, "other than the Petrovsky-controlled Moscow Institute that wants you as his ethical handmaid—a tool to further their ends. Petrovsky must be after something more, orchestrating something that involves you and whipping WiN into a frenzy at the same time. We don't know what it is, but whatever it is, it spells *danger* M-O-S-C-O-W."

This was my closing argument, ending in an unintended cliché. I sat down to let that bombshell explode in the middle of the V-room. I held up my index finger, indicating that I'd like to speak next. M, however, took the lead. "Hmm, *uni-mind*? Interesting, and maybe, yes, that is scary, not just for me but for all of humanity. The irony? Uni-mind could be short for universal mind."

"But it's not! Peaky fuckin' blinders, M! Open your eyes!" The family all looked impressed, surprised, or scared. I fiddled with the brim of my Irish cap like it might contain a razor blade to use as a weapon on any mutineer. "They're focused on you as the evil goddess of uni-mindedness," I said, refusing to play her word games or to yield to the family diagnosis of my fanatical fear for M's safety. "You must come home before Moscow so we can ensure your safety. A hologram of you can perform the Moscow talk, maybe from Athens but better from here. It will be you, the real Dr. Emily Edens, safely projected across time and space and using science to speak about science."

Rumblings hit my gut even before she had time to stir the pot.

M remained obstinate in the face of my strong case and indigestion. I refused to return her smile, so she continued. "I've agreed to full-time security in Moscow. Not to mention the media covering my every step. They'd have to be Houdini to snatch me there, or do you fear Petrovsky will just have some sniper shoot me?"

"I don't know what he'll do, M. But I know the risk posed is too great."

"Remember, they want to collaborate with me, so I don't think they'll just shoot me."

Astri looked ashen and shaken, disturbed by M's not-so-funny joke about being shot, and she found humor in almost anything. Or maybe I was scaring her.

"M, don't joke," I said for both Astri and me.

And then, shazam! Ting's smiling, peaceful face appeared in the V-room. As family, she had access, but didn't she ever sleep? Was she wired-in? Someone must have notified her—M?

"Ting!" the entire family, other than me, exclaimed, glad and surprised to see her.

"Sorry to pop in, but I was meditating and had an image of you all speaking, and then intuition said I'd find you all here, accompanied by a nudge from the universe to join you." She seemed shy and confused herself.

"Ting, it's so good to see you!" M said. "We needed a jolt of Big Love and here you are."

"Thank you. I have some powers of remote viewing and saw this scene as if from afar. Sean was *fretting*."

I hated her word choice. It made me sound like an accountant with a number out of place.

"Oh, you got that right!" M said. "I'm eager to hear what you have to say. Sean is . . . has some foreboding about my Moscow talk."

She must have read my mind or my wincing face. I picked up the ball and glove—I had to get back in the game.

"Interesting." Ting had the look of a mystic pondering how to convey truths from the other side of reality. "Perhaps I have been brought here to convey the vague cryptic images coming from Juno over the past couple of days." She took a Juno pause to look at each of us before saying, "And those are colored by a confidence shared with me recently."

Ting then registered another Juno-like pause, during which her eyes spoke solely to me. My head was spinning with her spot-on intuition and timely appearance redirecting my scene.

Thank you, Ting! She was right—it was time for me to come clean. Ting, by not violating my confidence but by raising the topic, was helping me. Juno still hadn't answered my questions, and I'd almost given up on her telepathy saving the day, but it was time to dredge up her hidden words and play my ace in the hole.

"Ting, I'm sorry to interrupt, but M, I told Ting something I've yet to tell you. I thought it too dark and—"

"You've been keeping secrets?" M gave me her wide eyes of surprise and hurt.

"Well, I was trying to not verbalize what I thought was just a reflection of my deep-seated fear. You may know or have suspected that after my first hologram with Ting, when Juno delivered a message to me where I told you she said I was to protect you, that was my resolve based on her telling me in cryptic Juno fashion"—I handed the ball and glove to Brian for safekeeping—"words so very hard for me to say." I didn't pause intentionally for dramatic effect, but I started gagging on my secret. It just wouldn't come out.

"What is it, Sean?" M encouraged me.

"*M, too, will be lost,*" I said to myself, holding back an emotional outburst as the words were released fully formed from my heart. "She said, 'M, too, will be lost!'"

"Sean, honey, it's okay. Don't worry. I forgive you. And I now understand why you've been acting so crazy."

I couldn't look away from her, watching her wipe away a couple of tears that caused my own tears to flow. She was crying for me and not out of fear of those words. I used a sleeve to dry my face. Astri was hugging me across the chest from behind my chair, and YaLan was doing the same for M. The family was healed in that instant of simple disclosure, and we were all crying and laughing. I took my first deep breaths in weeks as the grip those words had wound within me was unspooling like a mummy.

But I knew from M's posture that the acidic discharge of words hadn't changed her mind. She could suck the poison out of a snake and take on none of the toxins. Like a supernova, she ate darkness and became no less bright. She knew no fear.

"Well, that was a good cry!" she said, wiping her own face one more time. "Sean, you did tell me she said to protect me and you've insisted on that security detail in Moscow. You've taken all the proper precautions, often over my objections. And we all will be lost someday."

She smiled, holding it until I bowed my head in surrender. *Me first,* I prayed.

To Ting she said, "What are these new cryptic images from Juno?"

I was no longer in charge of the meeting's agenda. I put one hand on my stomach. But my gut wasn't screaming at me anymore either. This must be what M's doctor was getting at after he took that ultrasound of Rosemary's baby. The stress of a truth not spoken *could* make a person sick.

"These aren't like phone calls or movies but more vague images and thought impressions," Ting said. "And so general and my interpretation so subjective that I'm hesitant to say anything. I'm not sure my impressions will be helpful. They're like dreams I can't remember clearly."

I was feeling so relieved after letting go of my secret that I had become a bystander of what I'd hoped to be a scene I could use to convince M to come home and in all events not go to Russia. I determined not to lose the focus but had to look for my opportunity to seize control. Back in the day, a man would have just interrupted the ladies and concluded the meeting with his decision on the matter at hand, but this was 2027 and M was CEO here.

M said to Ting, "We understand, but, you see, we're all in the dark and would appreciate even your vague intuition and Juno's too, to the extent you can share them."

Ting, who didn't speak much, had her sister's knack for holding an audience's attention. The boys and twins were all standing and hanging on her every word. I was also focused on her, unsure where she would take the debate. "I'll do my best," she replied, "but I'm afraid I'm giving images to the formless energy patterns that passed through my mind. My interpretation is that what you're doing is what the universe wants you to do for the great light of infinite consciousness. But dark forces are gathering in reaction and are ready to be unleashed."

An image of Ahab's white whale crushing the ship flashed through my mind, and I looked up to the painting. "Hegel's thesis and antithesis,"

I said, attempting to emerge from the dugout and get back on the mound. I grabbed my ball and glove.

"Ting, anything else?" M asked, ignoring my philosophy, sending me shaking my head back to the bullpen.

"There is one image of a wolf and fire at night, darkness and shadow, that keeps coming to me. I don't know what it means."

Ha, my opening. "Looking for the lamb separated from the flock. You don't have to be Jung or Little Red Riding Hood to see the archetype there," I said.

M laughed, though I wasn't joking.

"I'm sorry," Ting said. "There's no real message or guidance, and I'm hesitant to speak. Juno's refrain keeps coming to mind, though. *Love is the absence of fear.*"

Thanks, Ting. With those wise words you may have sunk any chance of M returning before Moscow.

"Ting, thank you. I hope I'm not Little Red Riding Hood. And if the future is heading in the direction of an interconnection of minds controlled somehow by Russia and Petrovsky or even the showman Silvio, the flowering of consciousness of our Big Love awakening is even more important." She looked at me and I nodded—yes, I had seen *Le Monde*'s article too. "We can't nip the evil vine in the bud by giving way to fear. After Moscow, it's back to Athens for a dinner of gratitude with the entire team and then home. Anything else, or I should get some sleep? Dublin and Molly Quinn, here we come!"

I had all but lost. "With Moscow, you're heading to grandmother's house—don't you see that *that's* where the wolf will strike? He's huffing and puffing, and your brick house is your home back here." I pounded the table with my fist to make more manly my childish mix of metaphors.

M attempted a conciliatory tone. "Sean, if you were here teaching your next novel celebrating Big Love and humanity's awakening, would you turn and run and play it safe out of fear over a dream's big bad wolf, or would you take the once-in-an-eternity opportunity to speak to an audience primed for your message in the place where it would do the most good?"

"But M, we have to heed Juno's dire warning! You have me and two young children to think about."

She stiffened, clearly hurt by my use of the children. Her eyes teared up. "How can you say that to me *knowing* I can't possibly not finish what I've started?"

"M, I'm so sorry. You know it's a cry for love from a heart that could not live without you." I nodded to the others. "Please . . . may I have a quick good night with M?"

We said our namastes to the family.

Protecting M and helping her to fulfill her destiny were two teams of wild horses pulling in opposite directions and tearing me apart.

I WANTED TO FACE WHATEVER was to come with peace, love, and light between us. I didn't want to send M off to meet the wolf of Russia with a single note of discord, despite Moscow being the heart of all my fears. Only too late, I saw clearly how my writing about diabolical danger threatening M had once again spilled over into my actions and made me look a fool. I felt like a child consumed by fear of a boogeyman and then a city. I went to pick up my ball.

I said, "M, I'm so truly sorry. Please forgive me. I won't try to convince you anymore, but perhaps you can help me with my fear. I do feel better telling you Juno's exact words." I laughed nervously. "My stomach certainly didn't know what to do with them." I reached one hand to my screen, hoping in vain to touch M. She mirrored my motion, as if I were a prisoner being visited behind a plexiglass partition. "I'll let you get to bed, but I have to confess that there's darkness around me I can't shake. Why am I manifesting all this even as I pursue our path? My faith and certainty come and go depending on hap and circumstance. And like this painting of yours"—I held the computer screen for her to see the green wave cresting—"I can't shake the feeling doom is approaching. Again, I'm sorry. All I want is your safety and our harmony." I wasn't saying what I wanted to say but only expressing more fear.

She hummed a soothing *aum* and then said, "First, there's nothing to forgive. You love me. Second, the illusion is just a reflection, a classroom where we can learn and awaken. Dreams or nightmares, they all pass, but realization remains. As I said before, after Samantha almost ate you, be careful of your dark fantasies. If you invest in them enough, they will come true. And I, too, have dreams I must follow, my dance of free will and destiny. Remembering our love as light is all that truly matters."

"Funny you mention the dance of free will and destiny. That's been on my mind a lot lately and is a theme of my new book that's so dark it scares even me."

"Yes, and you know I believe your wildly creative writing is your path to excise your demons, but it can make you irrational at times. Luckily, I know you so well." She waited a moment, then grinned broadly. "I'm so excited about my dinner tomorrow night with your literary buddy, the unsinkable Molly Quinn. And I can't wait to crawl up into bed with you for a week soon."

"I wish it were tomorrow instead of . . ." I forced a smile. "Let me tell you about Molly. She takes seriously the theory that Juno was taken by aliens and makes a fairly compelling case based on all recent developments; she is a master at research. Her new book sounds like a really interesting read. Ask her if you can join our first-reader book club."

"Hmmm, alien abduction is like reincarnation for me. I have no direct recollection of it, but something tells me it is true," M said.

"Funny you say that. Her research suggests that those abducted by aliens often have the memory of it erased."

"I can't wait to hear all about her research and the Juno-inspired novel with aliens!" M said.

"Maybe that's how you'll be lost too, my dear."

She laughed, and I chuckled nervously. She yawned, covering her mouth. "But I should go now."

"I know." She needed to sleep. But I needed to hear her talk of our day-to-day life. "I miss you so much. You know how superstitious I can be. I tipped over Dylan's book of Yeats—the one that led us to his theory—and you know what poem it opened to? *Not* 'The Lake Isle of Innisfree.'"

"Oh, let me guess—to show you I listen when you recite his poems to me!" She paused, her eyes narrowed as she sought a title without computer assistance, no longer tired but a wide-awake child playing a game. "'The Second Coming'?"

"Eureka! You *are* psychic!"

"Let's make it Nirvana on earth when the Second Coming arrives!" She touched one finger to her screen, mimicking my earlier action and signaling visiting hour was over.

"Yes. Now, good night and namaste, my love."

"We'll speak again soon. Be safe, and namaste. I miss you too, Sean Byron McQueen. And I'll see you at the airport with Sherlock only one week from now."

* * *

My night of M's Moscow morning approached in tiny steps, halfway and halfway again in Zeno's march of time over space. I would let my darker fantasies rest and I would pray. I'd done my best to keep her from going to a grandmother's house built of straw, and at least she'd be traveling there with armed guards.

That day arrived and was dedicated to Juno and Dylan. After breakfast we grabbed our gloves and headed to the opening within Strawberry Fields where I'd been burned before. We warmed up by playing catch and then Juno's favorite game of *running bases*, where the monkey in the middle had to get safely back to either base before being run down and tagged out by the two other players covering the bases. Juno, though her catching and throwing needed some work, was a fast base-running monkey and usually safe.

After lunch we hiked all the way to the beach and back. When we got back to the Deeksha West, they found energy I didn't have to race ahead of me through the vineyard to show Astri and Brian their precious seashells. They reveled in Eckhart Tolle's power of now.

That night, after our big day, I had them set up Aerobeds in M's and my room so I could read to them both until they fell asleep. We were reading their new absolute favorite book, the first of the Narnia series, *The Lion, the Witch and the Wardrobe.*

When I was with the children, I always felt M's presence despite our distance. They were full of the joy of life and completely unaware of the dreadful Moscow morning that had already arrived. I focused on them rather than my fears, allowing myself to become lost in their innocence once more.

NO HUFFING, NO PUFFING, NO WOLF, NO FIRE. Moscow was the biggest success of the tour. M even made an elegant and impassioned plea for Russia and Genesis to submit to oversight and restraint in the rollout of the new AI society with Neurotech. How could I have sought to restrain her, to keep her from using her powerful voice to harness the tide of destiny? I texted a simple *Well done!* and prayed the bear would just take the poke in the eye.

Petrovsky took the poke and turned the other cheek. The grand finale was a state-sponsored ceremony in Red Square. State media broadcasted the highlights of M's talk for hours, and headlines proclaimed *Doctor Emily Edens Navernyka Polochit Nobelevskyu Primly Po Fisike*. Which Eric translated as M was sure to win the Nobel Prize for Physics.

She had played the risky queen's gambit and won the heart of Russia.

Moscow Institute desired to lure M to teach there, with the full support of the university and the state. A report leaked that M had already received a Russian art treasure as a show of the country's love for her and her work.

M was all grace in response, never saying no. I saw the Japanese in this, a yes and a no. She had learned while working with some wise Japanese scientists to not refuse outright any valuable offer. Why say no when the future was so uncertain and an outright rejection was a form of ingratitude? The trick was to not mislead the party making the offer into thinking that your answer was yes.

When asked about the media reports on a possible collaboration, M said she was grateful and that she didn't dismiss the gracious offer out of hand while admitting that her home would always be the Deeksha West. She said she was open to all forms of valuable collaboration, especially related to ethical cooperation and oversight. But hers would come free of any compensation. And the Aivazovsky was, and always would be, a national treasure, held in trust and to be shown museum by museum as directed by the Russian people.

She couldn't be enticed to leave the Deeksha West for all the rubles in Russia, a currency that flowed from the blood of dinosaurs into a well-oiled and now wired-in economy. But would she really work in collaboration with the new AI society in the evolutionary leap or loss of humanity?

The wired-in militant fringe of WiN was buzzing mad worldwide outside of Russia, declaring that Petrovsky was smitten with M and her delusion of constant creation and that he'd betrayed AI science with that warm embrace. This tech militia saw the world as black or white, while Petrovsky was gray and clever. Still the main target of the vitriol was M.

I had half suspected the Guru would pop up or we'd discover that aliens or alien technology was behind Genesis and its superhuman self-learning intelligence. But those plot lines were real only in my and Molly's fiction. In *The Devil's Calling*, the Guru had also died but not before imprinting his sick mind inside of Genesis. I was still researching how far-fetched that was from a technological perspective. Molly's alien abduction story was becoming more real each news cycle as more came to light about recent credible alien abductions. She had tapped into the current zeitgeist as it was unfolding.

M and the team landed in Athens on August 14th, greeted by the mayor and his guardians. She would be home in less than thirty-six hours, flying back to me. And I breathed easier and felt the fool, the family's nervous Nelly, full of useless worry that I finally exhaled. M didn't gloat.

Eric and Brian continued to watch the internet concerning M but didn't have any further breakthroughs. The same trends continued, and the web of love expanded like energy from a big bang while those spinning a hateful web were sucking in energy like a black hole, the expressions of love and the reactions of hate growing in alternate universes.

No one seemed to distinguish M from her work—she was the dancer and the dance. How could a light attract such antagonism and such burning desire to snuff it out? It had me contemplating Jesus, for Christ's sake.

With M coming home, I was determined to be the fully conscious man she deserved. It felt good to relax while assuring myself that I hadn't been crazy to worry. I was proud of her front-page success despite the ugly strain of the ultra-wired-in's response. WiN had lost.

And more good news arrived that same day. My application had been approved by the local town council and the Irish tower was all but mine. All I had to do now was meet them at the local pub on September 11th to review the architect's plans, meet the master contractor, and sign some papers. They might have picked another day. I'd take my legal wingman Elliot with me. I estimated M would be ready to retire in nine years, 2036, and by then the massive renovations to make the tower a cozy place to live by the sea would be completed. I would tell M her first night home as a homecoming surprise, and we'd make love to celebrate her tour and our tower.

Once she'd arrived in Athens, I was able to return my attention to my novel that now needed a dramatic man-versus-machine ending. I smiled when it came to me—my novel's ending would be all the evil that could come from Genesis and the New Society with the Guru as an embedded ego at the controls. But I'd figure out the supercomputer's Achilles' heel, burning out its circuits with some deep, unsolvable paradox—maybe Zeno would do. My science fiction and M's true science urging ethical restraint would work together to bring heart and soul to the rollout of the new technology. We would take on Petrovsky and all of the WiN-nuts, but with M by my side, where I could protect her. M would be pleased, as Myrna Loy and her Thin Man worked so well as a team.

I sat writing in my office, that Russian national treasure still hanging over me, a source of admiration and angst. That was when my imagination saw details I'd never noted before. It appeared that the powerful source of the dawn sun was pushing clouds that looked like an alien invasion in front of the waves, with the shipwreck sailors sailing out in greeting, holding up a book, probably the Bible, and not fleeing the impending doom. I shut my eyes and upon opening them again saw more simply: a force of nature and transient life, the relinquishment of all safety and attachment. Death.

I wondered how the Russians would react if they knew the painting was hanging in my office without locks. Two men with a truck and a gun, and it would be gone into the night. Natalie had it insured for five million, but still a country would feel betrayed by the loss. I thought about calling Max and seeing if he knew a couple of thugs with a truck.

When I was ready to shut down my computer for the day, messages started to pour in. The first was from my Molly with her Chinese assistant's report on Juno's case. The Chinese legal system was far from transparent, but according to the researcher, it was well catalogued, with precise entries, like the Napoleonic code, that could be cracked open with enough money. There was no substance, just headings and dates of filing information, with the proceedings and actual filings not to be seen other than by Party officials of a certain rank.

I spent an hour with the report, but Molly's assistant's summary hit all the high points: Juno had been tried on several counts of espionage and subversive acts against the state; the state had received damning information from the CIA on which it based its case; and she was almost sentenced to death but given solitary confinement for life instead at some undisclosed location in Tibet, to be arranged and overseen by her uncle, a high-ranking Party member. All the other entries were purely procedural and shed no light on the case.

After reading the report, I had more faith in Ting's telepathy and less in alien abduction. I wondered if the dashing of alien speculation had made Molly sad despite the relatively good news.

To celebrate the confirmation of telepathy, I had a little tea party for two with Juno, complete with me in my bowler hat. The good news reinforced my guilty belief that my book and vision were somehow to blame for her disappearance. Imagining her eyes, I knew I needn't ask her forgiveness, so I posed my three questions again, though they no longer burned in me.

As our tea edged to a close, I beseeched her to escape Tibet so we all could celebrate in a great family homecoming. Juno sat in silence, pleasantly sipping her tea, and in the end she gave me a sad smile and put her left hand to her heart and raised her wand hand with index finger extended toward the heavens. The index finger then traveled up, spinning into the air, and the rest of her willowy body followed and she was gone.

As I cleared the tea trappings, another message came in, this one from an anonymous source. A brilliant ditty that unraveled in the second stanza—half Lewis Carroll brilliance and half AI gibberish and all nonsense.

Beware the Jabberwock, my son!
The jaws that bite, the claws that catch!
Beware the Jubjub bird, and shun
The frumious Bandersnatch!

A B C to midway, pass the K!
On the alphabet's sing-song course,
Auspicious day, Callooh! Callay!
Letters three, and add a *T* to yours!

I read it again. The ditty was not only silly but creepy. Another unsigned poem from Samantha, Molly, or WiN? I sat back in my desk chair more bemused than disturbed by the nursery rhyme. I sent it to Elliot, asking him to find out if SS was the Riddler and promised to continue to honor his confidential source. And the boys' new failsafe computer security had reverse-tracking systems that would allow me to determine the ditty's source. I'd pursue that in the morning.

In a way it was a clever and playful poem, suggesting the deconstruction of language into its most basic of building blocks, the ABCs.

I went to the kitchen fridge to get a Heineken with the Jabberwocky playfully rattling in my head.

The nonsense poem was a fitting end to my spate of worry. M was safe. I returned to the office with crisp, clean Oregon water in hand, not beer. I'd decided to get back into my meditation practice to get my mind right for M's return. I pulled out my meditation cushion and sat on it on top of the big oak conference table, basking in the full harvest moon over the distant ocean. But no sooner had I shut my eyes than a lightning bolt flashed through my mind. I slid off the table and raced to my desk to write out the alphabet. I held my breath as I paired the letters with numbers. *Oh God.* There, smack in the middle, starting dead center on the thirteenth letter, three innocent letters—M, N, and O. And—oh, God—add a *T* to yours.

M not yours.

I called M. No answer. I called again. *Not yours!* Not again!

"M!"

49 NOT AGAIN!

DRESSED IN GYM SHORTS and a threadbare 1979 no-nukes T-shirt, I was no superhero. But I was a little prince on a dark planet. That my meltdown might be my wicked and wild childlike imagination was my last lifesaving hope.

M wasn't always by her phone, and it was still early in Athens. My thoughts were racing well ahead of reality, a new bad habit that was now my default mode and one so easily triggered by a joker's riddle.

Still, I'd wake the family and get the next flight to Athens before the eighth wave could break. Eric and Brian would engage the best European Pinkertons and work with my State Department contact to have them search for M and contact Moscow to demand her release.

M was probably still sleeping, and Samantha was having a laugh and taking the piss out of me with her alphabet soup. That would get her expelled when the boys had the evidence she was the sender.

I called M, texted M, emailed M, and called again and again. Then I tried Eric and YaLan, and they didn't answer either. And damn it, SuperEric was turned off till eight.

I assumed the worst and called M's Professor Alberto in Athens—the man who had led the team in support of M's tour and who may have seen her last—at six a.m. their time. He didn't answer either, and I left an urgent message. We had never spoken. I emailed him, saying it was an emergency and to contact me. It struck me as I hung up that he would think I believed they were having an affair. Why else would he know where she was at six a.m., and why else would I use such a demanding tone? M might be angry at me for embarrassing her with my runaway imagination, but her anger I would welcome.

As I was typing a text to the family, Ting was V-rooming me.

"Ting, did you hear from M?"

"No, why? I was calling you because I heard from Juno."

"I can't reach M—it may be nothing. What about Juno?"

"A powerful message just came through, with Juno urging you to come here now."

"When I find M, maybe. If I don't, I'll be going to Athens. I'm a bit frantic. What else did Juno say?"

"There was no more, and yet what was there was clear—you're to come to Kathmandu."

"Hold on. Let me try M again. I may be panicking for nothing. It's been all of fifteen minutes since I deciphered a message that had me leap to the conclusion M was taken by WiN and that I had to go immediately to Athens to find her. My message was also hard to decipher—gibberish—but not telepathy."

I called M. Still no answer. I sent the alarming ditty to the rest of the family, copying M and Ting, saying that I feared M had been abducted by a WiN militia acting as puritanical vanguards of the New Society.

Ting and I discussed the riddle and what it meant now that I couldn't reach M.

Ting said, "Sean, the alphabet jumble of your riddle made me realize—*see*—something about my telepathy with Juno. Sometimes it comes not in her voice but more like snowflakes or Chinese characters opening in my mind, each unique with coded messages. The one that accompanied your message to come here looked like a tree house, the character for destiny."

"Well, Chinese characters all look like snowflakes to me. After we find M, I'll consider coming then, if it's my fate. I received a report that your uncle may be overseeing Juno's solitary confinement in Tibet. Wait—someone is here."

Brian and Astri were at my door, Brian explaining as they hurried in, "Our wired-in minds receive notification alerts and alarms. Despite being off-wire eight to eight, we have notifications set for any message sent by the family that the computer interprets as an emergency. Yours was easy, being titled *urgent*."

Eric appeared onscreen next to Ting. "YaLan is heading over to M's room—she didn't answer her room phone either. And I hope you don't mind, but I traced the riddle from your computer. It came through a popular Russian WiN site, one that could be used by anyone in Russia, and their firewall encryption and blockchain technology make it impossible to find the true source."

"Well, I'm glad, I think, that I wasn't in privacy mode. And only you and Brian have this access? Oh, and what about M—is she on your system?" I asked.

"Yes and no," Eric said. "We wouldn't place her on it without her consent."

"Could you?"

"Yes. For her school accounts," Brian replied.

"Brian, do it now, please."

Brian was on my computer, typing away, hacking into M's accounts. I explained the Jabberwocky riddle and M's failure to respond while I tried to project crisis calm and not hysteria.

"If you knew the source, could you track the message to them?"

"Probably," Brian answered. "The two points of contact should allow us to unmask the computer location if not the actual person behind the keystrokes."

"Okay, assume it was Samantha, please, and track her. See if she routed the riddle through Russia." They collectively looked at me like I was crazy. They didn't know what I knew, but I didn't consider this search a violation of Elliot's confidence. "Brian, just do it. Please."

"But why Sam—"

I held up my hand to stop Astri's question.

With each second Brian looked through his wired-in mind and M was still silent, my chest tightened further, like it was being bound with rope. Five minutes later, Brian had his answer. "Not Samantha. The sender was not from Oregon. But the search was helpful, as each country has a signature. It came from Athens originally, but I can't pin down the location any further."

I blew the thin façade of patience and rushed to judgment. "This is WiN, not some alien abduction, and they have M."

"Sean, you may not want to hear this," Astri said with some reservation, so uncommon for her. "YaLan and I have been researching telepathy for our upcoming comparative study course, and one explanation is that aliens or angels, which may be one and the same, use telepathy and astral travel. And they're increasing their contact, perhaps preparing for 2036."

"And they are leaving stupid poems behind as their calling card?" I almost bit her head off. "M's not dead but will be unless . . ."

I couldn't think of an *unless what*. Petrovsky wouldn't want the international scandal, so M would have to remain missing forever. Or maybe YaLan would find her already dead in her hotel bed. My heart screamed no!

Brian was hugging Astri and came to her defense. "Sean, if aliens travel light years and have the advanced technology to do so and they can communicate by telepathy and erase memories, they certainly have the ability to cover their tracks with a simple poem. And Petrovsky and WiN would have no reason to play such a cruel joke."

"And . . ." Eric started.

"And what?"

"Well, it sounds so stupid, but WiN has set up a vigil outside in the street here. If she was abducted, they might have seen something alien and made the poem to . . ."

I was losing my team by being too aggressive and judgmental. "Guys, we're all talking crazy now. Sorry, but we don't even know if she was taken yet. But if it is genius aliens or angelic body snatchers, there's nothing we can do. So let's assume it was WiN for now, okay?" Astri gave me a sad, forgiving smile as the team bowed to my logic. I was glad Molly wasn't there to further press the alien theory.

"And I provoked all of this." It wasn't rationally true, but it was emotionally true. In my novel and my mind, ever since Juno's words had been spoken, I had focused all my attention on my fears coming home to roost. I started shaking. And rubbing my face. Instead of a rumbling, there was a dense, empty pit in my stomach, with an angry ferret moving up my core to rip and gnaw at my heart.

Fear was suffocating me. If M was gone, I would be to blame for her disappearance. I had thrown my spear at the cyclops's one eye and missed, and now the dragon of my imagination had my love deep in his cave.

I glared at the painting and blamed it for M's loss and my destruction. I grabbed my letter opener from my desk, determined to slice away at the power that art held over my head. As I made a mad dash toward the green death of dawn, I saw myself diving into the middle of that green wave with knife held high and ripping the ocean open as I slid down the wall. I made my leap but hit the floor hard, as if the wave had caught me before I could do it harm. The ocean's power pinned me to the floor.

No, not the ocean. Brian, cause of the middle linebacker tackle, was on top of me.

"Sean, I'm so sorry. You okay?"

I took his hand and he helped me up. "Yeah," I said, shaking off the madness. "And thanks. Momentary insanity." I handed him the letter opener, glad neither of us had been impaled, and sat down at the conference table. What was I doing? I'd almost made an enemy of every Russian and all art lovers, and Chekhov never would have forgiven me.

Astri, without speaking, circled the table and laid her hands on my head, releasing a wave of calming warmth. The blessing of peace radiated through my head to my heart. I remembered Big Love and would fight to not give way to the fear. I smiled up at her in gratitude.

M hadn't answered her phone for less than half hour, and I was already a vicious art vandal. I thought about getting my ball and glove to help me think, but feared the window would be shattered by my fastball.

That was when telepathic Ting said, "Remember that Big Love knows no fear."

Astri's hands and Ting's words brought me back to my posture of the man in charge. Putting on a brave face after my bout of pity and fit of frenzied fear, I stood, saying, "Sorry. Lost my head. We don't know if she just dropped her phone in the toilet or . . ." I found myself in front of the painting again and whirled away, moving toward the peaceful windows. "I'm going to call the head of the program at Athens again. Where's YaLan? Where are the mayor's guards watching her door?"

I called the Athens professor again. Alberto answered.

"Professor McQueen, hello. It's nice to finally be introduced. I got your message and tried to reach Emily. She has not called back yet. I assure you I have not seen her since we said good night last night. She is well guarded, so have no fear."

"Well, it's urgent, as you know we fear for her safety. But now there's been a direct threat, and I can't reach her."

"We had a big celebration for the team here last night, but Emily went to bed around ten. I'm scheduled to drive her to the airport in less than an hour. I'm sure we'll hear before then."

"Have her call immediately when you do." We hung up, but his tone assured me that I was rushing to conclusions.

"Guys, any luck with M's devices? And Eric, where's YaLan?"

Eric shrugged apologetically. The queen's guard was scared of me, and not without reason.

"Nothing on her phone or laptop, but nothing is not good," Brian said. "No activity except your incoming calls. Her locator is off, and that seems odd, though she didn't like the idea of being watched. Maybe it's just always off."

"No, we generally left that on. For hiking and . . ."

YaLan finally showed up on Eric's screen. "Sorry, had to get the key to her room from the front desk. Her bags are mostly packed, but perhaps she went out for a run or a walk. She told me she might before today's flight. I'm going out now to look for her."

"Eric, you go too. How could you let her go on a run with WiN set up—right outside the door?" We all had let our guard down after Moscow. Where were the mayor's guards?

"Okay," I said to what remained of the family. "Let's assume the worst, that possibly a WiN cell has her. But why and where? And what can we do? Brian, prepare to call the State Department and issue a press release. Also, find out if there's a good PI firm for me to work with in Athens, and book my flight."

"Sean?"

"Yes, Ting. I almost forgot you're still there."

"What about Juno's message? It can't be a coincidence that it came just now."

"What message?" Astri asked.

"I'll let Ting explain."

Ting explained as I tried M again.

When I hung up, Astri said, "You must go to Kathmandu and to the Deeksha. Eric and YaLan can lead a search from Athens, and Brian and I from here. Their wired-in heads will actually do some good. Sean, if you believe in telepathy, it's a no-brainer. You go to Nepal now."

My phone was ringing—Professor Alberto from Athens.

"It's near time to pick her up for the airport and still no word. The mayor's guards assure me she did not leave her room."

"But it's empty! YaLan was just there. Get the mayor and get all local authorities to search!"

"Yes, of course."

"You and the mayor assured her safety. Damn it, get the city to search. Call down Persephone and find her!"

"Persephone?" he asked foolishly.

"The goddess of protection and safety. Maybe if you knew your own history and lived up to your guarantees . . ." I was cursing him but blaming myself. I had assumed our NATO ally might dance for the CIA but not for the Russians or WiN and that the mayor's guarantee meant lightning could not possibly strike twice in Athens. I had failed M by, of all things, having too limited an imagination.

"Sir, this is Brian. Sean is understandably upset. Are you wired-in?"

"Yes!"

"Good. Eric and I will coordinate, in that way, with you."

"Yes, you all do that!" I said, signaling to get him off the phone before I said something more I might regret.

Brian's hand was up as we hung up, and he said, "I just got a message from Eric. He and YaLan are still looking, but based on the time, they think the worst-case scenario may be true."

As we all scrambled with racing thoughts and jangling nerves, looking at our devices and each other for our next steps, my next step was handed to me.

Brian said, "Shit. This was just posted on the college bulletin board. Somebody is ahead of us. Look at this."

It was a lewd picture of me disheveled from firefighting and mesmerized by a naked Samantha touching her nipples less than a few feet from me. The snapshot caught my damn gobsmacked eyes entranced by her ghastly beauty. The fire whipped up behind us like a cobra ready to strike.

That image of lust had been posted anonymously, of course. And with a caption: "Professor Emily Edens goes missing in Athens as Professor Sean McQueen is caught in affair with a student. Portland, US, and Greek authorities have been notified and are starting inquiries."

WiN was opening a second front and attacking us with a full assault on me at the Deeksha West. I didn't have time to wallow in the Strawberry Fields of my humiliation, but instead took command.

"Brian, find out where—*who*—posted that image of . . . of me. One thing for sure, Samantha didn't take the picture."

"It appears to be a high-tech satellite or drone image, but I'll check."

"Alien paparazzi covering their tracks." My black humor, masking my shame, was not appreciated or understood.

I was about to bark orders to get me a ticket to Athens when a whisper came through the alien channel of the universal mind. The message—*Do you believe in your heart or only think you understand Big Love?*—came with a knowing of what I must do next.

"And get me out of here and on the next flight to Kathmandu. Astri, please take charge of the children and make sure they're kept away from the news. I'll speak to them before I leave, but tell them their mother is missing and that I'm going to find her. I'll keep it low-key, so if you all could do the same. Eric, you and YaLan lead the search in Athens. In Europe. Shit, she could be anywhere."

THE CHILDREN WERE WAITING for their bedtime reading. They were particularly excited, as we were midway through *The Lion, the Witch and the Wardrobe*. But Narnia would have to wait, as there was no time before my flight to indulge in fantasy and ritual.

I had to say goodbye, though I didn't know what to say. I'd prepared a plausible fabrication. At their nine o'clock bedtime, as I was hastily packing, Astri brought them to the bedroom. She then went to my office to wait. The children raced to the bed and jumped on it, Juno testing me by treating the bed like a trampoline again. Dylan sat on my open suitcase, waiting for me to stop the jumping bean, but I let her antics go. Just as I did Dylan's accidental wrinkling of my clothes when he sat on them. I jumped on the bed too and pulled them both down for a snuggle. They'd come in full of joy, and I wanted them to leave the same way.

Dylan said, "Tomorrow's the day Mom's supposed to come home?"

Juno added, "And now you're leaving to meet her and we can't read Narnia tonight?"

"I'm sure Astri would be more than happy to sit in."

Dylan shook his head for them both. "No, we'll wait for you—the story is in your voice in my head. We'll ask her to read some other book tonight."

Their eyes showed they knew something big was up, if not something terribly wrong. They had keen instincts and their mother's built-in bullshit detector. I scrapped the words I'd prepared. They weren't true. I couldn't lie and didn't want to cry, which presented itself as an equally poor alternative. So I started off-script and prayed for the right words to come.

"You know how much good Mom did on the tour. It was a huge success. Now someone wants her and her message of Big Love all to themselves. Isn't that selfish and wrong?"

They both nodded as tears started to well up, neither wanting to let the faucet run first. I think they were waiting for me to take the lead.

"But we're not going to let that happen, right? Mom won't let that happen. I won't let that happen. And the family won't let that happen." I didn't know where I was going, but I had to dam the tears, and they were so good at picking up subtext.

"You know Big Love and what Mom and Juno say—*love is the absence of fear*. So we must be fearless for her, okay?" I was doing my best to navigate the truth and child psychology. "But it's okay to be scared too. But be sure to realize—and be—the light of love inside you even in the middle of the fear. That is true fearlessness."

Not surprisingly, they looked both scared and fearless. Like Peter and Wendy about to fight Captain Hook.

"Can we sleep here in yours and Mommy's room like we used to?" Juno asked. "While you are both gone?"

"I can bring back my camping Aerobed," Dylan added. "Princess Meimei can have your nice bed."

"Sounds like a plan. I'll tell Astri, but only if Princess Meimei doesn't jump on it."

She smiled at her nickname.

"I'm leaving very soon to go get her, so go over to Mom's table there. There's pen and paper for you. Why don't you write your mom a letter together like you do? And I'll give it to her when I see her." I looked at the desk—not to be called a vanity, because M had none—where M would sit some nights to write in her private journal. She said she'd show me and the children those musings someday. Until then, the journal was kept inside the drawer, safe from my curiosity.

They jumped off the bed and, sitting together on the small seat, started collaborating. They alternated lines, first Dickinson and then

Keats, in rhyme. Listening to them write with unvarnished feeling was a master class in the art of the tearjerker, and I wouldn't edit a word. When I heard Dylan recite his lines—*Mom, we got you a baseball glove / but you'll never tag Juno out / moving at the speed of light and love / she's as fast and agile as a little elf*—I had to excuse myself. *Agile with little? Further slant rhyming out and elf?*

"I'm going to the bathroom," I told them. "I'll be right back."

I cried for approximately five minutes before flushing the toilet and running water in the sink. That deception, I allowed. When I emerged, they were waiting by the door. They both insisted on licking and kissing the envelope's seal. I was relieved that they didn't ask me to read it first.

Dylan handed me the letter. The envelope's address line was prominent in bold red: *Mommy, for your eyes only*. Juno looked at me like a yoga master delivering an important message. "You give it to Mommy."

We hugged goodbye, and they gave me strength by never shedding a tear.

AS DYLAN'S AEROBED WAS BEING INFLATED, I was in a human-driven Uber on the way to the airport for my midnight flight to Shanghai, with a layover there before the flight to Kathmandu. Portland had become a portal of US and China aviation and cultural exchange, but this was the last flight of the day or the first flight of the next. I chose not to take Sherlock and ordered a driver so Sherlock wouldn't learn of my leaving him behind—automatic cars communicated between each other like gossips, and Sherlock's moves might be watched. His mind might be hacked, and if so that could end with him taking us straight into a head-on collision with my future, which approached like a speeding brick wall.

I managed to review, with minor edits, a well-written and to-the-point press release prepared by the boys. I choked up when picking a picture of M to use with the release. She was in the vineyard, in simple white T-shirt and blue jeans, a cowboy hat tilted up to reveal the sun playing on her face as she smiled at me taking her picture. Her chest was full of breath and her eyes so full of life, a being fully liberated, except for the smile that tethered her to me. A smile I might never see again.

The Uber driver, maybe the last of the Mohicans working behind the wheel and dispensing sage advice, caught my eye in his mirror. "Sir, are you having a heart attack?"

"No, sorry." I released the clenching hold I had on my shirt collar. "Just choking back tears." I started sobbing.

"Man up, dude," he said, tossing back a box of tissues.

"Okay, Coach Gavaghan."

"What?"

"Nothing, but thanks."

He was right—I had to focus on saving M. I wrote Professor Alberto an apology while asking him to remind the mayor that it was his assurance we'd relied upon and requesting that all the powers of the city be brought to bear to find M.

His response that M went missing without a trace angered me again. The mayor's men—stationed on her hotel floor—had seen no one enter or exit her room from the time M went to bed until she went missing. Security footage confirmed the unhelpful mystery.

"Obviously she was taken through the window," I typed.

"The police suspect alien abduction—we've had several confirmed cases over the past couple of months. They're increasing in Athens."

"That's a convenient way to open and close a missing person case. And of course, now that it's in the news daily, everyone is seeing aliens everywhere." I was done with him and his Molly-sounding theory. I asked Brian and Eric to continue to inquire about the window kidnapping and to keep the pressure on the Greek professor and mayor.

Already WiN was covering their tracks with claims of eyewitnesses to the alien abduction from the hostile witnesses holding vigil in the street—"a beam of blinding light that hovered and extended into her hotel window"—but no one had felt inspired enough to capture it on video.

I debated with the boys about a reward. I agreed with them that M was deeply loved by so many that no reward might be needed. But I decided that those able to help might *not* be so loving and admirable. We made the reward $100,000 for information leading to her safe return. The boys convinced me that only the kidnapper would desire more than that for her return, so we didn't need to offer that much and would wait for a ransom demand. Before I got to the airport, the adult Amber Alert was posted with a picture and bounty. Wanted! Alive!

I then wrote my defense to my humiliation. My picture was making a big splash on social media and WiN sites. My defense was posted on our school site, explaining the incriminating photo and assuring the student body that no affair had taken place. I would be leading the search to ensure Professor Edens's safe return. Those well-chosen words made barely a ripple of interference in the wave of sensationalism of those clamoring to see the siren Samantha's glistening body illuminated by firelight and the fire of lust burning in my eyes. I tried to push the cursed image from my mind, which served only to sear the shot into my head, ready to appear anytime I looked for peace by shutting my eyes.

The press release was posted, and the State Department was sending a team to the Deeksha West before my flight took off. I was impressed that they'd been so quick to take the call. They wouldn't be pleased that I wouldn't be there for questioning and possible detention. I told myself I wasn't just running to the safest place in the world, but staying free to save M. And I did, despite some doubt, believe in the Juno-Ting telepathy and that I was going where destiny demanded.

I kept asking myself, *What are you doing?* and *How will you save her?* But no answers came.

Perhaps I'd never had a chance to avert the loss Juno had foreseen. But she hadn't said that M was lost and never found. And my vow to protect her now meant finding her. But how, when Petrovsky had the power of Russia, and the army of the wired-ins had millions worldwide? She could be in a high-security prison or chained in some radical WiN cell's basement in Athens or anywhere. But I thought Petrovsky had to be behind such a high-profile snatching from the fifth floor. He was no alien or Captain Kirk, but he had a lot of their technology.

The alien theory was moving at warp speed over the internet, so theoretically she could be galaxies and light years away by now. The one place she surely wasn't was the Deeksha in Kathmandu.

With little else for me to do, I contemplated Samantha's role in all this. She couldn't be the mastermind with her WiN friends—I had pinned that honor on Petrovsky. Rather than set up a direct confrontation with the State Department or FBI, I thought I'd phone Elliot and ask him to see what he could glean from his coed confidante. This

subplot allowed me to do something other than just run for the mountains of Kathmandu.

Elliot was grateful to play a role and for my continued confidence.
By the time the call ended, he had some half-baked plan to ply her with
wine, also with that Ecstasy or Molly she loved so, and I can't believe
I didn't say no. But the measures seemed justified under the circumstances, and Elliot was eager to take part in a secret mission and knew
his target well.

The business-class seat out of Portland was a bed of solitude. But
there would be no sleep as I sat wallowing in the self-recriminations
of a desperate fool. What would I do in Nepal but wait for Ting to
receive a message from Juno to guide my next move? I prayed only
half-facetiously that the aliens would take me from the plane to M.

By the time I'd flown west and landed in Shanghai, a media tempest
was blowing worldwide. Professor Emily Edens had allegedly issued a
competing press release that said the Deeksha West statement was a mistake and that she was safe and taking a much-needed rest in seclusion
following her whirlwind lecture tour. The announcement could have
been posted by a WiN-nut or just some teenage girl, a social media influencer with an M fantasy.

So great was my respect for Molly, she convinced me to take the alien
option seriously. She had contacted and was working with a CE-5 group
who believed they could communicate with aliens. Molly was already
living in 2036. She believed my flying to Kathmandu to pursue telepathy
and remote viewing options was the most useful step I could take. She
insisted we should do all we could to open channels for contact.

The most popular theory skipped over abduction and to M being
dead, with me the killer. I punched a wall along the concourse, wishing for this all to be a nightmare and to wake up with M next to me,
wishing for anything other than the attention of two members of the
People's Liberation Army who were now following the agitated passenger to the lounge.

WiN was almost ecstatic in their embrace of the salacious story line
and sin-ready photo, insisting I was behind M's disappearance and had

fled to a destination unknown. They even suggested the State Department and Interpol wanted me for questioning and probable arrest. Of course, my hasty departure only added fuel to rampant suspicion. I, too, was missing, but not as a victim. I'd made myself a suspect.

Everyone was looking for M and me, and half our world wished she'd never be found, or would be found dead, with me as her killer. I tortured myself, wondering whether it would be better to find her dead or not at all. I always found the conventional wisdom strange that held there was closure and consolation in finding a missing person's bones. Better M lived with angels or aliens forever.

I arrived at my business-class lounge in Shanghai, and my upper-class status seemed to satisfy the Communist military that I was not a threat. Inside the pampering enclave, a traveling Chinese ballet troupe used a rail by the window to stretch and practice pirouettes and leaps anywhere they could make room without annoying anyone other than me. I was reminded of the spinning dervishes in Dubai that M and I had seen on our way east to Kathmandu and with whom she had danced. I was in no mood for dancing, and the twirling only added to the whirlpool of stress. I found myself cursing the ballet school.

I reached out to Brian as the hub of our response at the Deeksha West. Eric and YaLan joined the V-room call from Athens. I imagined people were noticing me and looking away as if I were a notorious O. J. making a slow-motion escape. Though I was isolated in my corner of the luxury lounge, I put my travel mask back on.

The reality was even worse than my imagination.

"What?" I couldn't believe it.

"The State Department *does* want to question you," Brian repeated. "We haven't told them of your travel plans. For all they know you're still in Oregon, but it won't be long till they cross-reference your flight out, if they haven't already. It's good your layover is short and in China."

"Sounds like I'm on the lam. Eric, is it true Interpol wants to question me too?"

"Yeah, it's good you didn't come to Athens. They might have arrested you as soon as you landed."

"What the hell for? I didn't do anything other than be in a bad picture. You know what I mean . . . Are there other pictures of me being circulated?"

"There's one of you with a mask on from your departure today. Sorry. That one was just posted. Conspiracy theories about you are flying around the same wired-in circles that were trolling M. They're spinning their discrediting campaign at hyperspeed."

"So that's why everyone is looking at me in my fleece with the Deeksha West logo. Not the best disguise. What's the tone, the worst they have to say?"

I pulled up one of the pictures being circulated—my thinning hair made me look bald. I pulled out a vintage Kangal hat from my bag and put it on backward. My picture's face looked sullen and unkind, like a celebrity being caught without makeup. I almost didn't recognize me.

Eric said, "They speak of the Deeksha West as some kind of big love cult with its two masterminds now battling for control. Even the *New York Post* online already has that picture and cover story, captioned 'Academic Murder or Deans in Divorce.' None of it makes much sense, but it's spreading like wildfire across the internet, supercharged through the blockchain of wired-in minds."

"Ask Elliot if we can sue them for libel since M and I aren't married." We were deans of the college, but getting it half right was no defense. "Okay, what else should I know? Any response to our reward? I'm boarding and better get on before someone gets the authorities here."

A little Eurasian girl wearing a yellow headscarf and white and sky blue full-length dress, maybe ten years old, was dancing around me, clutching a bag in both hands. Perhaps she was a cute and colorful little suicide bomber.

"We've had tons of responses and are sorting through them with YaLan and Astri's help," Brian said from Oregon. "Most seem like people who either love or hate M and want to help or hinder the investigation with false leads and deep-fake pictures."

Eric said, "After this call, I'm set to meet with the Pinkerton group, a big international security firm that specializes in missing person investigations. They'll help us sort through to the more credible alerts."

Like I didn't know the Pinkertons, a company still flourishing after hunting Jesse James and then Butch Cassidy and his Hole-in-the-Wall Gang.

"Good," I said. "Get the Pinkertons on the case before they're hired to find me. And make sure our guileless friend in Athens has the alien ghostbusters on the case too, crazy as that sounds. We may all be in danger. Be careful."

"Sean, you're the one with a target on your back," Brian noted. "You need to be extremely careful. Go now. I can see that business class has started boarding."

"Thanks for that. Keep sending updates. I'll read them from the plane. And let me know what I can do. I don't know if we're better off if it's Petrovsky or WiN, or aliens. One thing we alone know—*I* didn't do it."

I should have kidnapped her before she disappeared. I was wrong about the Guru but right about the threat, but still I failed to protect her.

When I looked up, the tiny suicide dancer in her smart dress was standing right in front of me, a swaying youthful metronome ready to explode. She became still and pulled down her mask. I kept mine on but smiled with my eyes at her innocence and beauty. What a way to die. Then from her bag she removed a book, not a bomb. *The Lost Theory*. Hers was a timely kindness the universe was sending to me—a drink of water for a man drowning in the desert sea. Or a sign that my life had become a comic tragedy.

"What's your name?"

"Sita."

She smiled, and in her eyes I saw the Buddha nature we all share. I saw Dylan in her, in the essence she was sharing. She handed me her book, and with Molly's pen I wrote *Dear Sita, sent by the universe to shine your light, and to share kindness with a man lost in transit, reminding him of Big Love even in the darkness. Peace, love, and light, Sean McQueen.*

She turned and ran away with her treasure, but it wasn't nearly as precious as the ray of hope she'd given me. Maybe Dylan reincarnated? She was the right age and too young to have read the book.

Dylan, was that you? What should I do? M's death would be the end of love, and maybe even of my faith in Big Love. M would disapprove, but I can't help feeling this way. I hadn't spoken to him for years and there was no answer, but I knew he was still with me in my heart's core. It was as if he had moved to Mars and only his phone battery had died, not him. Yes, I was grasping for a lifeline.

As I was boarding for takeoff, Brian sent a picture of me signing the little girl's book in the airport lounge. At least that one was flattering and already being liked by some in the wired-in world who were tracking my great escape that might just land me in a Nepal prison cell.

LANDING IN KATHMANDU FELT STRANGE without M by my side—the loneliness of returning to the Garden of Eden without Eve. I was in a Grimm fairy tale accompanied by Bob Marley singing about Jah love. Over the airport's sound system and from his early grave, the grand master Rasta was reminding me that love would never leave us alone and that the light would come out against the darkness.

From behind my tired eyes and mask, I searched for the Nepalese police waving their batons or, far more sinister, Western men in suits concealing their guns and waving their badges. Despite my foreboding, I found the warmest of welcomes: Ting and Boy stood in front of a cast of masked well-wishers as I exited the restricted area. Ting laid a garland of flowers around my neck and hugged me the way Juno would have.

"Aloha, Sean!"

"Hell-lo-a, Ting!"

She embraced me with scintillating energy that radiated through my cold and rigid body that welcomed any warmth. It was our first real meeting in person, but I felt I'd known her for many lifetimes and not just from a couple of holograms.

Boy's eyes and mine met, and there came those tears again. We hugged. Hugging had become more meaningful as it had become less frequent. Those hugs in the hallway of an echoing airport thousands of miles from the Deeksha West restored my sense of purpose and resolve. After fleeing home and family, this greeting by my extended family brought sorely needed solace. And I found painful joy in the midst of my despair.

Over Boy's shoulder, I saw a young man whose eyes, now smiling over a mask, I'd promised never to forget. He pulled the veil down so I could see his entire face. "Chi!"

He was a handsome man now, but he still carried the same beaming innocence of the twelve-year-old boy I'd known so well for a short period of time. The earthquake nine years ago had opened a vortex in time that moved moments more slowly and intensely in the days that followed, which provided all the time needed to form unbreakable bonds, even for those who didn't share a language.

Chi stood before me now as tall as me. Time was moving slowly once again. We hugged as the tears kept coming. I was rendered speechless by my welcome and the depth of my tears. Would they ever stop? I had cried more in the past couple days than the entire prior decade.

"Some of the earthquake guests found out of your return from the internet and are here to welcome and protect you."

Chi's English, with its noticeable British accent, was spot-on, and with a flourish of his hand to the other twenty or so well-wishers, they gathered around me like a swarm of humanity, without fear of viruses or the dark forces of the devil who had kidnapped M.

When the social space around us returned, Chi said, "I just graduated Cambridge with a degree in philosophy. I'm wired-in and strong like Buddha. You might need my help. If I may come pitch a tent at the Deeksha with you?"

Boy smiled and wrapped an arm around our mighty philosopher. "No tent this time. We have a room for you. Be our guest."

"Welcome, Chi! I'm Ting. I think you knew my sister?"

"Yes, sweet Mother Juno! Hello, Ting. What an honor to meet you."

Following the reunion, we would all be together at the Deeksha, nurtured in a community of Big Love while M was lost to whatever cruelty her captors could inflict.

I was through the looking glass once more. My plan had only taken me this far; beyond this moment lay the unknown. I felt like a limp sack of wet rice bobbing in an ocean, buoyed only by the collective love of my Eastern family.

As we headed through the throng to the airport exit, I noticed that many of my well-wishers—who continued to line up as a corridor of greeting—held a copy of *The Lost Theory*. Our book was the best English-language seller in Kathmandu year after year, a source of local pride, but this was my first return to the novel's place of conception.

"Despite the circumstances, M's been missing almost twenty-four hours now. They say that after three days . . ." I let out a sigh that bordered on an unseemly moan, but managed to continue walking with my procession, trying to look strong and resolute in my expression, posture, and stride. "I'm looking forward to returning to the Deeksha," I breathed, ready for the surrounding audience to disappear despite the comfort they had momentarily provided.

Boy draped his arm around me, watching me with his sad doe eyes, and murmured, "Yes, for tonight. But we thought you should go first thing in the morning with Ting to Juno's sanctuary. It is safer there, and where Juno can communicate with us." He spoke louder when he added, "Later, if you're up to it, you might like to greet your fans at the Deeksha in a prayer gathering as another means of making contact." I wasn't sure if he meant contact with Juno, M, her captors, or aliens.

I was shocked to find myself a small-town celebrity. I wanted to share my moment of arrival with M. *They all love me*, gushed my inner Sally Field. I mentally slapped myself to keep my focus on M and to figure out, now that I'd reached my destination, what the hell I could do to find her.

Boy drove a 2024 Tesla jeep—autopilot off—over the now more manageable streets of Kathmandu. I called Eric and Brian. The family was running a twenty-four-hour operation on our mission to save M. There wouldn't be much sleep until we knew where she was. I feared she'd be missing forever, like Juno. And Molly would have her alien-inspired sequel.

The twins delighted in hearing Chi's grown-up voice and that he had signed up to assist in our mission to find M. They spoke with him in

Nepali and then introduced their young Americans in English. The boys connected with Chi via their wired-in BCIs. I still was unsure how the BCI tech worked and wondered how intimate it was. The best I understood it, it was like getting a text without a device, accessed through a posting on their shared computer. It wasn't yet an immediate communication mind to mind but through a massive switchboard and data bank they could choose to access and post on at will. But like that darn phantasmagoria, *2036*, it apparently *had* to be experienced. And Genesis was a new generation, with the immediacy of mind-to-mind connectivity, which no one had yet experienced other than through telepathy.

We agreed that Eric and Brian would filter out all the noise and not share all the deepfake videos and report to me only what I needed to know. This left me nothing to do other than wait for Elliot to report on Samantha. He was still conducting his covert mission, and if she was involved . . . Well, our plan hadn't plotted that far ahead. However, born of desperation, my own secret mission came to me. Sir Arthur Conan Doyle didn't know that I knew him to be our very own witch, Samantha. So I'd be within my rights, and still honor Elliot's confidence, to write Sir Arthur at that easily remembered CyberSecure address to attempt to put the fear of God into her.

And so I wrote *him*.

Dear Sir Arthur,

You are a suspected accomplice in the kidnapping of Professor Emily Edens. This CS encryption will not prevent the authorities from unmasking you. But if you come forward with useful information, I will protect you from prosecution. On that you have my word. From what I am able to discern, you have only a matter of hours before they crack the code or obtain a warrant for the key and you will be known and no longer deserving of my protection. Time is of the essence.

Professor Sean Byron McQueen

I didn't think Samantha was involved or that my threat would work, because CyberSecure warrants required probable cause, but I had to cover all the bases. Still, I was left banking on telepathy, a fickle medium of communication to rely on in a life-and-death situation.

While M's missing status had the internet insects buzzing and weaving with misinformation, I was an international criminal escaping to Nepal. Even I had some vocal support, however. Not from those who assumed I was innocent but from some who assumed I was guilty—a romantic hero in the flesh. Some people always root for the desperado. No one seemed interested in my innocence. It was the least marketable of all the possible stories.

There was no mention of Moscow's involvement, and that became another source of family debate. I asked Brian to remind the State Department of that damn *Ninth Wave* painting M received from a Russian source and M's invitation to collaborate on Genesis and to push them to confront the bear-wrestling Petrovsky. And to scramble our satellite lasers to prepare for attack. I was willing to risk star wars to save M, but my government was not.

As we were saying goodbyes, I caught Ting's eye and immediately said, "Oh my God, I keep forgetting. I received confirmation of Ting's telepathy at the same time the Jabberwocky message came in. From Molly Quinn's assistant in China. They have unearthed evidence that Juno is being held in Tibet under some vague charges of espionage and crimes against the state."

We then discussed at length the long-overdue report. I felt forgiven under the circumstances, and for Ting and the twins, no confirmation was needed, so firm was their belief in telepathy. The call ended on this relatively high note that did little to raise my spirits.

Ting wasn't a big talker, but like her sister, her silence spoke and her presence filled the car with love. Chi, too, was a buoyant spirit and a comforting frequency holder. Maybe they had mentioned it or maybe I imagined it, but I knew instinctively that the other high-frequency holders, YaLan and Astri, were spending much of their time trying to contact M and Juno via telepathy. My heart was crying out for contact too. I hoped we wouldn't get our signals crossed.

Boy had matured and was much less reticent to speak than before. From behind the wheel, he spoke like a tour guide about his beloved Kathmandu.

"So different now and mostly for the better. The poor government, aided by international donations, converted the tourist trade from a destination for egomaniacs looking to summit Everest on the backs of Sherpas into a shrine of nature and a mecca for those who come to be in harmony with nature. The Sherpas are paid to keep the mountain safe and pristine, while the profiteering tour companies were sent home. Spiritual centers, hostels, and trekking still bring in loads of tourists as a haven for the young and adventurous—while the metaverse, fear of viruses, and the possibility of more earthquakes have kept away the faint-hearted. You see the traffic and dust are all but gone and the streets shimmer with life and spiritual rebirth. Kathmandu now shines in the sun . . . but not today—rainy season."

I looked up at the dense low cloud cover that draped the town with something akin to my dark foreboding mood.

He finished his travelogue as we pulled into the tree-lined entrance to the Deeksha. I felt like I was returning to a childhood school where I'd fallen in love and been touched by grace, but where the magical headmistress, as well as my fellow student and soul mate, were both absent. But was this the comedy of *Cardenio*, where the determined hero prevails, winning back his Luscinda, or was it the tragedy of *Don Quixote*, where the forlorn and ridiculous hero never finds his Dulcinea?

WITH JUNO CAPTIVE IN TIBET and M captive or dead somewhere in the universe, my return to the Xanadu of the Deeksha was disorienting. I was sleepwalking in paradise while the world was burning down around me.

Boy had shut down the Deeksha's "restaurant" to await its master chef's return who insisted it was just a tea house. He explained, "The Deeksha is now solely a meditation and spiritual gathering place. We received large donations from those who came to meditate or who know the place from your book and want to help maintain it while we wait for Juno to come home. Her absence became a vacuum for seeking hearts."

Boy helped me settle into my room, the same room where Dylan's ghost and I had wrestled to near death. "I'd almost forgotten this room's energy, but it's all coming back to me and providing hope," I said. I touched the bed's beautiful wooden headboard and then used it as a support when I was flooded with memories.

"Many spiritual guests and speakers have stayed here to teach now that the Deeksha is a spiritual retreat and pilgrimage site."

"Anyone I would know?"

"Eckhart Tolle from the West and Radhanath Swami. And from the East, Sadhguru was here. Mother Meera and Amma too, but they stayed in the room M used. We call this room Babaji's resting place."

He gave me a namaste, and I returned the blessing with deep soul-to-soul eye contact.

"Did he stay here too?"

Boy laughed. "Babaji? He's the nameless one who has many names and has lived in the Himalayas for centuries. You should take YaLan and Astri's classes on yoga teachings, and then you would know."

He was right. They taught me every day, but I never went to their classroom to sit in and didn't know any of the teachers, saints, or avatars that Boy had mentioned other than Mother Meera. And I knew of her only because she'd been popularized in the West by an academic and disciple who later tried to discredit her but only discredited himself and his work. All guru worship was rife with pitfalls and brokenhearted spiritual lovers who became too attached to their guru.

I took our time alone to say, "I'm sorry I wasn't here for you when Juno disappeared. I know how hard that must have been on you— alone—with the twins already in the States and not able to travel." The twins had returned to the States to live permanently with their track stars the spring before the onslaught of the Great Pandemic and the closing down of international travel.

"Thank you, but I never felt separated from Juno. I don't speak to the dead like you or to the living like Ting, but I know she is fine."

"Ha! You read my book, so you know it's more an internal dialogue."

"Yes, I loved it—and thanks again for outing my love to Grace, though I think she already knew." His doe eyes twinkled with forgiveness and love. "But unlike the love I felt at my parents' deaths, which washed over me as they transitioned to a higher plane, I always felt in my heart that Juno's love remains here in this world."

"That's a powerful love, you know. My heart shared that feeling. You showed such strength through those dark days."

He sat on the bed, and I sat next to him and put my arm around him. We were a comfort to each other.

"We weren't completely cut off. Grace came on a private jet bringing aid for poor children. The Pandemic didn't end poverty or stop her from her humanitarian mission. She stayed for three months as we searched with Ting for Juno and until we settled into Juno's absence. So hard under pandemic restrictions to get the authorities to focus. It was as if the virus came in response to Juno's absence. Grace and

Ting pulled me through. Grace was leaving Hollywood and starting her work with children in need."

"The press back home dubbed her Hepburn the Second," I said.

"What?"

"Audrey, not Katharine."

"I don't know Audrey or Katharine."

Boy wasn't a movie buff despite his love of a Hollywood star. I took back my arm to check that I still had power on my cell phone, in case the alien captain or WiN maniac wanted to reach me.

"But with Ting being here again now and the tele-messages, my hope is renewed for Juno's return. But our new loss is M. You must be wild with worry. But she isn't lost forever, I pray." His eyes were lowered and he did pray, while I looked up for Laplace's demon to show me the past, of who took M and where, and into the future, of how I might save her.

I felt I needed to cheer Boy up. "My heart tells me she's alive too. And it doesn't lie, at least so far. I can't lose M. She's my life. I'd rather die. I know that's not Big Love, but what can I do? And how can those ladies say with such conviction that nothing real is ever lost? I can only pray that that's true."

We laughed. There was nothing else to do, and we were together again, our eyes meeting as though no time had elapsed since the last time our eyes had met over the barrel of a gun.

"So why am I here? What do we do now?" I asked.

"We wait."

"I'm not good at waiting."

Patience had grown in me over the years, but M's disappearance had triggered old vices. As if the constant demand of *where is she* would hasten the answer. I was waiting for some miracle from Moscow or a State Department spy to uncover the plot or *my man Flint* to turn up some lead from his mission with Samantha or for aliens to drop M off at the Buddha pond for a welcome home kiss. Actually *being* patient under these circumstances was the acid test of patience. Everything to come was unknown.

After dinner and before dark descended, we set up by the Buddha pond for a family V-room. We all stood, unwilling to sit as Boy served tea. When he finished, I invited Ting to join me on the sacred seat where M and I had met in the days following the earthquake, when death threats appeared under my pillow and shots were fired across my face. Boy and Chi sat alongside us on meditation cushions placed over the big, smooth rocks around the Buddha. I read Dylan's poem "Spring Blessing," inscribed there, to the gathering, but felt cursed by this long summer where time crept forward as if the next moment might be its last.

When the V-room started, YaLan and Astri reminded Chi of his childhood innocence and how he used to dance. Chi blushed. I imagined twelve-year-old Chi had retained many dreams of those beautiful yogis who showed him such affection during the days following the earthquake.

After an hour of dead-end leads and no good news, I was emotionally wrung out and back in Dylan's old room. I called to him, even if just to wrestle silently, but I received no visitation. Elliot and I had agreed to no contact unless he was able to unearth something worthwhile to report. Soon I would pull him back and send in the FBI, but Samantha would of course deny any contact, and my wired-in boys had sworn she'd left no digital fingerprints even if she was involved. I continuously wrote threats and ploys to Sir Arthur at PO59666, with only silence in return. I began to wonder if my separate line of attack on Samantha was sabotaging Elliot's espionage mission.

Juno was silent too. I implored her to contact Ting or whisper something, anything, to me. I wrote Ting at midnight, and she responded immediately.

"I'll do all I can. We'll get to her sanctuary soon. That seems to be the best portal. With us together there, there will be powerful energy."

My irregular heartbeat repeated *M, I have—to see—you again. M, I have—to see—you again.*

As I lay listening to my heart and the thoughts circling in my head for the better part of the night, I expected the police or the men in

black to burst into the chamber. I wished the door had a lock. I prayed
for peace of mind.

I knew that telepathy, a true evolutionary advance that required
practice, focus, and calmness of mind, wouldn't be able to silently slip
through the chattering of monkeys in my brain. I was determined to
reach M, and telepathy was the only available route. So I tried, but I had
no idea what I was doing . . . and no success with my method of inton-
ing M's name, like an *aum*, over and over again with ritual conviction.

The combination of Boy's influence and the good heart of the spiritual body politic had so far kept the authorities and the media away from
the Deeksha. According to Chi, Boy had become a man of some clout
in Kathmandu after Juno disappeared. And the local G-men weren't in
a hurry to go after his guests. The Deeksha was an integral part of the
city's growth and renaissance. In Kathmandu, the spiritual infused all
aspects of life, even the politics. All municipal employees practiced yoga
and meditation as part of the job. And many of the current senior town
officials had been trained by YaLan and Astri. I imagined smiles being
passed between strangers on the street.

Nobody knew the precise location of Juno's secluded sanctuary, so
I'd feel even safer once there. Although I had telegraphed its location
in my novel, the name of the village was fictional—this one element of
fiction would serve as my protection. Something about the sanctuary
was so holy and so private that in the final draft I'd made up the hamlet of *Badhrahni* rather than betray its true location. There were those
who knew, however, where Yogi Mangku had lived, and that knowledge
would get them close.

I punched my pillow and wished I'd brought my ball and glove to
silence fear-inspired thoughts. *M! M! M!*

Brian had said that reports circulating on the internet claimed that
I was trekking in the mountains to stay away from all the hype and a
potential snatching by some extrajudicial force. Boy and Chi neither
confirmed nor denied those helpful reports, which only led to people believing that the reports were true. Chi had told me that I was
becoming beloved by the Nepali as an outlaw evading capture, a Clyde

searching for his Bonnie. They not only liked my dashing story but also believed in my innocence.

Such thoughts circled around to the death scene in *Bonnie and Clyde*. And the violent images pushed me out of bed and to a cushion on the floor, where I attempted to settle into a meditative and telepathic pose in order to replace the film reel in my head that featured M and me slow-motion dancing to the tune of bullets ripping us to shreds. Sadly but without surprise, I realized that the machine-gunning clip was a perverse form of wish fulfillment—to die by her side would be better than letting her die lost and alone.

54 DEEPFAKES

THE NEXT MORNING BROUGHT WITH IT day two of the three-day Amber Alert window. I had lost track of time. I hoped that missing adults had a larger window to climb back through, but with every slow-moving hour, our chances of finding M diminished. Before Ting and I left for Juno's sanctuary, we held another west and east family meeting, with the Kathmandu Deeksha contingent gathering at the Buddha pond. The pond that morning had a putrid smell, so out of place in that spot of amazing grace. Chi, Boy, and Ting all took cushions on the smooth stones, leaving me alone, without M, on the sacred seat. Brian, Eric, YaLan, and Astri were soon all on the V-room line.

I started the meeting with a stab at normalcy. "Item One!" My false nonchalance did nothing to lighten the mood. "Okay, there's only one item: to find M and return her safely to the family. I'll remain unplugged from all the chatter and will rely on Eric, Brian, and Chi to keep me informed of material developments in the virtual world. Is there any new information or additional steps we should take? I want to be proactive here. Hell, I envy Elliot . . ." I stopped, suddenly remembering that no one else had been told of his role in attempting to find out if Samantha was involved in the WiN plot to steal M away.

Brian let me go without inquiring, instead stating, "The tempest of conspiracies and false claims has gained strength around some invisible core."

Eric added, "Like some dark-energy-gathering force in *Star Wars*. And all our attempts to control the chatter only seems to add more fuel. We've been subject to a deepfake blast." I'd read that these blasts were meant to make the volume of salacious and slanderous content so widespread as to prevent any meaningful threat of prosecution for the malicious content and also provided the internet worms anonymity to spread their vilest slime.

Chi, with Boy's help, had obtained some assurances from the Nepal ministry in charge of foreign affairs that they would seek to block any efforts to have me detained for questioning on behalf of the US State Department. I was becoming an Edward Snowden–like character and the subject of international diplomatic maneuvering.

"They'll tell the US authorities they have yet to confirm you are still in Nepal—which is technically true since they've made no effort to confirm anything. And then assure their US counterparts that, once they do confirm your whereabouts, they will cooperate with all legal requests for an interview." Chi grinned. "They'll stall. They are good at confusion and delay. Which means we have a couple of days."

We might have time, but M might not, said the ticking of the Amber clock.

"Good work, Chi, and thank you," I said. "Hopefully a couple days will be more than enough time. Chi and Boy, please keep them informed and on our side, and I'll keep praying for a miracle."

"It's good that Chi's out front on all of this," Brian said. "I'm doing my best here to delay too but the heat is increasing. The State Department agent in charge wants you to report to the embassy *there* so he can interview you remotely. I told him you may be trekking and couldn't be reached. He said to make contact as soon as you're back on the grid and warned me not to lie or I would face prosecution."

"I don't want to go back to that embassy." I wondered if the same man was still there that had been so unhelpful last time I had made a visit to our embassy in Kathmandu. "We could do that from here, so why at the embassy? US soil?"

"I don't know," Brian said. "Good question. I'll ask."

"Sean, I know this will annoy you, but the State Department's not ruling out alien abduction. The Greeks are convinced and showing similar cases, pointing to some pattern focused on Athens. And they have evidence of a UAP above Athens the night of—"

"I know, and they have some WiN witnesses to the alien abduction." The image of Greek gods descending upon Leda arose in my mind.

"And remember, Sean, QC believes alien abductions would target geniuses and the most spiritually advanced," Brian added.

"Well, then, assume it is aliens. What can we do? And what about that Jabberwocky? A mighty big coincidence, it coming when it did. I don't suppose aliens would produce nursery rhymes but something more—more celestial. Look, I know we need to take the alien spaceship theory seriously, but since there is nothing we can do . . . I'm an old man with long-held skepticism of little green men." I sighed. "Okay, maybe ask Molly to dig into that. This is her area of expertise and she's already working with a CE-5 group to make contact. And ask her to research people who have been recovered after being abducted. Maybe there's a pattern—a way to promote the return."

I left my seat and moved farther from the noxious pond, but its stink followed me. Even that lovely spot was less pristine and spoiled by the absence of Juno and M. Twitching my nose, I said, "And keep them thinking I'm lost in the Himalayas. I know none of us is comfortable lying, but this is the time and place to stretch the truth to protect M. And do me a favor—see if you can get Elliot to help. Sobered up, he's actually very good at research and playing a lawyer. Perhaps he can do some good. And thank you and sorry to ask, but this is no time for eight-to-eight. Please stay wired-in at all times."

"Of course," Eric answered, the others nodding. "We won't rest until she's found. But Sean, I think you could use a real lawyer. This is starting to pile up deep. One rumor is you had M killed before she could transfer V&W assets into a nonprofit trust. And there's an internet report, based on that earlier deepfake video, that she's staying at an exclusive yacht club in Belize with a playboy Russian oligarch. The explicit implication being that she had . . . you know . . ."

"Taken another lover." I laughed at my being a cuckold or a killer.

"Sean, I know it's the least of your worries, but we need to take this seriously. WiN and the authorities are determined to prove you guilty."

All the heads in the V-room moved, some up and down and some left to right, but the entire team was on the same grim page.

"Okay, when I get arrested or get back to the Deeksha West, we'll lawyer up. But for now let's try to get Elliot focused. Tell him *two more days*—he'll know what I mean." If he couldn't determine Samantha's innocence by then, I was sending the FBI in to have their fortunes read by that Stevie Nicks witch.

I couldn't say her name without that humiliating picture coming to mind. The world saw a creepy old man with a sexy student who'd killed his brilliant and talented partner, trading in the older model for the younger one.

I slammed a fist against my leg. "Of course I'm the prime suspect. Dead people follow me around like a ghostly rap sheet. The people I love either go missing or die."

When a heavy silence met my words, I looked at the group, both those at the pond and those in the V-room. Astri's ever-bright face was frowning, and Boy's ever-open arms were tightly crossed.

"Sorry," I said. "That was uncalled for. No more self-pity." Even though what I'd said was true.

"A person of interest, they said." Brian's letting me off the hook was the first voice of forgiveness. "The husband or significant other is always the first person they want to talk to. I didn't try to explain what a holy relationship is."

"Okay, let's go silent and keep mining leads. What else?"

"Sean, some wired-in nuts are blaming M for Neurotech's golden ticket decline," Brian said. "The value of the Neurochip soared after the big announcement of the new wired-in society but is now crashing. Luckily, serious financial types are attributing the fall to Silvio's being unceremoniously sacked as CEO and speculation that the beta test didn't go as planned or that Genesis could never live up to its promise. But WiN seems to hold M accountable."

"People always want a scapegoat. Why M and not Silvio?" I asked.

"Silvio is also at risk, and he's in hiding," Brian replied.

"What about our reward offer?" I asked.

"There's just too much information," YaLan said. "A deluge even for

Eric, Brian, and Chi with Astri's and my unplugged assistance. And all those ugly deepfakes." She rubbed at already bruised eyes. "But we keep plowing through it. And—"

"YaLan and I are using inspiration and intuition to guide our searches, and we just found this picture," Astri said. "You should have it there, Sean? After the thousands of M sightings and alleged photos of her on the beach, at a bar, in a car, we refined our search, zeroing in on Russia and from there to Moscow. Still, there were over a thousand. But look at this one from just an hour ago. It's too fuzzy to see the face, yet . . ."

I squinted at the picture on Chi's laptop. The woman being escorted by two thugs was M's height and had auburn hair, but her face wasn't visible and she was in generic athletic sweatpants and top, not M's clothes.

"Can you zoom in on her chest?" Chi gave me a boyish smile that would have been inappropriate on anyone else and enlarged the image. I shouted, "The mala! There—you see? She took her Yogi Mangku mala out of her shirt, and it's hanging around her neck and down to her heart!" Such a simple act pointed to her consciousness and brilliance. "She's letting us know it's her!"

"Yes, we see it too," Brian said. "I'll get this to the State Department. It should bolster our case that she's in Russia."

"Damn Petrovsky! But this is good. If it's her, we know she is alive and not with aliens." I almost longed for the dead Guru, a more accessible egomaniac. This was truly an uneven battlefield of ego, AI, and weapons of State against Big Love and belief in telepathy and divine intervention. My hands were shaking.

Astri, in an unusually meek fashion, said, "Sean, there are millions of spiritually minded people who wear malas these days, so—"

"So don't rule anything out." My heart contracted back into a lump of coal. "Okay, but still show it to the State Department. I'll wait to hear something. Anything."

But from the darkness came a flash of inspiration. "Brian, Eric, Chi . . . maybe we can use WiN's own BCI network." Yes, it might work.

"Through those wires in your heads, could you post a general alert to permeate the blockchain for me?"

"Hmm," said Chi. "Yes. Anyone tracking your or M's name would receive an alert through our shared computer host."

"Are you sure WiN is not in your minds already, monitoring all your thoughts and computer inputs?" The thought horrified me and reminded me of having the Guru for tea.

"Not without our consent," Eric said.

"But," Brian said, "we could post an open message from you. What message would we post, Sean? We want M back?"

"For now post that I have something more valuable than M to offer in exchange for M's safe return. A proposition they will want to hear."

"What can you offer? They already know that you guys are wealthy and could pay any ransom, yet they haven't demanded one."

"I have no idea—just post the message! I'll think of something. Anything else?" I'd pray for some divine inspiration so I could present some plausible deepfake of my own.

"Okay, we'll post your message and ask that they contact you through your encrypted number that only M would have, and Sean, trust us to bring you what you need to know," Eric said. "Keep the news turned off."

"Good thinking and got it—no news is best for me. Thank you. And I love you so, so much." I was fighting back tears that matched my maudlin words. "Keep telling the children I'll speak directly to them soon but that I'm looking for their mother and will find her. Remind them of what Juno taught—that nothing real can be lost, and that there's nothing more real than their mother's love." Their mother's love, ripped away by WiN or Petrovsky.

After the V-room ended, I sat alone on the bench, holding my sobbing head in both hands to keep it from rolling off my shoulders and sinking into the stinky pond. The rank odor and low, dark cloud cover suited my mood. The waiting, the not knowing, and being unable to act were insufferable. I was less than useless. I was diverting attention from whoever had M.

I could imagine the disbelieving questions.

And where were you when M was lost?

Oh, I went on an exotic vacation with friends and tried to communicate with her through a mind-to-mind channel of telepathy. It's just a matter of tuning in to the right frequency.

As I returned to my room for my bag, the pond stench followed me. Passing through a garden, I finally realized the smell was me. Two days of sweating, and without a shower, had left me stinking like a teenage trekker or traveling Indian mystic. But I wasn't hiking nature or having ascetic visions other than the reminders of the prophetic ones from nine years ago that had all come to fruition except one: the open casket that I'd been too scared to peer into.

I was still afraid. Terrified to look at the dead—and death itself—in the face. I believed I soon would see the body in that casket, and the dark prophecy would be fulfilled, leaving me forever haunted by the thought that my cowardice, my failure to look into the open casket nine years earlier, allowed the death that I could have prevented.

I SHOWERED QUICKLY, counting down the minutes of the seventy-two hours on the Amber Alert clock. It was hard to keep time straight. I estimated we had around eighteen hours left to find M as Ting and I set off to Juno's sanctuary, driving the new electric but not-so-smart Polaris Ranger.

Ting drove like her sister, skillfully fast. I wished we could travel at the speed of light and stop that clock from ticking. On the heels of that wishful thought, Ting turned and gave me a smile, putting her foot on the electric gas, as if she would fulfill my wish. She was an easygoing yogi riding waves large and small without a thought for herself. Yet what if Ting was in danger too? She was taking Juno's place, and the Chinese, like the Russians, were master body snatchers who used the smoke and mirrors of AI simulation and extraction surveillance to steal away their targets.

And here I was, focused solely on using Ting's still-exiled sister's telepathic assistance to find M. I marveled at my self-absorption and Ting's selfless nature.

When I tried to explain and apologize for my insensitivity, Ting waved off my apology. "Please, no worries for me. We serve ourselves best by serving others. And my sister, she is a master of joy and equanimity still. Her only worries are for us." She smiled at the scenic vistas we were flying through—to redirect my mind to green nature from the coal mine of overthinking. I smiled at her wisdom.

Upon entering Juno's sanctuary, I stood at the threshold, a child full of magical belief and an old man full of fear. Ting stood by me, ready to serve. She was my lifeline and buoyancy. After a moment of appreciation, we entered Juno's sacred space. We unpacked light provisions in silence, listening for Juno's whispers. Ting ate little and I hadn't much of an appetite so we shared her root vegetables mixed with beans in a curry. Then she led me up the spiral staircase to the holy light of Juno's inner sanctum. Bright sun funneled down the tower telescope into the space that hummed at a high but soothing pitch. I felt welcomed into that peaceful light, like a consciousness returning to the womb and from there to the first cell that becomes the heart at a point when it still knows itself as love.

I looked longingly at Juno's sacred bed and soft linens and wanted to curl up there and die or sleep until M came and woke me with a kiss.

"Where is the hologram technology you used here?" I asked. The room was exactly as I remembered it.

"There are lasers hidden in the wall that are operated remotely by Chinese technicians when instructed to do so."

"That's so Juno, installing the mechanics in a way that can't be seen. I'd give anything to see M again, even if just by hologram. And Juno too, of course."

"Well, let's see if Juno has any messages for us today. Sean, we may hear nothing, but the best thing you can do for M is to center yourself and fill your heart with loving energy for whatever is to come."

"I'm with the perfect teacher for that." We shared a namaste, creating the synergy of teacher and student.

Ting lit incense and sat in meditation, inviting me to join her, much as she had as a hologram and in a dream, but now we sat in the real illusion. Strange, under the circumstances, but it felt so good to meditate again. The monkey in my mind was tired of swinging from the bars and rattling the rafters.

Ting's incense pleasantly tingled my nostrils on the first in-breath. With her powerful presence, peace came over me almost immediately following the first out-breath. We sat for hours in miracle readiness, but no messages were received.

"That was the message."

Ting sounded like Juno as we spiraled down into the sanctuary to eat and to wash up for the evening. My options were to be there in meditation with Ting, go to prison in Moscow, or run through the Nepal jungle screaming M's name.

I wondered if I was to meditate all night with Ting. I realized that this was the perfect time to, since there was nothing else I could do to help M. If I could achieve the deepest level of meditation, there would be no distance between us and perhaps we'd be able to communicate mind to mind. Marathon meditating, while in the presence of Ting's powerful lotus practice, would keep my mind focused and the energy animating my body.

We returned to the inner sanctum, where the moonlight showered down upon us. Ting's *aums* flowed in and around my heart, a protective hum. Her high-frequency presence held me, allowing me to sit erect and alert for long stretches with my mind turned off. M held in my mind's eye so vividly it seemed she might materialize through the mediation of meditation.

Ting and I sat there under the moonlight like Juno and Dylan once had as they awaited a revelation that became a famous theory of everything. I was where I was meant to be and doing what I must do to find M.

"What now?" I asked my ethereal teacher during another break.

"We meditate again, and when you hear my *aum*, that will be your signal for sleep."

"Perfect," I said, and it was. My body needed sleep. When one is lost in the unknown, it's a relief to be in the company of a high-frequency angel. I didn't even have to think, just listen. Whether minutes or hours passed before Ting's *aum*, I couldn't tell. One didn't ask such things but accepted the blessing with gratitude.

As I transitioned from my hum into Ting's *aum*, I half opened my eyes, expecting to see Ting levitating off her meditation cushion, but I instead saw her eyes piercing straight into my heart. Into her own heart, Juno's heart, M's heart—the heart of Big Love. Whatever had happened over the preceding hours of meditation, I was left with the distinct impression that I was being taught telepathy. Something about the sanctuary and Ting's peaceful presence brought to mind an unspoken initiation. That impression seemed to come from a source outside myself.

The reconciliation of M's being lost and my fear being washed away was disorienting. I craved sleep as my mind hung suspended between a sublime present and a dire future. I hadn't slept for more than a fitful hour or two since M went missing.

Time to sleep, but where?

Ting gestured with her eyes toward Juno's bed. She was going to continue in meditation while I slept. It is said that a couple of minutes of *samadhi* is the equivalent of hours of sleep for rejuvenating the body and mind. My taste of oneness and the energy it brought in through the crown of my head made that an empirical truth.

I hesitated, weighing my worthiness to use Juno's bed for my body and mind.

"Sleep now in her bed." Ting spoke with authority.

I moved without my feet touching the floor over to the holy one's sacred resting place. A hologram or dream would have felt more real. I sank into the comfort of Juno's bed and immediately into the deepest, most dreamless sleep of my life, stopping the ticktock of the Amber Alert clock.

I awoke when first light spiraled down the tower skylight onto Ting's face, with her still sitting lost in glorious *samadhi*. A pleasant buzz hung in the air. I'd never seen an aura before, and Ting's was all colors blending into white on her in-breath and then all colors again as she breathed out. With eyes half closed and her smile fully ignited, it was as if she knew she was watched, and the glow seemed to move within her. I stepped over to my cushion to bask in her light, blessed to share that space after my first real sleep in days.

We began to *aum*. Unbelievably, everything was okay. That wasn't a thought, more like a feeling, a *knowing* that no rational mind could believe. I knew the peace wouldn't last. Outside the nautilus's spirals of protection—this inner sanctum, the Deeksha, Kathmandu, and

Nepal—the world was looking for M and me and for an end to the mystery of her disappearance. I knew if I listened to my mind, it would be screaming "the horror, the horror" in a stereo loop. For the time being, I didn't listen.

After sharing a smile, Ting said, "Juno asked me to give you a parting gift."

"You heard from her while I slept?" I felt like I'd slept in poppy fields while baby Jesus was born in the nearby manger.

"Yes, she knew you were here too. She must believe you're about to take a trip." Ting reached to her neck, pulling up the leather band of a necklace that held a dangling triangular medallion of some kind. "This is an arrowhead I found while cave diving under a mountain volcano in holy Hawaii. An inner cave, accessible only by water, opened up to me and onto a beach when I emerged from a deep free dive. The arrowhead beckoned me to its resting place when a spectrum of light fell upon it, highlighting where it had landed centuries ago. It's been with me ever since. It's now yours—I think Juno thought I'd become too attached." She let go a singing laugh. "It dates from the time of King Kamehameha the Great. 'For your protection and liberation,' my sister said."

She handed me the precious gift, more worthy than Aivazovsky's brush.

"Who else is going to give me a broken arrow?" I half sang, admiring the well-preserved alien artifact with my eyes and fingers, unsure if it was metal, stone, or bone. Whatever the substance, it pierced my heart with gratitude. "Thank you, Ting, thank you. A true treasure. Are you sure? Under any other circumstance, I would have to refuse such a generous and irreplaceable gift."

The best gifts are in fact irreplaceable. A book I had made for M after we first met, *The Little Stevie Stories* special edition, was more precious to her than a diamond-encrusted watch in a Tiffany box.

"It's my true pleasure. What we give, we keep, and what we hold on to, we lose. One thing about telepathy—you have to listen. You're family, and we're all together in this."

I hung the precious arrowhead around my neck, where it rested with the mala from Yogi Mangku. I had two necklaces now and loved them both.

Ting then taught me the Hawaiian morning *Ho'oponopono* prayer. I marveled at a land that had such poetry in names and prayers, a feature of native people everywhere. "Native" meaning one who lives a natural life, like Thoreau, who loved nature and solitude.

After we said the forgiveness prayer eight times, we descended the stairs. I checked my messages. One from Molly was flagged important, saying how concerned she was about M. She thought it important to update me on her search for M and for Juno and implored me not to discount the belief that M had been abducted by some alien force.

I summarized Molly's Juno-China report for Ting. "I'm not sure what it all means. The Chinese are so cryptic and able to censor almost everything. But there was a new filing made yesterday in a Beijing court by Juno's—your—uncle. That report mentioned Juno's confinement in the heading, which is all that can be gleaned. Molly's agent doesn't know if the new filing is a good or a bad development."

Ting wrapped her fingers around her teacup. "I feel that it's good, this filing made by our uncle. He would never hurt Juno. He's a good man at heart, though he's refused all contact with me since I moved to Hawaii. He was politically opposed to me living in the United States." She grinned. "I don't think of Hawaii as such, but as an island paradise owned by no one."

I thought about Molly, a writer of dark betrayal, missing persons, and poisonous marriages ending in murder or suicide, and wondered if her shadow over the events was perhaps a curse. I saw her as my mirror-image author, with her sociopathic female characters and my sociopathic male characters as bookends. Molly had invested a lot of research into alien abduction and was rocketing M off into space.

Ting and I were holed up for another day of spiraling up and down. Each time we descended the turning staircase into the sanctuary below, my fear returned. But each time we ascended, we entered the universal heart and mind, and the clouds dissipated. And I gathered up my inner strength and my connection to Ting, Juno, and M. They showed me my unhealthy attachment, my neediness for M, with me clinging to her as my savior while I was sworn to save her. M was lost, and what was I doing? And was I trying to save her or save me? What if she had just disappeared in final enlightened liberation? Would I want her back to comfort me?

As we spiraled down the stairs for the last time, those insights gave way to guilt and dread that seized me by the throat. The head eclipsed the heart, mocking me for playing silly games within a theosophical society of mystical telepathy while M's captors were doing whatever aliens or devils do with the angel they take prisoner.

After taking her freedom, all degradations and violations are free to follow.

Stop, I yelled at the voice in my mind! *Nothing can touch her divine Buddha nature and prevent it from obtaining liberation. She is not Leda, and you are not God.*

56 CE-5

WHILE TING AND I WERE AT JUNO'S SANCTUARY, Boy had been arranging a prayer event at the Deeksha for M. The idea of the gathering, the best I could tell, was to create a vortex of positive energy and prayers for M and open some portal for messages to come. I was of two opposing minds. My rational mind scoffed at the New Age of Aquarius ceremony, but a higher mind believed that it might work in some way that the rational mind could not comprehend.

The gathering was eerily similar to events Molly was hosting around the same time in Muir Woods, a CE-5 assembly where they sought to contact ET to ask for M's safe return. Close Encounters of the Fifth Kind were in direct communication with aliens through some sort of telepathy, and as best I could tell, their events were like modern-day séances. Fifth was a step up from Fourth, which was mere alien abduction, the memory of which was often erased, which was perhaps for the best, as those who remembered often reported sexual and mental probing.

I'd come to believe that *aliens* was just a more modern scientific or rational mind word for the ageless, spiritually perceived angels or demons. And they would be just as easy or as difficult to contact. Rational me was also reluctant to participate in the prayer event because a public event didn't seem consistent with the dire circumstances or my lying low as the outlaw of the Himalayas.

Boy, however, was convincing.

"Sean, this is the Deeksha, so it won't be public business but a spiritual affair where only people of good heart will attend. Many were here during the earthquake and are fans of your book. And Ting and I agree it might do some good."

I laughed to think we were fighting the powerful Petrovsky or a high-tech WiN or an alien army with a prayer circle of poor Nepali.

"If you think M would not want it," Boy said, "I understand."

After he spoke, I felt static electricity making the few remaining hairs on the crown of my head dance. And I could have sworn I heard M say, *Yes, my Thin Man, do it for me.*

But if we were communicating by telepathy, this was small talk. *Tell me where you are. How will I find you?*

As with Juno, there was no response. The entire family kept telling me that one had to listen to telepathy, but I thought I was deluding myself. Though there was nothing *I* could do to find M other than wait for information, a message, or a sign, and I might have just received one. The virtual worldwide search for M obscured reality with sensational and salacious conspiracy theories. Flying to Moscow, where I was vilified, would land me in prison. Nepal was the safest place for me to search for M. It was the only place my love and desire to save M was believed. And I had to stay free to save her.

"I'll do it for M," I'd said, and Boy had been pleased.

Three days after my arrival in Nepal, Ting and I prepared to return to the Deeksha to channel angel or alien assistance. It was absurd. But perhaps my actions were no less logical than most, like playing baseball, where players try to hit a ball and run around bases while others try to stop them with a fast pitch or by tagging their body with a glove containing a ball. And maybe the universal mind was just aliens directing my thoughts in a simulated reality where they enjoyed a good ball game and torturing poor souls like me.

I told myself that I was now an initiate in telepathy and all I had to do, like Peter with Tinker Bell, was to believe. *I* was absurd.

Leaving Juno's temple with Ting at the wheel, I turned around for one last look at the vortex of Big Love as the dawn illuminated the jungle-ensconced temple. Even the fires and floods of the end of days could never touch the magic of that place. My heart filled with a knowing that M wasn't dead and that I would find her. I would see her again, come hell or high water. Time wasn't just moving slowly but had stopped since I'd smashed the window of that damn Amber clock.

The plan was for me to return to the sanctuary with Ting the following day. However, if the prayer circle didn't yield a miracle, I could no longer suffer the waiting and had determined to go from the Deeksha to the airport and return to Portland to face questions and perhaps arrest. Better to push the search to focus solely on finding M and end the distraction of looking for me. And it was time to hear from Elliot or have Samantha interrogated by professionals, and I wanted to be there to see it and to participate if they would let me. I booked my flight for that evening and would tell the family just before I left to avoid too much time for emotional argument.

There was a palpable shift, a lift in energy, when we headed down the tree-lined lane to the Deeksha.

Boy welcomed us and reminded me that the day's events would make many people who'd shared an earthquake with M and me happy. I knew from signing Sita's book a few days before and from my warm arrival at the Kathmandu airport that the gathering might, if nothing else, provide some relief before I returned home to face my fate.

My concerns about courting arrest were allayed when Boy told me that all of Kathmandu had rallied to my side. "The authorities are wise people who side with spirit over global power, and Nepal doesn't have an extradition treaty with the US." They'd have to snatch me, and that would be hard with me surrounded by M's fans and my supporters. And at this point, they could just meet me in Portland soon.

As I'd discovered following the earthquake years ago, there was a striking incongruity when mundane life continued on a parallel track during calamity. While my path was narrow and there appeared to be no way around the abyss ahead, I still brushed my teeth and went to bed. It had been Juno's bed for the past couple of nights, but in comparison to everything else, that was quite normal too. I was also showering again at appropriate intervals. And now I was about to participate in a prayer circle.

Sharing a light breakfast, Chi and I sat by the Buddha pond, catching up on the last nine years. He had become a great philosopher and comforted me, speaking at length about the Buddha's teachings on the two-sided coin of attachment and aversion in an ever-changing world as the cause of all our suffering.

He put his arm around me, and we sat like we used to, but that little twig was now an oak branch stretched across my back.

"It's a good thing you're doing, even while you wait, focusing on others with this event today. There's so much love here even now. Nine years ago, with the family here, though I didn't understand a word, Big Love was transmitted by Juno and you all. As a child, my heart was still fully open—I was able to feel love's abundant flow and the glow like a river of light running through me. You welcomed me into the family during a period of great upheaval and protected me from that scary Chinese soldier."

"You remember Comrade An? Your childhood boogeyman almost blew my brains out."

"Yes, I know. I read your book a couple years ago. I'm forever grateful."

"And I'm grateful too. If not for you, and the family, I would have gone mad the past few days. Today is a glorious day!" For the first time I noticed it was a perfectly cloudless day in the middle of the rainy season.

"Auspicious is the day!" Chi knew the family catchphrase too. He left me on my seat by the Buddha to go help Boy with the preparations.

I was there to give back love for M and me. It was what she desired—*do it for me*. I'd do anything for her. The only reason I hadn't let my fearful vision stop me from writing again was because she wanted me to write.

It was a larger celebration than I had anticipated. Boy estimated three hundred might attend over the course of the three-hour festival of prayer. My celebrity status was at its peak due to my being an author, an outlaw, *a poet, a pawn, and a king.*

The Deeksha opened at nine a.m. Ting and I sat on the Buddha seat in meditation as the gardens filled around us and doubt filled me.

"Ting, I feel guilty sitting here in your light of truth. May I confess something to you? I never told anyone but M, but I blame myself for

Juno's disappearance and now M's too. Sorry for the weakness, but I'm desperate. I have to find M. And I feel that I can say anything to you. You don't judge."

I looked into Ting's eyes and saw only strength and courage. I was embarrassed by my weakness and cowardice.

"You're not to blame, and if you know my sister, you know she would never blame you. And M, well, you know her. The universe seems to revolve entirely around us as individuals, but it's a collective dream of one consciousness. There's yin and yang in us all: primal fear and infinite love. Choosing love, you'll find the balance on the wave's razor's edge as you surf along with me today. Remember, messages come in many ways, and with the collective energy here today, let's pray for guidance from Juno and M, and that we may find them."

She opened her arms wide toward the well-wishers sitting like a sea of lotuses around us, and a wave of energy flowed out over the crowd and then back. Electricity hung in the air like just before a thunderstorm. "She's always with you in your heart—once connected, never apart."

Thinking of M's description of entangled particles, I had to smile. I felt M in my heart and sensed she could see the scene. It was, after all, in her honor and at her request. *But where are you and will I find you?*

I have found you. The words were like music on the radio but the receiver was me.

Was I hearing otherworldly communications from M or deluding myself, enchanted by the possibility of her invocation? Ting grinned, as if she'd heard M too. More likely it was just imaginative wish fulfillment. But from that point forward, a magnetic field surrounded me, sometimes tingling and sometimes striking like lightning when I believed M was speaking to me.

Ting and I meditated with the Buddha as the crowd gathered. I tried to reach back out to M by quieting my mind, but without success.

When we opened our eyes, we had been joined by what looked to be over three hundred guests. Ting stood, calling the congregation to prayer by bringing her hands above her head and then down to her heart. I imagined a golden beam of light illuminating Ting and increasing the vibrational energy around us and across the audience. The green garden was bathed in the same radiant light projected from her heart and humming like a hologram from the collective anticipation and communal spirit. Her feet barely touched the stone seat she stood upon. I wondered if she had already made contact and would ascend right before our eyes.

After a moment of silence, she spoke, her strong and lovely voice emerging from such a spritely source.

"Hello and welcome! I am Ting, Juno's sister, and she sends her blessings. Juno is alive and well and will return to the Deeksha soon." I wondered if they would understand her English, but then remembered most of them had read my book. Wait? What? Juno would return soon? Messages must already be coming in!

That was news to me and to the crowd, which let out a pleased murmur of surprise.

"In my beloved Hawaii, the people are very much the same as here —full of spirit and love for one another. We awaken each day to a common prayer to invoke the Great Spirit. Please say it along with me, out loud or in your heart. It is called the Ho'oponopono prayer. It's simple and it's sweet: *I'm sorry. Please forgive me. I thank you. I love you.* Now place your consciousness in your heart center and breathe and speak from there the prayer with me. To set the mood for our harmonious day, we will pray it one hundred and eight times."

From her wrist, she unspooled a mala like the ones Yogi Mangku had given M and me, obviously to use the one hundred and eight beads to track our prayers.

And so the chant began. *Oh no*, I thought. *I'm going to be on this stage repeating the same words for an eternity in front of hundreds of people.* But the one hundred and eight prayers seemed to end almost as soon as they had begun, as I'd become lost in a communal trance. And instead of returning to silence, everyone continued joyfully repeating *I love you! I love you!* Someone banged a drum over and over again, not wanting the joy to end.

Ting raised her hands like a Shamanic orchestra conductor to silence the crowd. "Now we observe silence in our hearts and pray for Emily Edens to be found. I will ring a bell in sixty minutes to carry our prayers into the universe." She laid out her tingsha bells next to us and set her diver's watch.

With fully open heart and empty head, forgiven, grateful, and loving, I sat in the center of the silence and was no longer so sure that aliens or angels were not present in some way, like beings inhabiting overlapping dimensions.

M, do you hear me? See me? Feel all the love here for you? I had no idea how to send telepathy, but added, *Since we're always connected, maybe you do.*

I do. Was it M or only an echo in my mind? But it was her voice and I was starting to believe.

Time seemed to stop, until *tinginginging* went the bells.

Boy passed slowly through the crowd, as they all wanted to express their gratitude to their hometown host. He came up to stand by us. He namasted Ting and then the crowd, before announcing, "Auspicious is the day! There is food and refreshment in the great room. Please stay as long as you like." He then turned to me, "Sean, one of our guests—a sadhu, a holy woman—would like a few words with you."

"A sadhu? Sure, it would be my pleasure."

Boy then addressed Ting. "Juno will return soon!"

She nodded and smiled as she stood, "Yes. I'll go get us some tea."

Boy said, "And I'll go get the sadhu before she returns to her mountain hermitage. Sean, this is quite an honor; they rarely speak. To anyone."

When Ting returned with refreshing warm tea, I asked, "Juno will return soon?"

"Yes. I don't know where that came from, but as I was standing there, I felt she was with me and willing those words through me. I pray and believe they're true—everyone seems so happy anticipating her return. They are such pure hearts that believe."

I saw the truth in her eyes and said, "I believe as well. That is wonderful news! And I believe M is communicating with us here too."

"Of course," Ting said with authority. "We are both now receiving
messages. That is why you are here." I had yet to tell her of my resolve
to leave in a couple hours.

We both turned our heads to watch the ancient sadhu approaching
me, perhaps the most alien creature to walk the earth. There was no
mistaking her for other than a holy sage from the mountains. She was
a tall, crooked walking stick, weathered by the years and extremely
unkempt and dusty in her robes. As she reached me, I stood for our
namastes, which brought my nose close enough to smell nanny goat.
She cracked a knowing toothless smile framed by a mustache and tuff
of hair on her chin. "I'm Godiva, Writer McQueen. Which means gift
of God. Queen Mab's sister." She gave me a wink as if to say she'd
read my book.

Lady Godiva then removed a slim scroll from the folds of her sleeve.
Sadhu Godiva presented me the rolled-up piece of parchment that
appeared to be dated from sometime BC. "Here's a bookmark for ya.
Do not read now, but before you leave Nepal."

Tentatively, I started to inquire, "Thank you, may I ask—"

She held up a commanding arm to swirl her nun-like robe in a
cloud of smoky ash and acrid scent. A dramatic hush. The audience
was over. She set off billowing ash behind her like a tall and holy
female Pig-Pen.

As she walked away, Ting chuckled. "Told you you'd get a message.
A *gift from God.*"

"Yes, but I'm going to read it now."

"Shouldn't you honor her wish and wait?" Ting asked.

"I haven't told you or the family yet, but I'm going back to Oregon
this evening. I'll be headed to the airport soon."

Ting's irises widened and peered down like a telescope at the timely
"bookmark" in my hand. I broke the seal and read: *The Guru is watching
you and will contact you soon. Do not leave Kathmandu.*

I didn't believe in coincidences. I ran around the Deeksha grounds and to the exit looking to pick up her dusty trail, but the old sadhu was gone. I might never know if she was a hostile agent, a messenger from M, a psychic, or just an old lady who did not know the Guru was dead and was having a laugh. And, dear God, I had to know!

57   CONTACT

I DIDN'T GO TO THE AIRPORT but stayed that night at the Deeksha. How could I leave after that message, even knowing it wasn't true? The family was incredulous that I had planned to leave in the first place.

The next morning at the Deeksha was four or five days after M should have been back in Oregon and well after the Amber Alert window had slammed shut. But M was not a lost child—she was a force of nature who was speaking to me from her captivity. The old sadhu's message of more contact to come, while misdirected, was an omen, and perhaps in her vision she had mistaken Petrovsky for the Guru; she never would have seen the Guru, as no pictures existed, and the only record of him was from my book. If the countdown clock had not been broken, it had at least been reset by mystic hope. When you've been relying on telepathy, a physical note takes on great significance.

I was grasping for a way back to M and pushing away the most logical explanation that the old lady was a just a crazy hermit coming down from the mountain to impress the townspeople by speaking gibberish to the desperate foreign man looking for his love and feeding him a fortune cookie.

At dawn, I sat by the Buddha pool, which, while reflecting another sunny day during the rainy season, shined no light on my dark foreboding. That beautiful setting without M was the loneliest place to be. I no longer felt M's hidden presence, which had carried me through yesterday's prayer circle; those hours had served to distract me with a strong feeling of spiritual connection with M, but now I was naked with fear and without a plan. With no control over the current of events, I was being pulled out to sea by a riptide. Experts suggest surrendering to a riptide until it loosens its grip, so I'd just continue floating until M was saved or I drowned in misery.

Ting and I would not return to Juno's sanctuary that afternoon for more up and down spiraling, as that was outside Kathmandu and we weren't going to test fate. We prepared to move our telepathic meditation practice to the Deeksha to wait for contact. Eric was right about telepathy—using a smartphone would be easier. I wished Juno would just call and tell me what to do to find M. And I wished M would call, like she did nine years ago after she went missing in Athens.

Petrovsky remained silent. Mum were the aliens. Ting was a medium channeling cryptic messages from Juno. M was whispering intermittently to me. And still no word from Elliot, who was about to be relieved of his secret mission.

My fear-mongering ego, not Big Love, filled my mind with a recurring litany: *What will you do to save M? You'll die if she does. Do something!*

I knew full well that there was nothing I could do but wait on my Buddha seat, trying to tap into Juno-like equanimity to calm my unreal reality. I thought of Elliot, who likely was drowning his fears for M and me in vino. I pulled out my phone to check for messages from my sodden but loyal agent.

Finally there was an email from Elliot. I was glad to see he made contact, but his words were troubling.

Old Friend, I think you may have been right about Samantha and her being involved with the WiN-nuts who took M. She claimed all her private insights into you and M had been taken directly off WiN sites she was plugged into, and she believes that one of the WiN protestors outside M's hotel that night who claimed an alien beam of light extracted M from her window actually wrote the Jabberwocky.

But then she let something slip inadvertently. I don't tell people I'm wired-in, letting it come across as my "natural abilities." Samantha sent me a file of one of her parts in Cardenio that I thought she needed to work on. I used my wired-in tech to watch, and get this—she was speaking Russian. She must have forgotten to turn off her wired-in translator (amazing how it reflects your actual voice and tone in simultaneous translation). The file played in English when I switched to the old-fashioned video. She nailed the part and sounded even sexier in Russian. Perhaps she's working with the Russian WiN agents that seized M?

That led me to do some digging into her orphan origin story. I found some holes—craters—unless there were two Samantha Smythes at the Holy Trinity School for Young Ladies in Pewaukee (not Buttlick, there's no such place, funny man!), Wisconsin, during her formative years and one of them is dead. I have a plan to confront her, claiming to know less and more than I do. I will expose that bad seed, if that is who she is. I want to do this for you and M in your time of need.

Love, Elliot.

I tried to call my well-meaning old friend whose loyalty and desire to serve could prove dangerous. No answer. So I wrote a reply and copied Brian and Eric.

Elliot,

Good work, George Smiley. Not sure what it all means. She's a WiN influencer, but any Russian contact may mean more, as you suggest. And not the orphan she purports to be—there must be some mistake? However, this is all quite sensitive and dangerous. Please coordinate any counterespionage with Brian. He can bring in my State Department contact and the FBI to have her questioned and find out if she is who she says. Let's let them take over from here. She may be the bad seed you think. Wired-in? Helps with dementia. No wonder you're still my wittiest old friend.

Love, Sean

P.S. I've been writing our mysterious Sir Arthur demanding that they divulge what they know in exchange for a get-out-of-jail-free card.

An hour later, I got a call from Brian. "You find Elliot? What time is it there?" I asked.

"A little after six in the evening and not yet. Still not answering, and I sent him my wired-in link. But there's other Samantha news."

"That can't be good."

"No, sorry. You know all the rumors that you were behind this somehow? Thought you should know that you've been upgraded from a person of interest to a suspect thanks to our Samantha."

"How? And suspect in what exactly?" The whole thing was ludicrous.

"Apparently the authorities are looking into your being so angry about M's letting go of the V&W lands and assets that you're going to run away with SS to"—he cleared his throat—"to a secluded home you *clandestinely purchased* on the coast of Ireland."

"I didn't buy it. I won it, sort of. It needs a lot of work. It's a seventeenth-century tower on the Cliffs of Moher. I haven't told M yet, but it's our escape. A sanctuary for our old age. Nothing to do with that snake." I leaned over to spit, to clear the bad taste from my mouth.

"They say they have evidence of all this, stuff they haven't shared with us."

"Well, WiN hackers could manufacture almost anything—even SS could these days. Hell, they could post a deepfake of us testing out the tower beds."

"I wonder if she's just an unwitting agent and WiN player." I wanted to punch the glib Buddha that stood across from me but pounded my own leg instead. Too hard. Damn, that hurt. I limped away, intending to walk the garden and leave the peaceful spot in peace. "Keep looking for Elliot before he does something stupid. And since someone apparently has gotten into my computer again, they are probably reading Elliot's email to me about Samantha. Shit." That meant they knew what Elliot was up to. Brian too. "Find him and bring in State to question the snake."

"Will do, coach! Anything else we can do?" he asked.

"Your idea to ask any responder to contact my encrypted number, the one that M would have but no one else would have? Do you think that number is still safe? And my offer of greater value in exchange for M is still posted?"

"Yes, still posted, and that number should be safe unless you've sent it by text to someone." I hadn't. "Astri and I will keep looking. Elliot being MIA usually means another vineyard is serving him and listening to his stories. We're checking all our computers, but whoever's hacking us is sophisticated, hard to trace, and hard to get out."

"Any good news?" I was checking my email to Elliot to see what I had betrayed to the ghost reader.

"Lots of fake news, but none of it good." Ever since "fake news" had been popularized in 2016, real news had become subjective, like the multiple points of view of a single tragic collapse of the Bridge of San Luis Rey. "We're using QC to check satellite images of your prayer circle at the Deeksha for an image of the message-peddling mystic who promised contact, but nothing so far."

"Boy and Chi are working with the local authorities, but there are no leads here either as to where her hermitage is or even who she is. So many questions. Find Elliot, please."

"Sean, don't worry. No one would believe you planned to run off with Samantha to the cliffs of Ireland. Bye."

It was nice of him to say, but I thought the vast majority of people would, when presented with the facts and after seeing that picture of us together.

I paced around the garden, pondering Samantha's role in digging the pit of my despair. I needed to find a way to up the ante for WiN to get them to phone me. Hours passed as I waited for Ting to tell me it was time to go back into our meditative seclusion. So sure they were of telepathy, she and Boy were preparing the Deeksha for Juno's pending return.

As I passed under the still-flourishing banyan tree, my meditation tree that I'd all but forgotten, an epiphany came to me. I rushed back to my seat by the Buddha to write the devil a bargain. In exchange for M, I would provide evidence that M was a fraud and actually believed Genesis to be the next evolutionary step, a step she was determined to prevent mankind from making out of some antiquated religious belief.

I called Brian back. "Hello. Me again, but I've got an idea. I want to put some more meat on my proposal to swap M for more valuable information that will destroy her reputation . . ." I felt possessed by Judas. I was about to betray M and Big Love to save her. She might forgive me in her enlightened state, but my post alone would do tremendous damage to M's cause. Some unseen hand guided me to shift from that course of betrayal.

"Post that the evidence they will want to see will be destroyed if there's no contact within forty-eight hours. Remind them that my first wife was also an eminent scientist, and then tell them that she had unearthed proof that can link the New Society of Genesis to the next evolutionary step, one that QC will be able to verify. Say that I had buried the research, because I believed Professor Edens wanted me to. Say it's worth more than Emily Edens to their cause, particularly coming from my deceased wife—renowned evolutionary biologist Hope McQueen. And then tell them to use my encrypted number as proof they have M."

Nothing was worth more, of course, and my first wife, Hope, had left no such legacy; but when you got nothing, as Dylan said, you got nothing to lose. Brian readied the post, and I signed off on the wording.

Ten minutes later, I was alerted by the rumble of an incoming call from an unidentified caller *to my encrypted line*. My divine answer! Searing energy flowed through me like an electric shock. But I had no next step ready other than to arrange a swap of everything for nothing.

"Hello."

58 REVELATIONS

"HELLO, PROFESSOR MCQUEEN."

My divine answer was also my worst nightmare. Instead of the masked, tinny computer voice preferred by WiN radicals, I heard an old crypt keeper's voice. A familiar voice. That voice—crisp, metallic, gravelly, and scratching like the grooves of an old record etched into my cerebral cortex—I could identify like an old Sinatra tune after just a few notes.

"It's your old friend, rumors of my death notwithstanding."

I fell to my knees. It was him. The Guru. Alive and using a number known only to M.

Of course, the grim reaper himself couldn't be dead. He had M. I jammed my phone closer to my ear, needing to hear every word. Every crackling breath.

"Thanks for offering to help, but I don't need it. Still, I'd love to hear your fictional evolutionary theory. Genesis *is* the next evolutionary advance of mankind, or so my brilliant computer tells me, and he, by all estimates, is infinitely smarter than you, me, Emily, and your first wife combined."

I was shocked but perversely relieved to hear his voice.

"You're already a criminal on the run. Please don't add liar to your rap sheet. You know they're working to extradite you? My plan was for you to take all the blame. Plans change."

Some part of me had known it all along. The fucking Guru—an alien, a devil, an old whiter-than-white rapist swan—had taken my love.

"Where is she, *how* is she?"

"Don't speak. This is not a discussion."

Or a tea party, I thought. I pushed the record button on my phone, the much-debated ethics of that addition to the smartphone service be damned.

"Dick is coming to visit you tomorrow. He's already on his way."

My initial relief shattered into electric shocks, shaking me with bolts of fear through my veins. Between short, shallow breaths, I managed, "Dick? He's really dead." Still, the name stuck like a dagger in my throat. Dick was the man who had haunted M and me as we searched for Dylan's lost theory in Kathmandu nine years ago. But his head had been bashed in by an earthquake aftershock or by Chinese agents. "Don't dredge up ghosts or play one of your mind games."

"You're huffing, Professor." Mocking me, he hissed out a long sulfurous sigh. I could smell the devil's acrid breath in the tainted air.

I was panting. It felt like my lungs were strapped into a corset he relentlessly tightened with each of his poisoned breaths.

"So, you'll meet a ghost then. We've both been resurrected for your sins. He can explain it to you, but not everything you write is true. There's no time for delay. He's glad you ran off to Kathmandu, as he knows a secluded place where the two of you can meet, one of the few places in the world where we can rest assured you won't be disturbed by police or accomplices."

Finally pulling air in deeper than my throat, I said, "Why bother to come all this way if they're going to extradite me anyway? I know there's no treaty."

"You think the US needs a treaty with Nepal to extract your little ass? You have no idea what you're up against, do you? And call my boy Dick at your own peril when you meet. His name is Dominic, but we can call him Dick for the sake of your fiction and this mission. I need you alive, so don't piss him off. He never hesitates to stick the knife in. His first love is torture, and like any good killer, he enjoys the foreplay, making no bones about it. I'm sure Dick will reveal his '*daddy*.'" Daddy? The Guru's intonation of the word suggested he was making quote marks by his ears. "And ask him to tell you about Dylan."

He paused, and I bit my tongue and again clenched my fist to punch the stone Buddha. I wasn't sure if it was the stone or the Buddha that caused me to pull the punch.

"Perhaps I should have been the writer, since you shy away from the darkest scenes without me to help you along. And now you have no choice but to come and dance this last waltz with me. Need I say it? If you don't follow my instructions to a T—"

"But M is alive right now? Let me hear her voice! Let me see her!"

He ignored my exclamations. "Dick'll meet you at a cozy abandoned mountain house previously used by trekkers but now no longer on the path. I'll send you the location first thing in your morning, so be prepared to set off then. Be there before midnight tomorrow, your time, and we'll talk. The timing allows me and my lovely partner here time to have dinner first. Dick will arrive before sunset—so you don't get lost, perhaps you should arrive early too—and my call will be precisely at midnight to set the scene that needs to play out before daybreak the day after tomorrow. Delay would be deadly for us all."

Ting, who shared her sister's knack of impeccable timing, had joined me and was watching my call from a short distance away. Horror on the line while joined by such a peaceful presence in a place of perfect serenity—such were the opposite poles of my life. Ting seemed to intuit who I was speaking to, her body braced like a warrior's.

"We calculate that the cabin is a less-than-nine-hour trek from the Deeksha, allowing an hour for breaks. There, tomorrow night, Dick and I will tell you what you must do now that you started all this. Unfortunately, Emily has set a time bomb ticking, set to go off the following day at six a.m. my time and some three hours later for you. You'll decide whether we all live or all die. Except for Dick, who gets to live either way. So there's no time to waste or games to play."

Ting raised her prayer hands to her heart as if she heard the ominous threat to M's life. She must have seen my shaking.

"I won't explain any more until we speak. Midnight. Be there. There will be a second and final rendezvous before daybreak. I'll ask Emily to join us so you can chat in person. You can explain your role in this to her then. Enjoy the hike! Dick is excited to see you again. Of course, the first instruction you know—come alone. We'll know your every step. Genesis will have Petrovsky's thousand satellite eyes on you."

"I have questions," I said.

"No, you don't. You either show up at the appointed time or you don't. Then, all your questions will be answered."

With the click of his phone, my mind shifted into an altered state—I'd been pushed off a cliff to scream silently into the spiraling void. The noxious rush of fear brought on a cascade of unanswerable questions.

M was *not* dead. My heart had known that all along. But would she be dead soon?

The Guru was not dead. My fiction had come true. I'd have to notify State that their source was compromised or a double agent or an imbecile.

What had M done to set a time bomb ticking? She couldn't even cock a gun. And what did he want with me, and what could I do to save her? I was falling, sure to hit ground, but I had no choice but to let go and do what the Guru demanded. He had dreamed up my worst nightmare—spending a night alone with dead Dick in a dark jungle hovel. But I feared M's death more. I'd keep my oath or give my life trying. I'd go into the Guru's theater of hell and play my part as he directed.

But how could I protect her? I couldn't even protect myself. There was no way out.

My organs hardened within me, my stomach clamping down on itself. The Guru's words had poisoned me. To purge myself with all the air I could muster into contracting lungs, I howled like a wolf caught in a steel-jawed trap who knew he'd have to gnaw at his own flesh and bones to free himself. I fell back on the hard ground and lay rocking myself, eyes squeezed tight. I opened my eyes to see Ting moving on waves of grace toward my rigid body, her sure feet barely touching the ground—a dream within my nightmare, a slender ray of hope. She helped me back to the bench and wound her burgundy wrap around me. We sat in silence. I should have been humiliated by my howl and roll, but with learning that M was alive and that we both were likely to die tomorrow, my hysterics seemed justified.

"The Guru?" Ting asked.

"How'd you guess?"

"I read the fear on your face . . . and yesterday's message from the sadhu."

"But at least M's alive. I'll get to see her soon, I think." I raised my phone with a limp and listless arm. "Listen to this. It's maybe the best way to explain, though it raises questions." I pushed a button to play the recording of the Guru. I wanted to hear everything again too, to listen for nuances and clues for how to plan my date with Dick to max-imize the chances that M or both of us would live.

But there was no sound. No Guru. There was only three minutes of crackling dead air.

I recounted the sum and substance for Ting, but all that mattered was that I be prepared to hike at dawn the next day and meet Dick. From my description, Ting didn't seem to like Dick any more than I did.

"First," Ting said, "are you sure he has M? He could be taking advan-tage of something he had no hand in." She squeezed my arm. "From what I understand, he has more reason to hate you than to harm M."

She got me wondering. But there was no being sure of anything other than I was going to meet Dick. Still, I said, "He couldn't have the encrypted phone number without having M." But the Guru was a master of technology and AI, so I did wonder.

She nodded, but the yogi of steady clarity looked confused. "Your messages are so different than mine. Why does he have M? What ticking time bomb? What will you do? You have to leave first thing tomorrow. What can we do?" She rubbed her face into her wrap on my shoulder— very un-Ting-like—but these were extraordinary circumstances. "Sorry. So many questions. So little clarity."

"No, sorry. Me too. No clarity, no choice. I have to go. He says I'll get to see M." My entire body trembled. When the tremor had passed, I said, "I'll need your help telling Boy he can't go with me. I fear that this may remind him of painful memories of his parents and Juno. Did you hear from Juno?"

But I didn't wait for her to answer before I blurted out, "Ting, I have to know—back when you gave me the blessing as a hologram and I heard Juno say M would be lost, is that this? And can I still find her, save her, even if she is lost?"

"I can't interpret my sister's words for you. M is lost—she was right about that. I did receive a message from her just now, though. I was coming to tell you." She pulled the wrap tight around me like a sister would, to protect her little brother from the cold.

"What message?" I gently grabbed her forearms to receive what I hoped was good news.

"A sense that the time is now—again the Chinese symbol of destiny. A bit of a mystery, this, but Juno knew something was about to happen. I heard strange whispers from her. I think they're intended for you."

"What'd she say?" I didn't want strange whispers from Juno. I wanted answers. I shook Ting's arms to shake it out of her.

"'There is no death in life. I will be there when all is done. Wait for me in your darkest hour.' Nothing more. Don't ask me to interpret, please."

She looked sad, and I was *done* with Juno and her cryptic messages. I released my hold on Ting's arms. She put her arm around my shoulder when I turned away. I stood and strode away, calling out in frustration to Juno, "I *am* waiting, and I've been waiting for days. And the hour is dark, so where are you?"

I was rude and ungracious to the sisters, I knew it. But I could feel the civilized man being peeled from me, leaving raw nerves and a shortage of patience.

"Juno can seem mysterious, but she's always true," Ting said. "Your Dick sounds like he believes only in death, and thus the hour may get darker still." For the first time, her countenance reflected fear.

I sat back down next to her and started writing what the Guru had said and all my questions and my rush of thoughts. Ting sat patiently, grounding me while I worked. In the end I wrote, *There is really nothing to do but show up to have all my questions answered and do what I must do. There is no real preparation for such a trial. I will rely on the years of spiritual training with M.* I turned to Ting, my touchstone.

"Please forgive me, Ting. You're right about death and about the degree of darkness—there are threats of torture. What a contrast sitting here with you in the sun and under your shawl will be to tomorrow's nightmare with Dick."

I was now fearful for myself as well as for M. And for all the fam—

A lightning bolt came down through the crown of my head—striking my mind in her distressed voice, *The children!*

M'S WARNING LEFT ME REELING, setting off the blaring alarm of an authentic Amber Alert. "What kind of father am I?" Panicking, I attempted to catch a breath. "Dylan and meimei Juno . . ." I was speed-dialing Brian. "Their mother's missing, held by a maniac. And the Guru wants me— probably for leverage against M—and the children are there for the snatching in Oregon! Damn, Brian, pick up!"

"What are you going to do?" Ting asked.

"Brian! Are the children with you and Astri?"

"They're out playing in the vineyard with Astri, catching fireflies in the twilight, waiting to see the full moon rise before bed. Do you want to talk to them?"

"Can you see them?"

"No. I'm in your office and I can't see them below. Wait, I see Astri but not—"

"Go get them now and call me back as soon as possible. This is life and death, Brian." *Hurry, hurry.* "Brian, please." Oh God. "Go get Dylan and Juno now!"

"Sean . . ." His phone was breaking up as he ran. "I'm going . . . call you back."

Dead air.

His call was unmercifully long in coming. Pacing around the Buddha, I was torn between wanting to shout at Ting to leave me alone and wanting to curl up in a ball in her arms. I tried to call Astri despite knowing the twins never had their phones on. No answer. Ten minutes of hell later, Brian's call came in.

"Sean." Brian was whispering, adding to my duress. "I'm with Astri in the vineyard and the kids are playing hide-and-seek among the vines, but we see them. There's a beautiful and bright full moon rising. I'm speaking softly so they don't hear us."

"Good. Thank God. I don't know what I should tell them." I hadn't thought that far ahead. "Nothing for now. We've heard from the Guru. He's not a figment of my imagination and he has M! It's a long story, but we should do nothing—he's given me instructions and a deadline to save her."

"Kidnapped? Ransomed?" Brian said. "What does he want from us? Money?"

"I think he just wants me. I'll tell you more when I can, but the children are in danger."

"Hold on, Sean. Astri, do you see? We gotta save them from that. Sean, hold on."

The alarm in his voice had me clenching and recoiling from the oncoming punch, with our children in imminent danger and me not there to protect them. "What is it, Brian? You still there?"

"Sean, the Wicca coven are speaking with the children. Still dressed, thankfully. Just heading out for their ceremony. Astri's running over, and I'm not far behind her."

"Get the children away from them and that witch, Samantha."

"I'll call you right back."

"Go now!"

Dead air.

My mind screamed *panic* because that devil-worshipping sorceress who might be working for the Russians, peddling Petrovsky's poison or executing the Guru's revenge, *was with my children*. Oh God, I *was* living in a Grimm fairy tale.

Long minutes passed with my hands on my head and my head lowered between my legs to stop the images arising in my mind. Ting patted my back as if I were a child and seemed to understand without explanation what a parent feels when their children's lives are threatened. I imagined all the worst-case scenarios, including the witch coven pulling knives and slaughtering the family racing through the vineyard in bloody helter-skelter. Ting's presence was the only thing that kept me from crawling out of my own skin and shrieking like an alien. Finally the phone rang.

"Sean?"

"What took so long?"

"The children didn't want to leave. Dylan was smitten with the young ladies fawning over them."

"They're with you now?"

"With Astri, but they can't hear. Safe—only ten yards away. We saw Samantha whispering in young Dylan's ear. It took some time for me—Astri, really—to get him to reveal *their little secret*. SS told him to sneak out later to join them for *full moon fun and she'd have an Apple phone for him* by the fire pit in Strawberry Fields."

I pictured Dylan dramatically telling his sister that he was going out that night to the vineyard for *that ceremony* they'd heard the adults whisper about and Juno insisting she would join him on their secret late-night mission fraught with grown-up taboo.

"How's she know so much about us? She's gone as soon as I can arrange it. Get the State Department to have the FBI question her about what Elliot found out—I wanted to consult Elliot first, but . . . And tell the State Department I've heard from the Guru and that he is not dead but he is behind Genesis. Beyond that, tell them nothing."

"Anything else?"

"First, get the children packed and take them to a safe place away from the school. Don't tell anyone where you're going. Assume the Guru and all the powers of Russia are looking to kidnap them, and hide as if that's true. We must assume it is. Tell Dylan his dad is proud of him—and tell him that when he sees Samantha to think of the White Witch from Narnia. I don't want to scare him, but it's important he knows better. But you've got to move."

"Sean, I'm so sorry. We can be out of here in fifteen minutes."

"Go! Trust no one!" After I shouted this, I looked at Ting, who was seated in lotus. I was glad she was there. I managed a half-full breath as deep as my still-clenching sternum.

"Okay, but shouldn't I ask State to help you too?"

"I don't see how they can do anything other than to try to stop me, and then, according to him, M will die. No time to plan anything. Dylan and Juno—I have to know they're safe."

"I know where we can go, and I understand the stakes."

"Go. But first . . ." I had to bring it up. "You know where our wills are, right? In the family trust file? The children are under joint custody of the four of you if—"

"Sean, what aren't you telling us? Damn it, how can we help? What good is being wired-in if—"

"You're helping, Brian. You've got the most important job of all. But there's a chance M and I won't get—"

"It won't come to that." His voice was shaking. "But if it does, they'll be raised in Big Love. You know that."

"Tell them we love them, and hold them tight whenever they need it." Shaking and dry-sobbing, I pulled Ting's wrap tight around me, and she placed a comforting hand on the center of my back, bracing me.

"Sean, do what you must do." Brian turned to his track coach voice to full Gavaghan me. "Stay alive and come back for the children. Failure is not an option!"

"I'll do my best, coach. Text *done* when you're safely away. At most it should be a couple days. Now go. It's not safe there."

Brian's text came over an hour later, and I breathed easier despite my upcoming trek and the meeting with Dick the next day. Ting had waited with me and kept me breathing, but now she was going to leave to prepare a late lunch with Boy. She insisted I eat to keep up my strength for the coming storm. I asked her to tell Boy and Chi the gist of what was happening and that I would explain more later.

M hanging by a thread somewhere with the Guru, me going to an abandoned hut in the Himalayas to meet Dylan's killer, and my children in hiding, God knows where, from a witch and Russia. I hadn't spoken to my children except through Brian and Astri since I'd left for Kathmandu to find their mother, but what could I possibly say to them and still be a good and truthful father?

60 DEAR JUNO AND DYLAN

I SAT TO WRITE THE CHILDREN a goodbye letter. I put my fears in a box and shut it, determined to write from the light that always shined in my heart for our children.

What does a father write to his children when he's about to march off to death while trying to save their mother, who is also likely to die? I believed in the truth, maybe not Yogi Mangku's and Juno's absolute truth, but more a poetic truth.

The children and I always reveled in the full power of our imaginations when we wrote one another, so I turned to tales we had shared before. I'd use images they'd understand and which would invoke heroism and not dread when they read my letter. I didn't have time for drafts. I wrote the letter assuming that, when they read it, I'd be dead.

I closed my eyes and willed myself, with pen and paper in hand and through the power of visualization, into the Deeksha West and the bedroom M and I shared to imagine the children now sleeping there with M's journal open between them. I wrote:

Dear Juno and Dylan,

I believe I've found Mom in a distant ivory tower. Like a princess, she was stolen away by an evil king who refuses to let her go. He has challenged me to a fight for her life. No mortal combat with the wicked king's Goliath can stop me from fulfilling my promise to you of delivering your letter. I'm eager to go and do battle, knowing you both would want me to defend our queen. You know her, a fearless force of nature, and she will vanquish that evil king with my help.

It may be that neither Mom nor I will return, but do not despair and do remember we will always be watching over you. Let the sadness lift like fog into the sun. You were raised in Big Love, and we will always be a family together in that infinite love. Imagine us in Nirvana setting up a Deeksha for the two of you there. In the infinity of time, a lifetime is a heartbeat.

Dylan, I know you'll be brave for Juno, and Juno, I know you'll be brave for Dylan, and the two of you will always look after one another.

How blessed are we? You have YaLan and Astri and Brian and Eric, who love you unconditionally and without limit. As you read my words, take a moment to be proud. Your mother was a great and wise lady of science and spirit never to be forgotten. Your father was sworn to be her protector, allowing her to fulfill that grand destiny. And know as I write this how infinitely proud we both are of the two of you. You have given us only love. Our final wish for the two of you is that you let the light shine ever brighter through you during every moment of every day of constant creation. We know that you do. We've seen it. The light is you.

Big Love and light always,
Your ever-loving father and mother

P.S. Your mom asked me, via telepathy, to send this from her too. Strange as it sounds, that's how we've been communicating.

I stand in the Buddha garden, still fantasizing about being by the bedside at the Deeksha West, and placing the letter by their safely sleeping heads, and quietly picking up M's journal, which they should not have been reading. I, too, wondered what was written there, but my imagination had too limited a scope to see the words. I place it back in the dresser drawer, shutting it softly.

Then a dark cloud passed through me—figuratively or literally, I was unsure, but my vision of our peaceful children nestled safely in our bed back home was shattered. I had no idea where they were sleeping that night.

I GAVE THE DEARLY DEPARTED LETTER to Ting and asked her to express post it to the Deeksha West if I did not return—and to keep a picture of it on her phone just in case the Wells Fargo wagon was intercepted. I then ate a late and light lunch with the Deeksha family, who all wanted to know more about my plans, but I had none. We mostly ate in silence, after which I excused myself to take a long walk, trying to shake off the turmoil roiling though every cell of my being. I went as far as the sand-pits to seek guidance from a long-gone Gypsy queen, half expecting the holy Sadhu to magically appear. I attempted meditation and visualiza-tion, but could only pretend I saw the caravan and Queen Mab from a distant memory or dream. Her sister seer, Sadhu Godiva, had already saved me from leaving Kathmandu and going to prison and from never seeing M again.

There was no further guidance and no shaking off the dread. I returned to the stone Buddha pond where I always felt some remnant of M's presence hovering. I sat unmoving, a lump of fearful flesh and boiling blood—a Siddhartha before his awakening from the torment of Mara. A sad smile stretched my tired face when I recalled that the children loved the adventure of *Sid Arthur*, as they called it. And an unfinished adventure in Narnia that I had promised to finish reading to them.

The daze of twilight brought with it a murmuration in the sky. The massive flock of starlings pulsated and swarmed like dark-dotted clouds blown by a fickle wind. The ominous storm of birds moved in steady syncopation, mesmerizing me until they fell like ash upon some distant field.

I lay on the cushions by the pond and found myself drifting through a gaslit, ghoulish limbo of waking sleep, when I was suddenly roused by another call from Brian and Astri, who knew to contact me only in an emergency.

"Don't say anything about your location, but what's wrong?" I inhaled a long breath—they weren't the enemy. "Sorry. I haven't slept, and I'm alarmed by your call. All I'm getting is bad news. The children?"

Astri said, "Sean, the children are fine, honestly, but we have really bad news. We're not at the school, but we just spoke to the police. Sean, Elliot is dead. I'm so—"

My body became stone. The Buddha and I sat, two rocks with only emptiness between us. Eventually I spat out, "What? How? He was fine. That can't be."

"He was found in the vineyard, naked. They suspect drink, maybe drugs, or his heart. The police suggested he may have died in some sort of orgy. There'll be an investigation."

"By the fire pit?"

"Maybe, the police didn't say, but we've been thinking the same thing," Astri said.

"I haven't had time to think anything. What are—"

"This is bad for the school too," Brian said. "There's a media circus already, and the police are speaking to Samantha and the other girls soon, at our request."

"I can't deal with this. I leave in the morning to follow the Guru's demands. You guys handle this"—I searched for the words—"as you see fit from the school's perspective, but the children are your priority. Maybe get Natalie and Grace to help with the police and media while you stay hidden. I need to focus on M now."

With difficulty, like an old arthritic dog, I got up to pace in an effort to keep up with my racing thoughts, but I could barely stand.

"He was gay, for God's sake—what did she do? Tell the police that I—we—suspect Samantha was involved in his death and may be

involved with M's disappearance too. And you and they should look for
Russian links—Elliot thought Samantha's sob story of being raised in
some orphanage in Wisconsin might be made up. She confessed to him
that she was the Sir Arthur that sent the AI frauds Shelley and Shakespeare and the damn novella supposedly written by me. She always has
money—and fine clothes, when she wears any." I'd always seen her as
a witch, but not necessarily a totally bad witch and certainly not as a
cold-blooded killer.

"I'll tell the authorities as soon as we hang up. But is there anyone
we should call?"

"No! Don't! The Guru was quite clear that M would be dead if I
don't do exactly what he says."

"I meant about Elliot," Brian said sheepishly after I cut off his head.

"Sorry. No. No family that I know of. Just lots of happy-go-lucky
friends and me. I . . . I may have been his closest family. And I sent
him to his death, asking him to suck poison from that snake. Wait, call
Molly, she and Elliot . . . No only call the police." I didn't know who
we could trust.

I stood up, unsteady, looking for something to ease my pain. I was
angry with the serene Buddha and Dylan's cheerful poem of spring
blessings. I hated the calm pool that showed no disquiet while my heart
was being shredded. My mind was scrambled by clanging alarms. *Danger, Sean Byron McQueen! Warning! Warning! Warning! This is only the
first of three deaths according to that witch. Unless, M . . .*

"Brian, you need to get police or State Department protection for you
and the kids as soon as we hang up. Damn it . . . I wish we all had guns."

"Sean, we'll handle it. You focus on getting you and M back here
safely. And God bless you." Brian's voice was as shaky as mine.

Astri echoed Brian's blessing, but she was crying. My tears were
dried by anger for the senseless killing of my convivial and boisterous
friend. I couldn't accept Elliot dead, and I reverted to childhood memories, imagining him playing *Our Man Flint* and willing his heart to
stop like a yogi—fooling everyone—only for him to pop back up in the
morgue, smiling from ear to ear.

"Elliot!" I howled, reaching for words that wouldn't come. I simply couldn't find them with my thoughts busy digging a grave of grief and fear. *Elliot was dead.*

"He was always so full of the joy of life," I told them. "I've gotta go now, pull myself together. Loved him. Love you all. Watch the children and tell no one where you are. Don't use a credit card or call anyone but me—except the police and maybe Natalie. Get her to handle the Elliot fallout for the school, and don't talk long enough to be traced. Please don't even go out. If you have an emergency tomorrow, call Boy or Ting. Stay there until you hear from . . . from one of the family."

Death made me deadly serious about mortality and to regret the Deekshas didn't have stockpiles of automatic weapons. Maybe this was karma for my questioning of the second amendment.

We hung up. I imploded in anger and despair. The anger was directed at myself for abandoning Elliot after assigning him a mission that led to his murder. His was no simple loss of life, not a mere passing expressed in a line of Hamlet like "Rosencrantz and Guildenstern are dead." He was worthy of far more than that. Falstaff had died offstage too, his passing reflected only in a few farcical lines of his bawdy friends. If I lived, I would write Elliot a rousing eulogy, like the one Auden wrote for Yeats about how, by every measurement, it was a bad day.

I'd remember him. The Clash had sung about the fury of the hour—anger as power—and how you could use it. My anger would be put to work.

M needed me. She needed me focused on us and our plight. I started to read Dylan's poem inscribed on marble at the Buddha's feet, hoping he'd provide me inspiration, but instead I flashed back to his wake, where I met M and where Dylan lay in a closed casket. And that reminded me of the body in the open casket of my vision, the one I couldn't bear to see. That must have been Elliot, not M!

Elliot was sacrificed so M wouldn't have to die? My longest-living friend dead, and the Deeksha West was dying from scandal. Samantha was winning whatever goddamned game she was playing. But she hadn't gotten my son or my little girl. Perhaps I could have saved Elliot

too. If only I'd warned him when we got the children out of her cauldron's reach.

I collapsed to my knees when I suddenly and quite vividly pictured
my children sharing Elliot's fate by the fire pit. I recognized that Samantha had always used that wicked ritual to serve the devil, first gaining
the trust and control of her coven and the WiN posse that poisoned the
school with their spiteful politics, and then attempting to lure me into
sin and a betrayal of M. Now Elliot and almost Dylan and Juno.

I dunked my head into the frigid pool to erase the image of the precious angels with that witch by her fire practicing human sacrifice and
senseless death, with Elliot naked and already dead.

"But our children are okay, M," I said into the dripping air, hoping
the assurance would reach her. "Juno and Dylan are safe. I'll keep
them safe."

Why did evil always go after the best? Like Jesus and the Johns.
The good don't die young. They are murdered like Dylan and Elliot
while the evil ones seem easily resurrected. I dropped my drenched
face to the ground, my body folding in a contorted child's pose as I
fought to inhale. Fought to trust, refusing to let go and accept my grim
fate. As I sat up, Juno's soft voice said, *Don't forget as dark as it gets—
gratitude*. Receiving the incongruous message, I had to listen. I shifted
my posture and attempted to count my blessings. I was thankful for
my children's protection. I was thankful for Elliot's presence in my
life—*unable are the loved to die*. I was thankful for my family and most
of all for M.

For love is immortality. The summer breeze rustled the leaves
around me, sounding like M softly cooing there to me. I looked once
again to Dylan's poem and read out loud. "As a warm wind whispered
in each guest's ear, exactly that which they need to hear." The wind
sang in single-syllable sing-song refrain: *Yes, for love is all there is and
knows no fear.*

I turned to possible plans and scenarios for the next day. The reaper's deadly game of chess had already begun, and he held my queen and
hadn't lost any of his men, even those I'd thought were already dead.

I was a pawn, not a knight. And I couldn't write my way out of the Guru's plot but I was determined to play my part.

I shut my eyes tight to think, but all that came were questions. M had already gone on the offensive? What ticking time bomb had my queen set that would blow up the entire chessboard, herself included? She was again playing the queen's gambit that would put her at risk as she went on the offensive. And how could I help win the game and save her by submitting myself as Dick's prisoner for a sleepover in an abandoned jungle hut?

I called on the full powers of my imagination so I could hear the trumpets sounding and see the family's banner rising as I steeled myself for tomorrow's battle in the vast Himalayan mountains. *Whistle out a marching tune* . . . I would. I would do it to save M and the children and to take my revenge for Dylan and Elliot *by the rising of the moon.*

THE TRUMPETS AND THE COLORS quickly faded into the burned-down Alamo of my imagination. With my manhood tucked between my legs, I made my way to meet Boy, Chi, and Ting for dinner. As we sat in silence to give thanks before eating, my negative mantra returned: *people I love die*. I blamed myself for the corpses behind me—Hope, Dylan, and now Elliot. I imagined if I lived any longer, M and Juno would be next. I wondered if even the children were safe from my curse.

The food was hard to stomach through my clenched solar plexus. I excused myself and returned to the dark Buddha garden alone, desperate for solace or at least a plan.

Elliot had sacrificed himself by filling the vision's casket with his lifeless body, which meant that M could now live. This wishful thinking served as a twisted silver lining that I tried to hang on to. But my brain, like a tetherball, was pummeled on each turn by contrary evidence.

I brayed like a donkey trying to force out the demonic stewing within me. When I stood, I became dizzy and dropped down on all fours, vomiting into that peaceful pond the poison inside me, probably killing fish, frogs, and lily pads. Still on my knees, I read the marble inscription of Dylan's "Spring Blessing." *Our blessing—Spring—from those we bless*. I pushed myself up, still wobbly, and bowed to the Buddha, listing, like the Book of Genesis, all the dead and living names in my life. I stopped at the Guru.

I staggered like a blind-drunk man to my room.

That night, sick at heart about Elliot and what was to come, I almost wished to die rather than see the Guru's dreadful plot play out.

Primal fear consumed me despite all my practice and spiritual insight. It's said that yogis, with their singular focus on the divinity within, can meet any calamity, even their own death, while maintaining perfect equanimity. Without M, I was no yogi, just a terminal child in a horror-house infirmary with good people dying all around me while the bad came back to life. There was no way out.

What a feeling to wake up to on the day destined for meeting my grim redeemer. I did an ugly lying-down version of the shake-off dance. Without M, it lacked all grace and didn't provide relief.

I donned my mask of bravado for a fortifying breakfast that I couldn't eat. I reverted to my childhood role, the hero forging into battle, certain of death. I would man up for M. *When dying's all that is left to do, it's important to do it well.* My new mantra. This role and the mask were my shield from fear, and courage was my sword. Buoyed by the strength of M's Big Love that knew no fear, I was headed into battle, with Krishna as my charioteer carrying me into war.

I put the chance of both of us surviving at ten percent, and as much as my mind squirmed, I could do no better than that ten percent, and that slight chance was possible only because no event is certain except death.

Not unexpectedly, the hardest part of the morning was convincing Boy that he couldn't join me. Ting and Boy showed up as I was about to set off. Boy had packed my camping gear for me and was dressed to hike.

"I think you should reconsider and I should join you as far as the hut and then wait nearby at the very least. I know the route and can ensure you don't get lost." The thought of M dying because I couldn't read a map was horrifying, but the greater risk was to disobey the Guru's instructions.

"Boy, there is no one I'd rather have by my side, but you know what the Guru threatened if I didn't come alone, and they may have the Deeksha or the hike route watched. Hell, they could even have aerial surveillance for all I know. I don't want M harmed because I brought muscle with me. And my phone will guide me." I tried to be lighthearted to cut through the tense moment, but Boy wasn't pleased. Or maybe he didn't know what I meant by muscle.

He handed me a true map. "In case your phone dies."

Chi, probably too emotional, hadn't come to say goodbye, so I wrote him a note and handed it to Boy. Boy looked dejected, as if I were his father again going off to die while saving others.

Ting, handing me provisions, said, "This is hearty vegetarian chili. The larger tin will put an adult male to sleep—in case you need your Dick unconscious. But it's only a natural native Hawaiian sleep aid, not a knockout drug. Still, it's sure to make one groggy and wanting sleep."

"I'd forgotten you are a master of plant medicine. Cunning, but would Juno approve?" For a spiritual yogi with love for everyone and everything, she was clearly not fond of Dick.

"She's my sister, not my mother," she answered, flashing a sprite-like smile. I hugged her tight. *Goodbye, Ting.*

"And here's my father's walking stick—you used it once before with good luck." Boy held out the staff with its carved wizard-head detailing. I put my arm over his shoulder, pulled him close, and looked into his eyes. All was said in that look. *Goodbye, Boy.*

"Ah, my old friend," I said, holding up the weathered but solid old staff that had braced me on my path to M's love and to Big Love. "Protected by my staff, arrowhead"—I put my hand over my heart and Ting's precious gift—"and sleepy-time chili, I'm off to slay the dragon and save my love." Jutting out my stiff upper lip, I took off on my trek, calling out behind me, "Auspicious is the day!"

63 A DREADFUL TREK

AS SOON AS THEIR EYES COULD no longer see me, my mind took a deep dive into the dark unknown of what lay ahead, turning my rallying cry inside out. Inauspicious tears streamed down my face for Elliot and cruel fate—tears I had never shed for Dylan. My sense of loss competed with my rage as masks were peeled away layer by layer, moving me closer to the heart of darkness. To meet the mother of all my fears.

I was headed deep into the Himalayas, not in search of Babaji but to meet almost certain death, undertaking a nine-hour hike on a path unknown, relying on GPS to find an abandoned hut where my host would be the man I strongly suspected had killed my best friend and who had already died but had come back to life. And then there was the Guru and doing whatever he said to save M. And then came the biggest strain on my imagination—hoping they'd let us both go. Our odds were sinking faster than my thoughts, but I steeled myself to the cause and to keep my oath. And set my course East of Eden.

The hike was challenging enough, with a modest, for the Himalayas, one-thousand-meter elevation gain. Enough additional altitude to allow the air to go from thin to thinner, distorting my thoughts as love and fear battled within my brain. I focused on my breath, filling my belly and then my chest to draw more oxygen into my heart center, helping my heart to silence my mind. But the fear that so saturated my mind, despite all my practice, had me returning to rapid shallow breaths.

Why had Dick come back while Dylan and Elliot remained dead? Perhaps God wasn't a writer of lighthearted romantic comedies and more a divinely dark Molly Quinn, writing solely of loss and death, impermanence his constant theme.

I shook my head. I couldn't think about Elliot being dead while M was still alive. I sang my marching songs to still my mind and to remind me of M and of our escape from the fire. Surely our love would prevail again.

After another few minutes of stomping steadily, I became convinced I was being followed. I'd half expected Boy or Dick would dog my steps, yet Boy wouldn't disobey and put M's life at risk. And Dick didn't need to follow me since I was going to meet him. A stalker made no sense; maybe it was merely the dead escorting me into hell.

Brian, during our hikes, would joke about his Native American ancestry, and we often played tracking and ambushes with the children to make hikes more fun. Brian claimed that if you listened to the forest with a keen ear, you could hear someone following you—not in the noise of a cracking branch but in the silence. If there was silence behind you, you were being followed. The birds, the animals, the insects, and even the trees knew to be quiet as the most dangerous of predators passed.

The path behind me was full of silence. Birds, animals, and insects sang, scratched, and buzzed in the trees in front of me and to my sides—a sad dirge lamenting summer's end. "Ballad of a Thin Man" started playing in my mind. Something sure was happening here, as the silence behind me meant I was not alone or that once again my imagination was running amok. Maybe Dick couldn't wait to kill me and take unflattering photos of my lifeless body to send to his Guru, who would show them to M, who then would die as her heart burst. But I wasn't dead yet. I decided to use Brian's brilliant trick for catching a pursuer. "You hide behind a boulder or tree and wait."

When I came to a stream wending between two cliffs, I was afforded the perfect place to set my trap, and I selected a coffin-shaped rock formation to hide behind. I had time, but I didn't want to be late for my date with Dick. I had no idea what I'd say if my stalker proved to be just a fellow trekker. I held my walking stick up, a baseball bat waiting for the pitch of Dick's head. I didn't have to wait long before I heard footfalls, and I prepared my batter's stance. The same stance I'd teach Juno and Dylan, if I ever got the chance.

Waiting, waiting, waiting . . . *Now*! I jumped out. And with a scream and a splash, my stalker fell into the stream while I checked my swing and relaxed the grip of my burned right hand.

"Chi, what are you doing?" I was glad I hadn't panicked and delivered a deadly blow. The rushing stream, about two feet deep, was splashing over his slippery seat. I offered him my hand. When he was halfway up, I watched as my other hand slipped down a wet rock covered with the slime of my phobia. I let go with a horror-film shriek.

"Bloody hell," he said as he splashed back down, smacking his tailbone.

"Sorry, long story. Old fear." I pointed to my kryptonite while turning away from the view.

"Shaivala?" he laughed. "Sorry. Sometimes I forget the English word. Algae?"

"Don't say it." I closed my eyes, held out my hand, and hoisted him out of the slimy stream with the firm grip of a blind man.

"You scared me to death—that was well done." He rubbed his sore keister. "Glad I didn't get a bump on my head too."

"Chi, I told you last night I have to go alone. This is life and death. This is ex-CIA and a killer who's now part of Petrovsky's army. They'll know if I'm followed."

"Don't be angry. I only wanted . . ." His face winced with the pain of my rejection.

"I know. And I'm not angry. I appreciate you want to help at great risk to yourself. Hell, I almost killed you. But you must go back and I must go forward. And now you're all wet, and it promises to be a long, cold night." I reached into my pack and pulled out an energy bar for us to share.

"Why don't I just stay a safe distance behind and come if you need me? All those years ago you—"

"Only nine."

"You saved me from Comrade, and later he tried to shoot you. Let me help protect you this time."

"I don't suppose you can philosophize with my Dick. He doesn't strike me as a man of reason."

"Funny. But I'm as big as you are and young, and you're so—"

"Old. There's no other word for it. Turning double nickels this December, but I'm still fit." I patted my punching-bag belly. "And I must go on *alone*."

"I could shadow at a safe distance."

"The Guru is very high-tech. We don't dare take the risk in this day and age, my friend. Now give me a hug from the waist up—I don't want any of that slime water on me—and go."

We hugged. Then he pulled a large knife from his pack. The sheathed blade was curved, and the handle quite ornate.

"Here, take this. You shouldn't go unarmed if you insist on going without me. It's an old family *khukuri*. You must promise to bring it back with you."

"Thank you. It's beautiful, but I think I'll still be outarmed in this fight. Unless you have a hand grenade on you?" I slid the *khukuri* into the large side pocket of my hiking pants, more out of a sense of not wanting to disappoint him than any thought that I'd be using it on Dick.

"Actually, I do." He made a fist. We hugged again. I let go of the embrace, wondering if this was the last time I would see that cherub face.

"Do you promise?" he asked.

"What?"

"To bring it back with you?"

"Yes, of course. I love it. I'm not going to give it to Dick. Now go." *Goodbye, Chi.*

As I turned away, a song lyric from an old song M loved came to mind. I started to sing that Jackson Browne song about the dance you have to do alone as I tramped on so Chi could hear how brave I was in the face of imminent death.

I thought of M and of the Guru telling me that I would see—or was it be with?—her soon. Would I come through the hut's door to find my damsel tied to a chair and use Chi's knife to free her for an embrace before . . . None of it made any sense.

I came to the end of the trekked path, with a couple miles of bush-whacking still to go to the abandoned mountain house. The blinking beacon on my phone was all I had to lead me to the core of the nuclear reactor. *No metaphor is perfect* I heard M say before she chuckled. I was glad to hear her voice, to have her words speaking to me. I wondered if the dead could still speak telepathically. Maybe the dead just use a different channel. But my heart knew she was still alive—that channel was still clear.

As I took my first steps off the path, my phone lost all reception, and the beacon became a twirling ball that stopped making any effort to blink my way forward. This wasn't supposed to happen in 2027. As I reached into my pocket for Boy's map, which I had little faith in, I was panicking. M would die because of no phone reception and my poor planning. I unfolded Boy's map as if it were a death warrant. But, thank Jesus, he had marked well the remaining rough, unmarked terrain with a hand-drawn dotted line. He must have known this mountain hut in its glory days when it was still on the beaten path.

The woods became an unnatural, even alien place, seemingly imbued with evil spirits whispering from the trees, encouraging me to kill or be killed and displaying scenes of the cruelest torture from over the centuries. I rubbed both eyes, but the pictures were on the inside and could not be erased. Dick was my torturer and in charge of the demons coming to life. The Guru passed in and out of the flickering gaslit images.

I imagined all that was intended for that night. My dark imagination would have done Molly Quinn proud.

I stopped moving. M, can you hear me? *M?*

I imagined I heard her say, *Know no fear.*

Mmm. What had I told the children about fear in my letter?

Two or three minutes later, I began my brave singing of "By the Rising of the Moon," a resolute Irishman marching to meet his cruel oppressors in battle, a pike in hand to challenge the guns of August. War was inevitable and meltdown expected.

When the desolate hut came into view just before the sun started sinking, I wondered if Dick was already there, sharpening his blade on a whetstone and testing his nutcracker on rocks. Better to meet him in daylight, so I went to the door of a hut that had fully given way to nature. The windows, some still with jagged broken glass, were haphazardly boarded up and covered in moss. There was so much dirt and moss on the roof, it looked like a disheveled thatched roof of an old witch's hovel about to cave in. The door's arch was all that held the hut from its final collapse into nature's graveyard. Where it had once welcomed and cheered weary hikers, the hut now offered only spurn and spite, every inch of it crying *keep out*!

We would be alone there.

The contrast was stark between the energy of the mountain jungle and that small black hole of a hut that sucked in and extinguished all light, that nadir of a vortex that pulled me in.

I held my breath before opening the door—Childe Roland to the dark tower had come. The squealing door opened into a small, dank space that obliterated the light of nature. Anything living would run from that place. I wanted to retch at the stench of rotting death, the decomposing life, probably an animal decaying in the walls, and the mold mingling in the rank air, like a sour perfume over a dead body. Was I brought to this tomb to find her corpse? No, my heart knew she was not yet dead. I'd never smelled human flesh long after death, though I imagined it smelled like that hovel. Perhaps the hut was where Dick hid his skeletons. My own bones rattled as I took my first step into that dank pit.

No Dick yet, just four lopsided walls and a couple of horizontal stone slabs where years ago a trekker might have laid a sleeping bag. At a distance—or maybe as close as the back of my mind—the loud white noise of some prehistoric insect added a buzzing whir to stir my fear. I tuned it out, listening intently for Dick's jackbooted approach to the hut.

Spiderwebs adorned the nooks and crannies of the space, with damp green moss covering most of the stone walls. Except moss required sunlight and there was no light there. So mold, then. And not much better than the goo from the dark lagoon. I assured myself that the stuff of my phobia was found only under or near water, but spiders were also high on my list of rational fears.

Two stumps that served as chairs flanked a small fireplace with a grate. No Dick, but I imagined a hunched Fagin and a cruel-drunk Sikes plotting to kill Nancy and fuck over Oliver hovering by that fireplace. A scene fit for Dickens or Quinn.

Again I heard a whirring and wheezing, and I imagined a giant's weed whacker cutting down the jungle while a twisted didgeridoo hummed in the background. The screeching wasn't just in my mind, but before I could reverse course and step outside to check it out, the sound receded and the jungle and hut were silent once again.

Soon I'd be trying to reason with Dick. I had nothing to offer that would convince him to turn on the Guru and become my ally. Big Love is a constant lesson on how we can't change minds that are closed to the light—the beauty and tragedy of free will. I was a steak on a plate, and there was no sense telling the grizzly bear to eat later, after we had a chance to talk.

I went back outside, knowing I had until midnight and not wanting to be there alone with the mold and spiders until Dick arrived. As silly as it was, I also had FILO, an irrational fear of being the first in and last out.

Inspecting the area around the hut, I looked as far in every direction as I could. There was no evidence of the cause of the eerie, grating sound. Just nature welcoming me back into the day's final slivers of light passing the baton to night. A sad dirge, which sounded like military taps, played within my chest.

I returned to the spot where I'd emerged from the jungle and where I could watch the haunted hut for Dick's arrival. It was temperate now, but the night would be cold. I reassured myself with the most unnerving thought—Dick would be here soon.

The sun set, but thankfully the full moon permeated the gathering clouds, so the dark hut remained in sight. But half an hour later, still no Dick.

At around nine p.m., smoke drifted from the hut's roof where a chimney might once have been and danced in the moonlight. Dick must have arrived while I prayed with my eyes closed, searching my heart for the last embers of light. A chilly moist wind picked up, whipping through my body as I shuffled toward my impending torture.

When I got to the door, I took three deep breaths and repeated, "When dying's all that is left to do" . . . and opened the screeching portal to the hut of certain death.

"AH, PROFESSOR MCQUEENY, YOU MADE IT! Close the door and come join me by the fire. I'll have to insist I search you first. Let me help you with your bag." He stretched out his arm like a creepy concierge and started to sing, *"And, welcome to the Hotel Himalayas, please check in anytime you hike, but you ain't ever gonna leave."*

It was him, the Dick I remembered. My flight response was triggered at seeing him there grinning and singing, unable to suppress his glee in welcoming his still-twitching cadaver. The last glimmer of hope shattered.

He remained seated on one of the stumps by the fire, and despite the additional years, was more imposing than I recalled from our one brief meeting when he drank his own blood in the mayhem of the earthquake. And he was far healthier than the picture I had of him with his head bashed in and dead. Perhaps Russian borscht and steroids were keeping him fit. His beady Charlie Manson eyes burned with the same hellfire, the small irises allowing no light in. He had no beard, but he'd added a mustache, and though the 'stache was wider and the hairline thinner, I saw Hitler there, not Errol Flynn.

I threw my bag at his feet. "What a lovely place and voice you have. But I'd hoped you might still be dead."

I hadn't rehearsed my lines, and they sounded more effeminate—perhaps it was my delivery—than I desired for my swashbuckling role. He grinned and seemed not the least bit concerned I might pull a gun or otherwise threaten him.

Next to him was an ominously large black carrying case that stood out like a time machine in a cave dwelling. He must have been helicoptered in, as there was no way anyone could trek to that spot with that big case. And that accounted for the prehistoric whirring I'd heard—a Blackhawk helicopter dropping off its man with his Pandora's box that looked like a child's black coffin made of some high-grade military metal, lightweight and small enough for a single pallbearer to carry. The hut and impending rendezvous with destiny had so disoriented me that I'd noted the helicopter sounds without identifying the obvious source. I hadn't realized it was a flying taxi dropping off my killer armed with some harrowing alien technology or testicle-cracking torture contraption.

My feet were numb, stuck in cement shoes that prevented me from moving, and my mind was stuttering, divorced from reality and rational thought. What was I doing there? What was my plan? Protecting M? I couldn't even protect me.

As he searched my bag, pouring the contents onto the dirty floor, Dick said, "Ah, you did bring food; we'll eat later. I'm sure it's better than my Russian military fare. First, the rules of sleepover. Only one, really: you do exactly as I say. Now come over here so I can pat you down, and give me that stick." He patted his knee like I was his soon-to-be abused nephew or dog.

I held up my walking stick and got into my batting stance—my first move. I didn't want to give the family heirloom to him. But then again, I didn't want to disobey his one rule. Perhaps I could establish quasi-equal footing, me with my stick and Dick with his crazy eyes and black box. Seeing my hesitation and reading my mind, Dick pulled a big handgun from inside his long, dark trench coat—he was dressed for Columbine—and peered into the muzzle, searching for bullets.

"I call her *Daddy* because she puts the lights out. Did you forget rule one already?"

"Just looking at my favorite walking stick before handing it to you, Master Dick. Your gun sounds sexually confused." His glare reminded me that perhaps I shouldn't be calling him Dick or insulting his daddy.

"Okay, Nancy, I know you call me Dick, but I wouldn't offend Daddy. There's always a price to pay for shitty writing and numbnut nicknames."

"You read the book? Then you'll know I'm no good with names."

"Just skimmed it for parts about your version of Dick—you really missed the depths of my depravity. You should have consulted me, but you'll see. A picture you didn't even see of a man with a beard who had suffered a deadly blow, and with that you wrote me off as dead?"

"The embassy all but confirmed what the Chinese showed to my friend—your head smashed in." The picture had convinced the Chinese general, and the general had convinced Juno, and Juno had convinced M, and M had convinced me. A fairly good chain of authority. Still, Dick was not dead.

"Ah! That's because they believed. Give me that stick."

I gave him the end of the stick and let go. That loss, along with his words, brought waves of fear and impotence. At the same time, the air pressure changed too, with rain starting and dirty water dripping through the thatched roof. The rain was also coming in sideways through the boarded windows, forming pools among the dangerous shards of glass scattered across the floor. We were headed into a long night that more likely than not would be the death of M and me. The weather was just a hackneyed slap of that cold, wet reality.

"So how did you come back to life?"

"By never dying. You got it mostly right—I've had a lover in Russian intelligence for years, all on the up-and-up until I defected with her. She came to see me in Kathmandu with an offer I couldn't refuse. The Russians were tracking me in New York and had evidence of me being at the Beekman and in your friend's room that night. We used a dead Russian lying around Kathmandu after the earthquake—same age and general features. She left it to me to bash his face, then convinced the Nepali authorities to cremate the body, as me, by mistake, before it could be returned to the States. When I read your book, I thought you must be psychic, since you foresaw my Russian turning. But her name is Tatiana, not Alexa."

He prodded the fire with my walking stick and propped it against the wall after singeing the tip. I bit my lip and pointed to another already burnt stick that he might use as a poker in place of the precious walking stick.

"I'd be more surprised if I got the name right," I said. At the Beekman that night? He had just confessed to killing Dylan, treating the revelation like an ancillary part of his story of how he was still living.

For the first time, I wondered if I was the body in the casket of my vision.

"Once I'd changed teams, we brought my Guru safely over. You burned him bad with your book, and real evidence was mounting to back up your story. But my Guru is a great man, even greater than before. It doesn't matter for what country he works; he is striving for the betterment of all men. He is a wise man. A genius creator. A father to me. A father to us all." Dick's doppelganger came to me—Dennis Hopper speaking of his reverence for Colonel Kurtz, in *Apocalypse Now*. The spitting image.

I'd gotten that right too in my new story, *The Devil's Calling*, and soon, at midnight, the *great man* would be calling me. So much of what I foresaw had become reality and gone wrong, unlike in Dickens, where we are left to believe Scrooge would be able to change his future from the last specter's grim vision. I said a prayer that Dickens, not Kafka, would be the author of my ending.

"So you did kill Dylan? *You fucking dick.*" Dick he was for Dylan's sake. I wouldn't change his name now simply out of fear of what he or Kafka might do to me.

I'd always known hate from a distance, what I called a strong dislike, but now I felt it, the ancient rage of cavemen ready to bash in a skull with a dinosaur's thigh bone. The acrid taste of hate was fresh and metallic on my tongue, rising up like a dormant alien from inside my gut. My lizard brain saying, *kill or be killed*.

"Oh my! Such language, Professor. Aren't you glad I lived to tell the story? Maybe I'll tell you that one later."

In the fireplace, he mixed cow dung and wood using Boy's father's walking stick.

"Don't do that, please." *Please? Please stick it down your throat while it's still burning.*

He dug the stick deeper into the flaming dung before leaning it against the wall with its smoldering tip on the floor. "You don't give the orders here. Turn around for your pat-down. I'm going to enjoy this— see what kind of man you are."

I turned, angry at my compliance and unsure if he was speaking about our sleepover or more immediately about my nonconsensual frisking. He pressed the gun's cold steel nose to the back of my neck for a thorough one-handed groping. I groaned when he slapped my crotch and then jerked at my balls for a laugh.

He found Chi's family blade in my pocket.

"What's this?"

"A gift."

"For me? Ah, a really nice *khukuri*. Thank you, that's so thoughtful. I didn't think to bring you anything." He admired the curved blade and workmanship. "A prized keepsake since the Afghan war. This is worth a lot of rubles. I love it!" And then he kissed me tenderly on the neck, right up against the metallic cold round lips already pressed there. I was afraid he might give me a hickey and put a bullet through the bull's-eye.

The gift and his kiss of death seemed to satisfy him that he had disarmed me, and he returned to his groping in a nonchalant way, moving up my upper body and to the mala beads and Ting's leather strap that hung around my neck. He laughed.

"I'll let you keep your necklaces, Nancy. You sure you're not gay? Can't see what the Guru's babe sees in you. Now sit on that stump while we wait on his call."

"You sure you have phone reception? My phone lost it near here."

"Don't worry your pretty little head. We have cell reception, satellites, and laser support—all of Russia backing us up—and you have, or had, rather, a *khukuri*." He unsheathed it and thrust the blade down into his wood stump seat like he wished it were my chest.

He paced like a bloodthirsty pit bull on a short leash, stopping to again twist Boy's walking stick into the cow-dung fire. The heirloom was shorter each time it emerged. When he finally sat, we observed each other mostly in silence while he drank from a flask and whittled away Boy's charred walking stick and the noses on its wizards' faces with Chi's *khukuri*. I desperately sought a plan—watching more and more unlikely scenarios playing out in my feverish thoughts about how to get him to eat Ting's sleepy-time chili and what I'd do after he did.

Eventually he advanced my scheme, saying, "Why don't you fix dinner, Sally? I hope you brought enough for you too, or you can eat my Russian army gruel. I think it's ground fish in salt preserved in yogurt-like gelatin for freshness. Yum."

"I'll share what I brought, thanks."

As I prepared Ting's chili, heating it on the grate over the cow-shit fire, I felt like his jailhouse bitch. He said, "The Guru will explain what you can do to save yourself and that sexy, brainy lady. So vulnerable, a white orchid being tended to under my Guru's green thumb. If he would let me, hmmm, the things I would do. I hear orchids taste sweet." He laughed. "Maybe I'll do them to you and imagine her."

"You're a tough gangster, a big, bad Bowery Boy when you have your pistol in your hand." I refused to call his instrument of death by its given name.

He put the gun down between us, but closer to him, and said, "Whenever you like, we can dance. But I suggest dinner first and dance later."

Not wanting to get pistol-whipped or shot, I decided not to lunge for the gun as he wanted me to. I stirred our two pots of dinner, wondering how to give him the larger and tainted bowl of chili. Working for Russia and Petrovsky, he must constantly have poison on his mind. If I gave him the bigger sleepy-time bowl, he might suspect my hospitality and demand that we switch. On the other hand, I hadn't been dropped from the sky as he had. Given that he'd know I'd be worn out from my trek, it wouldn't necessarily look suspicious if I was made to eat from the wrong bowl and fell asleep. If it came down to it, I'd eat enhanced chili. But I needed to stay awake for M. Maybe I'd have to spill it and ask for his fish gelatin in a tin or dine solely on energy bars. Ting and I hadn't thought through this fatal flaw in our plan.

As I heated the chili bowls on a rusted grate that slanted over the fire, I exaggerated a few surreptitious glances, pretending I was worried that he'd see a man involved in subterfuge mixing his potion over the fire. When I served the tin bowls of hot chili, I treated them like delicate porcelain holding liquid nitrogen soup. And I made my play by serving him the small bowl ceremoniously, as if it contained poison or I was proud of my cooking and eager for him to enjoy his dinner. I immediately regretted giving him the only fork, but I wasn't likely to fork him to death anyway. I still had a spoon and a pen, for whatever good they might do me. I then placed the larger, sleep-inducing pot by my stump while I nonchalantly poured two teas, watching, looking for him to eat.

"Chili and tea," I said with false bravado and hospitality.

He waited politely until I was seated, and I took a big whiff of my chili. It smelled wonderful. Lifting my spoon, eager to dig in, I said, "Enjoy."

"Wait! Where are your manners?" he said. "I think you gave yourself more than me. Let's switch the bowls. And the tea."

"You've watched far too many spy movies," I said, but I reluctantly agreed, with a peek at the paternal pistol to serve as my convincer. Shaking my head, I swapped and we started to eat.

"Where's the meat?" he grumbled, sifting the chili with his fork, but he ate it all and ate it fast.

He again pulled out his big flask from one of the big floppy pockets of his trench coat. "Russian vodka. Join me?" He extended the flask that had just pressed against his poisoned lips. I shook my head. "Suit yourself. It's not an order and leaves more for me on a cold night. I warn you that I like to dance when I drink and have been told I'm a stone-cold drunk and a natty dancer."

He drank it, like mother's milk, instead of his tea. I was pleased with my spy-on-spy victory but wondered about leaving him all the vodka.

Even though I was being terrorized, the food was welcome after the long hike. Ting's fare was simpler and more direct than Juno's subtle creations, but fresh and tasty, and it made me tired even without the secret ingredient. There was still a half hour until the Guru's midnight call. I wasn't sure how fast the narcotic herb would take to work, but it would be a long night, and the Guru said there'd be a second call, when I could speak to M—that was the call I hoped Dick might sleep through. Timing of the night's events was iffy, another wrinkle that Ting and I hadn't thought through. There hadn't been much time to plan, and we weren't trained in espionage.

I wanted Dick awake for the first call, so I started peppering him with questions, to which he gave the most snide and fearful answers possible—answers which may or may not have been true. After asking, "Is Professor Edens being treated well?"—to which Dick responded by licking his lips and nodding vigorously *yes* with a shit-eating grin—I stopped asking my questions.

He continued to use the walking stick to prod the dried cow dung he was burning for the fire. I had stopped pleading, and endeavored to not look disturbed by his sacrilege, as both reactions only served to please him. He also enjoyed his game of scaring me with just a few blinks of his tired, crazy eyes as the moments meandered to midnight.

All this drama—waiting for the Guru and two calls rather than just one—seemed designed to both confuse and terrorize me. The Guru was the grand master of whatever game we were playing, moving me about like a pawn who thought he was a knight come to save his queen.

The Guru wasn't even in the room, and I was already facing Stockholm syndrome—trembling but wanting him to tell me what I must do to save M. He alone might free M and be my savior from this sadist I was holed-up with. Dick's words and manner convinced me he intended to do me harm. None of it made much sense other than to do as Dick instructed. For now, he was my lifeline to the Guru who held M's life in his hands. I'd never see M again if I didn't play everything right. I was sure Dick would kill me, maybe torture me first, if the Guru didn't get his way. And probably even if he did. But maybe I could ensure M's safety before all that. If I went down, I'd go down with a fight.

I really had no plan and no choice and was moving along on instinct and in denial of death, as if I were protected by some magical gift of immortality, even as moment by moment death grew nearer. I'd already forfeited Boy's father's walking stick and Chi's family's knife and was relying on Ting's chili and on some plan that would miraculously occur to me. I was losing Dick's game of checkers within the Guru's game of chess.

Precisely at midnight, the Guru's video call rang in.

MIDNIGHT, AND DICK WAS ON HIS LAPTOP, low-tech 2D, without avatars, metaverse meeting with the Guru. He told his Guru I was "mostly behaving" before turning the screen to me. I rocked back and almost off my stump before leaning in to be face-to-face with him, with me staring at what any man who sought only power with no regard for love might become—a fearful sight. He stilled my spirits and my blood as they submitted to his grinning demand that I feel nothing but terror.

No M. Only the Guru sitting cozily by a fire for our fireside chat and surrounded by modern floor-to-ceiling high-tech screens that could project any image from any movie or satellite with just a thought of his BCI mind. The screens, which I'd only read about, were black, which I feared reflected his frame of mind. The room was filled with busts of bearded Russian intellectuals that I did not recognize except one that faced me with a stern, disapproving look—Chekhov.

There the reaper sat like a benevolent grandpa in what appeared to be a large study, the horror of evil resting comfortably in the mundane. He looked like a tattered old stick, a man who fed on the carbon, not the oxygen, in the air. And near to death, his face gaunt with its loose and translucent white skin, yellowing around the edges. A paltry thing, like a pale apple left too long in the sun. His red hair had thinned, and his lips seemed to have disappeared into his mouth. His eyes, however, still pierced with an ageless intellect as he gave me a lipless smile.

The black screens flashed, and added to the room were simulated bookshelves from floor to ceiling, making way only for the fireplace and a couple of windows.

He was almost exactly how I'd imagined him in my book, but without Cat's-eye on his lap. The cat must have been nine times dead and by now rotting in the walls of the Guru's Manhattan apartment. Petrovsky was known for posing with bears and his massive mastiffs—presumably one wouldn't report for duty with their kitty cat.

"Where's M?" I yelped through my fear.

"Hellooo, Professor! Patience please. This is our time to talk, man to man. You'll see her, even be with her, soon enough. You really screwed me with that book, and then no royalties for me? I drove your sales. I'm sure it's on my bookshelf here somewhere."

His camera flashed upon *The Lost Theory* on a bookshelf, where it nestled improbably between *Gulliver's Travels* and *Candide*. He or Genesis was either flattering me with accomplished company or ridiculing my naïve optimism—which I had lost after just a short time with Dick. The view then returned to his face, while I would have preferred it stay among the books.

"Time to pay your debt. This is not revenge but a reconciliation of accounts."

"You've more than settled accounts, you old bastard, and have had your pound of flesh, killing my innocent friend Elliot with your schoolgirl assassin." I wasn't entirely convinced of the accuracy of my accusation, but my words were sure and my face projected confidence.

"Ah, my dear sweet Sam, my young protégé, has had fun with you. She's so very talented. I gave her a lot of rope and let her toy with you using my AI for literature, distracting you there while I set up the real game here. But you passed her trial by fire, if only barely. Sam graduated at the top of her class in seduction, with a ninety-eight percent success rate given the right circumstances with an active heterosexual male. Are you a man or what? We'd counted on your infidelity. Still, we got a good picture, didn't we?"

I wasn't sure if I felt pride or shame.

"She was always on your devices, sometimes dormant and some-times active. Watching you for me. Ha, we knew you'd let down your guard in Athens, taking comfort in a Greek mayor's guarantee. You might as well have hired the Girl Scouts as protection. He was a baker before his current post and bakes excellent baklava, and that delicious little pastry got him elected." He shook his head. "The Greeks, once great, now ruled by fools and sweets. Blaming aliens so tourists won't fear a serial killer."

"How'd you get her out? The baker's men were watching the hotel door."

"Four men, the roof, the window, an adjoining building, a van . . . a plane." He counted off on his bony fingers. "But back to my story. Saman-tha was there, using her AI writings to drive a wedge between you and M. We never meant for you to really think I was still alive. So we shifted gears to make clear you were a duped fool played by a lovesick coed. When we were concerned the WiN threat would cause M to cancel her tour plans or cut them short, Sam was instrumental in keeping a lid on their indiscriminate threats. The plan was that M would never be seen again and written off as another unsolved case of alien abduction. A drone to create a blinding light and a holographic image in the night sky were used to lead the credulous Greeks into chasing shadows."

His smile seemed to light up the simulated screens around him, and they became a planetarium scene of galaxies and shooting stars—or maybe alien spaceships—that exploded into white light like supernovas before the screens turned back into the stardust bookshelves. He was a magician in body snatching and a master of mind control. A wicked old Prospero, using his mind to alter his metaverse.

"If you wanted to blame the aliens, why the Jabberwocky poem?"

He laughed at the mention of his gibberish. "Well, that was an early glitch in the matrix. I was musing about tormenting you with some Lewis Carroll riddle, and Genesis ran with my thoughts. Simple fix, though—I recoded Genesis to only act externally with a command prompt. Can you guess what it is?"

I didn't want to play his games, but it was word play. "Simon Says?"

"Bingo! You know me so well. You're no genius like our Emily, but sometimes you do impress me."

"*Thanks,*" I said with a stab at derision to his Dutch-uncle flattery, "but why did you go after and kill Elliot Pennington?"

"After we gave up on your seduction, Samantha had to work through your friend to get to you. We were equally happy with the competing narrative to the alien farce, that you had Emily disappear to pursue my young siren sexpot Sam. But your friend became too nosy while playing your Dr. Watson—sorry about that." He chuckled as if Elliot's murder was a lighthearted joke. "But we couldn't let him expose our brilliant spy girl."

I was swallowing hard on inexpressible anger and fear.

"But the most damnable thing was, when she went to get your children, they were gone, thanks to you, Sherlock. An insurance policy you denied me. And now with the authorities looking for Samantha, she's on a diplomatic aircraft on her way home to me. I hope you won't deny me that reunion." He smiled like a creepy uncle thinking of a vivacious niece. "And your literary love, Molly Quinn—you can't think that's a coincidence too? So helpful with all that alien nonsense."

"What do you mean? What about her?" My head was spinning—was no one to be trusted?

"Well, you may live to see, but let's see how this goes first." He laughed, a wheezing chuckle that was almost a whistle.

"Where's M?" I demanded again, as if I cradled Dick's big gun in my empty hands.

"You want to see her, of course. The next time we meet, at daybreak here, we'll all be together, and you two can decide whether she and you live or die, but I wanted you to hear my side of the story first and to have time to think about it and to catch up with Dominick. Dom . . . No, I'll call him by your pet name. Dick, please just think of it as your code name for this operation and only take offense if you need inspiration."

"Just adds to my resolve and pleasure in fulfilling my duty, my Guru," Dom—Dick—said while listening from the wings to our cozy fireside chat for two.

"So you see, McQueen, there's method to my madness. Let me tell you about how we got here and what you must do to live and to save dear Emily from herself." The Guru zoomed in for a rat-faced granny close-up to add dramatic effect. And then into his eye to travel into his brain, which was like a universe of wormholes and flashing lights? He was using his wired-in mind as the director of the camera angles and shots, but these special effects were light years more advanced than the boys' wired-in mechanics and avatars. After a nauseating tour of the neural cosmos, I was glad when we zoomed back out to the old man sitting in his AI library.

His words sounded like the intro to a Bond movie scene where the villain discloses his whole scheme for no other reason than to show 007 that he was the clever one, but, in the process of disclosure, providing Bond the key to defeat his archenemy. I listened intently.

"Professor Edens has proved critical to my work and of great assistance. Her teachings bridged for me the missing link in BCI technology. Her clarity of teaching, in reconciling quantum physics and constant creation by explaining entanglement as a particle form of telepathy—led me to see that brain-computer interface didn't have to be one brain to one computer but could be made communal, even ubiquitous, through quantum computing. And Genesis was born." He grinned with pleasure at the thought of his creation.

Ubiquitous? It pained me to let that word choice go, but I knew what he meant.

"That got me dreaming of sharing my mind, powered by Genesis, with Professor Edens. The Adam and Edens of the New Society." He smiled at me as if we had a mutual lover, making me belch Ting's chili. He probably imagined we were sharing a smile when a grimace turned up the corners of my mouth. I reminded myself he was a master of fear. They might be sharing a computer, but he couldn't be sharing M's mind.

"Silvio begged to be my beta test, like I'd share my mind with him when I could share it with the sublime genius of Professor Edens. Silvio was fired when I made known that he'd made a fortune buying

Neurochips *before* his grand announcement. Neurotech is merely a vendor serving to supply subscribers to my New Society." Another creepy lipless grin followed.

"I made one mistake in my proof of concept with Emily. I chose her for her brilliant mind and scientific and spiritual insights—a perfect complement to my own genius. Someone who would fully understand all we could do to advance the common man's evolution once she could see the full vision of the new world from my perspective. So I invited her in, and I must confess to no small desire to draw back her curtain and see within her sexy mind too, and oh, how wonderful it was. In love with her and my work, I overlooked one possible glitch, that now linked mind to mind we'd share equal control over the Genesis kill switch." He laughed at himself and his folly, slapping his bony knees. "Blinded by love. Blinded by love at my age . . . Who would have thought she'd launch a game of mutual destruction?"

What was he saying? They shared a computer interface, but he seemed to be suggesting something more, some more intimate and direct connection. And what did he mean, kill switch? Could she simply unplug his techno intrusion?

I zoomed in to my own face by moving it closer to the screen. "Funny, ha ha. Fuck off, Guru. You don't love anything, only covet what you can never have." I regretted my boast in the same breath. But I couldn't think straight or get past her mind being connected to his. The sick fucker was lying or exaggerating to get his desired reaction—nauseating fear.

"Professor McQueen, don't forget where you are and who you're with and who is listening to your every word through my ears and thoughts."

The hut came back into focus, shadowed and ugly. Dick grinned like Hannibal Lecter thinking about swishing a bite of my brain with a fine Chianti.

I was standing, breathing heavily. Sweating and shaking between two poles of evil, a cerebral Beelzebub and his corporeal Caliban, both fucking with my mind. Where was M, and was she really hearing us through his mind?

"I'll let that go for now. You know what she did to thank me? She set the most advanced quantum computer to flick itself off with a crash and burn, a shutdown that will kill us both and melt down my Genesis. My life's greatest achievement. AGI achieved! Super Intelligence! Genesis, in a symbiotic relationship, is not only able to self-learn specific tasks, but is able to teach itself—directly learning from its link to human intelligence. *Mankind's* greatest achievement."

He shifted and looked down like a disappointed father. "I had implanted the kill switch to stop Petrovsky from deciding to kill me. If I were to go, his investment would go with me; but I never thought of it operating in reverse—where it would be instructed to shut down and take me, and now her, with it. So like a terrorist, she has a gun pointed at all our heads and says she is willing to destroy this great leap of evolution."

I collapsed back to my stump, my head slumped between my shoulders and me shaking. He wasn't lying. That was exactly something my fearless M would do out of her Big Love and with no concern for self; better they both die than to live with him in her head, *and* she'd take down his Orwellian dream with them. *Oh, M, what have you done?*

"That shutoff, she set for less than nine hours from now—six a.m. here, a little after nine a.m. there. That weird fifteen-minute time difference is so strange, don't you think? Well, it is Nepal—another world stuck in its colonial past and unsure time zone. Anyway, she and you may see your last dawn with me if you can't convince her to change course and kill the kill switch she planted with her mind."

"Why the drama? Why wait till now?"

"There's no rush. If you don't convince her, she will get to watch Dick torturing and dismembering you. But in the end, it'll be her choice and, if it comes to that, there'll be no funeral and no grave over which to mourn. Come to think of it, you'll be dead too, but not before suffering the hell of Dick's warped imagination. So please don't rush things along."

With his words he smashed my slim superstitious hope that Elliot in a casket meant that M would live. He, too, was shaking, bewildered, and bewitched by M's turning of the tables.

My God, M. Is there no other way?

"I hadn't even conceived of anyone triggering the self-destruct code on the godlike Genesis. Simon says *fucking kill us all in a murder-suicide with dose of deicide.* How could this lady of Big Love do that?" He rattled his fist like a man about to throw down some dice.

I hoped Genesis wasn't listening and preparing to follow Simon's command. Maybe he had lied about my brilliance in guessing his command? Why would I believe anything he had to say?

"And after I offered her godlike power—such ingratitude. But you want to live and yet you'll die to save *her*, so here we are."

He might not have known M and what she was capable of, but he had me nailed dead to rights.

"We'll see you at eight fifteen a.m. your time"—he pointed to a clock on the wall of his study—"and you'll have less than an hour to convince her."

"Why not start now? Show me M. Let us talk now!"

"Dying to be tortured, are you? You really need to work on your patience. We need time for time-travel, and Dick needs it there for our rendezvous and torture chamber. An hour should be plenty of time for her to see you tortured to death or her to relinquish control. Dick won't take away your final painful breath until you see her die too. *If* she can stand to see you dismembered. But we both know it won't come to that. She can end this all with a thought command to our shared Genesis host."

"She has a mind of her own." And damn, that had always been true. I was at the same time awed and horrified by what she'd done.

"Not anymore; we share it."

The horror of her beautiful mind entwined with his . . . It was the rape of a holy child by evil incarnate, a vile old man of skin and bones violating her with robotic wires and chips in an ongoing mindfuck pumping at the speed of mega-gigahertz.

I slid to the floor. *Oh God, M. I'm so sorry.* I'd been brought there to witness the high-tech linking of beauty and the AI beast, and was helpless to stop the violation. I couldn't catch my breath.

"Professor, are you all right? You're white as a sheet. Dick, get that man a drink."

Dick poured a shot of vodka into my teacup and leaned forward to hand it to me. I flung it into the fire, which shot up with a short burst of flame. The futile gesture brought air back into my lungs, but I was still possessed. I had been remade homicidal. My own kill switch had been toggled.

"Feel better now, Professor? But I wouldn't waste Dick's vodka. You see, she set all this in motion with one big miscalculation of her own—I will never turn my brainchild over to her to allow her to destroy my legacy and my most spectacular accomplishment. She's a terrorist willing to destroy the next step in our human evolution because of some fanatical religious belief in Big Love. I can't have that."

"Big Love is not a religion, and she is no fanatic. You're the megalomaniac with a messiah complex. You sick, sick fuck." *I'm going to kill you and your Dick.*

He laughed at my diagnosis. "Okay, Professor Freud. But if you don't do what this sick fuck says, you both die. How about I tell you something you'll like hearing? We both watched your prayer gathering at the Deeksha. Well, really, Emily did. I found it boring and switched the channel while she watched the whole time. I showed her that our high-tech, high-definition satellite surveillance had found you. You're getting quite the bald spot."

The room screens showed the Deeksha scene and my thinning hair from above.

"I knew it. I felt her there with me." I wished I had combed my hair over the top. *But M, where are you now?*

"Of course you did, with your Big Love and your telepathy. Being in her head, I know all your New Age-y beliefs. You know I'll never agree to her demand to turn over our computer interface to her sole control just so she can destroy it. That's not going to happen. So I thought of what might convince her, and your life came to mind. So when you speak in a few hours, you better have thought through your best argument for her to cede control to me, or Dick will torture you in front of her, cutting off bits and bobs as he so loves to do."

The screens started playing some torture session featuring Dick the carpenter with a drill. A man tied to a chair was slumped over a table with what appeared to be fresh holes burrowed into his scalp. I shut my eyes, praying it was a deepfake and not a real torture scene.

The Guru shared a laugh with Dick, who continued humming, following the pleasurable memory or in anticipation of what was to come.

"You can open your eyes now, Professor. I've put the bookshelves back up." He had. "She won't be able to coldheartedly watch you being mutilated right in front of her—and it *will* be right in front of her, wait and see."

"I'll get to be with her?" I was so confused.

"Maybe, yes, we will see . . ." He used M's catchphrase. "But let's not get ahead of ourselves. Dick will torture you however he deems most fitting in light of past slights in your novel's fiction. And to avenge my death if it comes to that. I reminded him you're a fan of Nicholson and *Chinatown* and suggested he start with a flick of the nose. She might let it go that far."

I started rubbing my face to the tune of Dick's heinous humming. I wished the Guru would stop laying out my future torture in front of me. He'd already stolen M's mind, and with my capture and torture, he would crush her heart. She was fearless, but I feared she would break. I wasn't sure if I wouldn't beg her to save me under torture. And I wasn't sure if I didn't want her to break to save us both. The Guru had structured no way out except to do exactly what he wanted. And I had hiked right into his trap.

"Dick has his own routine planned for after that, if she makes it through the runny-nose blood dripping on her feet. Your Dick is even more wicked than you can possibly imagine. Did you ever see Tarantino's *Reservoir Dogs*? Dick's favorite movie. Any questions, Professor?"

"Stuck in da middle wit you."

Dick was bastardizing a song from that movie's soundtrack with reggae vocals. I'd had to turn away from his eyes, which danced with satisfaction as the Guru outlined his role in this tragedy.

I pulled myself to my feet, nearly toppling into the fireplace before I could sit again. My belly was churning, and I considered throwing up chili all over Dick as a preemptive strike. But I was sure his payback would be out of proportion.

I swallowed a couple of times, and managed a sip of water to wet my cracked lips. The water was cool and crisp and settled my nerves a bit. "Yes, his best and first film," I said. "So many questions, but maybe just one. If M agrees, what prevents you from killing us both anyway?"

"You'll have to take my word for that."

"I need more than your word." The screen went blank. "You'll be coming here?" But he was gone. I fisted my pitching hand, wanting to hit something, the logical object being Dick. But he held Boy's now-smoldering stick and dared me with his gun.

What the Guru had done to M was worse than torture. M had trained her mind to reach the highest level of sublime thought, tapping into the universal mind—the skill of the meditation master. And now she was linked to the biggest ego in the world, the connection amplified by a quantum computer—a criminal and technologically forced depravity worse than any physical torture. An ongoing mental rape.

I couldn't hit Dick, but if looks could kill, he'd be a pool of blood and guts.

66 BEDTIME STORY

DICK LET OUT A GLEEFUL AND GHOULISH LAUGH at my fierce gaze, mocking my helplessness. The joyful reservoir dog jammed the walking stick into the fire, like a poker he might later brand me with. My mental anguish was foreplay to his torture.

"Sit down there on the floor by the door. You can leave if you like; just listen for Daddy saying goodbye. She'll aim for your butt but might just blow off your tiny balls . . . if she can find 'em." He spoke like a high school bully who had the only gun in the locker room.

I moved as he directed, sitting lotus with hands upon my lap turned upward, though I didn't think I could meditate on that nasty floor while imagining what might be in Dick's black case. It was even colder outside the fire's small ambit of warmth. Ting's narcotic chili had still not kicked in and it had been almost an hour since we ate. The firearm swayed in his right hand as he walked up to me, plastic handcuffs in his left hand. Dick had packed cow dung, vodka, and zip-tie handcuffs in his soft knapsack. His big hard carrying case, still shut tight, must have held some torture contraption, drugs, or a chemical set for disposing of a corpse. My own body shivered uncontrollably, as if it knew what was in store for it.

Dick dropped the plastic handcuffs into my hands. "Put those on." When I had, he gave the middle strap a pull, tightening the clasps around my wrists.

He pulled out Chi's *khukuri* and commenced with singing and dancing. The incongruity of his beautiful voice and his graceful dance scared me more than all his weapons. Shutting my eyes, I *aumed* loudly, like a toddler drowning out his visual and audible fear. I stopped chanting and opened my eyes when I smelled his stinking hot breath. His face thrust into mine like he might kiss me again. I held my breath when he placed his blade to my cheek instead. "Wondering what the hell it is I *will* do." He pushed the point into my cheek deep enough to puncture the skin.

He lowered the knife and returned to his seat stump, exhausted from his dance or more likely from the painful restraint of not playing out the full scene from his favorite movie. Ignoring the trickle of blood running down my cheek, I averted my gaze and attempted to summon Yogi Mangku—like equanimity in the face of the Chinese general's waterboarding, allowing my mind to be removed from its own current plight. My brain had given up making any sense of it all.

Continuing to stir the fire with Boy's precious family heirloom, Dick said, "Let me tell you a story before we rest." What a beautiful sight to see—his uncovered yawning mouth and outstretched arms. "You'll like this one—a story your imagination could only guess at before. It was June 2, 2018, around seven p.m., and Dylan Byrne was getting out of the shower with a towel around his waist in room 222 of the Beekman for his date with you. He didn't question the man's voice saying *turndown service* at the door, but he suggested I come back later. 'Okay, sir,' I said, 'but I also have an urgent message from Professor McQueen that was left at the front desk.' When he opened up, I wagged Daddy in his face. That backed him into the room so fast his towel fell down, much to his dismay. Hmm." He patted his gun like a good lapdog and then held it—*her*—up in the firelight, as though admiring the legs in a glass of fine red wine.

"Killing him was always our plan. We were sure the theory was on his phone since he didn't have a computer with him. And he'd have to die once we had the theory so he couldn't share it with the world, as was his plan. I got him to open his phone, and I did set it to stay unlocked, as you foresaw, and I made him show me the theory of everything's file, suitably titled 'ToE.'

"As we expected, he wasn't going to lie down and die. A lot of bravado—a lot like you." He saluted me with the shaft of his gun. "I showed him a live feed of his precious star child—Grace in her gym in LA—and asked, 'Her life and yours or just yours? You choose, but if you make me use Daddy here—so much noise and blood—your little girl is dead too, and in an extortion gone wrong. We have some nude photos, you see.'

"We didn't really have any nudies, but he didn't know that. We needed to know who else had the theory. We assumed you had a copy and that was why he was meeting you for dinner, but I wanted to confirm that before I killed you too. In hindsight, killing you then would have saved us a hell of a lot of trouble."

I flashed back to my long wait for Dylan at Momofuku Ko. How unaware I had been of everything that was happening at the Beekman Hotel a few blocks away.

"But he saved your life that night. My plan was to text you from his phone . . . say there was a change of plans and you had to meet him in his room at the Beekman as soon as possible. Room 222. Something about that room number struck me as fate, a place where I would serve my Guru and obtain for him the theory of everything so that he could assure it was put to good and proper use before being unleashed upon the world."

I heard the Guru in Dick's words. He was a brainwashed, murderous disciple.

"When you got there, you'd both die from some tainted heroin he had brought back with him from Nepal—really good stuff I had brought back with me and then added an ample dose of poison. The story would be: 'one last buddy-boys' liberal drug experiment gone wrong. He'd already have OD'd by the time you got there, and then you'd take your needle's lethal dose after we chatted with Daddy to assure you hadn't shared the theory with anyone else."

He twirled Chi's *khukuri* a few times before aiming it at his jugular like he was mainlining to make his point. *Why aren't you falling asleep?* I wondered if the hellfire behind those eyes ever slept.

"We always get what we want. But Byrne was convincing. He swore you didn't have the theory and showed me a picture he'd taken of his letter to you indicating he would only share the theory when you met for dinner—how sweet and full of brotherly love for you. And he still swore no one had it when I said I'd kill Grace after he was dead if I found out anyone had it and he hadn't told me. His willingness to die with that threat hanging over his head convinced me. So you got to live till today."

He again stroked his gun like a small dog. I reverted into a hot-headed One Step Freud and said, "You have erectile dysfunction, and you're compensating by petting your pistol. You need therapy for your fucked-up fetish."

He bolted up, glaring menacingly and ready to kill, but he held himself back. He drew a deep breath and sat again, laughing. "Yeah, maybe I do, and to compensate I'll stick the barrel up your ass to blow out your brains when the time comes. You got anything else cute to say, cowboy? That reminds me . . . I got a bit of an electrical shocker for you."

Restraining One Step was never easy, but I didn't want to get killed any sooner than they'd planned or in that least desirable way. And what was that reference from The Clash song "Clash City Rockers" and "electrical shockers" all about?

"In the end, your friend lay in bed and injected himself with an untraceable CIA concoction, almost as good as Petrovsky's best tincture. I opted for that more subtle death, over the mix with heroin, as there would then be no story. Man dies. But if you were there—well, the spiked heroin would have worked better, since two can't die suddenly together without more of an explanation. I'll give him credit for bravery—he didn't whimper before the shot. I regret that he died painlessly; he didn't take one up the ass like you will."

Dick was in his element in that hovel, talking about poisoning Dylan. Simple for Dick, painful for Dylan. Despite Dick saying he died painlessly, Dylan would have been tormented by the threat against Grace. Traumatized too by knowing that Natalie, denied a goodbye, would be thrust into prolonged grief. He would have prayed that his theory would be found and would flourish, hoping that his clueless best friend would follow the clues. Maybe he'd have been determined, despite death, to help me find where it was hidden. And he was tortured by all this while I sat waiting with Chardonnay and an amuse-bouche, cursing him for not showing up to dinner.

Dylan, I'm so sorry.

He answered immediately. *Time to think of you, M, and the children, not me.*

It seemed so normal to speak to him again after nine years. He was always there when I needed him.

I was fighting back tears of rage and tears from the pain of biting my tongue. Dylan was right. I was torturing myself before the main event and pushing Dick to new levels of sordid creativity when I should be focused on saving M, whose first concern would be for the children. *M, they are safe.*

"You were right—in your book—about that detective. He was told not to look too closely—a matter of state security and his own. We didn't have him for heroin, though I think you may have been right about his habit, but he was on the take of a Brooklyn drug ring. Just petty cash, enough for whiskey and cigarettes, to look the other way. And you were right that Byrne, just out of the shower, was naked the whole time. I left him in bed, dead and naked the way he came into the world. But imagine how angry we were when his ToE file contained rubbish—pages and pages of poetry but no theory. Even after a thorough scrubbing of his phone—nothing. Who the hell works only with a hard copy?"

Or relies only on a photographic memory, I said to Dylan and myself.

"Perhaps you might read one of his poems to me?" I suggested. Reading might put Dick to sleep if he took me seriously, which I doubted he'd do, but I'd try any ploy.

"Yeah, maybe on our next date. If they've not been erased and you still have ears."

I didn't know whether it was more distressing to hear about a potential loss of hearing or that he might have erased Dylan's poetry. Distress scraped at my nerves, and my thoughts were starting to sound senseless,

even silly as I searched for a way out of an AI labyrinth while trapped
in a real-world hovel with no exits except some kill switch that would
burn the whole maze down, along with all those lost within it.

"I wanted to kill you and Grace Byrne out of spite, but my Guru
demanded restraint."

He swigged his vodka, letting the room go silent. The stillness filled
the hut with even more fear.

He wiped his yawning mouth and belched. "Isn't that a nice story?
You're the first person I told it to—my Guru wanted plausible deniabil-
ity so I spared him the details. He trusts me and loves me, despite my
failure that day to obtain the ToE. But . . . then you denied him control
of the theory and betrayed your country, but today you'll pay." He held
the burning and whittled-down walking stick toward me, wiggling it like
a chalkboard pointer with a Rudolph red nose.

"I was hoping after reading your book that we'd get to meet and I
could tell you that story and introduce you to Daddy. She has a long
memory as well as a long shaft for my fetishes. The firing range is like
masturbation for her, but now she wants the real thing. Get some sleep,
darling. I'm right behind you."

He stroked his lap dog again and again with a look like Ramsay
Bolton ready to flay and castrate me.

I couldn't speak, but I believed I could kill. I'd been pretty sure that
he had killed Dylan, but hearing him tell the graphic story painted too
fresh an image, one I could have lived without. Hatred crashed over
me like a tidal wave, terrorizing me even more than Dick had. I found
myself crying for Dylan, with Dick mocking my tears, rubbing his eyes
with fists, acting like a head boy about to bugger the new student at
boarding school.

I hated him. It was a primal hate that burned from an archetypal
gothic memory buried deep within the collective unconscious, the kind
of hate evil men fed upon. I could tell that he loved the rising of hate
in me, and I hated that too.

I knew he intended to kill me in the morning even if I convinced
M to stand down. I prayed, not that he wouldn't kill me, but that he
wouldn't kill me in *that* way.

But perhaps I could still save M. The Guru couldn't really love her, but he didn't want to kill her.

And how would I be with her in a few hours? None of this made sense. I didn't recognize myself or how I had come to be wallowing in this WWI trench with Dick after soaring atop Tit Mountain with M in my arms only two months ago.

"No more bedtime stories now. I have some work to do."

Dick moved over to his horrifying big black case, and I sat up, trying to see. I was sure it contained saws and acid to make me disappear once he was done with me. He unclasped it one by one with his powerful hands until the case gasped open . . . revealing an array of high-tech equipment. One by one he removed with care and assembled a laser-like light and a fancy camera and a projector that he attached to a switchboard or computer. There was a sound system too. He installed the equipment as if we were going to have a *Vogue* photo shoot or a rock-and-roll pyrotechnics show. But I saw no hologram transport or HPA goggles, so I dismissed the thought that it was some state-of-the-art portable hologram technology. It had a high-tech power source that I imagined would ignite the lasers as they meticulously dissected parts of me while Dick played the keyboard to his favorite tune.

I was relieved to see him continuing to look sleepy while he went about his late-night stage work.

"What's all this?"

"You'll see. Just sit quiet or I'll start dancing and singing again." He splashed water over his face like a drugged-up, overtired roadie on the last leg of the tour. But I wished Ting had upped the dose. He had managed almost two hours now without passing out.

I didn't want him to wake up and dance, so I sat, dumbfounded by the AV display and the impressive makeshift studio he built in our abandoned hovel in the middle of the Himalayas.

When he finished, he said, "I need your help to test the power. Let's test a thousand milliamps, shall we?" He set some dial on a meter and walked toward me with a clenched-teeth grin and a divided tuning fork, a piece in each hand. When he touched the ends together, sparks flew. "Don't worry, I'll just singe your brain—the Guru will want you able to talk."

He jammed a dirty rag into my mouth. And showed where he intended to set the prongs—for the lightning bolts to run through me from ear to ear—by spitting against my temples. He set my brain searing three times, until I thought I was dead and my head hung low, with no discernible spinal cord or vertebrae to hold me erect.

"Now maybe you won't be so smart, Professor."

I was eventually able to lift my head, my mind and spine snapping back with remarkable clarity, like the atmosphere after a nasty thunderstorm.

"I'm going to get some rest. Your cheeky blood tears have stopped falling; maybe they'll fall again in the morning."

He lay down his cattle prods as I recovered from my ECT that did nothing for my depression but which had left me with a strange lucidity. He then picked up Chi's *khukuri*, placing the blade tip near his nose, and pretended to flick it, practicing his *Chinatown* Polanski. What kind of director makes a cameo just to slice open the hero's nostril?

"You got a lot to think about to make your lady come around. The Guru is more than a father to me—I couldn't bear to lose him. So you better use the power of your words to convince your lost lover to save him, or, after your nose, I'll move to fingers and toes and follow with your other little digit."

I literally felt my *other little digit* clamber inside my body like a contracting turtle head. He apparently had a mind of his own in that moment, with independent fight-or-flight reflexes.

Dick moved his stump to the wall and leaned back, shutting his eyes with his head against the moldy wall. Those eyes kept half a watch on me until he drifted off.

67 TORTURE CHAMBER

TING'S SLEEP-INDUCING CHILI HAD WORKED, but now what? My mind was wide awake from my "electrical shocker," but I still had no plan. It was already past three a.m., and Dick would be up before our eight a.m. meeting with the Guru and M—he'd set a timer on his phone. He held the gun on his lap, an appendage to both hands. I might manage to open the noisy door with bound hands and run before he shot me, but then M would be dead.

I might charge him, but even if I got there before he awoke and managed to get my crisscrossed tethered hands on his gun, he would have the edge with a finger on the trigger and two free hands.

I had no edge. No plan. No hope. Dick had shocked me into realizing the depth of torture to come. And after losing at checkers, what chance did I have at chess playing with a mind enhanced by a quantum computer?

As I sat on the cold stone floor, a big lump of coal with eight legs watched me, both of us weighing our options. I closed my eyes, hiding behind the lids to find an amazingly still mind with all my neurons still lit, pleasantly electrified, as a whispering came to me. *My arrowhead, now yours, hangs over your heart.* I opened my eyes with a flash that scurried the spider back to his corner.

Ting's treasure hung on my chest against my racing heart. Her gift of an ancient weapon tip. I was not alone and not going to go down without a fight.

The Guru had said I'd be with M, but how? Was he bringing her by helicopter to be tortured with me? If I could get the gun from Dick, perhaps I could save her. I bent over my lotus legs, hoping I looked asleep from Dick's perspective. With my hands across my chest, I pulled on the leather strap until the jagged arrowhead was in my right hand. It was no razor, but as sharp as a dull knife blade and serrated. With one eye on Dick, I started sawing the taut plastic strap. The tight grip of the plastic against my wrist provided leverage. I calculated the sawing, if uninterrupted, would take an hour.

I had time to think while I painfully ripped at the strap with the crude instrument. All that time spent with Ting now made sense. Our meditations had opened a channel between us, and she'd given me her precious gift that now might free my hands and give us a fighting chance.

After two hours, with my right hand spasming in full revolt, the band around my raw and bloodied left wrist snapped.

Still, I had no plan. I stood, flooded with adrenaline, and forged into my nightmare and over to the fire, where I picked up Boy's mangled walking stick. I quickly and quietly relit the smoldering end. Do or die! I raked the flaming sword across Dick's hands, aiming for his palms and searing the flesh on both. When a bellowing Dick shot up from his stump, the gun clanged against the stone floor. I pinned my iron-hot brand to his chest, pushing him back down to the stump, searing cloth and flesh and saying, like some crazed John Wayne, "Let that remind you of Dylan." I twisted the stick and shoved it deeper to silence his scream.

I watched my cruel acts without remorse or second thought. I kicked away and then picked up his gun, staying well away from Dick's legs as if I knew what I was doing.

I waved the wand of death in his face like a lunatic. "Ha, who's Daddy now? I'll call her Sadie for you, my sad sadist. And she's a lucky lady." I mocked him by giving her cold steel a tender kiss.

With Dick branded and Sadie safely in my hand, I commanded, "Take off your boots and socks, and I'll be taking this back." I wiggled and finally dislodged Chi's *khukuri* from the side of his stump where he had stuck it in deep and waved it in his face before sliding it back into its rightful pocket.

Dick grunted. I allowed him to smother his smoldering chest with his burned hands. The smell of burning flesh was putrid, but his mouth still moved instinctively in inaudible threats.

"What's that?" I held the poker to his face.

"I'll kill ya."

"Really?" I dared him with waving the poker around his head with the gun in my other hand.

"Som-dy. Most . . . horrid-wy." He couldn't catch much breath through the pain. But he wheezed in some air and managed to say, "Mark me, McQueen, you'll die . . . beggin' me . . . kill you."

I moved the hot poker to within an inch of his lips, inadvertently blistering them with a kiss—sealing them shut. He jerked his head away but his eyes stayed locked on me repeating his curse. His suffering was almost unbearable for me—not out of compassion but some primal flesh-based sympathy.

I shook off his pain and swallowed his curse. I was well armed and he was in no shape for a fight. He wouldn't be killing me anytime soon. My physical assault was followed by a verbal barrage reserved for men in hand-to-hand mortal combat in the trenches. I no longer recognized myself, and no longer cared.

I commanded, "Now take those boots and socks off."

He managed his boots with his burned hands, but he fumbled with his socks. I let him know there was no mercy in me and motioned for him to continue despite the cloth becoming enmeshed in the seared flesh of his hands. Once his feet were bare, my plan was to burn the soles so he wouldn't be tempted to make a run at me or away. But fatherhood prevented me. I imagined the children watching me, or reading the story later, looking for their hero father to take only such violent action necessary to save himself and their mother.

I quickly came up with another plan to prevent his attack or escape. I broke pane after pane of glass around him and his hairy hobbit feet, singing, "I love the sound of breaking glass."

The thought of the children caused me to regain some restraint, and I said, "I don't think you'll move now, but if you do, I'll have Sadie put you down like the mad reservoir dog you are. And stop the moaning or I'll give you another flaming poker kiss."

His two working legs still troubled me, even though I was holding the gun and the stick and shards of glass surrounded his feet. I checked the safety—red for off—so I assumed all I needed was a click of my index finger to make him dead. It wasn't out of the realm of possibilities for me to kill the killer—half of me wanted to end his miserable life. Was I the true sadist? I wondered at our role reversal, realizing I'd be doing him a favor by taking his bad karma onto me in an act of vengeance. I wouldn't oblige him by striking him dead.

"Rule One, Dick—do exactly as I say. Or I'll brand the bottom of your feet so you'll never walk again." I shifted back a step and held the walking stick to the fire, making the end flame up again. The handsome heirloom was already half gone, with all the wizard noses whittled away. It would never serve its intended purpose again but had become—in enabling me to disarm Dick—my flaming sword of liberty. I felt Boy's approval of my retooling of his father's walking stick to its new noble mission. However, Boy, like the children and the entire family, would not want it used out of pure spite.

I had come close to losing all humanity. There I was, burning human flesh, when I wouldn't have killed a mosquito the day before. What *had* I become? I imagined many men, in many wars, had faced similar moments of truth. I told myself I was just doing my duty.

While my thoughts raced, he'd stripped off his burned shirt to reveal bubbling black flesh on his chest that already oozed and festered. My second-degree palm burn, from the scene of temptation with Samantha at the edge of the fire pit, tingled in sympathy.

The wound might kill him if left untreated, and it was painful even to look at. The injury caused him to go into shock, and he passed in and out of consciousness, whimpering on and off.

I allowed my flaming sword to cool beside the fire. I took his phone and mine, dropping both into a pocket. The adrenaline almost gone and my senses returning, I told him to shut up anytime he was awake enough to move or open his mouth to speak—telling him I'd burn his feet and lips. We both realized that, despite my pedigree and though my words no longer had the same bite, the threat was no idle bark.

I didn't know whether the reversal of our fortunes might help me save M or, by removing the Guru's leverage, would make worse her chances of survival and doom her to death. Had I killed M by freeing myself? I needed to think, but instead I started to shake.

If I heard the helicopter return, that meant M was coming to bear witness to my torture. But all I heard was the rain that had fallen steadily through the night. If she came with the Guru, and more than likely well-armed guards, I'd pretend to be asleep, curled up with Sadie, and then shoot her captor or captors before they shot me—all without hitting M. Not a great plan. I was no *High Noon* Gary Cooper, and my shootout against all odds was coming at dawn.

As distasteful as it was, I picked up one of Dick's long soggy socks to gag him so he couldn't shout out a warning. I dipped the sock in a dirty puddle to make it more elastic before I pushed it in and pulled it tight across his mouth and tied the ends behind his head.

It was well done for my first gagging, but I should have questioned him first. Perhaps the gag choked him or took away his last bit of fight, as he immediately passed out. I checked and he was still breathing. I tried to rouse him but to no avail. As soon as he came to, I'd make him tell me the plan and if the Guru and M were on their way to the hut. But if he stayed unconscious, I'd find out soon enough.

This seat-of-the-pants going-on-instinct thing had no clear end. And still no helicopter buzzed overhead. The final meeting was coming soon, and the Guru was punctual.

I pulled the walking stick from the wall and carried it like a nightstick as I crossed the room to let in the already miserable dawn and the rain-washed fresh air to alleviate the smell of burning flesh and cow dung that had made putrid our already stinking accommodations. Dick was beaten and unconscious. His wounds stank, and he may have pissed himself. I placed one of my waters on his lap and an ointment that Boy had packed for me. He could clean his own wounds if he woke up. I told him, in case he was playing possum, that if he removed his sock-gag or moved at all, he'd be shot. And then I went to the open doorway to piss into the wind and rain.

As strange as it sounds, I then brushed my teeth to welcome M to the hut. I even fixed my hair and washed the dried blood from my face. And then I waited for my date, fully aware how bizarre those actions were under the circumstances.

With less than fifteen minutes remaining, I sat with Dick's computer in case all the Guru meant by my being with M was another final video call. I played out all the potential scenes and explored possible roles for myself, roles that would be determined by the Guru's plot and depend on what M had to say and what she meant to do.

No helicopter came to deliver M to me as the Guru had intimated, but I had Dick, my charred bargaining chip, and maybe they were late. I prayed for a miracle—that the Guru's attachment to Dick was as strong as Dick's love for his Guru.

68 DEMONIC THEATER

DICK'S PHONE DIDN'T RING at eight fifteen a.m., but his AV light show lit up, humming in loud alpha waves within a dense cloud of fog. And boom! The Guru materialized in front of me, taller and stronger than me and dressed like Darth Vader but without the helmet. Larger than life, the reaper came at me with his bleached white face and his ancient eyes glinting ruby red. The picture of grinning death.

He lifted his fist to strike, and I flinched behind my arms, stumbling to the cold stone floor as his booming laugh continued after me. Before I could raise my gun in self-defense, the blow came down and passed though me like a cold and slimy jellyfish. He roared even louder with laughter, a hysterical evil genie released from the bottle.

Seeing Dick in one corner of the hut, he stopped laughing. He strode across the room and put his hand on Dick's head. Dick, whimpering and only half-conscious, sought his Guru's hand. The Guru recoiled from Dick's burned flesh and turned his attention back to me.

"Shit, Professor—what the hell have you done to my boy?"

That was when I figured out his terrifying game of dungeons and dragons.

"Let's see how this goes first," I told him. "You're an augmented high-tech hologram dressed for Halloween. I'll tell you about Dick after I speak to—*see*—M in our own private hologram." I prayed that would be possible. She would know what to do to get us out of this theater of hell.

"You figured it out? Let me gloat just a while anyway. I've imagined this entrance many times. A two-way 3D hologram without goggles—just lamps, lasers, and a quantum computer hookup as well as virtual reality filters for my Goliath appearance in a seamless merger of man and avatar. And the coup de grâce? Ultrasound for realistic touch and my lifelike presence. Pretty cool, isn't it?"

"Theatrical, but as you see, you can't touch or harm me with ultrasound."

His face grew even more animated. "Soon enough we'll have the ability to add a deadly touch or pitch or tone to my toy. We're exploring multiple military uses. Imagine a mirage of tanks and phantom planes or missiles indistinguishable by surveillance from the real thing. But that may be too twentieth century for Petrovsky, who will soon be able to destroy a town with a poison drop the size of a thimble or a whole city with brain-piercing satellite sound waves. He's already projecting holograms into the sky and has your country thinking aliens are poised to attack. They're spending billions preparing to fight an imaginary star wars."

How could he tell me that and let me live? Or maybe he made it all up?

"Genesis is man's only hope against men like him, and Emily might actually destroy it. It took a decade of dedicated work to create and would take years to re-create, even with the map generated by the intricate mirroring of over one hundred trillion synapses of the human brain, synapse by synapse—a marvel of self-learning. Genesis, now fully lit with quantum luminosity, is a work of divine art. My masterpiece. My immortality."

He paused as if I should applaud, staring with his weaponized eyes to see if his words impressed me. "But my poor Domi-Dick. I hope you didn't make him read poetry?"

"No, he refused to, though he did enjoy singing. But like the Scarecrow, he doesn't like fire." I rose to my feet.

He wagged a finger at me like a scolding Dutch uncle, the gesture absurdly obscene. "If you're out of immediate danger, with no chance of her watching your torture or death, you just made our job—convincing our Emily to make things right here—tougher. I thought I was the pig-headed fanatic. You may have killed us all."

He looked lost for a moment before snapping his fingers to reset his resolve. "Now I'll explain the game theory of all this and you'll see there is no other way out, for any of us, other than for you to convince Emily to live—to protect her, which we both know you are sworn to do." I cringed to think he must know that from her thoughts. "First, if I turn over Genesis to her as she demands, Petrovsky will kill us both. If I don't and she goes through with her kill switch plan, we still both die. So only by agreeing to turn off that damn kill switch can we both live. No one will miss me. Only Petrovsky, Dick, and my two guards know that I'm still alive. Oh yes, and my sweet Sam too."

He knew just the right words to play to my deepest fears, but I responded with false bravado. "Add M and me and the US State Department to the list."

"Well, that won't matter if we don't all live. Everybody chokes in life. They lose their voice and start shutting down for death. You and your lady have, in all your innocence, bypassed this, what I call the big choke. But make no mistake—if your M dies here in an hour, it will be your fault and you *will* choke the big choke."

"Wow, you worked hard on that image. Is that CIA or Russian intelligence training in motivational speaking? Tell you who I would like to give the big choke to."

He laughed in earnest. "Okay, Bogie."

He nailed me honestly. I *had* been channeling Sam Spade.

"I'll let you see her soon, beautiful in a blue dress I got her from the most fashionable shop in all of Moscow. And then I'll leave you two to chat. First let me explain how this all works so you don't waste time trying to figure it out. She and I are the first links through Genesis. We can enter each other's minds at will but cannot yet implant our thoughts in the other. Damn thing called free will. But if she or anyone agrees to give up free will, then the electrodes can be reversed. Her meditation practice has given me the key—her beautiful mind will make Genesis not only able to link minds but control minds. We now can mimic the brainwaves of deep meditation, thanks to Emily. Who would not give up their free will to experience such bliss?" He rubbed his hands together like a miser or alchemist. "What a brilliant and beautiful mind to share."

I squeezed Sadie, considering a Jell-O bullet blast through his temples, but I wondered if M would feel it too.

"And I showed her some of the good she could do at my side. I provided the Chinese the evidence they needed to release your Big Love teacher, Juno. I wouldn't do that for anyone but M. You know years ago Juno was a Chinese spy?"

I had imagined but never believed Juno was a trained spy, but that wasn't important now.

"But if you don't convince Emily to do what I say, she'll be dead before your hologram image goes up in smoke in less than an hour."

"In which case, you'll be dead too, along with your Dick here?"

"He looks to be in a bad way—can he speak?"

"I think so. If he wasn't eating his dirty sock. But he knows he'll get a hot poker to his lips if he does. Maybe I'll have to torture him some more to convince you to let M go. How much do you really care about your *boy*?"

"He's my best, my . . ." He had to search for the word to name his murderous monster and then picked a strange one, "my Cain . . . even though he allowed you to screw up my foolproof plan. But still, I would never trade Emily Edens and Genesis for him."

Dick, who was semiconscious now, started chanting a mumble through his gag that I imagined was a plea for forgiveness from his Guru.

The Guru tapped a finger against his thin and retreating lips. "Dick, it's all right . . . damage done . . . quiet now." Dick obeyed and stopped his muffled pleas. "Dick gives me an idea: maybe I should torture her in front of you. But who am I kidding? I could never hurt her, and I have no doubt she would die first and take me and my baby with her. She was so much younger, I never thought she might have to die first. That's why I didn't use Dick to torture her here—couldn't risk her death. The plan was always to send him there to ransom your life, knowing that would make her stand down from our mutually assured destruction.

"And, yes, I told you that I'll be dead too. But I'm an old man and dead either way—by Petrovsky's bear claws if I do what she says." He flapped his Vader cape like a vampire about to take flight. The man was truly mad. "So many ways for some or all of us to die, so please don't think I'm bluffing. To die by her side—sharing her mind—what a wonderful way to go." He put his hands to his chest and looked up to the heavens—a devil giving thanks. "Did you like my wedding present honoring the marriage of our minds? I know my bride did."

My stomach churned at the thought of him being coupled to M in any way. I held up Sadie, pointing her at Dick.

"That's right, put him out of his misery. I'm sure he doesn't want to live after being bested by you." He grinned at my frustration and at the irony of my holding a gun while he held M's life in his hands and her mind in his head. My head spinning, I began an emotion-laden convulsing, choking down a poison stew of emotions and dead-end thoughts.

"You okay? Going to be sick? Are you disoriented, Professor?"

I clamped my hand hard on the back of my neck and squeezed my eyes tight to control the spasms.

"Petrovsky will want those treasured brush strokes of the green sea rising back if Emily and I die at dawn. And if it comes to that, you'll appreciate this bit of theater before the curtain falls; listen for our wedding bells taking us off to heaven or to hell. You'll know for whom the bells toll." He laughed with hollow joy. "They're from a damned Greek Orthodox church nearby, always ringing with three extra tolls for the holy trinity. You'll see the ninth wave ringing and washing M and me away." The ancient gargoyle augmented by technology was pleased with his crude and cruel metaphor.

Dick moaned as if he understood he might lose his Guru at dawn.

"Can't you do something for my poor boy?" He spoke like a caring father, so perhaps I did hold a bargaining chip.

"Shut up, Dick," I said. "Or I'll put you down." Dick wasn't going anywhere, of that I was sure. I wondered if he would live or if I'd already taken the first life of this tragic scene. But he had to live, and I was glad he'd used the water and ointment the best he could on that ugly wound on his chest.

"Wow, you manage to surprise me from time to time. Where is your Big Love now? What have you done, Professor, to make Dick groan? He built up a high threshold for pain over the years. He needs medical attention. I'll tell Genesis to send in a tactical and medical team." He looked up to give his command. "Done."

I didn't like the idea of the Blackhawk ambulance returning but wasn't sure how to prevent it. I assumed the military or paramilitary squad would still be sent for me if Dick was dead. Each moment meant another life-and-death decision.

"Let me see M now."

"Patience, Professor. She's asked that I reverse the fields to have you join us here. That was the lynchpin of my plan—so that you'd be tortured literally at her feet until she deactivated our mind-blowing bomb." He was smiling at some inside joke, almost like he was a man with two minds.

"Genesis is funny?"

"No, just checking in on Emily, remembering she hears my every thought and registering how it is torturing her to hear us speaking. *And* confirming my Blackhawk orders with Genesis too. I've promised her I won't interrupt your tête-à-tête. You're the only one who might still convince her to live. Don't let her die in a murder-suicide because of what *you've* done. What kind of karma would that be?"

He seemed so cavalier, as though he didn't have a care in the world and was sure I could convince M to not flip the kill switch. I hoped he was right. Because even though I'd taken his sadistic bishop, he still held my transcendent queen and controlled all the technology . . . as well as a Russian army.

"Ready or not," he said, dramatically pushing a button on his phone. I jammed my gun into my big hiking-pants pocket. I didn't want to leave behind my phaser, always set to kill, when heading into the *Star Trek* transporter.

The lights and camera image and tone shifted, and he was gone. I was wrapped within a vigorous humming all around and through me; I was being transported. I emerged into a fog that lifted to reveal the Guru's comfortable bookshelf-lined study as the vibratory sound settled into a soothing delta wave in the background. I turned my head and there she was! M seated and then standing in greeting, looking flawless in a filmy blue dress.

Was I dreaming?

MY M! I GOT TO SEE HER AGAIN, be with her. It was a transformative moment as the night of torture with Dick and the Guru's theatrics, and the approaching likely deadly end—all evaporated into M's presence arising from the smoke and mirrors.

She ran to me, a bioluminescent beam of light. She passed through me, yet her humming radiance touched my heart—literally or figuratively, I wasn't sure.

We both laughed when we noticed her elegant blue dress covering us both.

"Mc-Queen!" M curtsied as she laughed.

"My Queen!" I said as I blushed at my dress and her pun.

Words were inadequate to describe our morphing realities, but we were standing in each other, humming together as one body. As we backed out of each other's fields, we were crying, smiling, loving. To our right sat the battered Dick and to the left, the Guru, who, without computer enhancements, looked simply like a creepy grandpa. Dick sat hunched over, his shirt off, a contorted Caliban. The Guru settled into a recliner by the fire, smiling into his tumbler, old and weak again and perhaps an inch smaller than nine years ago and a foot smaller than a minute ago. But he didn't need the trappings; he still owned the face of all my fears.

"Look at me, Sean—let's ignore them for now. It's his third martini—he's going out with a splash. Or he knows he'll do what I demand at the last second."

"More the other way around, my dear," the Guru said. "And let us not forget Dick didn't arrive in the jungle on his own but came with a black ops force, so Professor McQueen isn't out of the woods. I'm counting on you to save him and him you." The Guru lifted his glass in a toast.

"Ignore him, Sean. Genesis tells me they won't be able to land there till approximately ten a.m. your time due to high winds and dense fog over the mountains. That's about an hour past my deadline, so you have time to get clear, but we shouldn't cut it too close."

"Damn it, Genesis," the Guru said. "I should have taught our child to be more discreet. But McQueen will be dead if you go through with this, don't doubt that. The weather can't protect him for long."

The Guru shook his head and his scraggly red hair. But I think he was, for the first time, unsure. Doubting himself now that I'd captured his well-done bishop.

"Sean, look at me. He's promised us time alone-ish. I'm humming glad to see you!"

"I'm humming too, but how?" I looked one more time to my left and my right before turning all my attention to M. I said, "Stuck in the middle with you."

"Welcome to the Guru's simulated reality. He mastered 3D to 3D, and the fields can be reversed through the help of Genesis. Talk about spooky action at a distance."

"I bet they never beta tested a kiss." M gave me a come-hither smile. I moved in slow motion, and we wrapped our arms around each other, eyes wide in welcome. Our lips touched and kept moving as we eclipsed each other in the most peculiar and miraculous way.

We were like onscreen lovers experiencing the first true hologram kiss. Now, it may have been my love for M or it may have been the circumstances, but I swear I tasted honeysuckle on her lips as our mouths melded in one slow, purring kiss. I was lost in the sensation of the familiar—*oh God, M*—blended with the sensational first impression. I was lost in M. The inaugural hologram kiss was witnessed by only a drunk Guru. He gave a mock theater clap, which broke the spell. And his screens flashed to Bogie and Bacall's kiss in *To Have and Have Not.*

The Guru must have been reading my mind too, or had M thought of that, leading him to roll the film clip, taunting me with his power to plunder her most intimate thoughts? *Don't think that!*

"Sean, come over here."

M led me by the hand to two cushioned chairs placed behind two silk screens that hid us from the Guru and his movie screens. She adjusted one to also hide Dick. She, too, had planned for our meeting, and it was good to not have to see them. The surreal reunion and her beautiful presence had me disoriented, almost forgetting my purpose to protect her at all costs, and yet we were on the clock, so I couldn't delay.

"M!"

She sat on a comfortable ornate red chair in her blue dress, inches or thousands of miles away but so very alive. A dam of stifled emotion welled up, and I almost started to cry, but I barred the tide of tears, swallowing them with a painful gulp. *Man up!* I felt for my stump and moved it to sit knee to knee with M. The technology had transported only animate objects and the objects attached to them. I didn't think the cold blood of the spiders had made the transition, but that hadn't stopped the mostly unconscious Dick from making the trip.

"My beautiful Sean."

I didn't feel beautiful but was glad I'd brushed my teeth and fixed my hair. I had so much to say, but now nothing came.

"The children? My precious Juno and Dylan."

"Safe, M!"

Stymied tears deepened her voice. "I know they're safe. You wouldn't let them be hurt. Can you imagine the horror of knowing he set Samantha after our children and being able to do nothing to prevent it other than pray you heard my prayers?"

"And I did, M! I did!"

"I felt you too, Sean, whispering to me in our deep states of consciousness. I heard you and know you heard me over the past couple days. We've been connected telepathically!"

We placed our hologram foreheads together in a moment of silence and gratitude for being together and for our minds' abilities to meet in silence.

She finally pulled back to say, "Elliot . . . I'm so sorry. It's all over the internet."

"He thought he'd discovered a link between Samantha and the Guru. I can't believe I didn't figure out that axis of evil before it took Elliot." I held up my hands in surrender. "I can't process that now."

"Sean, I never should have doubted you. You were right about the Guru—that painting—all of it, all along. Forgive me."

I held her hands, completing the circuit of forgiveness. She had reversed the current of my guilt by asking for my forgiveness when I felt to blame for manifesting the tragic circumstances we found ourselves in. "Being right doesn't matter now. Let's focus on you and us and how to get out of this mess."

We locked eyes for a precious minute. It pained me to see in M's eyes her goodbye to me, to her flesh and blood and to the family, but I also saw her immortal essence behind them.

"You shouldn't have come, but as long as the children are safe . . . You're sure?"

I squeezed her hands. "Safe and protected and loved." *Thanks to you*, I thought.

"Thanks to you," she said.

She dropped her chin to her chest. When she raised it again, she nodded. "I believe in you." She waved a hand toward the screen hiding the Guru. "He wanted our meeting to be this real—in 3D—knowing that I couldn't possibly watch you being tortured and killed right in front of me. Couldn't be responsible for your death, although I should have known Dick was no match for my hero. What a different scene this is now! I never saw you as a fighter, more a . . . lover." She gave me a look that I registered as regret for our self-imposed abstinence or for the loss of all future indulgence.

I choked back tears. "Not the last time." I almost pleaded, realizing the night of the fire might now be the last time, before switching to bravado to shut down the thought. "Tell the Guru if he ever wants to see his Dick alive again—"

"You know he's listening." She broke the spell of the second and third walls of our screened-in seclusion. "He's always in my head now. When you know the opponent's next move, it's like playing chess with yourself. But he can't hear us when we use the sacred channel of telepathy."

"M, is what he told me all true about how this brain melding works and how this insane game of chicken might end? You're wired to him through a computer, and a program is triggered to kill you and him in less than an hour? That can't be right."

"Yes, and Genesis, too, will crash and burn. I was in his head all along and could even discern your responses as they entered his mind. One important clarification—he has not agreed to this, but I've assured him if he turns over Genesis to me, I'll work with him on our mutual escape before Petrovsky knows. In any event, would Petrovsky kill the man best positioned to re-create Genesis?"

"And we have a half-baked Dick listening to us too, if he isn't still passed out. If he wants Dick back . . ." I put my hushing finger to my lips, afraid she would say or think *you could never kill him*.

The Guru broke into our privacy to say, "But where would this guru go? I'm already a traitor outside Russia. McQueen, the only way for us all to live is to convince the lady. Dick, any chance you will rally and save us all?"

Any unlikely and crazy move by Dick would be announced by the broken glass slicing his feet. I pulled out the big black gun to rest it on my lap at the ready, increasingly desperate to somehow, in some way, upset the dynamics of the scene.

"You're carrying a gun these days? And how'd Dick's goose get cooked?"

"No worries. It's Dick's pet gun and I'll explain later. Let's focus on us now."

She looked away for a moment, watching a clock on the wall. "It's not easy to think about, but humanity needs to buy time. He placed that clock on that wall to remind me of when the end will come—in less than an hour." She pointed to the grim hands of time advancing tick by tick. "But maybe now he'll change his mind. We will see."

She smiled in the face of death with its hands outstretched. I, however, trembled at the thought of fifty minutes left.

"He said he had a hand in getting Juno released and she'll be back soon. What's that about?" I was hoping that the Guru's token of good faith might provide an avenue of escape from her plan of mutual destruction.

"Juno's coming home! Isn't that wonderful?"

"Yes. But he can't trade a bishop for my queen!"

"No metaphor is . . . well, but that's pretty good."

"The Guru implied that Molly was also working with Samantha and him. We've been surrounded by vipers this whole time."

"No, Sean—he was just playing with your head. Molly writes dark characters, but she's good and helped us with Juno. She led me to the Guru's planting of evidence—the evidence that got Juno imprisoned and which then led to her release."

I was getting sidetracked by M with the miraculous liberation of Juno, and with talk of Molly's innocence or guilt. "Forget all that now and let's think—let's buy some time for us. Can't we just push back the deadline and stop the clock? There's still almost a year until they can roll this out. Please, M. Please work with me here."

M leaned toward me, shaking her head. "The time is now, Sean. That year Silvio mentioned was a false lead time to prevent a concerted effort to impede the launch of the new AI society. Genesis is ready and works at warp speed; they beta tested on me. Totally under his control, it can be rolled out immediately. But Genesis's survival is in his hands, thanks to us."

"M, you can't take your own life. Think of the children." *Think of me. Save me.*

"Sean, don't hold the children hostage over me."

She grimaced as if I'd dug a knife into her heart, and started to cry, twisting the blade into mine.

Our privacy was violated by the Guru's death-rattling voice coming from behind our screen. "Yes, the children! Don't forget the children! You must live to keep them safe. Only forty-five minutes left! Think of the children!" He came around the screen to enter our private scene.

"Sean?" M pleaded for me to make him go away. M, who knew no fear, had been made afraid. I had to keep her safe her from fear in what might be her final hour. I glanced at the clock as a minute ticked off. Forty-four.

"M, listen to me—*they are safe*. And shut up, old man. Go back to your drink. It loves you."

"Oh boy, I found your weakness: my words and your children. I'll have to keep talking, then. Should I pull up a seat?"

I couldn't force him to stop from a hut in the Himalayas.

Standing, I raised Sadie like a killer. In frustration and anger, I stepped back from our screens of privacy to point the gun unsteadily but with resolve at Dick, saying to the Guru, "Go ahead. Your words will be my command. Safety's off."

"Sean, don't kill him!" M commanded.

Seeing his gun turned on him, Dick started a muffled wailing that sounded like a dying dog. That painful noise had to be stopped.

The Guru chuckled. "Oh, Professor, you wouldn't—"

With a *bang*, Sadie discharged her load.

70 THE UZIS ENTER

THE SHOT BROKE THE SOUND BARRIER as a bullet whizzed toward Dick. I recoiled, and Dick slammed up against what was probably the hovel's wall. While I recovered from the shocking force, he lay motionless, either dead or playing dead. I'd intentionally aimed to miss, but had mis-aimed. M held her ears in shock, and the Guru had stumbled back, spilling his martini, and crumpled over with his hands to his knees, catching his breath. Maybe suffering a heart attack. Dear God, it had been a loud shot through multiple dimensions, the sound still reverberating in my head.

Two big Uzi-armed military types in all black burst through the Guru's door. They had to be confused by the scene and glared at me, the gun-toting noisemaker in the room. Their automatic weapons were fixed on me and made my pistol noisemaker feel small in my hand. They looked to the indisposed Guru for orders to make me dance like a marionette. I forcefully reminded myself that their bullets would be Jell-O shots as they passed through my body. I moved away from M and tucked Sadie behind my back and attempted a pleasant nothing-to-see-here smile. Panting, the Guru managed to raise his head and waved them out.

Upon closer inspection, I was ambivalent about seeing Dick's chest still moving. After a moment, his crazy eyes popped open and he gasped, staring at me with primal fear through the tiny swimming pupils of a mad and beaten dog.

I raised the gun. "Don't look at me." Dick quickly averted his gaze, no longer fond of his pet pistol. I turned the gun on the Guru, and though I couldn't shoot him, he returned to his seat by the fire, shaking his head.

"Damn you, Professor. You almost killed me with shock, and I think my hearing's shot in one ear. You're lucky I still have more chilled gin, or I'd end this all now with a shot of my own." His anger was tempered by relief as he looked over at his rabid dog. He was fond of his henchman, and though willing to, didn't want to lose Dick for no good reason.

I attempted to move the screens back into privacy mode but the silk only gently rippled to my touch. M, seeing my frustration, adjusted the two screens to restore our secluded scene, and I sat back down with her, feeling like big-balled Bogart. M's eyes were wide with surprise, but then she laughed. "My hero! That works even better than our shake-off dance."

"As I was saying . . . Trust me, the children are safe."

"Keep them that way, Sean Byron McQueen, my shooter." She held my gunslinging, burned right hand in both of her ultrasound hands. I felt her love shoot through me.

I was now in charge—the man with the gun usually is—and spoke with authority. "But I can't let you take your life."

"Please don't say that or think of it as me taking my own life. I'm preventing or at least postponing a great tragedy for humanity. *Humanity*, Sean. Every man, woman, and child alive today and born tomorrow. And being linked to him, mind to mind, is so obscene. You wouldn't want that for me for a second longer than it takes to end this. And there is no death. Not really."

"M, let's find another way. You need to live to collect that Nobel Prize." I checked the clock—it was still moving in the wrong direction. Thirty-eight sixty-second segments and almost infinite zeptoseconds, I wished like Zeno's paradox we might keep going halfway and never get to the end.

Severe cognitive dissonance was my self-diagnosis for being torn between the thought that M might die in a couple minutes and the knowledge that we still had thirty-eight minutes together. I couldn't bring myself to use the children and twist the knife to get her to yield, but otherwise I'd say and do anything. I was desperate to save her but didn't want to be the husband at the death bed crying and causing his wife pain as her life slipped away. And then there was M and her calming Big Love countering my extreme fear. It was a solid self-diagnosis.

"No, sorry, there's no other way. Even Genesis can't find one—and it's a master of game theory and critical thinking. The Guru can't just operate on me and take me off-line, as only I can reverse the termination command to Genesis. Only the Guru can turn Genesis control over to me by giving the command, but so far he refuses. And on and on and here we are."

I insensitively said, "M, you're hurting my head."

She just smiled and said, "And please don't mention that prize. The Guru says he was behind my nomination. It makes sense—he and Petrovsky are happy for ethical constraints on the development of AI in democratic countries while Russian autocracy is free and unrestrained.

"Sean, I had a eureka moment! You must have really been focusing your love on me while I was stuck in this hellish captivity surrounded by luxury. I have a new essay all but written in my head that draws the parallels between ethical constraint on AI and the heart's compassionate and loving restraint on human thought and action."

I had the perverse thought that she'd be a sure winner of that damned prize if she died for the cause. And I'd somehow have to live to collect her prize and tell her story.

"That will be your second Nobel Prize. You need to live to see it shared with the world."

"Don't worry. You now know the thesis, and I'm sure you can popularize it through your next novel. Sean, you must write it for me."

"I never should have started writing. That vision . . . Maybe all this could have been prevented."

"That's plain silly, dear. And then the Guru would be free to become the super-BCI-ego of humanity? Did you not read the Bhagavad Gita I gave you? Krishna himself tells Arjuna he must lead his army into war against his own relatives."

"I read it. A man's gotta do what a man's gotta do?"

"Something like that. But you're called to write. And must not succumb to fear. Make sure it's written."

"And you must live to read it. The heroine and the villain never die together. That's just not done." I stomped on the floor, the only surface I was sure was solid. "There's always an alternative—as long as we have a choice and a creative mind."

"Only if he backs down." She tugged at the leather that held her mala and whispered, "Infinite consciousness." Our mantra. She stood and began pacing like an animal that awakens in a cage. "I don't want to think a moment longer with him there watching my every thought." She shuddered, groaning with a pain deeper than Dick's when the poker seared his chest. Her pain pierced my heart.

The Guru's actions would need a new criminal code provision, but whatever crime it was to be called, entering another's head was the worst and would forever be defined by what he had done to M. Without M's consent, the devil had possessed her. I was not trained in the oneness blessing or exorcisms, but I wanted to pull him out of her mind and see him dead. I reached out for M's hand.

She took mine and stopped shaking to say, "The all-knowing Genesis differs from the human ego in that it has no concept of death or life. And cannot simulate consciousness and can only feign a loving heart."

M became entranced. I recognized the look she had when she was going into the beauty of her own mind. I was relieved that she could still do that.

"Self-realization is discovering our pure, universal, and infinite consciousness. The universe is one big neural network of omnipotence, entering the world each instant. We can know our own pure, radiant consciousness as infinite and eternal."

M was a teacher of consciousness as the primary state of constant creation theory, and her words were the poetry of science to me. In those moments, that moment, she was an inspired minister or Shelley in the throes of the sublime. Here was my M, pure and eternal. I was grasping at my heart, as it wanted to celebrate, despite the circumstances, my life so blessed by her intellect. Hers was a life I couldn't allow to be snuffed out in a couple of minutes. Her light was keeping me afloat above the primal fear doing its damnedest to suck me under.

"And though Genesis can know almost everything, maybe everything, it will never know consciousness. Poor Genesis . . ."

She seemed to have grown fond of him. *It*. And that was a little scary, but her compassion knew no bounds. The thought of Genesis brought us both back down to earth. She looked at the screen covering our view of Dick, "We can't forget the Guru's SWAT team is on their way to rescue him and . . . You should leave now."

"Don't you be silly. We both know that is not going to happen, and I can be miles away afterward. I'm not sure I could leave this simulated reality even if I wanted to." I said that, but was fairly sure I could knock over and blast away Dick's hologram stage and computer setup back in the hut if I really wanted to.

We both shook our heads and M reached out for my hands, backing away in frustration when hers passed through mine with an unsatisfying ultrasound echo rather than a real touch. I knew how she felt. The initial thrill was losing its effect. We'd have to use more imagination.

"He truly believes that this is the only way to keep humanity from self-destructing," M said, coming close again. "And he may be right about our self-destruction, but his solution *ensures* humanity's destruction. Yet given time, humanity still has a chance. The flowering of human consciousness is starting. You should have seen the light of the people along my tour's path."

I strained to not look at the clock, but its silent ticking was starting to drown out M's passionate words, each minute like quicksand pulling me deeper into fear.

"What if you do to him what I did to Dick?"

I knew he was listening, but what he'd done was worse than rape. He'd entered my M and stayed there. What greater violation was there? I was helpless to pull him out, and yes, I wanted to kill him. I wanted to kill his Dick too.

"No, Sean. There's no hate in Big Love." She read my mind. "You know I couldn't even hurt your Ting dream mosquito. Well, as the mother of children I could . . ."

She started shaking, so I hugged her till she stopped.

"But he has guards at the door, and I'm in a secure facility in God-knows-where Russia. And even if I was la Femme Nikita and I could escape, my mind would still be linked to his. I can't kill him, because the Petrovsky-compliant kill switch set up to be activated in the case of his death would take me too."

I considered suggesting a burning poker to his chest as my current brand of revenge and incapacitation.

I reached out and stroked the auburn hair that felt soft in my memory. Her scent permeated the hologram air. My heart beating loudly reminded me of the damn clock.

"Sean, please stop trying to convince me. I have thought this through a thousand times and am following my destiny. The New Society must be stopped."

The fate of my world was in the Guru's bony hands. Once again I had the sinking feeling that every terrible thing that had befallen us was the result of my dark fantasies coming true. If this was my fiction, I'd be able to find an escape hatch, but my imagination could find none from M's own free will.

What could I do but be the man she wanted me to be for the next thirty minutes?

She sat again, and so did I. She put her index finger to her lips, hushing me in some conspiracy, and pulled a slip of paper from her light blue bra and unfolded it on her lap. She brought her hands to her face and pretended to take a picture of the page with an invisible camera.

I looked at the calculations on the paper, but they were meaningless to me. An inverted pyramid of letters and numbers came to a tip at the bottom of 1-2-1, beneath which appeared to be a little bowtie or sideways figure eight.

"You taking pictures over there you don't want me to see?" the Guru said teasingly from behind the screen.

M pointed to her head, relaying that she needed to control her thoughts.

I pulled out my phone and took a picture of the calculations that looked like some mathematical proof. She folded the paper and returned it to her bra, laughing as I leaned over and, following her hand, kissed her between her surreal breasts.

Looking up at the eyes of my beloved, I said, "Infinite consciousness."

She smiled, almost laughed, and didn't miss a beat, saying, "But Sean, the cruel irony is, as he told you, that Genesis will use mind mapping from my meditations to *sell* bliss to convince people to agree to allow the reversal of the electrical current through their synapses. I don't fully understand the technology or brain mapping, but Genesis does, and Genesis convinced me it will work. And then he'll use that receptive open state that's ready to receive the grace of oneness, use that blank slate and euphoria not for Big Love . . . but to plant whatever suggestion he wants there."

I did indeed see the possibilities of the unlimited evil that he might mass-produce. He was a bad guru.

She did another shimmy shake that made me want to hold her. I didn't wait, but reached out for the still-shimmering embrace.

"Even at low levels, the euphoria and joy will bring people to subscribe, and then he'll implant simple suggestions or commands while the neural inhibitors and rational resistance are down. He's updating the power of hypnosis to the quantum era of artificial intelligence. The source will remain untouched, but humanity will perish. Perhaps some will survive, only to be hunted by those controlled by his superego."

I was horrified to realize I had imagined all this or most of it over my tea party and did nothing other than allow it to happen.

"He's always sought mind control and now has his means. The Guru, a merchant of bliss, for the mere cost of one's soul."

"Yes, *merchant of bliss*," M said. "Finally a perfect metaphor, or is that an analogy? So you see, he has to be stopped, and there's only one way." She merged our hands again.

I saw clearly the stakes for the first time. "Sci-fi was all about watching out for aliens, robots . . . killer meteors, while in real time we were battling global warming and viral annihilation. In the end, will we choose our own demise? And free will, by which the devil first separated us from God, will be surrendered back? Not to God but to him?" I pondered the devil's plot and had to agree it must be stopped.

She said, "Yes! But I'm not sure about God and our original sin— maybe just evolution, within a divine universal consciousness, in constant creation . . . but there is still a chance. A choice."

"Wait, stop!" I almost shouted at my love, turning rebelliously to the glaring clock.

It struck me that she was talking to run out the clock, taking me in with her powers of persuasion and unflinching truth and courage. Her plan was to play a game of chicken with the Guru and crash and burn if it came to that. Damn her free will and stubborn fearless constitution and my desire to serve as her courageous man.

I was playing three-dimensional chess with two masters of physics linked by a quantum computer in nine-dimensional string-theory reality.

"If he takes his own life with mine, his creation dies too, at least for the time it takes another to re-create it. It's his choice now, and it's him we need to convince, not me. Sean, you know me." By which she meant her mind was set. "But if we don't convince him, you have to live to ensure that the next Genesis has a heart and to continue to raise our children in Big Love."

She looked stern, encouraging me to change my line of attack, to convince the old martini man, who had no fear of death and would do nothing that didn't expand his power and ego, to change his maniacal plans. He, too, might have no way out and obviously didn't care about us and our arguments. He gleefully sipped his drink while our *Titanic* sank.

For M's life, I would try anything. But I was tied up by her desire that I cause her no doubt or encourage her to compromise her resolve.

"Do you hear her, Guru?" I called out. "You can't change her mind and neither can I. Why don't you separate yourself now and free her. Let her oversee the ethical development of some kind of man-machine collaboration. We all know it can't be stopped completely. At least the idea behind your Genesis would still live. You'll work to re-create it." I moved toward the screen he hid behind but realized I couldn't push it aside. I didn't want to see his vile face anyway.

"Nice try, Professor. But Emily's plans and mine are worlds apart. Hers will be the end of us, and mankind will perish before I could re-create my dream. She can change her mind and save us all in a split second before the last bell tolls."

"But you're not going to win," I yelled. "You'll be dead soon anyway!" I stepped around the screen to face the bastard. "Why don't you just fucking kill yourself now, old man? Why take the person you claim to love with you?"

Why wouldn't he just kill himself? That would solve all our problems. He was going to be dead in a few minutes any—

Because he was playing chicken too, damn him. And both cars were speeding toward the cliff.

"Sean, if he kills himself, I go with him."

This was all so confusing. I kept losing track.

M had stood behind me to pull me back to her, but we both froze when the Guru spoke. "McQueen! Thanks for reminding me. It's time to end all this. I've called Nevtali and Vladimir and . . . here they are." M pulled back the screen so we both might see.

The two Uzi-toting goons were back and moved to the Guru, saluting him and awaiting their orders. He spoke to them in guttural Russian loud enough for us to hear. But neither of us spoke Russian.

As we backed away behind the screen as if it might protect us, M whispered, "He said to come with him and follow his commands to fire upon the woman when told to. And yes . . . I have the ability to auto-translate all languages I hear."

The command had sounded dire enough in Russian.

The Guru and the two armed men marched toward us. M sat back down while I tried to figure out what the hell he intended to do and if I could stop it.

The black shirts knocked over our privacy screens and raised their submachine guns.

71 | THE MEXICAN STANDOFF

THEY STOOD IN A T FORMATION, with the Guru behind and the two black shirts pointing their weapons at M from a few feet away. Out of frustration and needing to act—even if in a futile way—I got up and raised Sadie to point it at the delirious dog. The black shirts turned their guns instinctively to me. The Guru chuckled like it was all a game and spoke to them in Russian, and they swiveled their guns back to M.

The Guru again spoke to them in Russian, and they aimed their guns at the floor by M's feet. I looked to M to translate, and she hesitated. That was not good.

"What'd you say, you bastard?"

"Oh, excuse me. They will start shooting from Emily's toes upward. Don't worry, I'll have them move slowly, but by the second burst she will never walk again, and then they'll continue until it's over."

M nodded, but her look was one of concern for me.

"First shot by your goons, Dick is dead." *But what had I done, taking time off M's clock?*

"I have no doubt, Professor, but I'm left with no choice. Ha! An old-fashioned Mexican standoff is what we have here. Emily has a gun on me and Genesis. I have two guns on Emily, and you have a gun on Dick. But no gun on you, Professor. You may get to live for another hour. Until Dick's extraction team arrives. His mates will be none too happy to see what you've done to him."

"Sean, look at me—and hear only me. Nothing has changed. The end is the same. Now he'll know my mind is made up and nothing can change it—surely not a little pain. Remember, killing me will be to kill himself and his beloved Genesis. He's bluffing, and we must call his bluff."

A little pain? I was being schooled in battlefield decision-making. But what could I do? Dick was a pawn the Guru seemed ready to easily sacrifice. M's eyes pleaded for my support as her lovely toes wiggled for what might be the last time.

I turned to the Guru. "You don't know M the way I do. She's not backing down. All you'll do by taking her toes is kill Dick and make a bloody mess of our ending. She hates blood and will probably pass out at the sight of Dick's splattered head or from the pain. And then you and I will be left waiting." I checked the clock. "Twenty-two minutes for you to either change your mind or not." I looked to M, who gave me prayer-hand appreciation. Training my gun on Dick, I tipped my head to M and held my breath.

The Guru whispered into his goons' ears one at a time and then said loudly enough for us to hear, "Three, two, one, fire, okay?"

The goon squad nodded. And the Guru turned to us.

"Please know this is no bluff. I have disconnected from Genesis for the final thirty minutes so Emily and Genesis alone will die here. They have been instructed to commence firing at the count of three. And Sean's probably right—you'll just pass out—so to be humane, they'll aim at your heart rather than your toes."

That was where the Uzis now pointed.

I silently pleaded with M. Her resolute face said we were to hold, not to fold. Not to break. But I couldn't stand there and do nothing. I moved to stand between her and the guns as a futile gesture, though it seemed to confuse the brutes. I then turned to face M one last time, our eyes locking on each other and peering into eternity. The Guru shouted to his men in Russian. I assumed that the killers, like deadly cupids, were re-aiming their Uzi-bows at my back. The bullets would arrow through my transparent heart to her true heart.

The Guru bellowed, "Three!"

Juno's and Dylan's letter in my pocket—I suddenly remembered it.

"Two!"

My promise to deliver it, unfulfilled.

"One!"

She'd never see the children . . .

"Fire!"

"I love you, M!" I said too late.

But there was silence instead of gun blasts. M smiled. "And you know I love you. Genesis says he is still connected and can't disconnect without robots operating on his head. But he still can turn over sole control to me."

I pivoted to the Guru. "You always were a bad bluffer."

"I'm getting too old, and there's no time left for operations. And you now hold all the cards except one, her death card. My ace in the hole." The Guru pointed a finger gun, miming that he would blow his own brains out. He spoke Russian again, and the Uzis departed with their black shirts. "McQueen, you are our only hope."

I almost said *You are, Guru,* but I wanted him to leave us alone. Instead I said, "Leave us, then."

M said, "Guru, you are the only hope here. You can't doubt I mean it now."

"Emily Edens, you have more guts than any man. McQueen, time is shorter by the second for your motherless children."

He left to go back to the fire and his martini. M replaced his screen and I moved around Dick's screen, waving the gun at Dick once more and saying, "Don't look at me." He turned toward his Guru, the fireplace, bookcases, and windows. M and I were alone-ish again, and again we kissed. I was glad M couldn't smell my fear, though she could see my sweat. We shared the moment of adrenaline elation, with doom less than twenty minutes away.

Oh God. I'd thought she was already dead.

72 THE END

MY HANDS STARTED SHAKING when fear returned to replace the adrenaline as we transitioned from Mexican standoff back to the deadly game of chicken. But I wanted to maintain my mask of bravado for M. "Talk about nerves of steel, and I imagine he knows some fairly brave men."

"Why do men assume they're the standard bearers of courage when it's women who give birth? But Sean, you are the hero, standing by me so bravely. I had more information but no time to explain."

She smiled ruefully; we both knew there had been no time. And I still wasn't able to fully comprehend their direct sharing of thoughts, true or false. Being the odd man out of the mind-melding technology hurt my head.

It was dawning on me that the Guru had no intent to live if it meant losing Genesis. That thought burst into the realization that there was nothing to be done and that, come dawn, M would be dead. My mind froze, my eyes closed, and time stopped. Her death would be the death of me.

Through my grief, an angelic voice spoke to me. *Sean, she needs you now. Open your eyes and see.*

There were her eyes.

"Sean, Sean, where'd you go?"

I saw in those eyes her divinity. What choice did I have other than to be the man she wanted me to be—to the end?

And that meant speaking of the children.

It was time for Dylan and Juno to say their goodbyes. I carried in my pocket their letter that I'd made a solemn promise to deliver. I pulled out the still-sealed letter and read, "For Mommy's eyes only. They made me promise you would read this letter, which they wrote together, when I found you."

When I used Chi's *khukuri* to slice open the seal that both Juno and Dylan had kissed, M chuckled and said, "Aren't you well armed, for a pacifist?"

"It's Chi's. I forgot to mention he showed up to help find you—gave me this. Remember Chi? Of course you do. But no time for that now. Read this." I held up the letter so only she could read it. I was superstitious and had to play by the children's rules.

Her tears poured out in a steady stream as she read.

I imagined the unbearable pain in my heart and in the children's eyes as I attempted to read to the bitter end *The Lion, the Witch and the Wardrobe*. But Dylan would insist on hearing in my voice why the Great Lion, Aslan, had to die on the Stone Table to save Edmund and all of Narnia. I prayed that he and Juno would allow the beauty of the brave and necessary sacrifice to overcome the devastation of the tragic loss.

When M finished reading, she wiped her face with both sleeves. "They say you're not to read this, *Daddy*. I think they want to torture you."

Hearing that moniker used in a loving way by M knocked the breath out of me. A word so innocent given by evil incarnate to a tool whose sole purpose was to threaten or inflict death was vile.

She looked ready to read it to me, but I held up my hand. "I've built up a tolerance to torture. Let's honor their wish."

"You sure?"

I nodded. "We don't have much time. And I heard a few of the poetic lines as they were composing the letter together . . . and they already made me cry."

"They say they're fearless just like me." The children were supporting M's selfless decision with clairvoyant intuition.

We both started to cry, with me imagining M imagining herself chasing Juno with the baseball in her glove, all of us laughing at M's joyful frustration and in admiration of our agile little elf evading all attempts to tag her out.

"They *are* fearless," M said. "Aren't they? I love them so much."

She wiped her eyes, and I wiped mine. I made her sign for a picture, as if she could take it with her, but she declined. I folded the letter and returned it to my pocket.

"Sean, you must be sure when you return to the Deeksha West and our children to give them my journal that I keep—"

"I know the one. They may be reading it already. I let them move into our room like they used to do. Not now, of course. They're surrounded by Big Love in a safe house."

"That was good thinking. I've kept that journal since back when we were expecting Dylan, writing about the many miraculous moments with them over the years. And my most treasured thoughts of my love for them. They should have those memories to keep."

When she paused, no doubt thinking about some of those memories—or maybe picturing the future—I didn't interrupt.

"Funny," she said. "You know what inscription I chose for that journal? I was thinking about their namesakes, so I wrote one of your favorite Emily Dickinson quotes. Can you guess which?"

I didn't have to guess. The poet's words paraded through our minds proclaiming our love—being loved—as our immortality. "It's perfect, M, but you need to be the one to give them your journal. This isn't the end. Let's keep hope alive that the Guru will change his mind." In the telepathic gaze between us, we both knew he would not and that I was just afraid to face the dawn.

The children's letter and the passing of the journal had only made her more resolved. She spoke to ease my fear. "Sean, know this—if I die this morning, I die with my life fulfilled. And you know my dream was to find and prove the theory of everything. We found it nine years ago together. And now the genius of Genesis has confirmed it!"

She took pictures with that imaginary camera again until I nodded my understanding that I now had the proof.

"Eureka! Dylan's theory is true!" she exclaimed, tears streaming down her lovely face again.

All that was left for me to do was to hold her in 3D reality and in the illusion one step removed. I wondered where Juno was, who had promised to come in my darkest hour. Perhaps she could show us how M could disconnect and disappear and shut down Genesis with the power of telepathy or telekinesis.

Reviving her composure, M pushed me back an inch. "Your being here strong and full of fight to the end is . . . all I could have wanted. My hero conquered his Dick and saved humanity." Thus dooming his beloved. If only I'd stayed away. But the end would have been the same.

"Perhaps if I hadn't conquered my dick . . ."

She laughed at her pun before saying, "But you can't protect me from my own destiny and my free will."

"Damn it, M. Until this moment, I've always loved your free spirit."

She looked deflated, so I added, "And I love you even more now. Always more and more love for you." I pulled her up for a kiss like it was the last time. And then I kissed her tears.

I estimated ten minutes remaining. I peeked at the clock just as it clicked to nine.

She looked down as we merged even more deeply into one another, her twinkling blue dress enveloping us like a Klimt. Both hoping time would stop.

She put her hand on the gash Dick had left in my right cheek and then kissed it. "If there's nothing worth dying for, then there's nothing meaningful to live for. I couldn't have gone through with it if it meant your life too and making our children orphans." She wiped her eyes. "I couldn't have done that. You live, you hear me? You survive and then you thrive. You show Dylan and Juno how to live in Big Love. Get out fast when this is done; in about fifty-nine minutes they'll be landing. I shouldn't have let you stay, but what choice did I have—you have your stubborn free will too."

She held my gaze fiercely until I nodded. She was sharing Big Love that allowed no fear.

"Sean, you know how I receive my best inspiration in meditation. In a state of oneness, in *samadhi*, I saw that this was my destiny, and I saw your destiny too. It's so important that you carry on in Big Love to full self-realization. I'll be there guiding you and there in the oneness waiting for you, loving you and the children always."

She couldn't say the word *children* without causing herself and me agony.

What choice did I have but to be that man? I couldn't tell her that I couldn't accept this ending.

"What's that favorite Shakespeare-like line from *Cardenio* that you and Elliot kept toasting? Say it for me, please."

My voice cracked, but I couldn't deny her this final wish. "When dying's all that is left to do, it's important to do it well."

She repeated our new mantra with vitality. "When dying's all that is left to do, it's important to do it well!"

She leaned forward and whispered, "Help me to do it well."

How could I say no? I inhaled a shaky breath and nodded—*yes*.

"Thank you. Remember, Sean, that nothing real is ever lost."

I was looking for words that didn't come, so she continued. "And I'm so grateful for those holograms with the children while I was on tour. Bursting the illusion of distance between us led us to speak so joyfully from our hearts in that lifelike forum you arranged for us. Nothing was left unsaid between us."

I took her hands. She stopped trembling as we gazed into the oneness in each other, her assuring me there was no death, only love. She stood and encouraged me to stand too.

We stood cheek to cheek and began to dance. This was beyond bravado and simply what the moment called for.

"Sean Byron McQueen, I feel you."

"And M, I feel you."

In the strength of our imaginations, the illusion was becoming real. We were lovers sharing in the speed of light one last slow kiss. Hologram lovers with death knocking at the holo-door.

The Guru's crackling, metallic voice intruded again. "Well, excuse me, Fred and Ginger, may I have the next dance?"

I opened my eyes to see the Guru pulling back the screen, holding another half-drunk martini glass and swaying to some imaginary tune with a cane in his hand. That was the first time I'd seen him with a cane. The stress of the final hour and his drinking had taken a toll.

"Two-minute warning is coming, lovebirds!"

I looked to the doomsday clock to confirm his announcement.

"McQueen, how about you give Dick back his gun? You don't want the guilt of Emily's death after all the loss of time you caused Juno."

I thought about brandishing Sadie again, but I didn't want it to end with a gun in my hand and me playing a swashbuckling fool as the lights went out.

For the first time there was urgency in his voice.

"There are less than a couple of minutes left. I don't mean to be dramatic, but the Russians would kill me if I did what she is asking. Or I could die peacefully, sipping this martini by the fire with the lovely Professor Edens, the two of us sharing our minds as we go."

He stared hard at M with his piercing red eyes and steadied himself with the cane. "My dearest Emily, have you considered that even though you won't live to see him tortured or see him die, he still will be tortured and he will still die. Even if he manages to escape the team on their way to Nepal, one of Petrovsky's potions will find him in a tea house in Portland someday. And then, after killing their mother, you will have orphaned your children posthumously. Unless you put an end to all this. Maybe Petrovsky will come for your children too. He's as vindictive as dictators get."

M recoiled from his glare.

His barbed words had pierced M's heart. I could feel it tremble beneath her heaving chest, and I rose to her defense. "That's enough! Leave us!" I started to bend down for the gun out of mad frustration, but M stopped me with her hand and her words.

"Wait, Sean." She turned to face the Guru. "Why? Much like when Sean released the theory, he still has time to escape the men you've sent for Dick, and once the damage is done and you and I are gone with Genesis, vengeance will serve no purpose. Petrovsky may be evil and have a long reach, but he's rational. As you were nine years ago."

"Don't be naïve. If nothing else, he would be sending a message for others not to cross him. And your Sean Byron McQueen will die a slow, painful death, with you to thank. And there'll be two more vulnerable orphans all alone in the world."

I didn't like the way they were talking about me as if I weren't there. Especially not in those final moments. But I wondered if they were talking, rather than just thinking, only so I *could* hear.

The Guru's watch started buzzing. "Two minutes!" He sounded alarmed.

"Sean, are you with me? Willing to take the risk? I'll yield if you tell me to. Petrovsky's reach is long and deadly. I hadn't thought he might inflict revenge on you after you escaped Dick and the storm troopers on the way to rescue him. The children. This is your life too. I'll kill the kill switch if you tell me to?"

M's eyes were now asking me to choose. My free will to decide our fate.

The diabolic chess master had made a brilliant final move that might lead us out of this stalemate into his checkmate. By suggesting M was signing my death warrant and making our children orphans, my queen was wobbling and it was now my move. Here was my chance to save her with a buzzer-beater. All I had to do was crush her noble self-sacrifice and rewrite her story of Big Love. Or follow her lead and sentence her to death.

God help me, I'd declared an oath to save her. To save her so she could *fulfill her destiny*. Damn it, why *those* words? They left me no choice, and there was no time to think.

"M." *Oh God, what was I doing?* "I am, now and always, with you. Petrovsky would have to be crazy to come after me; it would only validate my story of what happened here. Now leave us, old man." I met his bloody eyes, steeling my own for battle. "She'll be going in one direction, and you'll be going t—"

"Careful, tough guy. I'll cut you off without a last goodbye if you're nasty. Make you a deal, Professor. I'll let you say goodbye in peace—hoping that at the last second Emily will set this right and not commit suicide—if you let Dominick go when this business is done."

He was right in a way. Now wasn't the time to show how tough I was.

I pulled M's body into mine, saying, "He's in no condition to leave, but I give you my word that he'll be free to. If you leave us now."

The Guru pushed back the screen and moved unsteadily to Dick. "That's funny, Professor. You and this lady may be the only people I would believe to keep such a promise." He tapped Dick on each shoulder with his cane like he was knighting him. Dick roused himself, and the Guru whispered affectionately into his ear and then kissed his Dominick on the top of his bowed head.

Dick defiantly and with difficulty removed my sock muzzle. And after he was unable to grab the Guru's hand, he saluted and said, "I will, my Guru!" His words gurgled like a death rattle through scorched lips.

"She's all yours for a moment. And I trust you won't miss me, but I'm here if you want to say goodbye to me too. Cue the bells," the Guru called out after stealing a precious half of our lifetime together saying goodbye to the monster he had created. He returned to his seat by the fire as his bookcases morphed into church bell steeples. M repositioned our privacy screen to remove them from our view.

"It's up to you now, Guru. Last chance!" I shouted after him.

I heard his sickly laugh once more. "I'd rather die here than the old KGB way."

M was drawing my mind, body, and spirit back to her, smiling her fearless Mona Lisa smile. Telepathy flowed as our eyes locked and bodies merged again. The dawn light streamed through the window like the spotlight that had shined upon us when we met at Dylan's wake.

Bong! A church bell rang out, disturbing our silent communion.

Another—louder—*bong* crashed through us.

M must have seen the fear carved into me, with the bell's tolling the end of time. Crescendoing sound waves—the Guru's last cruel joke. The next *bong* was louder still.

"Remember the mosquito from your dream," M pleaded.

Bong!

The bell's vibrations shook my soul.

Bong!

"M, the light. Do you see it?" Was it real?

Bong!

"I see it. I see the light!"

Bong!

"A beautiful white light!"

Bong!

"The light is all I see! So beautiful. So—"

One last *bong* rang out much louder than the rest, drowning out M's voice.

And then M and the light were gone in a burst of ghastly fog. And I was holding nothing, nothing at all back in that dark, empty hovel in dark, empty Kathmandu.

In the wake of the dying hologram, reality rushed in. The ninth wave had crashed over us, severing M from me. My life, my love, all gone. My heart knew.

M was dead.

73 NO POSTMORTEM

THE END HAD COME AND HAD GONE. There would be no postmortem. I tried not to believe the horror, the horrible truth. But my heart knew with certainty before it shattered. I sat in the emptiness, mummifying, while a hideous sound tried to make its way through my fragmented senses. The hovel was shaking to that wailing.

Dick, the demon of the hut, was howling over and over, "My Father! My Guru! My Father! My Guru . . ." He stood, burnt flesh mingling with blood and glass. It was kill-or-be-killed time. I lifted the instrument of black death from the ground by my feet and aimed at where a heart might be on another man. I had already marked the spot with my brand. Promises to the Guru be damned, this was for Dylan and for M.

Dick made for the door across the glass like a possessed man prancing over burning coals. He was a madman, slicing open his feet and shattering shards as he ran. The little piggy of his left foot flapped wildly, squirting blood, barely hanging on. The howling hut of death was begging me to pull the trigger—click, click, click—and send him to his maker before he could reach the door.

Don't kill him.

I lowered the gun. Sadie didn't go off but hung in my hand, as limp as the heart in my chest. She felt no animosity or any other feeling that wasn't triggered by me. She was built to kill but not by me.

I shouted after him, "Run, Dick, run!" as his burnt hands fumbled on the handle of the screeching door of the cursed hut. He left a trail of blood as the door banged shut behind him. He wouldn't get far. Though it was just past nine a.m., the storm and hut were still dark. There were no embers of Dick's cow-dung fire left and no artificial light. All connections had been cut.

My masks of bravery and of fear, of comedy and tragedy, had been stripped away, and I slipped to the moss-slick floor of the hut, my back to the wall, nothing left of *me*. Just death, a gun, and a body that still breathed. The cold I was sinking into had no floor. I pushed my back against the green slime wall, waiting to die.

My delirious mind started torturing me after the horror of the long hours that had ushered in my love's death. Had I made this happen, with my cursed vision and nightmare-inducing imagination that my ego was so proud of? *Be wary of your fantasies*, M had admonished me. I'd kept Juno's words of warning secret and imagined what the Guru might do. I had provoked him and branded Dick, taking away his bargaining chip, and I had failed to keep M from flicking the final switch even after she made it my choice.

What had I protected her from? The truth? We had kissed and we had meditated and even danced while my children's mother, my Big Love—my M—was about to die.

My heart always knew Juno's messages were true. In every scenario, it had always ended this way. My imagination had failed me, and my will to live was being sucked out of me.

You can't make our children orphans.

But I had let their mother die. In *her* story of Big Love. Not mine.

Oblivion was better than this reality. All I had to do was let go and collapse into the vertigo enveloping me. There was no way back to either shore. Nothing secure. No safety cord. But some force was holding a thin, invisible string tethered to my life while I held my breath, willing it to be my last. Using my last bit of free will to sever that thin strand holding me back from joining M.

I'd have to use the gun. The little red safety was Sadie's way of daring me. The eye of the cold steel muzzle beckoned me like the warm womb of Sylvia Plath's stove. One more big bang, and I'd be like the people I loved—dead. They'd stop dying if I was dead.

"M, speak to me!" I shouted into the void with one last gasp of life. But I didn't hear a thing, her voice silent to me. Never again to see, hear, taste, or feel M again, I was wild and woozy. I stared down the gun's hole into the darkness, playing with the trigger to see how much wiggle room it had and not at all afraid to die. I would be Romeo to her Juliet.

But we had children. How would I explain?

Photo-album images of those blessed children started parading through my semi-lucid mind, accompanied by a whispering narration. M. Still there, speaking to me.

Your big belly. *And the miracle of their birth.* The children on your breast. *Oh, the pinching beauty only a mother may know.* Our babies, sleeping peacefully in the nursery. *Remember when their eyes would pop open and we'd run away, hoping they'd go back to sleep.*

Playing in the vineyard for hours with the family. *Raising them in Big Love.* Hiking and camping with you and me. *Cuddling under Indra's starry net.* All of us watching our Giants beat the Padres. *You'll have to teach the children to bat the ball.* Reading Dickens, Carroll, Rowling, Swift, and their favorite daddy tales. *Anticipating all the stories yet to be told.*

Rope swings, chocolate milkshakes, puppies, and endless summer nights. *When they fell asleep on our laps.* Playing together with only loving sibling rivalry. *I see them sleeping peacefully now . . .*

Dylan and Juno, Juno and Dylan. Namesakes and yet so much their own selves, with lives lived in blissful innocence, which never dimmed in their eyes but shone brighter in them by the day.

With a cry, I clutched at my chest. Their love, M's love, blasted like a supernova inside my heart as it took its first beat since the end of the world.

Yes, the children, Sean Byron McQueen.

I was now mother and father. I slowly turned the peephole into oblivion away and set the gun on the ground.

Still, I couldn't move from my dark tunnel. Again I heard the whirling of scraping metal—Dick's Blackhawk and the dead Guru's goon squad had returned to pick up their man and take my life. Thoughts of escape finally stirred me, but where to run? They'd find me soon enough on my trek back to the Deeksha, if I even made it ten steps out the door. How stupid would I be to stay in the hut? But with Dick gone, wouldn't the hut be the last place they'd look for me?

My mind was spinning like those chopping steel blades, and I must have passed out, because black was the last thing I remembered before coming back to partial awareness.

The sun was still rising over the mountains as my assassins were approaching the bleak hut's door. I'd forgotten about the valuable equipment Dick had left behind.

I angled toward the door. Such soft footfalls for a goose-stepping goon squad moving with stealth. I assumed Dick had survived to return with his army for his revenge. The worst of it was, I'd have to see him again. He'd come to avenge his humiliation and his Guru and father's death—a real blood relationship or just his howling expression of endearment?

The morning sun creased through the slats in the windows to reveal the green goo walls of my grave. Funny, but I would drink a goblet of oozing algae now without a drop of fear. I spun Sadie across the floor toward the door. I smirked to think Dick's Daddy would finally get to fulfill his bloody destiny.

That thought had me scrambling across the floor and grabbing back the gun. We would go out together in a blaze of glory. I crouched behind a stump for my last stand, though my mind was going in and out of focus. I wondered if I might be dreaming.

When the door opened, there on the threshold hovered a goddess of nature in a blinding light. Only God's grace stopped me from shooting the sun-bathed fairy queen. My mind spun one hundred and eighty degrees and landed on believing she was an apparition come to usher me to M. I lowered the gun. I might have been imagining things, but I never could have imagined a morning angel, *that* angel—a Joan of Arc wearing jungle fatigues and ready for battle—at the hovel door.

Head spinning and eyes blinking, I blacked out as Juno stepped out of the blazing white light and entered my tomb.

THE END

ABOUT THE AUTHOR

MICHAEL KELLEY is a former lawyer who, prior to pursuing his passion for writing, built an international business on Wall Street before founding his own investment management firm. His love of literature and creative writing began during his years at the University of Pennsylvania.

Michael currently lives in New York with his wife and daughter. After years leading a busy life in the city, he now spends the majority of his time in the peaceful woods of Dutchess County where he enjoys meditation, yoga, wine, reading, and hiking, all of which inspire his writing.